What professionals say about:
THE PRIMARY OBJECTIVE

"The work is well written a⸱⸱ has a g⸱⸱⸱⸱ance
of success in the market plac⸱⸱⸱

SM

"We can confidently state that the work was found to be an
entertaining, intricate and unpredictable geopolitical thriller,
with a wide ranging scope and an engaging manner of dialogue.
The Board commended the ambition of your storytelling and
accessibility of your writing."

AH

"I have been discussing various aspects of your story and
have agreed that your novel is well-written with an absorbing
narrative."

JH

THE PRIMARY OBJECTIVE

MARTIN VENNING

mvenning.net

Matador
9 Priory Business Park,
Wistow Road, Kibworth Beauchamp,
Leicestershire. LE8 0RX
Tel: 0116 279 2299
Email: books@troubador.co.uk
Web: www.troubador.co.uk/matador
Twitter: @matadorbooks

ISBN 978 1800461 109

British Library Cataloguing in Publication Data.
A catalogue record for this book is available from the British Library.

Printed and bound in Great Britain by 4edge Limited
Typeset in 11pt Adobe Garamond Pro by Troubador Publishing Ltd, Leicester, UK

Matador is an imprint of Troubador Publishing Ltd

To Frances for the motivation.

To Samira for the inspiration.

To you, dear reader, for the acquisition.

The adventure begins...Enjoy!

ONE

THE RUSTING RUSSIAN-BUILT GAZ-66 truck groaned up the steep incline following the track to what looked like a redundant quarry in the half-light of dusk.

Jack was thinking.

Here he was, in the back of a clapped-out flat-bed lorry with an arched tarpaulin over the back, with five others who he had met hours earlier who could only be identified by their first names. God, after a few hours in this sort of comfort, he needed more than a cushion to sit on to stop his bum aching. But that was the least of it; despite being apprehensive, they were still alive.

Who were they again? He was trying to fix the names to the faces. The biggest, predictably looking like the Action Man of the group, was simply introduced as 'Dave'. He didn't look like someone he would want to have a disagreement with. Dressed in khaki fatigues, chiselled features and shaved pate, Dave either had a military background or the look of an extra in a Vin Diesel movie.

Preoccupied, this man didn't look the type to engage in small talk. At least, having spent the past five hours in the back of a truck, he had not spoken. His face was expressionless, but his eyes revealed an intensity – no, anger – which did not encourage dialogue.

The person next to him went by the name of Joe.

A slight figure (compared to Dave next to him), he chewed gum, had tied back brown hair and, judging by the amount of effort he put into it, didn't have time for a chat. He was fidgeting – tapping his fingers to some strange rhythm that would have looked OK if he had headphones – but didn't.

Next to him was Rodger – 'Rodg' – who, somehow, was managing to sleep through the quieter parts of the journey, although, a bit like a snake, he seemed to have perfected the art of snoozing with one eye open. Bookish, almost professor-like, with slightly greying hair, cropped beard and glasses, Rodg appeared to be the most unlikely member of the group. Complete with a knitted black 'beanie' hat, his gaping mouth exposed teeth that were his only bright feature, not dissimilar to the sharp pointed outcrops they were passing along the dirt track.

'Gil' sat to the right of Jack, closest to the exit, which had been reassuring. He had seemed more relaxed than most, probably because his hands were wrapped around an M16 carbine, and seemed quite happy to make small talk, especially football and Liverpool in particular. Listening to him, and the negative body language of some of the others, Jack soon remembered he had been warned to be careful about talking, in terms of both topic and language.

When the members of the group had signed up, they had been told to keep chat to a minimum and not to ask too many questions of each other. Really? Isn't that the natural thing to do when you get to meet people? Not in this case, evidently.

The final member of the assembled 'happy band' was clearly not fully Caucasian, but looked as though he could have been from a number of different countries on the edge of southern Europe or the Middle East. He showed little interest in Jack's attempt at banter; in fact, he started to wonder if he spoke English at all. They had been told to call him 'Fawaz' and all he did was to play with some worry beads tied to his left wrist.

The drive down from Baku had provided a cautionary introduction to their mission.

They had boarded the truck at an agreed meeting point, outside a warehouse on the private General Aviation side of the airfield. There was no other truck in the vicinity to create confusion, but it looked odd, a red-headed man who certainly didn't look like an olive-skinned local, dressed casually in Western clothes at the wheel of an old military vehicle. Seeing some of his prospective charges approaching, he had jumped out of the cab and come to meet them. Like any good tour guide, he had a piece of paper with some scribbled names upon it. As each of his prospective passengers arrived, he checked their passports and ticked them off his list. In the front passenger seat was a dark-haired woman wearing a forest-green T-shirt, who looked disinterested in her colleague's administrative duties and made no effort to climb out to say hello. Despite there being only six of them, space was limited as they had to fit round the sides in the back, as wooden boxes, covered by rugs and blankets took up much of the space in the middle.

A bit like the aircrew on a departing flight, their driver, a slightly overweight man with an Irish accent in jeans and a red check shirt, had taken the opportunity to explain about what to do in an emergency, before his passengers clambered in the back.

The man in the check shirt explained:

"Depending on potential bottlenecks, it will take between five and six hours to get to your destination. Once we get out into the country, the roads become a bit narrower and we won't be able to drive as fast. Also, some of the territory we are crossing can get a bit lawless in places, with local militia acting as the police. At the moment, we've heard there is a guy called Ruslanov whose causing trouble for the authorities on our route. Occasionally, his people stop vehicles and search them, sometimes taking anything which takes their fancy. We will resist them, but there may be some shooting. Those people like to feel important, so you should expect to hear some fire, but don't be frightened. They're shit shots, but you could catch a stray. If I think we are headed into trouble, I will bang three times on the back of the cab. If I do that, you lie on the floor and keep absolutely quiet. When the danger is passed, I will tap twice, meaning you can return to your normal sitting position."

He nodded to a stocky, tanned, bald-headed man in a flak jacket, finishing a cigarette a short distance away.

"If there is any shooting to do, leave it to us. Gil over there is here for your protection and will provide any other covering fire that may be required."

It would be a test to see whether there was sufficient floorspace for at least five of them to lie flat, if necessary. A few cushions had been thrown in to soften the likely numbing effect of sitting on the steel floor of the interior for what was going to be a number of hours. Jack soon realised they also provided some protection from the shaking and vibration of the crank shaft below as the ageing truck was stirred into life.

The first three hours or so had been uneventful. Lots of different vistas and sounds kept the uninitiated interested, but, as Jack had already discovered, did not do much to increase his circle of friends or their conversation. As they had been warned, the truck soon seemed to be occupying lower gear ratios and the road was becoming subject to more twists and turns. Through the gap in the rear tarpaulin, it was clear the daylight was fading and they could have little idea where they were, other than a general realisation they were a couple of hours away from journey's end.

That's when the threatened three bangs on the back of the cab was heard, creating an awkward scramble as five of the six passengers attempted to get down on the floor without landing on top of each other. It seemed to take an age for them to do this, but at least it was done. The truck's engine suddenly dropped a couple of octaves and above the roar there was, for the first time, a series of shouts and then the first "rat-a-tats" of automatic fire. Combined with the flash of sparks, the sounds of ricocheting bullets and the popping of a myriad of holes being punched through the higher levels of their tarpaulin cover, they understood what it was like to be under attack. Then, by way of response, a burst of outward fire which seemed very close, even if it hadn't come from the rear of their truck. The only person who had not gone to the floor was Gil, who had now wedged himself against a side panel, having got his carbine through the gap at the back of the tarpaulin. Although it was impossible to tell from Jack's position, he assumed these bandits were now giving chase and Gil was about to discourage them, by loosing off a few rounds in their general direction.

All went quiet soon after, but nobody moved, waiting for the agreed 'all clear' signal. It didn't happen for a good twenty minutes and, shortly after, they were surprised their vehicle came to a stop at the side of the road.

Their driver, 'Mr Check Shirt', came to the back of the truck with a torch and muttered briefly to Gil before announcing to the company: "We have passed the danger area, but one of our fuel tanks has been holed. At least they didn't get our tyres. We have a spare jerry-can to get through, but it will take me a few minutes to plug it. If you need a pee, this is your best chance. Don't go far from the truck and come back quickly. Gil will keep watch and we'll get moving again soon as possible."

As good as his word, he had them on the move after some twenty minutes.

Although they had not talked much, a moment of adversity was creating a bond between them.

This little group had shared each other's company in a cramped truck, packed with equipment, with the opportunity of looking at each other (or in some cases getting uncomfortably close) for over five hours, which was pretty good going, and they had only stopped once for a comfort break.

The occupants of the truck still had no sense about what each other were supposed to be doing.

Now they were here. Not at their ultimate destination, but at the true start of the adventure, in an old quarry 'heaven knew where'. They had lurched to a halt. Given the parlous sound of the engine on the incline, they weren't sure if they were the victims of circumstance or whether the act of the engine dying was premeditated, assisted by leaking diesel. Jack opted for the latter in response to more staccato banging, this time on the side of the truck with what sounded like a blunt instrument.

The instruction made complete sense to Fawaz, who was first to jump out, followed by Rodg and Gil.

The group were greeted again by their driver, and his assistant, the woman in forest-green combat uniform, now with an AK-47 sub-machine gun across her shoulder, which looked ready for use. Under normal circumstances, these two looked like a couple on an adventure weekend, but, so far, this could not be described as "normal".

"Welcome to Barthaz," the man said, in his soft Irish lilt.

Where? Jack thought. There were precious few landmarks that he could see which would turn his vision of Barthaz into reality. Behind them was the track which had weaved its way along the valley between two sets of high hills (not quite mountains, but wouldn't have looked out of place in the Cairngorms). To his right, a sheer cliff which looked like it had been shaped by an angle grinder and, to his left, low ground going into the blackness; but, most of all, the overriding first impression of Barthaz was the silence. Without the sound of their truck's wheezing engine and clanking gearbox, there was no other distraction.

In common with every other experience he had had on this trip, Mr Check Shirt wasted no time on introductions. Based on his initial experience, Jack now understood why it was important for all involved in this exercise to be anonymous – to know as little as possible about each other, just in case. But who were they planning on meeting and talking to? Although he had been tempted to ask for formal introductions, it became abundantly clear that information would not be offered, and the mere request would be unwelcome.

Their host (in the check shirt) continued:

"We did our best to get you as close as possible to your destination by road, but this is as far as we can go. We have about an hour's walk down there to your jumping off point, where we can get you properly kitted out. Don't worry about the truck – we'll take care of that. Follow me."

And with that he set off with the passengers following in single file led by 'Big Dave', as Jack had decided to call him. Although Jack's eyes were acclimatised to the dark, it paid to concentrate on following the person in front. A casual look behind convinced him of this, when he saw the outline of the woman with the machine gun moving a few paces behind. The ground was rocky and difficult to walk on without stumbling, but started to give way to thick, knee-high grasses which seemed to grow taller as their journey on foot progressed.

If the prospect of having some chat in the truck had been difficult, it was now certain that maintaining the silence of their surroundings was the order of the day.

Jack really couldn't be sure how long it took – perhaps a half hour or more – but, he reckoned soon after, the silhouette of a building came into sight. It looked a bit like a big shed, casually thrown together with rock, steel and timber, but it was nonetheless difficult to tell at a distance, especially when it appeared to be unlit.

If the walk, in darkness, seemed a little challenging, it had been made easier by the fact that the terrain was now relatively flat and their leader had a pair of night-vision goggles, which ensured they were able to take the shortest route to their destination.

Their host put his foot firmly to the base of the door and it opened with little resistance. Once inside the doorway, he pulled a torch from his pocket. Picking up a box of matches, he lit a paraffin lamp. With everyone inside and the door closed, he found the main lighting switch with spare battery packs and fluorescent strips stacked next to it.

The building may have looked ramshackle and anonymous on the outside, but its interior was tidy and organised. To the left were two trucks in military camouflage (certainly in better condition that the one they had travelled in) and one of them appeared to be parked over a maintenance pit. All manner of tools, parts and tyres were stacked nearby. Several metal pens, similar to those used on a sheep farm, with straw strewn on the ground, were next to the trucks. The rest appeared to be open space, other than a long trestle table with canvas webbed packs on and below it. On the right was another table with food supplies, flasks, water and cola.

At first sight, it was difficult to tell whether this place was a farm or military logistics base, but in either case, given the value of its contents, it was surprising it was deserted.

Although the night was warm and the weather dry, they were all pleased to have reached a place they could stop to get their bearings.

"OK, everyone – food is on the table over there – ham, cheese, eggs, soup, water, tea, coffee. Help yourselves. I will start the final briefing in fifteen minutes. Please put all your rubbish in the sack provided. We will be moving on in the next couple of hours."

They all started to fall on the provisions. Their "lady friend" and co-driver stayed by the door, gun at the ready.

"So now let's get on with it. I am delighted you had an opportunity to get to know each other on the way here and, whilst you are getting used to your new-found colleagues, you may not be clear on why you have been brought together."

To Jack, that was an understatement.

He recalled a chance meeting, only a few months ago, with an old friend at Piccadilly station in Manchester.

The conversation was predictable. "Is it really you?" "What are you doing these days?" "Got time for a drink?"

It was this third question which was the start of the adventure. They crossed the road and ended up in the bar at the Malmaison.

Sitting on high chairs with a couple of beers, the dialogue kicked off with their shared reasons for being in town – in Jack's case, it was really about seeing a couple of long-standing friends about work as an investigative journalist, which would involve finding injustices to right without getting beaten up in the process.

Life was uncertain as a freelance and you had to take what you could get.

"I'm normally here once a month to either get work or show potential employers I'm still alive," Jack joked.

His companion seized on this casual remark to make a point.

"Are you up for a bit of adventure, then? Don't you wish you could do something really different?"

Jack wasn't entirely sure how he was going to respond to that.

"You should take a leaf out of my book," his companion said. "I took a job with a charity and haven't looked back."

He started to explain.

"I joined Peace International originally as they were looking for field officers or observers to go to Africa to monitor the activities of some warlords in some of its less governable quarters," he said.

"My job was to get to know them, encourage them to lay down their guns and get into politics."

It sounded really interesting to Jack, especially as his friend was required to live a nomadic existence and sleep in a campervan most nights.

"Man, did I have some adventures – how long have you got? The scariest moment I had was in the Congo…"

And so the story went on.

It was now past eleven and, as creeping middle age confirmed, way past Jack's bedtime. Except by now he'd missed the last train home and needed a bed for the night. The stories he had heard were probably laced with bullshit, but he had to concede they sounded good.

It was clear his friend had packed more into his forty years than he had.

Jack's scariest moment hadn't been in an exotic location in Africa; it had been exposing a rogue landlord with ancillary interests in drugs and prostitution in Wakefield. His then editor had been pleased he had come up with the type of narrative that compared the streets of Horbury to those of San Francisco, but had not been unduly concerned about him being duffed up and threatened with worse in the process. Jack did recall, however, getting a cursory thank-you from the local police, who had an "off the peg" solution to multiple misdemeanours, which were attributed to the local Mr Big. Life hadn't been that much easier elsewhere either.

He had tried his hand as a data analyst working for a digital marketing company, predicting purchasing decisions from social media feeds, but it was dull and he really wanted a job where he could get out more. Last year, he had taken on a six-month temporary role as a news producer for a cable station, Press TV, in London, financed (as he discovered at the interview) by the Iranian government. He wondered why he had got the job. Either there hadn't been many takers or perhaps it was because buried deep at the end of his CV he had claimed he spoke Farsi. He had made reference to it really as a way of making his otherwise average background stand out, and to be fair it wasn't an exaggeration. He knew a bit of everyday conversational Farsi because he had an Iranian grandmother who had married and moved to the UK. She was a contradiction as she surrounded her home with pictures from her country but rarely went out socialising. The result was she hadn't learned to speak English fluently and insisted on using her mother tongue. She had spent many years looking after Jack as he was growing up, so it was inevitable he would pick up the language. Although he could read some simple stuff, he couldn't write any of it. It was a fact his employers at Press quickly picked up at the interview, but it wasn't a deal-breaker. His reports were needed in English anyway and at least he was able to discuss editorial angles in Farsi with his boss.

Although he had run out of interesting stories, his friend had not. The night was still young, and it was his credit card behind the bar.

"Why don't you join Peace International? We're always looking for volunteers. You won't get paid much but you won't be short of adventures and at least they will pick up the tab for the airfares."

Normally, if someone had come to Jack with such a proposition, he would have been analytical in his approach. But it was nearly midnight, he needed the loo and, unless he was not mistaken, there was a lady sipping a glass of fizz at the end of the bar looking short on company. In such situations, it was often difficult to get his priorities right and, true to form, he didn't.

Jack offered a mumbled acknowledgement it was his round again and headed barwards to place his order at exactly the moment the mysterious lady, and target of his most alluring smile, picked up her room key and headed for the lift.

Although he was feeling fairly coordinated, his actions did not allow sufficient time for the relief of his pressing personal circumstances.

Order placed, potential love interest denied, and credibility shredded, Jack downed the "one for the road" and headed for bed, with the words "I'll call you in the morning" ringing in his ears.

Of course, the next day didn't start well. Jack was in the wrong place with a bad headache and suffering a lack of inspiration to explain away the conversation of the previous night to his latest better half.

Gathering his wits from the four corners of the room, he quickly realised the focus of the day's activity was already lost.

Coffee, a sandwich and then the train journey home.

And then the phone call – "You haven't left town yet? Good – stay there – I'm with someone you need to meet..." and shortly after:

"Hi. I'm Edwin Wilson, Director of Peace International Europe

– I've heard a lot about you and hear you have an adventurous spirit…"

The day had, in effect, been written off before it began, so what the hell – for the sake of a couple of hours, why not talk? Jack thought.

Wilson proved to be a very engaging character – judging by his demeanour, clearly a military man – but his story was well worth hearing. Having got as far as colonel in the Royal Dragoon Guards, he had seen service in the Falklands and Afghanistan, but, more than that, he had a clear view that there was a need to find a way to bring warring communities together before fighting had started.

He had been in Manchester to address a peace studies conference at the university. His message was clear. Not enough attention was given to preventing war and regional disputes through conciliation and mediation. There was a need for some independent and neutral organisation to help empower communities weakened by conflict, to strengthen their civil society and resilience – essentially the purpose of Peace International.

This all sounded very worthy to Jack, but he guessed there were a number of organisations doing the same thing.

Well, he thought, maybe you can't have enough people engaged in such work, but what Peace International was doing was pretty unique, as he was to discover.

"There is another side to our work which is less well known," Wilson continued.

"We sometimes work with governments to support their objectives if we judge them to be working in the interests of peace."

The journalist in him was coming to terms with this thought, but really, as a conversation filler, Jack observed that seemed like a pretty wide definition.

Wilson agreed: "Sometimes in any diplomatic dialogue, there is a void that prevents meaningful engagement. This is a space we can operate in," he said.

"You see, from time to time, there are jobs that need doing on behalf of a government that they are unable to do for one reason or another. Our international network can be utilised to support them if we think their request fits with our own aims… and, of course, it can be a very useful income stream for us."

Wow! Now his reporter's brain was really running.

"So you provide a sort of general service function for the government?" Jack heard himself countering, rather clumsily.

"That is one way of looking at it," said Wilson, "but don't forget we are international. Our clients include other governments as well, and sometimes we just do things because our trustees think it is the right thing to do. Remember, unlike a lot of very worthy charities, our purpose is not to intervene after an event to provide relief, but before problems develop. Also, it is important to engage in a healing process after a conflict has occurred. Ask any soldier with first-hand knowledge of the realities of conflict whether they would prefer to resolve disputes without recourse to violence and destruction, and I can tell you what they will say. The victims are invariably the innocents. Our strict rule of confidentiality means we don't seek credit for our work, but influential people understand our capability."

This rather smooth understatement was calculated to dissolve his line of questioning and, coming from the organisation's chief protagonist, seemed at first to be entirely reasonable.

"Given the scale of problems in the world today, why wasn't Peace International more heavily involved especially with organisations such as the United Nations?"

Wilson seemed to commune with Jack.

"We all know there are plenty of problems out there to keep us occupied, but unfortunately we don't have the resources to be more directly involved. We are an active organisation which must pick interventions that we can reasonably expect to be able to deliver on. Managing expectations is also a key part of our relationships with governments. I choose to take it as a compliment that they often overestimate our abilities. Our skill is in managing cases where we can project a start and end date as well as being able to be confident about achieving an outcome."

Jack then started to understand where this conversation was going.

"A man with an enquiring mind and an eye for detail could do well working with us," Wilson continued. "We are always looking for individual volunteers with the right qualities."

Knowing the old saying "a bird in the hand..." drove him to respond.

"Give me your card and I'll send you my CV – and, by the way, I expect to be paid the market rate."

Wilson smiled. "Don't worry, Jack, that is not necessary. We know where to find you when we are ready. I'm sorry I've taken up so much of your time, but I hope you will agree this has been a worthwhile meeting. I am sure our paths will cross again before too long."

Jack's mate just nodded, and he disappeared with Wilson into the crowded broadway of Piccadilly, leaving him to reflect on the exchange and what it may mean for the future.

Needless to say, a couple of days later, his mobile buzzed.

"I thought it best not to leave it too long before we spoke again," came the now-familiar voice, "especially when I have a job – no, *adventure* – ready for someone with your skills..."

As Jack recalled, that was no more than eight weeks ago (he remembered doing his tax return at the time) – hah, and now here he was!

True, Wilson had been as good as his word. Here was the prospect of real adventure with a clear ethical base and paid to boot. Not only had he received a golden hello but an air ticket to a place called Baku.

As a single guy, what wasn't to like about that? Now, it felt like Jack was about to find out.

As a reasonably fit thirty-something with a penchant for the outdoor life, the prospect of a walking tour in the nether regions

14

of Azerbaijan (somewhere in western Asia, near Iran, he was told) certainly appealed but the working aspect of the trip intrigued Jack more – to copy and witness documents in a secret place that could prevent a Middle East war. Quite how someone with his limited knowledge of Farsi was expected to do that he wasn't sure, except, he guessed, there were people based in England better qualified than him for the task. But, as he reminded himself, he was expendable in a way that these others may not have been, so should celebrate the opportunity and get on with it.

"Everything you need is in the backpacks stacked over there. Please take one when we leave. You will each be issued with a Makarov pistol, silencer and ten rounds for personal use in an emergency if you need it. As you know, this operation is not without its risks. You have deliberately not been briefed on the personal details of your colleagues and will not carry any evidence of your nationality. Further, from the point of departure from this place you will only speak in Farsi. And, now, David here will brief you on your mission."

"Mr Check Shirt" had clearly been a boy scout.

"Big Dave" stood up: "Good to meet you all. My instructions are to lead you on a reconnaissance mission across the border in what must be assumed to be hostile territory. Our mission – our primary objective – is not about conflict but to gather intelligence – to improve our knowledge of the capability of a potential adversary. My job is to help each of you to deliver your element of the plan and get you back safely. The light armament you have is for self-defence purposes only. It will be considered a failure if anyone dies as a result of this operation."

Jack raised an eyebrow.

His ironic gesture was either missed or ignored.

"We are close to the Iranian border. About two hours hiking time from our present location over the other side is Ibrahim Sami. This is a village not a person."

Now that *did* get a laugh. Dave punctured the levity.

"Ibrahim Sami, or *IS* as I will call it, may be in the far north of Iran, but is central to our interest. The border between Azerbaijan and Iran has been closed now for a number of years due to regional disputes. Our mission is covert so we cannot access permitted border crossings. Our route in is across open country, a major river (which marks the actual frontier) and then a minefield, but more on that later. Outside Sami is a significant garrison of the Revolutionary Guard, Iran's elite fighting forces, and conjoined is a training facility used to provide terrorist field training for foreign fighters in the pay of the Iranian state. This in itself is not our interest, but nearby in the mountains to the north is a facility which is our target. Satellite imagery shows this to be a series of modern, low-level buildings without the apparent military uses of the Revolutionary Guard base, over here, at Posyan to the east. Yet what we don't understand is what is going on there. There is only one road to the site from *IS* and it is clear these nondescript buildings benefit from a high level of protection, including two levels of security fencing and anti-aircraft batteries."

Rodg interjected: "What's at this location which demands this high-level protection and why has it been built in an isolated location away from the garrison?"

"Our intention is to investigate and report back to PI. Our plan is to create a record of the base on the ground which will involve obtaining access and to log any documentation we may discover back to HQ. The mission is planned to take between two and four weeks. It is my job to ensure you leave Iran as quietly as you arrive, but once out of the country we will disperse, returning home under our individual effort.

"And now I would like to introduce you to your colleagues who are part of your team and to briefly explain their role. Firstly, here is Joe."

Joe stood forward removed a bandana and provided Jack's first real shock – Joe was not any old Joe but was a woman called Jo. Given her dress and unfortunate habits with gum, she had the opportunity to pass as a man in Jack's book, but, regardless of gender sensitivities, Jo was definitely here for a reason.

"Jo is a scientist who specialises in biochemical warfare and is an authority on the identification, manufacture and storage of carcinogenic agents."

Was this a clue about what Dave expected to find?

Clearly, Jo was an asset in herself and Rodg emerged in subsequent introductions to be her dedicated minder to provide full protection for her.

As Dave was in an expansive mood regarding introductions, Jack was intrigued to hear what he was going to say about him.

"And this is Jack," he said, acknowledging him for the first time.

"He is here to record evidence of anything we find."

And that was that – no more detail was to be provided about how he would achieve this aim and it wasn't his place to say more. Neither, as one of the people who appeared to be a non-combatant, did he suggest that there would be someone watching Jack's back when things got difficult. Jack waited for Dave to introduce Gil, but his fellow traveller was ignored.

Dave, clearly a man who was measured in his language, moved to the final introduction – Fawaz, who had been staring at his feet as the rest of them had got to know each other.

"This is Fawaz – I will let him tell you more about his involvement."

Quietly spoken, Fawaz began:

"Hello, everyone, I am looking forward to working with you in the coming days. I am Iranian. I was born and raised in Ibrahim Sami. I grew up in the early years of the revolution and witnessed the effect it had on my family's life. I had two elder brothers in the Iranian forces who were killed in the Iran–Iraq war and I followed them into the military when I was old enough. That was when I left Sami for the first time. I was posted to Lebanon to fight with Hezbollah but picked up a wound from a rocket shell. I returned to Sami and saw the changes at home. My community had become poorer. Most able-bodied men had been forced into the military and only two guys I knew from my schooldays were still there – and they worked for the intelligence service. The women of Sami, including my mother and sister, were working the fields and tending livestock. A new military base was being built out of town. The farmer who owned the land was not compensated and locals were told to stay away. The people who got work there were all outsiders. They had to get special passes to leave the construction site and when they came to Sami they caused trouble, doing drugs and hassling women. Incidents were covered up and any protests dealt with by military threat. A friend of my father made a complaint to the base commandant and subsequently disappeared. His body was found the following week next to a road with signs of being tortured. Since leaving the army, I had hoped to help my father on our farm, but permission has not been granted by the provincial government, as they think my mother and father are still able to manage on their own. I think it was bullshit because my parents had found twenty of the sheep on their farm dead for no reason. They hadn't been able to watch them 24/7. When the deaths were reported, the animals were not allowed to be buried. A truck was sent to collect the carcasses and take them away. Again, no explanation or compensation was offered. I found out the dead animals had all grazed in the area close to the compound we are due to investigate. I shared my concern with one of my old schoolteachers, long since retired. He told me to keep quiet to stop me getting into trouble.

"That is when I knew I had to leave. One of my friends from army days gave me a job as a research assistant at Tehran University, where I got to know Peace International.

"My plan is to return to Sami and take over my father's farm. I have no interest in politics but care passionately about the future of my community and country. I cannot stand by and see it ruined as land and property is taken and local people are disappearing as is happening by our present government.

"I tell all this to you because my focus is different. I want to use this opportunity to help build a better future for my country.

"I am part of this mission because I know, a short distance from here, something bad is going on. It has to be revealed and stopped.

"There is no formal border crossing point at Sami, which is understandable given what we know, but I grew up near here and know the local territory well. I will be your guide, not only to the boundary of the Aras river but across it, through the traps, sniper positions, wire fences and minefields that lie between the river and Ibrahim Sami village. I have checked and secured a base in a farm building away from most houses and I will get you to the target and back as safely as possible."

If he wasn't anxious by this point of the story, Jack now had a feeling of sickness in the pit of his stomach, a point noted by Rodg, who at the moment had read his expression.

"Don't worry – they certainly won't want to kill you on this mission. You would be a huge propaganda prize provided you do and say what they want. If you don't like the sound of that, the next best thing to do will be to go running around the border minefield. Although they will still get their story, at least you won't have had the pain of them extracting your agreement."

There was a sort of poignant silence at this point as the dark irony of his observation hit the spot. The mood was swiftly broken by Fawaz: "This is my home. I do not wish to die. You will be fine with me."

The simplicity of his words and the matter-of-fact delivery proved a counterbalance to Rodg. Whatever the future held for them, it was clear that, if captured, Fawaz had even fewer options for his recovery.

With the help of their guides who had got them this far, they got strapped up and kitted out for the start of the mission. This was the point when the support network, such as it was, would fall away. Gil was quietly helping them out, checking the rest of them had everything they needed. Jack guessed, as no one bothered with him, he was a bit player in the operation, although his animated demeanour had suggested otherwise. Their job was to clear up after them, leave no trace, take the truck and disappear into the night.

Fully equipped with night-vision goggles, they filed out of the barn following Fawaz and were enveloped by the silence of the night and the riot of stars in the sky. The ground, a mixture of grass and sedge, continued to slope away as they moved towards the base of the valley. To the left, the silhouette of the hills of Azerbaijan; to the right, a void of scrub. Occasionally their sights picked out the reflections of eyes watching them, but these shapes were just foxes going about their nocturnal scavenging. As the group moved forward, the sound of rushing water became louder and moonlight started to dance on the churning water – so they had come to the edge of the river – the border and the point of no return. Fawaz had told them of the hazards of their journey and the importance to staying in close formation, and that applied to the river crossing. The depth was deceptive and the current strong. There were places where they could cross at waist height but others where the water could easily overwhelm a person, especially carrying the kit they had. They were in the dark with precious few visible reference points to guide them – save their first sight of the opposite bank – the Islamic Republic of Iran.

Again – as Dave had warned – conversation was limited to essentials and Jack was using the silent time to follow Rodg and rehearse his somewhat limited Farsi. He was also a little stressed being at the back of the group, especially realising the reassurance of the gun-toting lady who had watched over them at the farmhouse was no longer present.

And, of course, crossing water – any sort of water – is a challenging experience. For starters, the distance they had to travel was deceptive. At the briefing, Fawaz had described it as being little more than a ford – what they were facing was much more of a wide, fast-flowing, if relatively shallow river.

The steady and measured manner of their approach from the Azeri side was now starting to feel like a horizontal climbing exercise, with tentative steps being made on the rocky riverbed and the chill of the running water enveloping their legs and thighs. For all his bravado, Jack noticed Fawaz moved forward with a pole, testing the depth of his chosen route. Despite the water-repellent drysuit, the force of the rising water was starting to reach the skin and, exactly as they had been warned, his body temperature started to drop. Now was not the time for delay and yet Fawaz seemed to have slowed. He was not going directly across anymore but was moving to his left into what appeared to be deeper water. The current grew stronger making it harder to keep his feet grounded. With his chin starting to get splashed, he guessed this was the point in any other scenario where he should start to swim, but the weight of the kit bag was always going to make that unlikely. Jack knew he would be facing greater challenges and that this wasn't the moment to panic. Remember – all he needed to do was follow the man in front.

While the water level around him was increasing, the randomly uneven footing was difficult to walk on and making solid steps was difficult given the sharp stones below. After what seemed like half a dozen strides at this new deeper level, he could make out that the water surrounding Fawaz was dropping away and the river's edge was now clearly in sight. Still struggling to keep his balance, Jack moved forward, following Rodg stride for stride, and gradually the effort seemed easier. Soon they were sloshing their way to the shore. Although not much was said, the collective body language had its own conversation – they were relieved to have landed in the Islamic Republic. The drysuits had largely done their job in keeping the ravages of the river away from their skin, although the price had been a strange, clammy, cold sensation. Not many people realise that a drysuit does indeed keep you dry in the wet, but fails to prevent you sweating as you exert yourself. They were still far from journey's end and the prospect of feeling damp was something they were going to get used to as a result of either fear or exertion or probably both.

Although stopping on arrival on the far bank, it was only to adjust their webbing before the 'yomp' and crawl through the minefield started. Whether the Iranian authorities had considered crossing of their border at this point, it was clear they did not intend to warn prospective arrivals of the dangers ahead. Maybe it was because they thought the prospect of people coming to Iran was so unlikely there was no need to offer a welcome.

Fawaz glanced around the route forward and then back at his charges. A nod of the head was all that was required to instruct them to follow him in single file. What lay ahead was more scrub land, only this time broken by several trees. These were not so extensive as to have constituted a copse or wood but provided some relief from the more barren landscape they had left. They moved around fifty paces before stopping and turning left. Twenty paces on, they went right and after another fifteen paces turned right again, before turning left this time after forty paces. They now had the relative comfort of a plane tree nearby, which told them this would not be an easy place to set a mine. With the river behind, a tree next to them and what looked like a track suitable for a four-by-four to use ahead, their collective confidence was growing. Yet, at this point, Fawaz signalled to stop.

Unexpectedly, a tripwire was ahead. Quite what the penalty might be for touching it was not clear. Given its relative height, it was a surprise, not least because it would presumably be triggered by local wildlife... or maybe it was a device to prevent animals wandering into the minefield. Whatever, its purpose was to tell someone in the locality they had visitors and they were not yet ready to announce their appearance. They had only just traversed the tripwire when, away to their right, they saw the lights of a SUV heading along the track towards them. The vehicle was not travelling at speed, but neither was its driver dallying. Fortunately, the lie of the land gave warning of the vehicle's imminent arrival, so they were able to use the nearby brush to take cover. As it approached, they started to hear the strains of what seemed to be local pop music blaring out of the vehicle. The tunes were not easily recognisable to the Western ear, but the beat would not have been out of place in a disco. On board were two soldiers laughing and shouting above the din. Was this a normal military patrol? They could not tell, except the two on board did not look either combat ready or concerned. They didn't stop nearby and soon their lights and noise disappeared into the night.

TWO

JAMSHID TURANI HAD NEVER really been interested in politics, probably because he came from what many would have considered to be a privileged background. His father had been a senior economics professor at Tehran University and his mother part of a very exclusive group of female entrepreneurs running one of the city's most successful tea houses. He had a sister with a seemingly unhealthy interest in boys, which really annoyed him, and his parents had always gone along with the notion she would, in due course, marry a successful figure in the energy business or government. That meant the pressure of family expectation was on him – yet the academic life was not where is interest lay. With the help of this father's connections, he had joined the country's merchant marine – in effect the non-uniform part of the Iranian navy. His training as a navigation officer had opened up a world of travel possibilities. Already at a relatively young age, he had sailed extensively in South Asia, especially visiting ports in Sri Lanka, Indonesia and China. The experience had provided him with a secure background and relaxed discipline. The Iranian navy had developed a friendly civilian face by providing a casual approach to religious observance, provided officers attended a daily contemplation meeting with the ship's imam. He was generally well regarded by his colleagues and if anything was thought of as being a bit too serious on occasions. Although personable with a generally friendly demeanour, few of his compatriots could remember times on board when he had let his hair down and consumed alcohol (which, privately, many of them had done).

He was, many thought, a good guy, but few could claim to know him well.

After nearly ten years at sea, the national shipping company transferred him to an administrative role at the southern port of Bandar Abbas. The job, scheduling Iran's fragile raw material exports to nondescript parts of the world, offered little stimulation apart from a pay rise and the pride of his mother, who saw the move as a perfect platform for finding him a wife. Careful selection of invitations to her Tehran tea house was part of her plan to find the right woman. This, of course, was a tried and tested route which had resulted in his sister being married off to a fairly beige bloke called Abdul, apparently some high-flier in the Interior Ministry. That had been less than a year ago and already she was expecting.

If daily work was a grind, weekend family visits to home were little better. He had forgotten how many times he had had the opportunity to tell his mother to keep out of his life, but always failed to bite the bullet and tell her directly. He guessed his father understood his angst, but he never intervened, preferring to keep his head buried in the latest Stiglitz assessment of the US economy.

Of course, one of the challenges of university life was separating the theoretical and the practical and in that sense his father had encouraged his son to explore opportunities when they arose. Given the responsibilities of the job, Jamshid was aware of the importance of his work – helping to keep his nation's struggling economy moving.

Every day, the task of scheduling deliveries of crude to countries choosing to ignore the sanctions of the US was becoming more challenging. Selling cargoes at sea, re-registering ships with third-party nations in transit and even managing access to overseas bank accounts still controlled by the state were becoming the rule rather than the exception. Markets remained thirsty for oil, but it was getting much harder to transact deals and the costs of the middlemen were rising. Watching the TV news, he saw no signs of life getting better anytime soon. Apart from the usual invective-laced utterances of the Supreme Leader railing against the Great Satan and his helpers – particularly neighbours in Saudi and the Emirates, time was taken up showcasing the daily moans about food shortages and the miscreants caught breaking the country's strict dress code or gathering to protest for freedom of speech.

It was Thursday night – the time to pack his laundry in anticipation of the trip home next day. The phone rang. Ravi, a college compatriot who lived nearby, had arranged for a few of his friends to get together for a meal. Normally his schedule didn't allow enough time to drive across town to the restaurant, but what the hell... why not? And, after all, their lamb kebabs were the stuff of legend. Leaving the laundry in his bedroom, he grabbed his keys and set off into the night. It was the end of the evening rush and so it took half the time of the estimated forty-five minutes to get there and there was quite a crowd when he arrived. His initial impression was he had been asked as an afterthought, and as it turned out, to an extent, that was the case.

"My best friend, Jamshid, is here," announced Ravi and almost on cue the assembled group roared their appreciation. Jamshid felt a little uncomfortable – yes, there was Ravi and a few other acquaintances he knew from the sports club they were members of, but also some faces he didn't recognise. A pleasant surprise was to note this was a mixed group and, although the girls there had their *hijabs* to cover their hair, their formal dress had failed to hide their looks.

Ravi continued: "This is Bandar's most eligible bachelor. The man with a real head for figures."

It was clear Ravi liked to be the centre of attention and his expansive introduction made Jamshid blanch.

"I wouldn't go that far," he mumbled.

"How far would you go?" enquired the woman nearest to him, seated to his right.

Before he could answer, his eye connected with hers and he felt like he was drowning.

"I…" he hesitated, but the woman moved on.

"My name is Mahta – pleased to meet you. From Ravi's description, I am not disappointed."

He thought Ravi's description would not have allowed for a tall, dark thirty-year-old with a mouth that couldn't close, but maybe he was wrong.

"Er… hi, nice to meet you…" he said rather lamely.

"Well, yes actually," she said, "the lamb here is the best in town."

He hadn't had time to ask the question and so she was already ahead.

"It's my first time," he said, "but I've certainly heard of the chef's reputation."

She laughed and leaned into his shoulder.

"OK, so, as a virgin, I should assume we will not get a conversation in before you have had your kebab?"

Given his flat-footed attempt at small talk, her confident approach and unexpected remark shut him up. He nodded quickly and pretended to be part of another conversation taking place to his left, managed expertly by Ravi. Subsequently, they both got caught up in the fizzing wave of chat, jokes and gossip which occupied the coming hours. As had been predicted, they really didn't start to talk again before the coffee arrived.

"So, what do you do?" he asked.

"Oh, nothing too special – I work for the government."

It was his turn to laugh.

"Hah! That's what everyone says," he said.

"And why not?" she countered, "The pay is OK, the work is not challenging and I get enough time to ride my horse. Do you ride?"

27

"I have done once or twice on holiday but I'm no expert. I do remember getting some bruises for my trouble, which seemed to last for ages after."

"You need to practice – call me and you can come and meet my stallion, Alazaha. He is used to taming the untrained."

She pressed her card firmly into his hand, winked, picked one of the other girls up that she'd arrived with by the arm and headed for the door. The group chat continued until the shishas came out. That was his opportunity to withdraw.

Driving home, he felt a strange feeling of happiness – a very un-Thursday-night feeling. The food had been good, and the company had taken him out of himself. And what about that girl, Mahta? She was something special. He touched the breast pocket of his shirt – just to check he still had her card – and smiled to himself as the looming prospect of the flight to Tehran brought him back to reality. Of course, with hindsight he had been set up, but at the time it seemed like fun and he was overdue some of that. While packing his laundry, he also looked out a pair of stout boots that he suddenly saw a future for.

Once the four-by-four's lights had disappeared in the distance, Fawaz pressed ahead. Since crossing the track, the landscape had changed dramatically with fields of potatoes and pomegranates, and, away to the right, what looked like an orchard of almond trees. The vista had been exposed by the light of the moon and Fawaz had quickly realised the disappearing cloud cover had improved the visibility sufficiently to make the night-vision goggles unnecessary. However, the pale moonlight was reducing his own cover. Turning to the group following, he gestured to lift up the goggles and to keep low. He followed a careful line at the edge of the fields, taking the opportunity not to leave any incriminating moving silhouettes against the declining cover.

They were now picking up speed as they started up the slope away from the river. The fields at this point were not only cultivated

28

but had clear boundaries, which acted as a stopping point for the team to get together. After the completion of the third field boundary, Fawaz signalled the group to come together and spoke in Farsi for the first time. Jack realised his colleagues had a quicker understanding than him and he became the one to have to ask him to repeat certain comments and speak more slowly.

Fawaz was happy to oblige but Dave wasn't impressed.

"You're going to have to do better than this in the next few days," he said.

"I don't want the locals getting any more suspicious than necessary."

Jack then silenced him by saying, "I wonder if they will spot a Mancunian accent?"

Their methodical movement on the edge of cultivated fields had brought them within less than a hundred metres of the first building that could be realistically described as being at the very edge of town. It was two in the morning and all was quiet. The team was now assembled, with full kit, in a boundary ditch. This was the point that Fawaz would continue the journey alone. Leaving his backpack with the others, Fawaz now climbed out of the trench and started walking up the track towards the town. In rough, stained grey trousers, soiled boots with worn stitching on the right sole, old shirt with a slight tear in the left sleeve and a heavy waistcoat, Fawaz looked like he had just finished checking the abundant quantities of pomegranate in the next field. Although the look was right for the occasion, his timing gave the wrong impression: that he was about to announce his arrival to the first person he met in his hometown. His progress was followed closely by Dave with his field glasses. Fawaz had arrived at the first barn door. From the viewer's point of view, Fawaz seemed to be leaning into the door and applying one, two, three major thrusting movements before the door opened. Fawaz slipped inside and the door closed behind him.

Given the tensions of the night and the journey, sitting in a hole in a field on the edge of a nondescript border town in north-west

Iran seemed like an anticlimax, but that feeling started to change as a result of an inordinately long wait before Fawaz emerged. His body language seemed more positive than his cautious departure. He came back to the group to collect his backpack and signalled them to follow. This was undoubtedly the scariest moment to date, obliging them to break cover and walk openly towards the barn, all the time trying not to make too much noise with their heavy boots. One by one, they slipped through the door within a door, which took them into the barn and the place that would act as their base in the days ahead.

The small electric strip light in the barn gave the impression that the place was much bigger than it probably was. They seemed to be close to a wall of straw bales that rose from floor to ceiling. Its width was accentuated by a mezzanine, again packed with neatly stacked straw bales. Access to the mezzanine was by way of a small ladder which looked flimsy enough to collapse if a man put any weight on it. Further, looking at the top, it appeared to go nowhere as it was surrounded by more bales.

"Winter here can be tough. My family have another three barns getting filled with winter feed so we can keep our livestock in here and not offer a takeaway service to the local wolf population," Fawaz joked.

Given the circumstances, Jack would have been forgiven for not detecting the irony of the comment. Fawaz then proceeded to test the strength of the ladder by climbing it, with the backpack on. Although the act of getting to the mezzanine was swift enough, what to do upon arrival became a bit more complicated. The principal gap between the bales was wide enough for a person moving sideways to get through, but not someone with one of their heavy-duty bags. Momentarily disappointed, Fawaz dropped his pack and pressed himself into the space. In the dim light, he disappeared from view.

"Hey, guys, if we can shift around some of these bales this will be ideal for us – come up and take a look."

Two hours later, the team had succeeded in rearranging the mezzanine to provide a wall on the side facing onto the floor of the barn but opening up a good space hidden from view. Further, Fawaz remembered there was a hatch at the rear of the mezzanine for dropping bales out directly to the field behind. It looked like an ideal site for an operational base.

Dawn was now breaking, and Dave wanted the team to get some rest – all except Fawaz. Now changed for a third time, Fawaz came down the ladder with a small suitcase looking like he had just stepped off the night bus from Tehran. It was due into Sami in around half an hour and he expected to be there to mark his arrival.

Although all had worked so far, this was the point when trust between the newly acquainted team would come into its own. Fawaz would be seen to arrive in the town and could be expected to stay in his parents' house nearby. He would have to work out how he would keep in touch with the rest of the team in the barn. Dave shadowed Fawaz to the barn door, looking out to see what the first response was to the local cocks crowing. All was still quiet. Dave let Fawaz out into the street. Fawaz locked the outside door of the barn and Dave looked back at the mezzanine to check that signs of the occupants were hidden. The elevated vantage point offered good sightlines to the door and darkness to assist their cover. At this stage, one person would be retained to manage the watch. Fawaz had been quick to point out that the ground floor would be used during the day and the team should be mindful that people and animals would be coming out of the barn at will. But, for now, it was important to rest and come to terms with their surroundings.

Fawaz had not been back to Sami for some years, but, as he moved cautiously from street to street and reacquainted himself with his surroundings, he realised little had changed. Rather than going the most direct route to the bus stop in the town square, he had opted to keep to side alleys, where his presence was unlikely to attract attention. His journey took him close to his destination, where an old acacia tree provided cool cover against the sun's first rays of the morning. As he approached, he heard a dog barking from the other side of the wall, followed by a muffled shout and a slamming of an upstairs shutter. The first business of the day was getting under way as farmers started bringing produce into the local market – some with the modern workhorses of the locality, Toyota Hilux flatbeds, or, in some cases, with more traditional horses and carts. Slowly, and almost methodically, the din of street business began as the arrivals set up their stalls. Of the locals, the first to open up was the town's café, anxious to catch the other traders offering the first sales of the day. Keeping his distance, Fawaz leaned on the corner with a Russian cigarette – the kind which acted as a calling card to the locals that its owner was involved in the smuggling business – something which in the locality would be regarded as a badge of honour and worthy of respect. Importantly, if challenged, it would save him long bullshit explanations about why he had suddenly decided to return home.

Seven o'clock in the morning. The overnight bus from Tehran was late. Given the distance, it was not a surprise, more an inconvenience. He waited some more, during which time a military pick-up arrived with soldiers keen to ensure they had first pick of the traders' bargains and some headed over to the café to place their breakfast orders. The pace of activity was now growing as mothers came out on the streets to escort their kids to the nearby school and stop to chat and find out the latest gossip.

He shook his head knowingly – life in Ibrahim Sami had certainly changed in recent years due to the military presence and growing population, but, to his eyes, this was based on the same timeless patterns of behaviour that he remembered from his youth.

And then the shouting and horn blaring and about a dozen adolescents on mopeds started kicking up the dust. This was followed by the outline of a coach which came into view through the ensuing cloud. Not bad, only about fifty minutes late. The bus ground to a halt in the market square, not in any prescribed position but in a place of the driver's selection. However awkward for the traders, this bus stopped right next to them, adding to the general cacophony of noise, people and animals – both pets and others, some in cages likely to be destined for the cooking pot. The bus door opened, spilling yet more people into the throng. This was the moment Fawaz had waited for. Approaching from under the acacia tree, no one spared him any attention as he mixed with the locals. He made a point of singling out the bus driver, who, clearly tired and wanting to get into the café himself, had jumped out to unlock the luggage compartment below at the back. As he dutifully attempted to remove bags, he was pushed out of the way by several of his passengers, anxious to grasp their possessions and greet their loved ones. By being engulfed by this swirling chaotic mass of humanity, most observers would not doubt he had just arrived in town on the bus.

He did not have to try to be recognised.

"Fawaz, is it you? Why didn't you tell us you were coming home?"

Almost immediately he had to drop his case and use both hands to steady the impact of his younger sister, Shimina, who jumped into his arms.

"I can't believe it – Mum and Dad have just sent me out to buy bread and now you're here! Have they just tricked me into meeting you? I bet they have known for days, weeks, that you were coming back…"

Fawaz managed the moment well.

"I just got fed up in Tehran and decided to come home," he said.

"Oh yes? And what about your girlfriend?"

He looked surprised.

"What you mean is: you have had enough of student life and fallen out with her." Shimina was confident she had the story.

33

Fawaz didn't do anything to make her change her mind. "Oh, Faz." She used his nickname. "Mum will be thrilled. How long are you back for?"

"Not sure, really – just want to get back to normal life for a while and clear my head."

"Dad will be pleased – he's getting on with the harvest now and I know he'll want some help. Sod the shopping; we must go and see them now," she added, putting her arm firmly through his and walking purposefully back to their house.

Alternate Fridays were always hectic from Jamshid's point of view. He had to get his weekly report through to the Transport Ministry, get to the airport for the flight north, get to his parents' home, then to evening prayers and, finally, the obligatory family meal. The weekend would involve a visit to his local sports club to play football and the regular visit to his mother's tea house. Despite the routine pattern of proceedings, it was no surprise that the visit to the tea house was at the back of the list. He really wasn't interested in meeting the daughters of the city's intellectual elite, but neither did he wish to endure his mother's constant nagging. After all, if he fell out with his mum, who would do his laundry? The most bearable way of dealing with the tea house ordeal was to ensure it was preceded by the football, which would at least provide the opportunity to exorcise the demons of the week.

Normally the football would happen in the local sports hall, but this particular week it was no more than a kickabout on disused tennis courts a couple of blocks from his parents' house. The result was that he didn't have to get his formal team strip on (red shirts and black shorts) but could turn up in his standard casual wear (white T-shirt and jeans). The football was a loose arrangement with local lads – some, who he had known for years, but others who were new to him. It was a mixed bunch – in terms of age and background. Everyone from a couple of old schoolfriends, the local baker, a train driver and even an electrical engineer. Apart from playing the games, there was also plenty of opportunity to have a chat about... well, anything except politics! Most people understood, particularly in Tehran, that discussion of politics was dangerous at the best of times and sharing a discourse in a public place was definitely not the thing to do.

This particular week, the football was different. Different venue, more players and fewer he recognised. As for the game, it was farcical – players of different ages and standards, horrendous tackling, non-existent refereeing and an incoherent, rag-tag partisan crowd, not supporting a team but individual players. At the end of the game, Jamshid estimated the score at 11–8 but no one was quite sure and, in the end, nobody seemed to care. Players sat on the ground sharing cans of cola and talking through the highlights of the game from their own points of view – a series of conversations as diverse and unruly as the game itself.

It was Jamshid's turn to enter the aimless banter, discussing a late tackle that had robbed him of a certain goal, as he saw it. As he talked, his eyes moved to the middle distance and settled on a woman laughing with two or three others on the far side of the pitch. Whatever point he thought he was making at that moment fell away as he stood, hesitated and sprinted towards her.

"Mahta? Remember me from the restaurant in Bandar Abbas? I was going to call..."

Clearly unimpressed with having her conversation interrupted, she made him wait before engaging.

She looked blank. "No, sorry, should I know you?"

"We were in the Apadana restaurant in Bandar on Thursday night..."

The two girls with her started to look hostile. She said: "Look I am really sorry, but I don't know you and I've certainly not been – where did you say? – in Bandar Abbas, wherever that is," and started to laugh – a signal taken up by her friends.

He mumbled an apology and walked away... after three paces, he turned to look at her once more and knew he was not mistaken.

Returning home, he showered and set off for the tea house, reflecting on the strange encounter and mentioned it to his father.

"Don't worry, son; that's the way women are. I remember your mother being difficult when I first met her. She should have been a lawyer – our courtship was like negotiating a contract; that was how she got her clauses into me." He laughed.

"Now, talking of girls, Mrs Alrakahthan is coming to see your mother this afternoon with her daughter Hanah – well, if I was your age that would give me something to think about. She is in advertising or something and I hear getting a date with her can be difficult. She has a brother, Hasan, who used to come along to my tutorials. I'm not sure what happened to him after university – there was talk of him going to Harvard – but you and Mum will probably find out. You see, your mother knows how to go about fixing these things."

His dad was right – Hanah was indeed a looker. A tall willowy figure with a bright patterned headscarf and a smile too wide to get through the door. Jamshid recognised her type – used to being the centre of attention and probably high maintenance.

Definitely with the wow factor, she reminded him of a baklava, the enticing honey-covered pastry – so often the best accompaniment to afternoon tea – attractive to look at, sensational to taste, but the ability to make you sick if you had too much of it.

The one surprise in the fragrant Hanah's presentation: she seemed to be enthralled to her mother.

After the usual pleasantries and small talk, the dialogue withered as the respective mothers took over and their conversation became transactional.

"Hanah and Jamshid would be great together, Mrs Alrakahthan."

"I'll have a word with my husband, and we'll see if we can arrange Jamshid to be transferred to Tehran."

Alarm bells started ringing in Jamshid's mind from this snippet of conversation and it was time to bring this chat to a close.

"Don't you get tired of being told what to do?" he said to Hanah, but without waiting for her reply he leaned across and gave her a long and unhurried kiss. The tactic produced mixed results. The target of his open affection was shocked, resisted but then responded. The respective mothers looked disbelievingly and were appalled in equal measure.

He too was surprised, nervous and exhilarated. It was a deliberately outrageous action designed to negate any cosy matriarchal scheme.

Surprised, as he was not naturally an impetuous, instinctive person; nervous, because he knew his flagrant move was at best impolite and at worst an assault in public; and exhilarated because, actually, he quite enjoyed it.

However, now was not the time to hang around.

"Great to meet you, Hanah, Mrs Alrakahthan, I hope I will have the pleasure of meeting you again."

And to his mother: "I'm sorry, Mum, but I've got to leave. There are a lot of things I need to sort out before I go back to Bandar – see you at home later." ·

Jamshid didn't wait to continue the conversation and couldn't be witness to the reaction he left behind.

His first urgent appointment was two blocks away at the twenty-four-hour fried chicken shop.

Ibrahim Sami was a relatively small rural community in a distant corner of north-west Iran few knew of or cared about. Although it was close to an international border, relations with Azerbaijan were basically good and until recently the area was not militarised. Locals were not sure what had led to the change of circumstance that had resulted in the construction of an army base nearby, combined with a garrison and airfield, but hadn't felt especially hostile to the prospect. To the casual observer, on the surface, life in Sami hadn't changed that much. The area's communications were limited to satellite systems, but the military kept a low profile. Their arrival had led to the emergence of a kind of "under the counter" cottage industry, with a number of local entrepreneurs starting to invest in shops selling Western-branded outdoor clothing and footwear, bargain designer fragrances, music and entertainment DVDs. The baker's café, the launderette and the general store selling food had expanded, a Chinese restaurant had opened and the daily market provided the focus of day-to-day activity, filling the air with the scent of spices and cooked meats. But the regular appearance of off-duty soldiers provided other opportunities for commercial activity such as the guest house, ironically situated next to the mosque, where, for a fee, alcohol was available and it was rumoured the company of attractive women (mostly smuggled in from Pakistan so it was said) could be found. The local entrepreneurs had been smart: they kept their new wealth hidden behind closed doors. It was not in their interest to cause a problem or have the eye of the state staring into their affairs.

As Fawaz left the central square on the arm of his sister, he noticed more signs of new prosperity in the village – buildings he could remember as looking ramshackle now rebuilt. Modern doorways with electronic intercoms for access and more and better cars. In his youth the Peugeot 504 estate was the vehicle of choice for those able to afford it, but today's equivalents were with Toyota Hi-Luxes or Mitsubishi Shoguns – even one or two had Mercedes, but the result was that, even in some of the village's narrower alleys, parked cars were starting to block access for the few still using horses and donkeys. Like so many parts of the world, Ibrahim Sami was starting to be squeezed between the old and new. Young people, particularly those educated at the madrassah, were moving away, rather than following in their parents' footsteps in working the land. There was no doubt Sami's farmers were now older and their working lives were that much harder. And, as for the new, they seemed to be outsiders – patrons of a new military economy.

Fawaz's father was well aware of the problem and had only recently taken a loan to buy new tractors as the physical demands of tending his fields with horses was becoming too much. Talking to his neighbours, he would use one of the tractors on their fields for a fee that would help them in the sowing and harvesting of the fruit and vegetables that were the life blood of the local economy. His use of automated equipment was still relatively new in the area, and as a result he was seen as one of Sami's elder statesmen, someone who was a pillar of the community and consulted on governance issues.

This influential position in the local community had also provided the opportunity to enter local politics and run for Governor Mayor, but this was a step too far. He was old enough to understand the dangers of political activity and the corruption it produced.

The regional Governor Mayor was appointed directly from Tehran, had absolute power over the local judiciary and civil administration and no connection with the locality, although he did retain a compound in Posyan, some eighteen kilometres away. As far as the locals were concerned, the governor mayor was God's representative in the locality and the sermons of Friday prayers would have to be submitted to his office in advance by the local mullah to carry his seal of authority. Despite the respect of his peers, Fawaz's father was not going to be able to compete with that and was careful to keep a low profile as a result. For him, keeping the right side of the military was a greater concern. When the new Revolutionary Guard base at Posyan, outside Sami, was established, it came by executive order from Tehran. There had been no consultation or compensation for local landowners and, although he specifically had not been affected, some of his neighbours had lost their livelihoods as a result. It had created a lot of bitterness and mistrust and for a while Fawaz's father had been caught up in it. Some of his neighbours felt his opposition to the central government's action had not been strong enough, yet from a practical perspective he knew that direct challenge was not the way to deal with the military. He resolved to work with them and to be a source of positive influence. His strategy had produced rewards but in a typically understated way. For example, with the tacit support of local 'off-duty' soldiers, he had, from time to time, been invited to participate in covert raiding parties which had crossed over the border into Azerbaijan to steal whatever they could find – money, girls, food, equipment, even guns. Just like similar groups over there who made a living doing the reverse. The pocket money it provided had been useful in hard times and these activities had cemented his reputation as a local 'fixer'. He won praise for not chasing land compensation payments, but his prospects to win preferential contracts to support the successful operation of the base were enhanced. The commandant, Colonel Rashid Rahman had become a friend, especially as he came to know Fawaz's father had no interest in military or security matters. From time to time, he would receive an invitation to have lunch at the base, which had proved to be surprisingly informal. Rahman would tell him something of what went on at the base and Fawaz's father was smart enough to know that he was being tested, in order to see whether he could be trusted not to tell others what was going on. As time passed, the relationship between the two became stronger, with Fawaz's father being able to access the sort of military intelligence a foreign power would pay handsomely for. But he knew the power of a quiet life without the scrutiny of the state, which did not need an excuse to arrest and imprison. His special relationship meant he was one of the first in the locality to hear of another state investment in the locality. Given the ongoing pressures of international sanctions, the state had set an objective to become self-sufficient in food production, but the strategy was not just about encouraging local people to get on the land; it was also about harnessing the power of science to produce more crops and meat. Sami had been selected as the place for a research station to develop fertilisers and associated chemicals that would accelerate production, so the story went. Clearly, because of the nature of its work, a secure site was needed. A place 'off the beaten track' that no one would know or care about. That was important as any plan to build a new facility on quality arable land would make trouble for the Governor Mayor. For Fawaz's father, the solution was obvious. The road north in Khoda Afrin Prefecture, towards Ashelqu, would offer suitable sites. A short drive out of town there were a couple of tracks to the left which hugged the barren hills away from the fertile lands of the valleys. Here no one would care what you did. A dedicated road would ensure only those with business would go there, and, let's face it, anyone who worked there would want to live in Sami or close by. Maybe there would be a need to build some more modern quality homes fit for those who would be required to move into the area. The Commandant had seen merit in the idea and had won the support of the Governor Mayor. The land was entirely in the gift of Khoda Afrin Prefecture, so the Commandant and Governor Mayor had put the idea to Tehran and it was agreed. With the two senior officials in the area backing the scheme, the prospect of success and profit was guaranteed. Fawaz's father would only benefit marginally, but, as one of Sami's leading entrepreneurs, he saw indirect benefit coming to the town, creating demand for new commercial services that he would invest in.

That had been a couple of years ago. The research base had been built as had the new ranch style houses on the edge of Sami. The Commandant and Governor Mayor had done very well selling the housing, as well as taking central government fees for building the research facility. Fawaz's father knew about the development of the plan and hadn't been happy when he found twenty sheep dead nearby, but had been rewarded for his silence by being granted additional land for cultivation on the northern side of town. Soldiers had taken the carcasses away and the matter was not talked about again. Sami had benefitted too, as new businesses were established, including a gymnasium, cinema and entertainment centre, consisting of snooker tables and internet café, which were already popular with the off-duty military. At last, life was looking good for all concerned until a local merchant from Ashelqu driving to Sami made an unfortunate discovery. Making the journey twice a week, there was little he didn't know about the constantly changing landscape, one minute verdant irrigated fields, the next barren rocky and empty terrain. Not far from the new research station, the merchant had seen what looked like a large sack about ten metres from the roadside. It was an unusual sight and very visible to anyone passing by, not least because a large bird of prey was also circling the site. He couldn't recall why he had stopped to investigate – perhaps it had been just a momentary hunch – but he soon wished he hadn't bothered. The hessian bag was big. Big enough to contain a body. The merchant had started to realise what it was before touching it and looking inside. The stench and flies wildly gyrating around the bag had given him due warning about what to expect. Upon opening it, he found the body of a man in blood-stained, ragged clothing curled in a foetal position. The body half fell out of the hessian sack, with the head and right arm being the only exposed flesh. Behind the beard the man's face and neck were a mass of boils and blisters – so too was the exposed arm and hand. That was when the panic set in. The merchant left hurriedly to continue his journey. Out of the corner of his eye on the next ridge overlooking his position the sun caught the reflection of a mirror or glasses looking in his direction. He had been over halfway to his destination and had relatively little time to work out what to do. If he went to the police in person, the chances were he would be arrested and held until his report had been investigated. If he failed to report it, the registration of his car would have been picked up on police speed control cameras nearby. He would be traced and asked why he had not reported what he had found. Either way, he decided his prospects didn't look great. Perhaps there was a logical explanation for what he had seen and all would be OK. In the end, his course of action was decided by the fact that a roadside parking place had just been vacated as he arrived, and right next to it was a public payphone. The merchant took the opportunity to deliver his cargo of textiles to his partner, who had a stall in the market. Normally he would have allowed time to chat how business was doing, gossip and take orders for later in the week – maybe have time for a glass of tea before departing, but this day was different; he was twitchy. He made his excuses – his new wife wasn't well – and had to depart without delay. He then went to the payphone and made the call. It wasn't a conversation – he did not identify himself and gave the bare essential information about what he had seen and when. He wiped the receiver with his sleeve and went to his pick-up. He hesitated before starting the engine, knowing that he needed to set off carefully to avoid attracting attention. His plan almost worked. As he accelerated out of the parking space a man on a bicycle suddenly appeared in front of him and was knocked to the ground by the impact with the pick-up. The man on the bicycle had not been injured but nonetheless vented his anger on the merchant, dragging him out of his vehicle and wrestling him to the ground. Surprised bystanders intervened to pull the men apart but by that time the damage was done. Through the melee and confusion, the merchant could see a uniformed policeman approaching.

For people familiar with the way things work in Iran, seeing a uniformed policeman was often a welcome sight. Most police didn't have uniform, carried guns and often had a very individual approach to law enforcement. In this instance, the policeman had been on a tea break in the market, was uniformed and clearly wasn't looking for extra work before the end of his shift. His powers of analysis were good. There was no damage to either the pick-up, bicycle or either of the protagonists and he'd arrived early enough before serious blows could be exchanged. He told the merchant to get on his way and took the man on the bicycle to one side to give him a talking to. Again, as is typical in Iran, the forces of law and order would make their own judgement and tended to favour the wealthier party regardless of who was right or wrong. The added piece of luck the merchant had was that it was clear the policeman he had met had no idea about his earlier call.

As he set off back the way he had travelled, he passed the entrance to the research station and saw a military patrol vehicle had parked nearby. Two soldiers, not police, were standing over the sack. His eye returned to the road and he continued the journey home.

There was a gentle knock on the door – "Come in," he called. Shimina walked in.

"Dinner is nearly ready," she said.

"Where's Dad?" Fawaz asked casually.

"On his way," Shimina said. "Should be here within the hour. He's really excited to hear you're back."

So much for the surprise.

"Shall we wait for him?" he asked. Then, answering his own question, "I think that would be best. Tell you what, I just fancy a quick walk to freshen up first, I won't be long."

Shimina had been about to say she would go with him, but his quick reaction had cut off the possibility.

THREE

IT HAD ONLY BEEN five or so years but to Fawaz his absence
had seemed longer – the poverty of Sami that he had been keen
to escape had largely disappeared. He remembered that some of
his compatriots as well as his seniors used to gather in the town
square, hoping to be hired for the day on local building sites.
Although there didn't seem to be much new construction under
way, the town centre, at least, looked well cared for and busy.
There certainly weren't numbers of youths fresh out of school
loitering around looking for something to do, but maybe they
were just hanging out somewhere else. The prime purpose of
social gathering in the centre of town had been for the monthly
executions. Usually half a dozen local miscreants – thieves of
one sort or another – would be presented for ritual charging and
humiliation, stone and shit throwing, before being suspended
on a construction crane to die. Bodies would be high enough
off the ground to be seen by those at the back of the crowd
and normally left for a few days, until they started to smell and
attract the interest of the suburban crows. Looking around town
now, it was hard to imagine the recent past.

Walking arm in arm with his sister, Fawaz left the noise of the
centre and headed off on the side street, where he had often kicked

a ball with his mates. It was relatively quiet now, save one or two passers-by, mainly women in *hijabs* on their daily shopping trip and a couple of war veterans, one missing an eye, the other a leg, having a smoke in a doorway. Two hundred metres further on, and Shimina brought Fawaz into a small square, and back to the front door of his parents' house.

Following his clandestine arrival, Fawaz had in the half-light approached his father's farm from the rear, where not much appeared to have changed. The front, facing onto the residential street, looked very different. Whitewashed with red painted window frames and shutters, the family farm now looked an imposing residence, not lavish in the way that would draw criticism or questions from locals, but a status symbol nonetheless.

Shimina opened the door and almost walked into a woman cleaning a mirror in the hallway.

"Khalifa, where is my mother?" she asked.

The woman pointed to the first doorway and purposely departed through a door opposite.

"Mum – look who I have just found in the market," as she propelled Fawaz through the door.

His mother, deftly sewing a *susani*, stood up, screamed with joy and hugged him, her face contorted in delight at seeing her boy.

"Why did you not tell me you were coming home? Why haven't you written? Where have you been?"

The three questions were clearly going to take some time to answer, so his mother immediately called Khalifa (who turned out to be the housekeeper) to bring tea and almond cake. Fawaz prepared to tell his mother and Shimina of his adventures in Tehran.

He had not been surprised by his father's absence as he had expected him to be out in the fields and on with the harvest. From one of the rear windows, he could see beyond the chicken shed to the land beyond and a tractor in the distance. He was also not expecting to hear the machine was being driven by Hanif, the husband of Khalifa, and that his father had driven to Posyan for a meeting. It was too soon to start enquiring about the reason or purpose of his absence other than to ask when he was expected back.

"He always returns for dinner," said his mother with a smile, "which will allow Khalifa to prepare your bedroom and finish the cooking."

Already Fawaz was seeing the changes in family life – his mother, father and sister living comfortably under the same roof with another couple who, to his eyes, were housekeeper and farm hand and presumably paid by his father. Life at home had clearly changed. Had his family become one of the middle-class members of local society? And since when had his father started attending 'meetings' – with whom, about what? Clearly there was much to think about. His expectation of home and the reality were very different. Heaven knows what he would say to his father and how he might explain the unannounced guests in his barn. For now, he had stuck to his prepared story about life in Tehran and his student activities, which had been largely accepted by his mother and sister, although in the case of the latter he seemed to think she had not really bought his motivation and reasons for dropping out of contact. He was also aware of what he had learned in London: not to be overly self-critical. Khalifa took his travel bag up to his room, which provided him with his next surprise. It was exactly as he had left it. The bed remained in the same position – so did the wardrobe and chest of drawers with the poster of the Barcelona football team and that view over the chicken shed, down towards the river with the hills of Azerbaijan in the far distance. It was now early afternoon and he had not slept for thirty-six hours. He lay on the bed and stared at the ceiling before falling asleep.

Dave crouched with his back against a bale and signalled to his colleagues to stay quiet and still. The barn door had opened and there was shouting as two locals herded some forty sheep inside. He was not sure of the exact time, but it was dusk and the shepherds had decided it was best to get the sheep in, as this was the time wolves would come down from higher ground looking for food. The shepherds filled the feeders, locked the sheep in the pen, pulled down the mezzanine ladder and left. The tranquil atmosphere of the barn had changed as a result, with animals jostling for position to get the best feeding places. The closure of the barn door resulted in the team relaxing on their makeshift beds. Dave and Rodg had blocked the back windows of the barn with bales which allowed the them to use their torches.

Dave said, "Fawaz will be here soon. Be ready to move in one hour from now."

Nobody spoke – each lost in their own thoughts, but all prepared their equipment and checked their pistols.

North-west Iran was a funny place at that time of year. During the day you could be sweating buckets but when the sun went down you could freeze. Stepping out on to the street, Fawaz felt the chill breeze and wished he was wearing his insulated combat fatigues from the night before. However, he consoled himself with the idea he wasn't going far. He looked left and right to check no one else was around and hurried off towards the edge of Ibrahim Sami. Coming to the third barn door, he saw it had been locked. His fiddling with the padlock was loud enough for all inside to be braced for trouble, but it was left to Fawaz to be surprised by the number of sheep inside. It would certainly reassure the uninvited visitor. Dave and Rodg had arranged cover firing positions on the door if needed. It was Jo who first answered Fawaz's call.

"Everything OK?" Fawaz decided not to waste time explaining his first visit to Sami in several years. He nodded and smiled.

"So far so good. But there needs to be a change of plan. My dad is not back for an hour and I have to have dinner with the family. I can't get to you before midnight. Are you happy to have a look around without me?"

Dave spoke for the group. "I think I know where the target is, but I could be wrong. Now it's getting dark, it's time we were on our way. Come back at midnight and wait for us. We can talk about what we've found out then."

Dave was now moving into leader mode. This felt like a suggestion but was really an instruction. Fawaz was first out of the door and moved right. Dave and the rest of the group strained to listen to the sound of the sheep and moved quietly outside to the left. After 100 metres the lighting finished and the road became a track and, shortly after, the track disappeared. The group skirted around the edge of the settlement, following a route parallel with the main road out of town to the north. It was more challenging than expected. Although confident with the direction, it was difficult following the matrix of field boundaries and ditches which would provide cover for the trip. The last thing Dave wanted was for the team to leave a complete set of tracks across a field shortly to be harvested. If the experience of trying to find a non-detectable route to a target whose location their leader was unsure about wasn't enough, the group had to come to terms with the sounds of the night. It was too cold for crickets, but the call of nightjars and owls were apparent, interspersed by the distant cry of wolves. The irony of circumventing a cultivated field against a background not of cars or people but of the wild calls of nature somehow seemed a bit weird. The juxtaposition was broken by the sound of a shotgun coming from the lower grounds towards the river. Funnily enough, it was this sound which gave Jack confidence. His father had been a farmer and used a shotgun to bring down foxes, badgers and other wild things that might be likely to attack his flock. This was an old-fashioned sound and probably a rifle, something akin to a poachers' .22, a weapon more likely to make a point than actually kill something it was directed at. However, it served notice that they may not be the only ones out in the vicinity at this time of night.

Dave was much better organised than Jack had given him credit for. The group leader had known that at some point on their journey they would need to cross the main highway to the north, a route well-lit as it approached the town with the added hazard of traffic cameras, at least as far as the junction for their target location.

The question was where? Logic suggested the best place would be immediately behind one of the cameras as if they were to be caught on film it would be at the edge of the equipment's focusing capacity. Now the group had got as far as the highway's edge, Dave was working out his options. Examination of the position put them close to a bend and a layby capable of accommodating three trucks. All available space was taken for the night thus cutting the field of vision. The result was a natural crossing point which the group used one by one at five-minute intervals. Their silent movement did not disturb the drivers, who had their cab curtains drawn. Crossing the road had also meant a sharp change in the terrain. Here there were no fields of pomegranate, almond trees or groves of olives – just barren rocks and scree. The stones were lighter-coloured and, although there was cloud cover, the brightness of the night would make them appear more visible if someone happened to be looking. This was a chance they had to take... and someone was indeed looking. He had only picked them up by chance but now watched intently. They were moving in the right direction and the watcher was generally impressed with the pace of their progress. He estimated they would get to the ridge above the camp in around twenty minutes. Although some distance away further along the valley floor, he would have to move to a new position to maintain his surveillance. The group were following in Dave's footsteps – literally – and kept their eyes fixed on the ground to avoid tripping up over sharp stones, or worse, creating even a minor rock fall. The pace was rapid, unlike their previous journey, as they knew there was no ordnance in their way. When Dave stopped to check his bearings, the whole group stopped – just as well, as Dave had adopted an odd semi-crawling movement, using his hands to support his crouched progress over the craggy terrain. His own grip and balance, although better than most, caused some cursing among his colleagues when he inadvertently put his gloved hand on a small black snake, which attempted a bite as he threw the writhing creature away to the boulders below. The muttered curse was only a minor distraction and certainly did not cause unnecessary delay. The moment of arrival at the target came suddenly and unexpectedly soon, pressing him flat against the rock and signalling his colleagues to come up either side of him. Here was the edge of the ridge above the target. He was initially disappointed that his elevated position did not give him the clear view of the compound below. Yes, it was well lit but between his position and the camp was a wall of conifers; some seemed mature, at least ten years old, but what had they been planted in to make them grow? There certainly wasn't any topsoil. Bet they brought it in, he thought. Now moving slowly, each in turn slid down the slope and close to the outer perimeter fencing. For tonight, this was journey's end.

The purpose now was to observe what was happening and Dave signalled Jack forward to record the scene.

Fawaz didn't have many clothes with him but his wardrobe afforded him choices of styles which he had forgotten. Inside the family home and not on show, a clean white T-shirt and jeans were easily available. He felt strange – a guest in his own family home. It was relaxing and stressful at the same time. Home had changed a lot: certainly not as spartan as he remembered it. His mother had always insisted on a daily family meal in the evening and tonight her wish of the past three years was about to be realised. While he had been out for his walk, his father had returned and had gone to his study to make a couple of calls. As Fawaz had come down the stairs, his father had heard his approach, had broken off and was waiting at the bottom, his arms wide in welcome. He engulfed

Fawaz with a firm squeeze, leaving him in no doubt he had been missed.

"I've wanted you home for so long," his father cried.

"Life here has been so hard; I needed your help. Why have you not called? We have been worried sick. It was only by asking your unit that I was told you weren't dead."

As often with families, there had been a communication breakdown. Following being injured after the last war, where most of his compatriots had been killed or maimed or taken prisoner, there was not a great welcome awaiting at home for a defeated soldier. It was hard to imagine that, back then, there had been barely enough to eat and drinking water had been rationed in some places, up to a year after hostilities had ceased.

"Enough of the questions, Hafiz," called his wife, Dilshad. "Our boy is back, our family is complete and we can catch up on all our news in the coming days. First let's eat…"

His mother had always been a good cook, which according to his father was the reason why he had married her. The real secret of cooking was always because they had a ready supply of fresh vegetables and meat, especially chicken and lamb. Tonight, they had planned a feast.

Typical Persian main dishes are combinations of rice with meat, or fish and some onion, vegetables, nuts and herbs. To achieve a balanced taste, characteristic Persian flavourings such as saffron, dried limes, cinnamon and parsley are mixed delicately and used in some special dishes. Many foods famously associated with Middle Eastern, and indeed world, cuisine have their origins in Iran, such as kebab, ranging from Chelow kebab, kebab-e barg, Joojeh (chicken) kebab to Ghafghazi. These are traditionally served with local, fresh herbs and could be accompanied with Mast-o-musir or Shirazi salad. Hafiz called for some of his best Shiraz wine from the Zagros mountains down south and they drank late into the night…

"Hey, it's Hanah – you asked me a question this afternoon and you didn't give me the chance to answer. Call me…" Jamshid hit the recall button on his phone. It had only been an hour since he had left her at his mother's tea house in Akbari Street. Seemed there was at least one person he hadn't managed to upset.

"Meet me on the observation deck at the Milad Tower – I will be there in thirty minutes."

Jamshid was impressed with the sense of purpose in her voice. He sensed this was an appointment he had to keep.

Of course, the tower was an unmistakable meeting place – not only easy to see but one of the few spots in the city where parking was readily available. It would have been quicker for him to have used the Hemmat Expressway but, given where he was, he would have to take the longer route via the Hakim Expressway and Milad Hospital. Congestion in the afternoons was such in Tehran that the concept of a rush hour didn't have any meaning and the term "expressway" seemed only to have psychological value. It had been some years since he had been to the Milad Tower and so he was pleased to have the excuse to go.

Arriving at the observation deck, he noticed that the queue to take the lift down had been greater than the line he had joined to ascend, so there was comfortable room to wander round, enjoying the views of the surrounding metropolis.

It was a rare opportunity to enjoy the panorama of western Asia's most populous city through the haze and pollution of the day. He used the capital's other iconic symbol, the white marble-clad Azadi Tower out towards the western entrance to the city centre, as his point of reference, working his eye slowly eastward, to work out where his parents' house was. Just when he thought he'd pinpointed it, a voice whispered in his ear, "Thanks for coming. I suggest you don't greet me in the same way as you did in the tea house." He turned and was immediately relieved she had approached him. Unlike their earlier meeting, Hanah was wearing a light brown headscarf, dark glasses and a Burberry.

The extent of her disguise made him wonder at first if it was the same woman.

"It was a real pleasure to meet a proper man, Jamshid. I really wonder whether there are many left in Tehran these days. She had now taken off her glasses and stood next to him, but her brown eyes were staring straight ahead at the view below.

"Your mother tells me you are living in Bandar right now scheduling sea exports." Jamshid stiffened slightly at that point. Sharing where he lived was one thing, but his mother telling anyone who may ask what he did for a living was a little unnerving. He nodded.

"I find that really interesting," she said. Now he was worried. If she found that "interesting", she couldn't have much of a life.

"I work in sales and advertising for my father's business, so I am always looking for export opportunities and I hear you are looking to come back to Tehran. I think we could help each other... once we can get acquainted."

The line sounded like something from a Hollywood B movie of the 1950s but, as Jamshid had already realised, this was a serious person, not like the usual parade of mothers and daughters normally served up at the family tea house on a Saturday afternoon.

"You must come to dinner at my villa in Karaj tomorrow and meet my father – eight o'clock. Don't be late." She put a card in the breast pocket of his jacket and walked briskly towards the lift, which was about to descend. The steel doors closing prevented him from joining her.

Jamshid had planned to get an earlier flight to Bandar, which would have meant the dinner engagement in Karaj was out of the question, but curiosity or just instinct told him to stay over. It was secret among his colleagues that he made his regular visit to Tehran, so, for the sake of a day, it was easy to call in sick and return a day late. His job scheduling freight movements out of the country was frustrating enough and his delayed return would hardly make his job harder than it already was. Returning to his parent's house in town, he saw his father reading in the study, puffing on his shisha pipe – his mother had already gone to bed.

"You know, she was really upset about how it went at the tea house," his father ventured. "She really didn't know what to say." A first, he thought to himself.

"It was just as well nobody complained, or you would have had the police on your back."

As they had met in a private booth in the tea house, Jamshid was not too worried as the only complaint would have come from Hanah's mother and considering he now had a dinner invitation it couldn't have mattered too much.

"Actually, Dad, I am sorry – I spoke with Hanah personally to apologise afterwards and she was OK and I'll tell Mum tomorrow. I was stupid and did it to shock her into stopping trying to organise my life – I'll be away to Bandar soon and expect everyone will have forgotten about it by the end of the week."

His father nodded and returned to his book.

The journey to Karaj was about a twenty-minute drive, but, as usual, when the congestion was factored in, the trip seemed a lot longer. He had risen late and missed his mother before she went to work so he had allowed a bit of extra time to drop in at the tea house and visit the galleria nearby for some flowers. The arrangement had gone smoothly – the satnav in the family car had taken him directly to his destination, a smart residential district and a tree-lined avenue.

Hanah had answered the door in person. Dressed in a cream, tailored designer-label silk blouse and brown culottes and dark green heels, she looked every inch a stylish, Western woman. Her shoulder-length brown hair was tied back, which had the effect of accentuating her high cheekbones. The hallway of her home was similarly affluent yet understated. High-ceilinged with a chandelier, large wall mirrors and a couple of landscape paintings depicting views of lakes and mountains. The floors were marble and featured a dark, ornately patterned rug which looked too expensive for people with shoes to walk on. And yet it also felt cold and anonymous. Jamshid reckoned he could have walked into several homes of the country's elite and found a similar scene. He saw nothing which had a personal or emotional connection. No family photographs, books or magazines.

"Great to see you. I hope our house was not difficult for you to find."

Her welcome seemed more formal on this occasion, although he had to concede he had started their relationship in a very forward way so maybe they needed to retrace their steps.

She was pleased with the flowers but left them on a chair in the hall before leading him straight through to the dining room, where a small, stocky figure of a man stood to greet him.

"May I introduce you to my father, Abdullo Alrakahthan?" she said. "We run some import/export agencies in Tehran together." Jamshid nodded, met his gaze and shook his hand. Sensing his hesitation, she quickly added, "My mother cannot join us as she has gone with Hasan to my grandparents in Tabriz for a family visit, so it's just the three of us."

At that moment, a male servant entered the room with three glasses of sparkling wine.

"Champagne?" Abdullo enquired, more by way of statement than invitation.

"I think the taste of Pol is so much fresher than the rest. Some of the stuff the French serve up these days is crap, but this is good."

Jamshid was initially surprised with the offer because, although consuming alcohol was banned in the country, the law was widely flouted in private, especially when there were no witnesses. Maybe he was being tested, but as he had not been offered an alternative he had chosen to accept.

"Let us drink to friendship," Abdullo suggested.

Jamshid briefly felt uncomfortable. Had he been lured here by his daughter to face some sort of punishment from the previous day?

Fortunately, Hanah moved the conversation forward.

"Your mother had told my mother a lot about you," she started.

Jamshid tried not to show his irritation.

"You schedule exports for the Port of Bandar Abbas but you are trying to get a job back in Tehran. We have some growing businesses and could benefit from someone with your experience."

Jamshid realised this conversation may not be going in a direction he could control.

So far, the private dinner for two with an attractive but as yet unknown woman had not come to pass. He had met a man he knew nothing about, who had offered him a job without much thought or research. Maybe he should just cut and run. He was normally good at making excuses, but Abdullo was right. The champagne was good and the dinner of lamb tagine with fresh rosemary was excellent. The alcohol may have been illegal, but it loosened up his tongue to create some great conversation, which moved away from business to food, fashion, football and fast cars.

From an uncertain start, the evening had passed quickly. Jamshid took his cue from Abdullo, who decided to leave after coffee.

"There's no hurry," said Abdullo, heading for the door. "You two have not had a chance to talk without me being involved. Take your time and use it well. I hope we may meet again soon."

With that he was gone. And, as had been planned all along, the real talking started.

"So our meeting was not down to fate," Jamshid began.

"I suppose that depends on how you define fate," Hanah countered, "I have come not to believe in luck," she said.

"I am surprised you had not heard of my father. He has done is homework on you. He is one of Iran's most successful businessmen who has managed to avoid jail. He is an entrepreneur. When he was young, he was selling American cigarettes in the bazaar, saved enough to buy a general store, which he grew to become one of the country's biggest supermarket chains. He was only able to succeed because he made friends with government officials and created opportunities for them to share in the wealth he created, eventually selling the business to a consortium led by a former mayor of this city. That wealth has enabled him to establish new broader import/export businesses where I work as his assistant.

"One of the lessons he learned in the retail trade was not to employ more people than necessary and make full use of technology when it can be accessed. So although successful we are a small organisation, but highly organised. It's funny: in this age of international sanctions, we only have to go to Dubai to buy all the expertise we need. Getting goods into Iran is not that difficult, be that luxury items from wine to cars. But our future depends on our ability to sell Iranian commodities and products overseas. The government gives us freedom to run our businesses provided we create opportunity for them to earn dollars to keep the nation solvent. They are not interested in what we sell or how we sell it, provided we can bring home money to the exchequer. The Great Satan is our competitor, constantly finding ways to prevent us trading. Our job is to find ways of countering their efforts. You will understand we are interested in how you are scheduling oil exports and how your expertise could be harnessed for..." she paused, "a variety of other products ranging from commodities to semi-finished goods."

"Are your problems about finding customers or finding the means to get products to them?" Jamshid asked.

"My father allows me to market our services in an appropriate way, but logistics are complicated so I think that is where you can help."

"Why me?"

"You are in the right position, are the right age and have the right ambition. Working with us gives you all the money you could ever want... plus..." she paused, "other benefits."

"And if I don't accept?"

"When you think about what we are proposing, I am sure you will. My experience has been that those who receive our invitations find the opportunity worthwhile, but those who don't... well, fate tends not to smile on them. You will understand, we have eyes and ears everywhere and have an ability to show displeasure if necessary, wherever you are."

Jamshid found his mind processing information very quickly. This was not the evening encounter he had imagined. Here he was, a young, aspiring middle-ranking manager for a port authority in the Islamic Republic drinking champagne in a luxurious villa, alone with a mysterious beautiful woman at a late hour talking of... of what the Revolutionary Guard would label "treachery".

He had to go and got up to make his excuses.

"Pity you have to go so soon. You are welcome to stay."

She placed a gentle kiss on his cheek. Jamshid had moved to the door.

"I will ask one of my people to see you out," she continued.

"Oh, and, Jamshid, take care on the drive home. I hear alcohol affects the senses, especially when driving at night, and, don't worry, I will be in touch very soon."

His car was waiting in the drive, engine running. He got behind the wheel and headed home.

He was on Highway 32 heading for the Mehrabad airport and city centre. The anonymous suburban vista passed him by quickly as he drove into the metropolitan area. Street lighting told him he was approaching the capital and he was following signs for Chitgar and the Lashgari Expressway. Traffic was understandably light considering the hour and yet, inexplicably, he had missed the flashing lights of the highway patrol coming up behind him, overtaking and signalling him to pull over.

He complied and drew to a stop. Two armed police got out of the car and came to the driver's window.

"Good evening. This is a security check. Please step out of your vehicle."

Jamshid complied.

"We have reason to believe you have consumed alcohol. We will search your vehicle and test your breath. If we find evidence, we will arrest you."

Offences with alcohol normally involved prison stays and public flogging.

His heart sank. He knew his accusers didn't need evidence to take action. Nonetheless, they went through the pantomime of a slow and thorough check of his car and then took the breath test.

The lead officer had told him to spread his legs and put his hands behind his back.

He was cuffed and kicked in the groin. The two officers stood over him. The junior pulled out a mobile phone and turned away to make a call. A short conversation ensued, before turning to his colleague and nodding.

"Seems Allah is merciful even at this time of night," said the senior partner. "You have friends who are concerned about your welfare. I have been told it is not necessary to restrain you with the cuffs, provided you drive home carefully."

The lead officer kneeled down to release the hand cuffs, stood and walked to join his partner in the patrol car.

"Oh, and Mr Alrakahthan wishes you a safe flight to Bandar in the morning."

Jamshid heard the slamming of the door and listened to the patrol car heading off into the night. At least his arms were now free to hold his crotch as he continued to writhe on the verge where he had fallen.

The thicket provided Dave and his team the closest cover to the camp perimeter fence, which he estimated to be fifty metres away. From here, the floodlighting provided a panoramic view of the facility and yet the nature of the light was concentrated so the area beyond its boundaries remained in darkness. There were four apparently separate blocks of buildings, each of three storeys with flat roofs. The central area looked like some sort of parade ground with a designated landing area for a helicopter. To the back of the compound (and the nearest part from his position) were storage tanks for fuel and water and a third which had a plethora of valves on it, which seemed to be for some sort of gas, but he couldn't tell at this range. The compound appeared to have only one entrance, protected by three checkpoints with heavy concrete blocks positioned either side. It was surrounded by what appeared to be a white wall, possibly two metres high, then barbed razor wire, then steel fencing. Dave couldn't be sure if the arrangement was designed to stop people getting in or getting out, but, on the basis that there were no watchtowers, he assumed the former. Again, it was difficult to tell from a distance, but there seemed to be a generous space between each perimeter boundary and he could see two uniformed soldiers with a dog patrolling between the outer wall and the razor wire. Interestingly, the anti-aircraft battery which he had heard about was a mobile facility parked in a layby outside the front of the camp, suggesting this was a temporary arrangement. Further scanning of the layout showed him a parking area with six tarpaulin-covered trucks and as many civilian four-by-four off-road vehicles. The overall impression of the place was that it was not a base focused on external operations and its size was correspondingly small, relying on one external entrance.

Given the small hours and despite the light around the compound, there did not seem to be much activity taking place, but, quite by chance, he was fortunate enough to see a camouflaged military truck arrive for entry. This wasn't a general transport vehicle but looked like a refrigerated lorry commonplace on any civilian road. His field glasses focused on the reception arrangements – guards meeting the truck, the driver getting out and taking papers to the guard house. A few minutes later the driver emerged together with a soldier and the first barriers went up. As they closed behind the truck, the second barriers opened and then the third. No vehicle could drive straight in. The truck moved to the furthest left block – ideally, the one located closest to Dave's vantage point. The driver and escort soldier got out, releasing the back door of the truck and the soldier gesticulating to others in the building to come out. More soldiers emerged from both the vehicle and the building – there must have been a dozen of them. Four boxes, perhaps a couple of metres long, were manhandled into the building, with those soldiers who had arrived on the truck getting in the back and the driver returning to the entrance, where he dropped the escort at the guardhouse. What was being delivered could only be guessed at, but what Dave had picked up was that the soldiers guarding the camp and those in the vehicle were not the same. Although the light can play tricks on the eye, it was clear that those guarding the camp had a uniform predominately blue in colour, while those in the vehicle were in green. The observation was raising a number of points that Dave and the team needed to think about. Why was this relatively small compound separate but close to a major garrison? Why did it have such a level of security and why were soldiers in different uniforms? The first light of dawn was now starting to spread. It was time to withdraw and get back to the barn. Although the four of them had travelled together, they had not spoken, preferring to use all their senses to absorb their surroundings. They had seen and heard much. They needed to talk about it and draw some conclusions about what to do next. The party had begun to retrace their steps back to the highway and beyond. The trucks that had been parked up overnight in the layby where they had crossed the road had now gone. They crossed one by one, waiting for a passing wagon to provide cover as it moved around the corner, back across the fields to the barn and their mezzanine base.

Shortly after their arrival, the barn doors were opened and a couple of young men came to take the sheep out for the day. This was a noisy and chaotic business, with the shepherds shouting and waiving to steer the sheep in the right direction. As the cries became more distant, the door opened again. Jack was on watch and nodded to the others. Fawaz climbed the ladder with a satchel around his shoulders. He pushed the bag ahead of him as he came through the narrow gap between the bales. "Morning guys. Here's breakfast." He pulled out a bag of pastries and a couple of flasks of coffee.

"How did you get on last night?"

It was Jo who spoke first. Fawaz was still feeling the effects of last night's Shiraz and arak, and certainly hadn't had the opportunity to come to terms with all he had seen and heard.

"It was a family evening, plenty to eat and drink and a chance to catch up," he said.

"Things are a bit tricky for me – the family want me to spend all my time with them and I have to tell them I need sometime on my own, so given the importance of our mission I'm not sure how the time will work out yet." That he did know.

"We got to the target and had a look," Dave said, chewing on his pastry. "It's difficult to work out what's going on there, but there's plenty of people to stop you finding out.

"The entry arrangements and perimeter security suggest there's something there that needs protecting but from the buildings we have seen there doesn't seem to be any clues."

While Dave was describing the scene, Jack had taken out a small camera from his kit bag, and started flicking through the images he had taken. The camera was passed around the group continuously while they all viewed the material.

"What I couldn't work out was there seemed to be people wearing different-coloured uniforms," said Dave.

"I think I have the answer," said Jack. "Take a look at this."

He had flicked back to some of the views of the central parade ground and some signage in the background. When magnified, the lettering was Chinese. Looking back through some the other images, soldiers wearing green were either delivering to the base or manning the anti-aircraft battery outside the perimeter.

"Did you know there was a Chinese base in Sami?" Dave asked. Fawaz looked blank.

"There's a lot of Chinese in Iran involved in state-procured construction projects but I didn't know their military was involved and certainly not here. If this is true, then the base must be leased to them by the government, who will provide external security."

"It also means that the base will be regarded as sovereign Chinese territory and they will have responsibility for everything that goes on there," said Rodg. "Isn't this going to give us a problem? I don't remember our mission ever factoring in this as an issue. It's going to give Peace International real difficulties if this goes wrong."

"Not just PI, but us and the Iranians," said Jo.

"Yes, I know," said Dave. "When a private mission such as this is undertaken, there is never direct communication with headquarters; it is the responsibility of the field commander – me."

"So that's it?" said Jack, "We'll cut our losses and go our separate ways now?"

"Not necessarily," said Dave. "The mission must be formally cancelled first – by me. I will have to report on the circumstances when I get back. Part of this will be to identify the factors that will mitigate against success. In other words, if I feel the changed picture will prevent us from being capable of delivering the mission, we should withdraw. And another part of the consideration will involve each of you agreeing that the programme cannot be delivered. Already a lot of risk has been taken to get us here in position so we must think carefully about our situation. We're all tired now. I suggest we get some rest and reconvene at 16.00. We can make our plans then."

FOUR

FAWAZ SLIPPED AWAY AND returned to the family home. His mother was in the kitchen.

"Allah is merciful," she said, "he has brought you home to us. Now we can all live together in peace and prosperity and plan for the future."

Fawaz gazed out of the window at the countryside.

Yes, he thought to himself, this looks wonderful, but is it real?

A couple of hours later his father returned from the fields.

"How are you feeling, son?" he asked, but didn't wait for the reply. "If you felt anything like me, I guess you have felt better," and laughed. "Country life has its challenges, as well you know. Getting the harvest in is only part of it. I have to get the wool sacks, and sheep to market and I've got to chair the meeting of the Sami Traders tonight." Seeing his son's surprise, he continued. "No. We didn't get the chance to talk about how I have been able to diversify my business interests," he said. "I need to think of the future when I am too old to work. We have done well in the last year and I have invested in a clothes and textiles shop, which your mother helps me run. I've even taken a controlling share in a Chinese restaurant."

Fawaz was curious. "You didn't tell me this last night – or, if you did, I can't remember. How did that happen?"

"When the military arrived, I helped them out by supplying meat and vegetables along with a few of my neighbours. We had land confiscated so we thought this was a way of getting something back for our losses. I think we did well. We didn't know how big the garrison was going to be and so there was quite a bit of money invested in the area from Tehran. Suddenly, we had a new market of soldiers to sell to. Soldiers had wages but nothing to spend them on, so I and half a dozen others set about building businesses in the town. We reasoned that soldiers needed feeding and clothing. People would want accommodation. Others have gone into entertainment and housing. My neighbour has set up a factory making boots, another making bricks, and someone else has opened a barber's."

"And the Chinese restaurant?"

"That is my newest idea. It's really the themed restaurant attached to the guest house. There are some Chinese workers on a research project on the other side of town. They are not allowed to mix with local people and don't get out of their compound very often. I thought it was a good idea to show them they are welcome and have a place to go that reminds them of home. I mentioned the idea to Colonel Rahman over lunch at the garrison and he fixed a meeting with the officer in charge of the research station. He was really great and arranged to lend a chef to teach a couple of my workers some favourite Chinese meals. Apart from the recipes, he even helped to get some Chinese furnishings in the place to make them feel at home as well as arranging Mandarin language lessons for my people. I'm also diversifying to keep pigs as sheep meat is not part of their normal diet."

Fawaz was taken aback with the energy of his father's description. He couldn't have imagined him even talking in this fulsome way a few years ago.

"Yes, there is no doubt I have been lucky to have been involved, but I was in the right place at the right time and have been rewarded. Now I don't have to do all the back-breaking jobs on the farm. I can buy machinery to help and have people working for me. That is why I am more than a farmer now and run the Chamber of Trade. Who would have thought Sami would have a Chamber of Trade?"

He shook his head in wonder; he was living the dream. Fawaz knew he should be happy for him, but in the back of his mind he couldn't reconcile his father's good fortune with his own struggles. His father may complain of a bad back, but Fawaz would have traded it for the shrapnel embedded in his left shoulder – his souvenir of war from the Lebanon.

Admittedly, when he had finished his conscription, Fawaz had never thought of returning to Sami but nonetheless he couldn't understand how he had not been aware of the life-changing circumstances in the locality. In fact, what was really surprising was that no one else seemed to know either. There had been no press reports on TV or in the *Tehran Times* about it. Was this just happening in Ibrahim Sami or were other new military zones being created? And how come such change was happening but seemed to remain a secret? The questions were running around in his head, but answers were harder to come by.

He had taken tea with his father and wanted to understand more of the story – especially as he suspected not all his friends from the madrassah had left town in the way he did.

He returned to the theme of the Chinese restaurant, fondly imagining the facility must be the only one in Iran north of Tabriz.

"So do you eat Chinese food now?

"Ha! No," he said. "Noodles give me wind and it all tastes the same when they put sweet and sour or black bean sauce over it. They often have cuts of meat we don't want and boil up the bones for soup. Occasionally, when one of their VIPs comes over, a week before they send special supplies for us to cook. Although the research base is the reason for the restaurant, I wish there were more of them working there. If there were, I would have invested more in pigs and kept the place open longer. Keeping pigs makes sense here. I don't have to look after them on the good land in the valley. They could go higher up perhaps, nearer the base, but then there would be a risk of theft and I haven't got time to deal with that. I suppose living in Tehran you've got the taste for it – you should go over there and see what you think. I am always pleased to see Iranians visit the Chinese restaurant – I'm trying to encourage more people to go. I think there is a way – the Chinese like to gamble; so do Iranians, provided they can do so in private. It's another business opportunity. Who knows? I may even extend the opening hours. I had enough trouble getting the permit to open from midnight to three in the morning. When the prefecture complained no one would want a restaurant open at that time, I had to tell them to speak to the Chinese! What a carry on: they don't want to eat before I go to bed."

Fawaz found himself warming to the subject.

"Doesn't it create problems with the neighbours?"

"I've not waited up each evening, but I haven't had any complaints. The Chinese run a truck down from the research station four nights a week and take them all away again when we close. It's great: they eat and drink, play cards and things and there's a couple of duty guards to do the driving and load them on board at home time. They are no trouble and always pay their bills. That way, I get a steady flow of paying customers on each visit, and they always come because it's the only time they are allowed out of the base."

"So how many are here at the research station?"

"I don't know. They all look the same to me. But I do know they don't stay that long. They fly into the garrison airbase every six weeks or so, one lot out, another lot in. I'm starting to wonder if they're here for some sort of holiday."

"What are they doing there?

"Oh, *researching stuff*, I suppose. I've never been allowed to go up there but Colonel Rahman has. The site was originally opened by the government to make fertilisers, but the Revolutionary Guard took it over to test chemicals, and that was when I had twenty of my sheep killed. But the government leased it off to the Chinese a while ago and they've been building it up more. Where they are is 'off the beaten track', so no one I know goes up there, although I think the garrison sends a supply truck up from time to time."

While Fawaz's teatime discussion with his father was taking place, the rest of the team had time to decide the future of the mission. Each had been thinking through the situation they faced and Dave seemed the most thoughtful.

Although part of the security protection they had was based on not sharing their backgrounds in case of capture, it was clear Dave and Rodg were military men, used to careful planning, and, as they had known from the beginning, in the field Dave was in charge. Seemingly calm on the outside, the others drew confidence from his grounded approach. The real man, however, had more than the question marks of the immediate situation to address and joining the mission in the first place had been part of the remedy to exorcise his personal demons.

Captain David Hebbert had been a soldier with a difference. Ever since he was a child he had been in love with the outdoors and had excelled at sports in school, but despite his love of competitive activity sport could not satisfy his hunger for action. It took a chance outing as a Boy Scout on a potholing experience in the Yorkshire Dales to really inspire him. Here was an activity that combined physical exercise with a purpose and risk, the rare quality he needed to fire his adrenalin. Education had a passing interest for him; although he didn't fulfil his teachers' hopes of an Oxbridge place, the doors of several quality UK universities were open to him. But it was the military that drew his attention. His parents, recognising his interest, wanted him to go to university on a military scholarship, which was offering limited opportunities to engage in practical exercises alongside reservists, but this didn't do enough to meet his appetite for excitement and adventure. In his quieter moments, he understood why – he liked to put himself in uncertain situations where he could make a difference. The idea that uncertainty also carried a risk of danger appealed in a way he didn't fully understand. What he did know was that the chance to join an entrance course to join the commandos was not to be missed – one of the most challenging options open to him involving extreme physical and mental tests.

They were not necessarily the elite of the UK fighting forces, like the SAS and SBS, but were not far behind. They were trained for heavy-duty fighting in hostile terrain from polar regions to the jungle. The enemy was not limited to hostile forces but circumstances where conventional fighting techniques were unlikely to deliver successful outcomes. His service record was unusual. Not for Hebbert the better-known theatres of conflict of the Middle East, but the lesser-known ambiguous proxy struggles involving the UK that were rarely discussed in public. Supporting government forces dealing with insurgents in northern Nigeria or Columbia and most recently working as a military adviser in Georgia and Ukraine. His success had been rewarded with promotions and the promise of a settled post at the MoD, giving him the prospect of settling down and starting a family with the right woman. That had been part of the problem. He had had many relationships with women; one or two he had actually loved, but they didn't love his life and he was not ready to change. He had to accept, albeit reluctantly, that family life was not for him and so he had put the thought out of his mind. He probably didn't have any close friends, but he had a quality of trust that enabled him to get along quickly. If he had, that person would have told him to hang up his boots by now because his future was being realised – as an ageing one-trick pony.

His present predicament was a case in point. *De facto* leader of a clandestine mission with no nation supporting or backing him up. This is what being lonely really meant. And now, in the moment of crisis, the moment when he was expected to be at his best, he wasn't.

Enveloped in a fog of memory fear and indecision, his mind went back to Horlivka in Donetsk Oblast, his last outing as a military adviser with Ukrainian forces fighting hand to hand and street to street against Russian-backed rebels. If ever there had been a chaotic military situation that had needed his skills, that was it. He had found himself leading a group of around twenty 'students' defending the rail head on the corner of Pushkinska and Petrovskho on the front line. It was an overcast day, the rain falling steadily almost in a metronomic beat, the dull thud of shells bursting in the distance. He was asked to take charge of a squad to remove snipers close to the town's rail station. When they set off from the army base to the south of the target, he had assumed he had a group of conscripts who, at the very least, had been through basic training. On the way to the checkpoint they were due to defend, the lads seemed in high spirits, probably from the local vodka that had been put in the back with the ammo, or from the pungent, tobacco-like substance which smelled faintly like shit when burned, which was also being shared around. They were laughing, stroking their Kalashnikovs and aiming at each other, fingers perilously close to the trigger. They stopped laughing as the truck turned right into Pushkinska and the shooting began. In a street with high-rise blocks either side, the lorry itself was hardly a difficult target for sniper fire. Those at the back of the truck loosed off some fire indiscriminately and were knocked back by the recoil. Dave had shouted for everyone to get out and run for cover to the checkpoint. Two of the lads were picked off as they scrambled out. From his position in the front passenger seat, Dave had leaped out, using the side of the truck for protection before running forward. He tried to offer some covering fire for the boys between zigzagging down the road to the sandbag-clad safety of the checkpoint. He had been around fifty metres away when one of the snipers had a direct hit on the ammo in the back of the truck. The force of the explosion surprised everyone, throwing

71

most in the vicinity, including himself, a good distance away from their position and shattering glass in the surrounding blocks. For what seemed like an eternity, hostilities ceased as the shards reigned down. He couldn't hear them and could only see a cloud of dust and flame where he had been moments earlier. Snipers were needing to reposition themselves and some of Dave's boys who had been quick on their feet got up and ran for cover. Only eight people from the truck arrived at the checkpoint, to find just two Ukrainian soldiers struggling to defend it. Those who had made it had their weapons but only one ammo belt each. Fortunately, there were enough supplies in the street corner bunker for them to keep going. Dave's job was to assess the position to see if it would be defendable in the long term. From his position, two sides looked out on high-rise housing; the other two sides looked out onto railway sidings. It was clear that the defensive effort was needed on the built-up flanks. The danger was identifying the position of the enemy fighters. In the main, they were in the upper levels of the buildings, yet in the basements the ordinary tenants of the block – the old, children – in fact, anyone incapable of fighting, cowered, waiting for the violence to stop before trying to pick up the pieces of day-to-day life. One such man broke cover, carrying a pillowcase attached to a walking stick, which he was waiving about and shouting. He shuffled towards their position before pulling out a machine gun from under his old, stained raincoat. Dave took him out with a short burst. To the left, an agonised cry came from an old babushka leaning out of a basement doorway. He was clear he had taken the man's life but hadn't understood what he was shouting about and why he had drawn a weapon in clear sight of their position. Whether his shot had an effect on the snipers, he couldn't tell, other than the pace of hostilities picked up and they were taking more incoming fire. There was no time to dwell on the moment, all his attention was now focused on staying alive. He had reported back to operational HQ that the level of opposition could not be endured without reinforcements and withdrawal was required. He had been one of the lucky ones. The Ukrainian Army ran a small train up the line from Donetsk to pick them and other stragglers up. The action had been instrumental in the rebels taking over the town and the small contingent of clandestine British forces becoming limited to advisory duties out of Kiev.

As a direct combatant, Dave's role had been surplus to requirements and he was flown back to Brize for debriefing. For reasons he didn't really understand, the twisted face of the older man in the raincoat stayed with him. They had only shared a moment in time but somehow it seemed precious to both of them. Dave could have been the very last thing the man had seen. The man for some reason looked like his image had been etched on Dave's memory for evermore, the stick and the white flag as well as the gun. Had this man been about to surrender? Why, oh why, had he shown his weapon? He had asked for it. It was the final straw. Dave decided it would be his last shot in anger as a British soldier.

He had no release for his emotion. He would not forget and would return one day to pay his respects. The commandos had been his family. Leaving was not easy; resigning his commission meant for the first time he didn't know where the next paycheque was coming from and when he would next see his friends. Now on Civvy Street, he had to find a job which could use his experience. It was his former commanding officer who had put him in touch with Peace International and the rest was history.

Here was Dave's dilemma – he was a fighting man who had lost his appetite for the kill. Staying in Iran increased the likelihood that death would knock on his door once again.

Alternatively, leaving without achieving the primary objective would leave him grounded in his regrets and perpetuate the continuing nightmare.

It was with a sense of relief that Jamshid slipped himself into the front passenger seat for the lunchtime Iran Air flight down to Bandar Abbas. He'd made it back to his parents' house around three in the morning, sat in a bath until four and slept until nine. His parents had left for work and he found a scribbled note in the kitchen from his mother asking him to phone her that evening. Given the events of the past twenty-four hours, he was pleased he was putting some distance between them and at least he now had a period of uninterrupted time to reflect on everything that had happened. Although sporting black eyes from lack of sleep, Jamshid looked pretty well and, although the soaking in the bath had helped his soreness, his body still ached from the kicking he had endured. He had to hand it to the police. They may have been under an instruction to rough him up a bit but not to leave him marked.

The plane had taken off on the western runway which took him over Karaj and he had gazed out trying to pick out the Alrakahthans' villa, which he knew bordered the Jahan Nama Park, an easily recognisable green oasis on an otherwise ochre landscape, on the capital's outskirts. He was clearly in a predicament but how had it arisen? At the end of the day, he was a young man with a respectable job planning a promising future in a difficult environment. His mother seemed to think he was incapable of doing this without first finding a wife. Whereas they could agree a wife would be a good idea in the long term, Jamshid did not feel ready for family life yet. What was the point in settling down until he had exhausted the thrill of the chase, courting several women, not just for sexual experience but also for camaraderie? He had gone along with his mother's tea-house assignations to keep the peace at home, but also perhaps with the outside possibility that he may come across a girl he fancied as opposed to someone his mother thought was suitable. It was also a good way of filling a slot on the twice monthly visit home. Although Bandar could not compete with the attractions or wages of Tehran, it was at least far enough away from his mother's interference. You could say that his visits home almost allowed him to live a double life – the problems in Tehran could be kept in a box only to be opened on his return. His real worry about the dinner in Karaj was that he could see that the lines between life in Bandar and Tehran were about to become blurred, and potentially that would not be good for him or his parents.

Back in the office twenty-four hours late, his story about being mugged in Tehran was accepted without question. After all, firstly, he had not told a lie, and, secondly, like many other cities in the world it was not an uncommon occurrence. His mood was also lifted by confirmation from a broker in Tashkent that a shipment of two billion barrels of crude, ready loaded in the docks, had been sold, subject to ship-to-ship transfer at given coordinates in the Yellow Sea. Great news for the country and for him personally, as he would receive a commission and congratulations from the energy minister. Jamshid's personal friendship with the broker from university had been the lynchpin for the transaction. Of course, all parties knew who the end buyer was, but Jamshid's job was to do the transaction and leave the politics to others. All he had to do was to reconcile the paperwork and alert the proxy bank in Karachi to secure the deal. Doing deals in oil was getting increasingly complicated. It used to be that transactions were always managed in US dollars, but as a result of sanctions that was now virtually impossible. The new currency of choice was Chinese RMB – increasingly secure and much harder to trace, as well as becoming more competitive in foreign exchange markets. Despite his success on this deal, his country needed many more to keep the economy from potential bankruptcy; Jamshid was one member of a large department, all focused on the same objective.

With the rise in his own reputation came opportunities not granted to many – to travel overseas, especially to industry conferences, where the prospect of meeting potential buyers on the fringes of recognised commercial practice was high. In the months ahead he would have the opportunity to travel to Pakistan, Serbia, Myanmar, Indonesia and Ethiopia – a visible sign of the shrinking global markets still open to his country.

Unlocking his door to his flat on a Tuesday night, he found his mail and newspapers backdated to the weekend, which he picked up and put on a side table. As he turned to close the door, Mr Tawal, a retired naval captain who lived in the flat opposite, had come out to see him.

"I hope you had a good trip north and that your family is well." His statement had the slight intonation of a question and his face had the suggestion of a smile.

"Yes, thanks. I was a little later than expected getting back," Jamshid replied. "Family business," he added with a slight hesitation. "But all is well."

Mr Tawal nodded, but made no move to go.

"I am pleased… and so will your friends…" Tawal looked at him directly. "I have always found true friends pick up the phone before they come knocking," he added.

And, before Jamshid could take in the comment, Tawal had withdrawn.

A split second later, the significance of Tawal's comment registered with him.

He was about to ask who these friends were or perhaps get a description.

Tawal had always been a good man whose heart remained at sea. Jamshid would ask him another day, sure in his mind Tawal would not forget.

His next move was to check his answering machine, which had three messages, one from his mother, which could certainly wait, one from Ravi about fixing a game of squash and finally a surprise: "Jamshid, Hi, it's Mahta. You remember? From the other night. Ravi gave me your number. I thought you were going to call… did you lose my card? You were coming riding with me and Alazaha? Or was that bull? Let me know. I am waiting."

A lot had happened in a few short days after first meeting Mahta, not least Hanah. Was this interest social or strictly business?

He would think it over before calling back. After all, he wouldn't have time before Friday.

A meeting with Ravi would come first. He called him back, declined the squash, but offered a fresh juice over breakfast in the morning.

In the half-light of the barn, Jo watched Dave seated on the ground his back against a bale staring into the middle distance. She had the opportunity for a snooze, but she had too much on her mind for that. Whatever he was thinking about, he seemed a world away from their situation. She was tempted to ask him if he wanted to talk, but got the impression he wouldn't be needing an invitation to do so. Despite his distracted manner, Dave had an air of authority about him that was both reassuring and worrying. Strangely, given their predicament, his calm manner made her feel safe like she was on some scientific field trip. He was organised and in control, and had the answers to the questions of the moment. That same sense of control was also unsettling. They had set out on a mission which, by Dave's own recognition, was unpredictable and dangerous, to them as individuals but also potentially for geopolitics. Although it was clear he had a plan and had the capability to deliver, she wasn't certain he would be flexible enough to adapt to change if circumstances required. Time would tell. The group had already learned much in the past hours and privately Jo wondered why their intelligence had been so limited before they set out. Had Peace International solid information about what was happening in Ibrahim Sami to justify her involvement? She had come to realise the risks of the mission extended into her professional reputation as Dr Joanna White-Smith, departmental head of biochemical remediation at Oxford's Thornberry Institute of Environmental Toxicology, as well as life and limb. Despite the worries, she maintained a quiet excitement about the task ahead – this was real-life James Bond stuff. She actually got to travel to a new part of the world and practise her Farsi, learned as part of a secondment to the United Nations delegation in Beirut investigating incidents of poison gas attacks. Although used to working with military professionals, she had not been trained to handle weapons and she had thought it unusual Peace International had insisted she attend specialist training provided by the British Army before joining the mission. She had always loved the outdoor life ever since climbing Ben Nevis as an undergraduate and had signed up as a medical officer in the TA, so the challenge of hiking over rough terrain for miles on end was not a problem. Even better, the chance to serve with Peace International came about at exactly the right time following the break-up of her marriage to Brian, a serving SIS officer. No real story in this other than the fact their professional lives seemed to be on very different tracks. While most of her time was spent in laboratories in Oxford, he had been in Washington, doing things that could not be discussed. Looking back on it, you would be forgiven for thinking they had married too young on the basis that their lives as students would, to some measure, just continue. Although she loved Brian, she had realised that she could not face the life of being, in effect, a military wife, moving regularly from place to place, especially if she was expected to have children. Peace International offered her a chance to use her professional skills in a positive way as well as providing the opportunity to reboot her life. She was clear that, whatever happened on this mission, her life afterwards would be different, more fulfilling. Thinking about the immediate situation, the newly introduced complicating factor of potential Chinese involvement raised her curiosity further. The previous year, she had spent time in Xi'an, working with the university on a research project to purify carbon emissions from cars. Her limited experience had taught her that the Chinese were much more innovative in applying technologies than developing new ones, so, if they were in charge, the work was probably less sinister and more benign. Alternatively, if their research was potentially dangerous, they would probably want to undertake it as far away from their own population as possible. Under normal circumstances, if she thought she was going to meet or read Chinese, she would have turned to her mobile app to help her, but in this situation she wasn't sure how she would understand what was happening if they ever made it into the compound. Her phone stayed home for this trip and, even if she had been able to bring it, she guessed getting a signal would be difficult. The thought of her phone made her remember she had left it in the top drawer in the bedroom of her flat – an easy place to find it in the event she did not return. Almost as an afterthought, she had recorded three goodbye messages – one for her mum and dad (who thought she was on holiday in India), another for her younger sister, herself a geography student in Newcastle (who probably thought she was still at work in Oxford), and a third for Brian (who she thought wouldn't give a shit anyway). Her messages had been deliberately and purely personal and didn't make any reference to the assignment of Peace International but had served the purpose of explaining she knew she was on a risky overseas trip that she may not return from. She had left the detail of explaining her demise to PI to deal with – after all, they were looking after her passport. Thinking about it for a minute, she was still surprised that it was them and not the government who were sponsoring the mission. She had thought it had the feeling of an operation best suited to the military, but maybe not being a soldier would make things easier if captured. Despite having a trim figure and no make-up, she had never considered herself to be a beauty. She tapped her left breast pocket, where she kept the cyanide-capped gum guard by way of reassurance, and took the Makarov out of the side pocket of her backpack. She felt the weight and responsibility of it in her hand.

Jamshid suggested meeting Ravi at the Pak Bakery on Azadegan at eight in the morning.

The Pak was always busy first thing with office workers and specialised in serving a black fiery liquid some called coffee with fresh pastries and for those with a really strong constitution, the sort of rich cake that even Jamshid's mother would admire. The location was convenient for both. Jamshid had a fifteen-minute drive to the Port Office on Ghadir Boulevard, and Ravi just over five minutes away from the Omm-e Leila Hospital, where he was registrar. It was just as well Ravi didn't have far to go, as Jamshid had plenty to share from his trip to Tehran.

Ravi had listened in a casually attentive way, keeping one eye on the screen of his mobile in case of an emergency call. Maybe it was because he dealt with life-or-death issues on a daily basis that those who didn't know him regarded him as a light-hearted, superficial character. Sometimes his casual or facetious manner was comforting to those facing trauma, but he had observed his friend closely enough to understand his fears. Ravi also had the advantage as a senior medic of being able to steer clear of politics. Although he went to some lengths in his fraternity not to be seen to be communicating political views, the essentially corrupt nature of government was known to him. For his part, he had opted for the quiet life and was prepared to tolerate it provided it didn't interfere with his career. It was with this thought in mind he made his observations.

"It was US President, Roosevelt, who said: 'there is nothing to fear but fear itself', and in my experience it's true. You and I must know of at least half a dozen families in Bandar who think they are the top earners and don't give a shit how they do it. These guys talk a big game, but so far all they have shown you is they have a couple of pet cops on the payroll. You are right when you ask why they are targeting you. You are handling big-scale commercial deals for the state, but you are one of many. Is it because you are relatively young and unmarried and fancy this woman? Unless I missed something, she has not offered herself to you, or is it they think you have a weakness in wanting to return to Tehran? Perhaps these Alrakahthans want to buddy up to your family for some other reason. Whatever it is, forget it. Do your job, live your life, screw who you like, provided you keep it private and wait for the next paycheque. I give you six months in Tehran before you're climbing the walls to get back here – at least you can go swimming in the sea at the weekends…"

"Or horse riding," Jamshid said, now looking a little less stressed. "You know that girl, Mahta, you introduced me to? I swear I saw her watching me play football in Tehran…"

Ravi just smiled and shook his head.

Breakfast over, the friends went their separate ways.

For Ravi, a cardiac arrest required his attention.

For Jamshid, he had the monthly port directors' meeting, where news of his big oil deal in the Yellow Sea could be formally reported. The weekend was fast approaching, and it was high time he returned Mahta's call. They arranged to meet on the following Saturday at her stables south of Rajaei.

Finding the stables wasn't easy. His Shogun was fully equipped for driving on rough terrain but the recommended route took him via a warehouse and industrial park behind the docks, where, in the far corner of the development, he picked up an entrance where a gate used to be and a small sign with an image of a horse. He followed the track for around half a kilometre before coming to what looked like a smallholding. It was a livery business – a sort of horse hotel – where riders without the space to look after their animals at their residences in town could rent a stable and, for additional fees, get them exercised daily. Mahta evidently had only just arrived, as she was tightening the saddle on her horse while one of the stable hands was 'tacking up' another in the yard. She was ready dressed for the occasion with her version of a traditional kurta. Below her *hijab* she wore a long smock which almost looked like a dress, jodhpurs and boots. She carried a short crop under her left arm, an essential tool for guiding her charge. Her stance reminded him faintly of one of his teachers at the madrassah – assertive body language with the capability to mete out punishment for misbehaviour without warning. It had been some time since he had last ridden horses and had only come part prepared, wearing a sun hat, T-shirt, jeans and boots. She laughed her greeting:

"Are you going like that? I think you will be a little sore by the time we are finished. I have asked for a quiet horse for you so you can relax."

They ended up taking the Arabian geldings for a slow trek in the foothills of the mountains behind the port. It was an odd location with contrasting views, looking one way at the developed port facilities and the Hormuz Straight beyond, and just seeing the shadow of Dubai on the far horizon, away to the right, and to the left an escalating primitive high ground of scree, rock and occasional vegetation. Mahta steered her horse along the narrow stone bridleway which snaked north towards the village of Garband. Jamshid's horse knew the route and followed up the incline, carefully picking its way through the sharp stones underfoot, ignoring the fact it was carrying 100 kilos of human on its back. The cloudless sky was azure blue, but the temperature had passed the hottest point of the day, making the journey comfortable for horses and riders. At the highest point of the trek, Mahta stopped, dismounted and gazed at the view over the straight and the busy shipping lanes serving the Gulf and across to Dubai.

"It's funny: when you look from here, you realise how many nations share this small window on the world – we are lucky to have it," she said.

Jamshid had jumped down too and stroked the neck of his horse.

"Yes," he agreed, "it all looks a bit better when you see it from a distance. It's only when you get close up you get to understand what's really happening."

He took off his sunglasses. She retained hers. "You were in Tehran last week. Watching me playing football," he asked, not sure if he was just making an observation or asking a question.

She laughed. "Don't think so highly of yourself. I wasn't in Tehran and I have been too busy to take a flight to watch you play football. Are you any good? Maybe a man like you isn't smart at telling us ladies apart from each other."

In his mind, he pictured his brief approach at the football last week and compared to the present. Then as now, the woman wore sunglasses, but they were different. The *hijab* was different, the coat was different, the hair was different; she had been with a group of other women friends. Was her face rounder? But the laugh. *The laugh.* He chose not to pursue the subject further.

"Maybe..." He paused and hesitated, returning his gaze to the horizon.

"When you realise how close we are to our neighbours over there, it's funny we don't seem to be able to resolve our differences."

"What differences?" she asked.

Jamshid looked surprised. "Oh, just people who don't live here telling us what to do and what to think..." He stopped himself. This conversation was starting to feel a bit political and this was not the time or place or even his interest, but Mahta pushed him on:

"What do you mean?"

"I can't help thinking we would all be better off without the Emiratis and Saudis running to the Americans when they think they have problems. They keep looking for confrontation with us to draw attention away from their own issues. I am sure the American sanctions are trying to force us into war, so we have to fight for survival, just like they did before the fall out with Saddam."

Mahta frowned and followed his gaze into the middle distance. Her headscarf had come lose in the strengthening hot breeze. Jamshid decided he had gone far enough with that topic and moved to a safe subject.

"And what do you do when you are not riding your horse? I remember you telling me the other night you worked for the government."

The change of approach broke the seriousness of the moment. She laughed.

"It's true, I do – but I am also a teacher, though not the kind who works in a kindergarten. I train engineers to design alloys and

83

compounds for industry."

She watched his face fall.

"It's not that bad. I keep people and families in work and help keep the country safe. From what you told me, all you do is help a few people get rich, and I bet you aren't that good at it because, if you were, you would be rich too."

"Well, you could say I have great prospects."

She laughed again.

He suddenly decided to tighten the conversation. "This is great – just you and me and the horses, but why are we here?"

"I think you know. I think this is as far away from other people as we can get, so I don't understand why you haven't kissed me yet."

Jamshid remembered his spontaneous action in Tehran with Hanah.

"Neither can I," he said, hesitated and duly obliged. Somehow the experience with Mahta seemed a lot more real and natural. Was it because he hadn't taken the lead? After all, it was Mahta who had invited him out, without really knowing too much about him, and again, here in the middle of nowhere, she seemed to be confident and in control of the situation.

In a country where women were generally regarded as submissive, second-class citizens, in the past week he had realised he had met two who were anything but. And yet they were very different. One seemed to use her femininity as a commercial weapon; the other offered it as a gift.

Both were skilled in the art of modesty and etiquette, extracting information without offering much in return.

The moments may have stretched to hours, but for Jamshid the time was passing all too quickly. It was soon time to return to the stables.

They made small talk on the descent and said a more formal goodbye as Mahta dismounted, loosened the saddles and handed the horses back.

"When can we next meet?"

"Next week. Same time, same place. I will bring a picnic."

He climbed into the Shogun. She had been right.

His thighs were sore and the complementary discomfort from the Tehran traffic police was still with him. He hoped he would recover in time. The sudden acceleration of the SUV made the wheels momentarily spin and he set off back to town, leaving a cloud of dust.

As she watched him go, she made a call on her mobile.

"Hi, it's me – I've made contact."

She closed the phone and went back to bedding down the horses.

She knew she wasn't a natural in the surveillance business.

FIVE

"**THEY'RE PRETTY CRAP, THOSE** Makarovs," muttered Rodg as he watched Jo passing the weapon from hand to hand. "Typical PI – they're so bothered about not being seen as mercenaries they won't even issue us with the equipment we should have for a job like this. They have only given us these, so when we get shot the ragheads will think we are Russians. You'd have thought they'd have given us Kalashnikovs at least, but I think they're scared we'd do too much damage. These take a bit of getting used to. If they'd given us enough ammo I think you and Jack the Lad over there need a bit more target practice.

"Let's hope we only get to wave them around without having to use them. When they sent you off for training did they tell you about the special quirks of this thing? Thought not. Best advice is don't expect to hit anything more than ten metres in front of you, aim high because it will shoot low, and pull to the right, so you really need both hands on it if you want to make it count. Silencer is pretty good. If you fire this at a party, no one apart from your victim would ever know. Still…"

He paused. Rodg – Sergeant Rodger Mbenza, late of the South African Army Medical Corps and more recently managing director at Elite Protection Services, was feeling the pressure of the moment. Although he had said nothing at the time, he had read Dave's expression clearly despite the growing twilight in the barn. It was a look he had seen many times in his career as he had been attached to small fighting units battling insurgencies in half a dozen African theatres, the Caucasus and Central America. The look of men playing the game of hunting and hunted, making up the rules as they went along – reconciling fear and aggression.

Rodg was an ambiguous character.

He had become a specialist in covert operations, which meant that, if he was successful, he earned a good fee; if he wasn't, he made sure he lived to fight another day. He often talked about death but had a deep confidence which had led him to cheat it. He had an inner belief, so strong he had flirted in his youth with the idea of being a missionary. Yes, he liked physical fighting, but not in the orderly situation of a boxing ring or cage – not killing. Death was wasteful and often pointless. Rodg saw victory in terms of dominating an opponent in such a way that they would recognise his achievement and be subjugated. An expert in field craft, he was practised at implementing medical procedures for wounds and trauma without the full range of drugs and equipment found in a hospital setting. In military terms, although most armies need people with his skills they were rarely acknowledged or rewarded with rank and recognition – cash was king and that had led him to a new career protecting VIPs. The big money had always been with African dictators and Russian oligarchs, many of whom liked having a personable guy with good English as part of their protection teams. It was a sort of badge of honour, although often his compatriots didn't like it because they thought he was better paid (which he was). But things were not like they used to be and the world had moved on. Since the break-up of the CIS, he had had a couple of personal protection assignments in Mosul and Baghdad. Fewer tyrants and more democracy were part of it, but there was a growing market in protecting celebrities and rock stars. As in Africa, the Bollywood elite were particularly good for business, but he'd done a couple of duties with rap stars in the States and specific assignments for Hollywood A-listers. He was even offered work as a stunt double in an action movie, but, having sustained his first real injury – a broken leg – decided to take a back seat, employing former colleagues in the military to do the dirty work. His way of life hadn't proved attractive in the marriage stakes and despite a steady stream of female admirers, including a failed marriage in Las Vegas, none had succeeded in getting him to hang up his boots. Although he had made his money, he became bored and wanted to get back to the action. He had come across Peace International's humanitarian activities in Syria and been impressed how they managed to continue their work in the face of constant harassment. In PI he saw an organisation that had principles and strength, something which he could relate to. In Rodg, PI found a rare commodity, a trained medic with proven battlefield experience – an ideal man for a crisis.

This was now Rodg's second outing for PI, having been part of a non-political combat group which had prevented a massacre in Kashmir last year. He was one of a small team privately credited in supressing a full-scale war between Pakistan and India. From what he knew from his briefing for this mission, the stakes were just as high.

Fawaz had a lot on this mind and had reflected on the matter-of-fact conversation about the arrival of the Chinese in Sami. Although the Revolutionary Guard garrison had arrived first and their presence was physically far bigger than the Chinese, he was interested in how his father seemed to relate their arrival to the incident of the dead sheep. He had asked how they died and expected to hear that the deaths had been caused by roaming wolves that occasionally came down off the mountain when other food sources were short. When he asked how they died, he was surprised to hear he didn't know. He described the ewes just lying on their side with blood oozing from their mouths. There had been no sign of violence and he thought they must have died late in the day as falcons had not attacked the carcasses for food. With so many killed in one place, he had reported it to the police as a matter of routine and had set about excavating a pit to put them in. He had been surprised when he got a call back within an hour of his report telling him not to touch any of the animals and that they would arrange their collection. He had recalled within two hours a sealed truck had arrived with a dozen or so soldiers in "white uniforms". They had gone to the field, loaded up the dead animals and took them away. Given they were worth about two million rials, he had asked about compensation. The supervising officer had smiled and said, "Your reward will be in heaven." The very next day another detachment of guards arrived. They did not ask permission to access his land but moved in with some strange hand-held equipment, like they were scanning for something. When his father approached them, he was told to go away and keep out of the field until further notice. That was that; he never heard any more and six months ago decided to use the land again. The field had been his most northerly, bordering the highway and about a kilometre from the research centre. For some reason his father had linked the unusual incidence of the dead sheep to the arrival of the Chinese but he didn't understand why. He also didn't want to alarm his father by continuing to discuss it. He knew another opportunity would naturally arise before too long.

It had only been a few days, but Hafiz was delighted at having his son home and his wife and daughter were in no doubt that the appearance of Fawaz had been a very happy, if unexpected, experience. Surprisingly, Fawaz had not been closely questioned about where he had been and the circumstances that led to his return. For most Iranian families, stories of their conscripted sons in the military were rarely regarded as positive experiences. While service was compulsory, the completion of duties wasn't, meaning a commission could extend over many years. The volatile nature of the Middle East meant engagement in conflict of some description was highly probable, and, like many armies, the Iranians sent soldiers into battle poorly equipped, often leading to unnecessary death and injury. Hafiz had his son back, albeit sporting a war wound, which was seen as a badge of honour in local social circles. Hafiz wasn't getting any younger and yet the sudden relative success of his commercial activities had fostered a youthful spirit which negated his years. The arrival of Fawaz made complete sense to Hafiz as he now saw a credible succession for his burgeoning businesses. Now was the time to make plans before Fawaz decided to go away again. Although he had gone to some lengths to explain his good fortune to his son, he hadn't had the opportunity to introduce him within the locality. But it was also important to do it in the right way. That meant starting with his most important associate, Colonel Rahman from the Revolutionary Guard garrison, and Hossein Moussavi, governor mayor of the prefecture, Tehran's representative in the community. These men had been the prime beneficiaries of the militarisation of the area and were naturally close. Arranging a place for his son at their forthcoming lunch was easy. The three would meet monthly to discuss how the region was progressing. The mayor provided an update on government initiatives, the commandant on military matters and Hafiz on developments among the civilian population. It was an effective forum, with each of them requiring action and support from the other two in order to ensure smooth governance. Every other month, they would be joined by the senior officer from the research base, if he had time. Hafiz knew that Fawaz would only be able to join when their business was concluded and was delighted that his son agreed to come along, but it would mean waiting several days longer than the original scheduled start of the PI mission.

For Jack Vass, joining Peace International had been an impulsive act, picked from a mundane series of fruitless business appointments on a random day in Manchester. It gave him purpose, focus and a chance to get an "exclusive" with national, perhaps international implications. Prior to his departure, he had recorded details of his seemingly casual recruitment and basic training, most of which had been about learning to shoot. He was still unsure why he had been picked and had concluded it was because he was fit and (oddly for a journalist) not asked too many questions. He was still having problems getting his head round the ethical purpose of Peace International, a registered charity with global operations which had the capability of making military-style interventions where it judged there to be a need to prevent wars. Some charity: a headquarters on the next block to the UN building in Manhattan, 25,000 paid staff, funding estimated at over a billion dollars and access to the political elite – presidents and prime ministers – and responsible for who knows how many secret operations, where, inevitably, some people may get killed. Whoever the shadowy people were on its board, these were the people with real power and influence.

As someone contributing to the realisation of their laudable objectives, he had more mundane issues playing on his mind, consisting of maintaining supplies of food and water and managing personal hygiene. The team had eaten well at their embarkation point in Azerbaijan, but had taken military rations and water with them on their journey east. Both needed to be replenished. Food was arriving intermittently in the form of bread, pastries, cold barbecued meat and watermelons supplied by Fawaz at different times of day when he was able to pass unnoticed. He also brought in a jerry-can of drinking water and a few paper bags for collecting and disposing of shit. This latter responsibility seemed to get delegated to Jack, who had to find places to leave the bags to prevent discovery. The usual place was the slurry pit outside the barn, but a couple of the farm hands were using it to collect the waste from the animals. Jack had to work out when it was safe to go with their own rubbish and had already nearly been discovered having a slash on an outer wall just when the farm hand had been closing up for the night. As for Jo, Jack didn't understand how she was managing without the aid of modern facilities. Jack was coming to terms with the big outdoor adventure and tried not to think too much about what was going to happen. He was trying to write notes about his feelings as a way of dealing with his own nervousness. A big gap in his note taking had been the lack of information about his colleagues. He had expected to find out more as the trip went on, and indeed that was his plan, but he had been reminded of the anonymity of each to their own might be essential for their survival. Notwithstanding that, he got the sense that Dave and Rodg were fighters. They seemed most at ease with their experience and weaponry. Jo seemed to be OK, but he was less sure she was not demonstrating bravado about their situation; maybe she was as scared as him. From the little he knew, her job sounded damn near impossible – to confirm the presence of something which might not exist. And, if that sounded pointless, getting killed into the bargain. What had happened to that other bloke who had crossed the river into Iran with them? None of the others had even mentioned him. And no wonder: this rule about speaking Farsi was getting him down. Not everyone had been compliant. He could only remember a bit from his granny and the others were obliged to keep using the language and not English. Why, oh why? Perhaps that was the real reason why conversation between them had been so limited. He hadn't expected to be spending so much time in the barn and he was getting too much time to think. He decided to lie back and imagine a dream with his girlfriend, Sarah, long brown hair, never-ending legs and tits to die for, astride him. It was only a fleeting distraction as the holster on the side of his thigh pressed into his guts, drawing his attention; at the same time, he heard the lock of the barn door opening. Instantly he rolled to his viewing position.

Fawaz was able to make short but regular visits to the team, slipping away from both parties as the moment took him. He would leave supplies below the mezzanine and go, or alternatively climb the ladder to their vantage point. Once Fawaz had heard his father's story of what was going on in the locality, he needed to share with the others and plan their next move.

It started to rain after dark, but Fawaz had already made his plans for the evening.

He had not yet had the chance to see Ibrahim Sami at night and expected to visit the local café, hotel and Chinese restaurant. Since his arrival home, he had already invented a job to do on behalf of his father to check the barns and livestock as well as their fodder trays. He worked his way round the farm buildings methodically, just in case prying eyes were on him. He need not have worried – the farm hands had gone home, the rest of the family had gathered to watch on TV the latest episode of a historical drama about Darius the Great and, because of the rain, even the homeless war veterans on the street had found suitable doorways to 'hole up'. He had slipped out with the usual jerry-can of water, bag of bread loaves, and home-made *lighvan* cheese. The sheep announced his arrival in the barn by pressing forward, expecting he may have brought them some extra delicacy to complement their already generous diet. He called to them by way of reassurance as he climbed over the steel barrier into their pen and mounted the ladder to the mezzanine. Once he had left, the sheep would settle down to sleep and would only get up if they sensed an intruder approaching. For this reason, if the team went out after dark, they would use a hatch at the rear that would provide a direct exit, although the same ladder would be needed. Care was taken doing this in the rain as there would be a risk of mud and leaving tell-tale boot prints. That was a problem for later – the challenge for now was much more serious – what was the future of the mission?

Late afternoons were a busy time in Ibrahim Sami. The steady stream of people visiting to buy the ranges of meat, fruit and vegetables was augmented by stallholders trying to park close by to pack up their goods for the evening, while others were assembling to enjoy the entertainment of the snooker hall and cinema. The main presentation of the day was Asghar Farhadi's Oscar-winning classic *A Separation*, followed by a midnight showing of *Operation Red Sea*, about a Chinese special forces unit rescuing their fellow citizens in a mythical country on the Arabian Peninsula. The chaotic atmosphere at this hour was accentuated by customers frantically haggling with stallholders, who were trying to decide whether it was better to let produce go below the advertised price or take it away. Other traders would keep a stall for a different reason, to drive customers towards their shops nearby. On such was Hashmi Kolani, a trader from the neighbouring town, Ashelqu, who had both a shop and stall selling carpets and rugs. His business in Ibrahim Sami was secondary to his operation up the road, but for him it represented a major expansion of his trade. Carpets, and rugs especially, although an essential part of an Iranian home, were like art, a very subjective purchase. Hashmi's challenge was twofold. Firstly, he had to move on his mid-market, high-volume rolls from Afghanistan, and, secondly, to grow his bespoke design ordering service, woven at the back of his shop in Ashelqu. Both activities were profitable, but it was his bespoke, locally made product which had the higher margins. Understandably, customers in this segment were part of the burgeoning middle class of the area, and sales told him the environs of Ibrahim Sami were on the up. Many sought abstract colourful designs, but at the top end rugs needed to be personalised, either by working the initials of the customer into a design or by taking the inspiration of a particular precious moment, captured in a photograph. Having packed up his stall and closed his shop around half an hour earlier than usual, he had arranged to meet a prospective customer in Sami's central baker's café. Although a short distance from the calm open lounge of the guest house, this was the domain of the local working man. At this time of day, it was noisy, sweaty and smoky – a strange venue to choose for a business meeting. The smell of fried food and the steam from the coffee machine aided by the revolving roll of lamb kebab meat sought to spread airborne fat around the premises. This, added to the condensation on some of its windows closest to the kitchen, created a natural drawing board for the irreverent and often phallic graffiti of its customers. In theory, it was a bit like deciding to impress a client by meeting in a rundown McDonald's as opposed to the nearest Hilton. Having said that, Iran is one of the few countries without a branch of the global burger chain, so, if there had there been one in Sami, it would have undoubtedly taken trade from the baker's café. But his instinct was right. His prospective customer, Jafar, a local builder, was himself growing his business, and starting to experiment with brick, having just invested in a kiln with a partner. Hashmi had a small photographic catalogue with him, demonstrating the quality of his work, and had arrived early, which was just as well, as seats were at a premium.

He ordered a milkshake and lamb burger, sat with a notebook sketching, imagining getting an order to carpet an entire house. He had taken the precaution of draping his jacket over the empty seat opposite for his guest and paid scant attention to a man enquiring whether the seat next to him was available.

"Excuse me, I couldn't help noticing your catalogue – are you the famous Kolani of Kolani Carpets?"

Kolani looked up, momentarily bewildered before recognising his inquisitor.

"No..." he said in disbelief. "Fawaz al-Fouadi, the 'Joker King of Sami', is it really you?" He put his spectacles down on the table in front of him, stood up and shared a hug. "Allah be merciful! You couldn't have been hiding in your fathers' house for the past six years?"

For the first time since his return, Fawaz had spotted a fellow former pupil from the madrassah. Kolani called Fawaz "the Joker King" because, as a boy, Fawaz had had an uncontrollable nervous twitch in his left eye which made him look as though he was winking. His teachers regarded it as a mark of disrespect and used to punish him as a result. Fortunately, he had grown out of it, and Fawaz told the short version of his story which had led to his return.

Kolani's story was different and more disturbing. The only son of his family, he had moved to Tabriz to work in a date-packaging factory, but moved home after his father had been arrested for joining a democracy protest march in the capital. He was held a prisoner in Tehran's notorious Evin prison and tortured to persuade him to sign a confession to say he was an agitator working for the United States. He had resisted and went on hunger strike. He was banned from receiving visitors and held in solitary confinement. After some thirty days he had apparently tried to escape and died in a fall attempting to scale one of the jail's perimeter walls. His family and friends knew he would have been too physically weak to make a break and the prison itself was the most secure in the country. Even after his father's passing, he was given a pauper's funeral at the prison. Hashmi believed he was killed by guards because he wasn't a high-profile dissident and no one would protest at his death. The family had been denied his body for burial because it would have proved he had been murdered. Hashmi had become the head of the family. The salary of a date packer was small and the location too far away to commute back to Ashelqu. His mother and sisters were weavers at home. He had started by selling their work in Ashelqu's market, then using his savings to buy rolled carpet from Afghanistan. His overseas trips were difficult to organise, so he had made a contact who helped him to get false passports, especially if he needed to go to Asia. That, in turn, had helped him to open his second stall and shop in Sami and so he had found success from a family crisis.

He had moved on to explain how he recently married a local girl from Sami and that as a result he would be moving to the town. He was hoping to discuss a swap deal with Jafar that would allow him to save money on the move. He explained he felt happier here because Ashelqu was "too tribal" and his female-dominated family faced daily discrimination and harassment when he wasn't there. Kolani said in recent times he felt the area was becoming more dangerous and recounted his experience some time ago of finding a dead body "with warts and lesions" in a hessian bag at the side of the road. His tale was interrupted by the late arrival of his prospective customer and his lamb burger. Flustered at the appearance of food at the time, he broke off their conversation to introduce Fawaz to Jafar, and ordered tea for his guest, while the new arrival studied the menu. It was the polite time to move on. Standing and shaking hands, Fawaz thanked Hashmi and promised to drop by the shop in a couple of days.

"Great to see you, my friend, I cannot wait to tell my mother. She remembers you. If I can help in any way, just ask," and with that he reached for his catalogue and started his sales pitch with Jafar.

The group sat cross-legged on the floor, facing each other, except Rodg. Had he been seated collectively, they may have constituted a circle. But Rodg was keeping watch – listening intently to the noise of the rain, the distant howl of wolves and faraway shots of likely poachers.

Notwithstanding these duties, he listened in as Dave started to talk: "We have only been here three days but it's clear we have already a great deal of information that we would never have known without coming. I am not sure where the original intelligence came from regarding the research base, but it looks like it came from aerial drone imagery, probably from the US. We knew about the anti-aircraft protection first when a missile downed an Israeli drone back in March. Although we were aware of the location of the site and the position of buildings, we were able to conclude that the complex must be much larger underground, given the projected numbers of personnel working at the site. We have not known, however, why this compound exists in this location. If it was for a military purpose, it would be logical for it to be located in the Revolutionary Guard complex at Posyan."

Jack was absorbed in Dave's commentary and had already picked up his use of the term "we". If "we" related to those in the barn, then the language was loose. If Dave was morphing into *Commander of the Peace International covert mission in north-west Iran* mode, then already he was imparting fresh information.

Dave went on: "We know there are regular personnel movements in and out of the compound, suggesting there is an active programme of work being undertaken, which is what we are interested in understanding. The most significant knowledge we have established is that the staff appear to be Chinese. Unusually, considering the compound is an enclosed base within a foreign jurisdiction, the Chinese operatives on duty are armed. Again, we don't understand why this is, given the forces are there by invitation and not in a frontline battle setting.

"We are aware also there are tensions between Iranian hosts and Chinese 'sponsors'. A relatively small group of Iranians charged with looking after their guests are profiteering from their presence, but the majority are not. Crime in the locality has reduced, largely because the perpetrators are off-duty militiamen and easily traceable. We are not aware of any capital punishment since the Chinese have arrived. However, most locals are aware of the slaughter of some twenty sheep in a field a few months back. The deaths have been attributed by some to the Chinese and has been a source of resentment as the state confiscated the carcasses without offering them as food. Thanks to intelligence from Fawaz, it appears that the local population have benefitted from the investments in the locality made as a result of the Chinese arrival, but no social or cultural integration is allowed.

"Nonetheless this factor considerably increases the complexities and dangers of our mission.

"Given the circumstances, the Iranians have done well to

ensure the extent of Chinese involvement in the area has not been detected in the outside world.

"I would remind you: as operatives in a Peace International private operation, our mission is to achieve our objectives without the threat or incidence of killing people. I must emphasise, in this case, mission failure, if attributed, could be regarded by a state actor as hostile, leading to far-reaching and unpredictable consequences.

"Part of my responsibility to PI is to fulfil the mission objectives, avoiding loss of life and to ensure your safe return to your homes. Given what I have described so far, I am no longer confident of being able to do this within the constraints upon me.

"I have two courses of action available, and neither can be fulfilled unless we all agree.

"The first option is to manage a withdrawal. Under these circumstances Fawaz will guide us back to the river where we can retrace our steps back to Azerbaijan.

"Or we can remain in the theatre and request additional resources in order to meet our obligations. In this scenario, it should be understood that, despite our own personal views, the extra resources may not automatically be provided. If that is the case, we may be obliged to withdraw anyway.

"Finally, we are in an unpredictable, hostile environment. There is an ongoing risk that our presence may be detected and challenged. In such circumstances, we are obliged to avoid declaring our nationality and purpose in the face of certain torture. Each of you, individually, will have choices to make about protecting yourself by using the gun issued to you by killing an assailant or by the use of the cyanide capsule each of you has been issued with. The cyanide alternative is quick and final.

"As Mission Commander, my advice is to request additional resources to complete our task. The additional time we have to commit waiting for these to be provided will not be wasted but will allow us to continue to research our plan and deepen our knowledge of this community. I'm happy to take questions."

Rodg was standing back from the group, his eye on the barn door. "How long will we have to wait to get the extra help you think we need?"

"Who knows? Because of PI rules of engagement on covert operations, we have no direct means of communication with headquarters. In this case, as some of you will know, we are being underwritten by the British government and we have a conduit for passing messages."

"What does that mean?" asked Jack.

"This information is beyond your brief and classified. It means that, although the British government does not endorse our objectives and will not reference this action because it is covered by a D notice, they are prepared to use us to support their army's own field training."

"And...?"

"There is a SAS team shadowing our work."

"Where?"

"I don't know. Their role is to monitor our progress and provide logistical assistance if necessary."

"What logistical assistance?"

"Exactly what it says. It's about helping us to muster and do what we have come here to do. In fact, one of the ways they are providing assistance is with communication. I have identified a location for a dead letter drop, which will be the method used to get our message out. Our job will be to sit tight until we have the response."

"And if we don't get it?"

"We break up and withdraw as we have already discussed."

"So that was who that guy Gil was?"

"Yes that's correct."

"And he's out there somewhere on his own."

"I have no knowledge about where he is, what he is doing, or who he may be with. In the meantime, with your agreement, I will send the message tonight. We need to make sure we are safe in the locality. The longer we stay here, the riskier it will be.

"Fawaz, could you be taking a look around to spot an alternative location if we need to leave quickly? Any more information on the locality and local military strength would be useful.

"Jo and Rodg, I need you to go and take another look at the research compound. We need to check exactly what we need to do to get in and out of there.

"Jack, you need to take over watch duties here until I get back."

Sensing agreement, Dave added, "OK, guys, let's get to it – remember, dawn is at 03.58 local. You must be back here by then."

He checked there was no movement outside the back of the barn, moved the ladder out of the rear hatch, pulled his night visor down and stepped out into the wind and rain.

Jo and Rodg prepared to leave but waited for a few minutes before following.

"OK?" asked Jo to the others.

"He spoke well," said Fawaz.

"That's as much as he has said since we arrived," added Rodg.

"Hope none of it gets lost in translation," said Jack as he watched Rodg exiting feet first.

Fawaz waited until Jo had followed and pulled up the ladder to allow his own exit in the barn.

"She has courage," he said. "I hope she doesn't get hurt. This is different to how I thought it would be."

"I know," said Jack. "I'm not sure what I expected; it's getting a bit scary, but she makes me feel confident."

"How do you feel about the gun?"

"Before we got here, I didn't see the point in it. Now it looks like we are up against the Red Army, I'm now sure I'll be needing it. I know I will only have a moment to decide when the time comes; just have to be sure I don't bottle it."

Fawaz put his hand on his shoulder.

"There are big uncertainties for all of us. At least you don't have to be a stranger in your own country." He squeezed through the gap in the bales and descended into the sheep pen, leaving Jack alone in the dark with his thoughts.

Another man alone in the dark with his thoughts at that moment was Dave. Running low at the field perimeter, he was moving to the prearranged meeting point with Gil. Before Gil left to go his own way, they had agreed a place next to a particularly prominent cedar. No appointment had been fixed but Gil said he would monitor the site each night between midnight and one in the morning. It had taken Dave some ten minutes to get to the tree and, having walked round its magnificent trunk, retreated to the shadows to wait. It was still pissing it down and, although the tree kept the worst of the wet off, he was starting to feel like he had done when he had emerged from the river. Again, it was not the dampness but the cold which was noticeable. Anyone who thought the weather in north-west Iran was all sunny days and balmy nights could not have been further from the truth.

While he waited, he checked that his Makarov was primed with the silencer attached.

It was a long fifteen minutes before he saw movement in the undergrowth and the black silhouette of a man emerged with a quick wave. The figure approached and slid into the ditch next to him.

"Fancy meeting you here," Gil began with some irony. "I wasn't sure if we would get to meet again."

"Come on, man; you must have known what we were coming into."

"I had my suspicions, but all this looks like a bigger deal than I was expecting. Guess that's your reading too. I saw you guys up at the research base last night. It's quite a place, isn't it?"

"Yes. I've sent two of my team back now to measure up in more detail."

"So why are you here? I wouldn't mind a crack at it myself but, as you know, we're grounded."

"Don't worry; I understand the rules of the game. But you are right: I haven't got all the tools to do the job. I need you to get me help or instructions from London."

"OK – what do you need?"

It was a short walk across Walpole Park, and past the tennis club to the west London Tube station. A crisp autumn morning, Edwin Wilson had an appointment first thing with the assistant permanent secretary at the Ministry of Defence. In a sign which he thought said much about their relationship, this meeting had only been set just before 10pm the night before and the venue was the distinctive red-bricked St Ermin's Hotel just behind Victoria Street, often used by civil servants and politicians when they wanted "off the record" conversations.

The APS was first to arrive and, having done a quick recce of the reception area, settled at one of the tables outside under the portico at the front entrance. He was less concerned about the chill in the air than bothered that his seat would put him in the best place to monitor comings and goings. For a moment, he had been distracted by the arrival of a black taxi containing a group of American tourists. It was remarkable just how many people had squeezed out and how many bags were accompanying them.

The arrival of the cab had scrambled the hotel's porters and even the cab driver left his seat to help. He assumed the summer tourist season was coming to an end and this must be the lull before the winter shopping trips arrived.

His initial scan into the foyer had taken him by the reception desk, where he was a known entity. His presence was noted, but no approach would be made until he had settled on a particular seat. The reason for having a quick look round was much more than choosing the best possible position but was more about checking at that moment whether any colleagues from Whitehall or indeed members of the Westminster rabble were holding court. In making the arrangement, given the hour, he thought it would probably be clear of people he would be obliged to acknowledge, which was a great advantage. The problem, of course, of meeting such people was that his presence would be noted and surreptitious questions would be volleyed into his office to determine what he was up to – all part of the "gossip go round". That was particularly the case in the Ministry of Defence. That's why, if he was going to be seen out of the office at this time, St Ermin's was the natural place. Convenient, but not so out of place as to raise undue suspicions about his activities.

His thoughts suddenly moved from American tourists to the here and now as he saw Wilson walking briskly towards the hotel entrance. He had already spotted him and was smiling with a spring in his step. He stood to greet him.

"Eddie, my dear fellow, good to see you and thanks for taking time to drop by. I do hope I haven't impinged too much on the day's activities."

His guest responded, "Sorry to have kept you waiting. Usual problem, delays on the District Line."

Both men settled down, pots of tea were duly ordered. The host was happy as he particularly liked the complimentary biscuits.

"You may know why we had to meet. I am the bearer of a strange message from your man in northern Iran – Hebbert. On a positive note, he seems to be doing quite well, getting himself embedded in the thick of it, but on the other side of the coin he bumped into one of my guys last evening and asked to pass on a message to you. Now I do know why you operate in the way you do – in fact, I commend it – but I have to say my chaps have their own pressing tasks to perform, and there are others active in the theatre. Chaperoning your people running around is only a sideline for us."

"Others?"

"Well, it's hardly surprising under the circumstances, but we've detected a covert unit of Russians operating in the area as well.

Funny lot, a bit untidy and certainly not as housetrained as our people. If we're not careful, they could create problems for us all."

"Well, you know, Roddy, we operate in constrained circumstances. No one understands the rules of the game better than Hebbert and, if he felt the need to use the back channel, I am sure he had good reason."

"I wonder – but anyway apparently he's moaning about being under-resourced. I seem to recall he said as much when he was working for us, when we had told the brass that getting our new aircraft carriers operational had to be our priority. But never mind: he is really one of us and apparently is *in extremis*."

"What has he said?"

"In essence, he's confirmed this research centre we have heard about is being managed by the Chinese and seems to have half a platoon guarding it. Presume that's news to you?"

"Has he asked for more weapons?"

"Not really – not sure what you sanctioned for personal protection, but he's looking for more ammo and another body. Are you sure he's not trying to start a war?"

"On this mission the guys were issued with Makarovs plus ten 9mm rounds precisely so they could avoid the temptation to launch a skirmish."

"This seems like a lot of fuss for the sake of a few bullets. Tell me about the body."

"He wants you to send over another superman or woman, with expertise in chemical warfare, capable of unarmed combat and fluent in Mandarin. Anybody spring to mind? I thought not. You had better go away and consult your contact book. I will do the same. If anyone springs to mind, I will call."

"That's good of you."

"We are here to help – at least in theory. I think your boy is probably onto something. One of my chaps observed a dead body next to the road leading to this base which, from what he could see at range, was showing evidence of extreme tissue scarring.

Apparently, some goons in protective suits came and took it away somewhere we may never know, but it looks like a potential smoking gun for your people to chase."

He finished his tea and got up.

"I understand Hebbert is sitting tight until he hears from you. I assume that means you need to get this sorted in the next twenty-four hours. Call me soonest on the private line, when you have composed your reply. Happy to help with logistics as before. By the way, the tea is on the department's account, but you do not need to declare it as a benefit in kind."

The contact known as Roddy buttoned his overcoat and set off at a brisk and purposeful pace.

Wilson watched him leave for the short walk through the assorted hotel greenery before turning left towards Victoria Street. He waited a short time and followed the route of his friend adding an additional left turn to take him back to the Tube.

Once back at his office, Wilson studied the database of other Peace International operatives worldwide. He knew before he did so that finding an individual who would match up to the requisite criteria would be difficult, and, even if he could find the person, he had no confidence of being able to get them at short notice. He was drawing a blank on his computer search, having thought the USA, Canada or possibly Hong Kong or Singapore would be the most likely places to find what he was looking for. One by one he started to drop his search criteria until the computer came up with a name – Dr Gulman Ehat, formerly of the University of Xinjiang in Urumqi but seconded to the World Health Organization, temporarily resident in Tashkent, Uzbekistan. An expert in radiation sickness, he had been given special permission to leave China as part of a multinational project to decontaminate former Soviet nuclear munitions in a remote region bordering the Aral Sea.

He had a mobile. Wilson estimated the time as early evening in Tashkent.

Dr Ehat was heading to his car at the Westminster International University when Wilson's call came through. They talked and Dr Ehat requested a brief was sent over to his secure mail account at the World Health Organization office. Although certified by Peace International as having attended basic training, he had not worked for PI in the field, but he spoke English, Russian and Mandarin and had a brown belt in judo, though he was not experienced with firearms. A native Uighur and a practising Muslim, he had done well to win his freedom from the Chinese state. There was little on file about his personal circumstances but had the benefit of being able to get a direct flight to Baku, where PI could look after him.

Having studied the documentation, Dr Ehat had confirmed on the basis he could take sickness or annual leave that would enable him to return in two weeks, and, within that timeframe, no one would be suspicious. At his request, he bought his own open return ticket to Baku on AzAir. He had a doctor friend there, at the State Pedagogical University, who he could contact, if necessary, to justify his journey.

It was already clear to Wilson that the present situation was becoming more complicated.

Even if Ehat was the right man, getting him firearms proficient and in position with the rest of the team at short notice would be difficult.

It was a gut feeling – a hunch – but Wilson decided he wanted to review his training and meet him personally. A quick check on plane schedules indicated he could catch a flight from London that would arrive in Baku four hours behind Ehat. Normally needing to dash to PI's headquarters in New York, he kept a pre-packed bag ready.

He called his friend on the secure line at the MoD with the response for Hebbert, saying he would need one of his crew (probably Gil) to take him across the border from the embarkation point to join up with the PI team.

Wilson would meet Ehat at the Four Seasons Hotel.

They would have dinner, and some sleep, before flying south to Minjivan for training and on to the embarkation point.

It was tight, but he estimated seventy-two hours to deployment.

His man on the ground, 'Bob' (Mr Check Shirt), and his lady partner (Anya), the one with a predilection for Kalashnikovs, were instructed to arrange the logistics.

Jo and Rodg made their way carefully to the copse behind the research station. The challenge was attempting to see all the barriers and hazards that would prevent entry. There was a mixture of physical deterrents (fences and walls) and practical hazards (dog patrols and observation platforms). But the real part of planning was trying to work out where to go when access was secured. Patient observation appeared to show a lack of electronic security on the doors to the individual buildings as people could be seen moving about the compound with relative ease, but still there was no clue about how the base worked. Frustratingly, the signage in Chinese characters offered little help but what was clear was that two entrances seemed to be used by those carrying arms. These entrances related to one of the four buildings but in itself looked too big to be a guardhouse. Was this place the main barracks? And what of the other buildings? Having previously identified changes of uniform which had led to confirmation of the Chinese presence, it was clear there were some in other forms of attire, some in blue boiler suits, others in white, what appeared to be laboratory coats. It was symptomatic of Chinese order that there was certainly some association between the operatives' dress and the entrances used. The other challenge for the observers was trying to estimate how many people were on site. There were three personnel carriers with what looked like thirty seats in each. Sitting through the night, there were only two arrivals at the base. The first arrived around 01.00 hrs which seemed full of 'off-duty' people, but there was a second, arriving at 03.30, which looked more interesting. This appeared to be a dozen long oblong boxes, heavy enough to be unloaded by four people at a time. Each was taken into one of the buildings without being stacked outside. Surprisingly, just as Jo put down her nightsight, four other individuals, in chains, were taken out and escorted through the same doors that had just swallowed the boxes. Given the distance of the observations, it was not possible to provide a more accurate account of what had taken place but nonetheless were helping to build a picture of its true functionality.

Dave returned to the barn before Jo and Rodg. He expected to find Jack on watch but the mezzanine was empty. He swore to himself under his breath; he listened intently to see if he could hear any clue above the shuffling of the sheep below. The rain was not as intense as it had been earlier and a glance at his watch told him dawn would arrive in less than an hour. Given the position, he could not waste time and effort looking for Jack; instead he repacked essentials into the backpacks in case for some reason Jack had been captured and their cover blown. Then he sat waiting, checking his Makarov was fully loaded and screwed the barrel of the silencer in place. Jo and Rodg returned ten minutes later. All three were prepared to make a swift exit but had no clear idea where they would go. The new arrivals joined him, listening intently for the sign of Ibrahim Sami waking up and, more importantly, for the sound of footsteps nearby.

The first light of the day was appearing over the mountains to the east when there was an early sign of a ground nesting bird being startled into life. Dave looked out of the back hatch, gun ready, to see Jack scrambling for the ladder. Swearing again he stood at ease, as Jack crawled through the hatch. Dave had been tempted to say, "Where the fuck have you been?" But he was smart enough to realise this extreme reaction was more likely to demonstrate his own fears, just at the time when he was about making his team as confident as possible with the task ahead. He chose a more emollient approach.

"So what's happening?"

"Sorry I wasn't here when you returned. After you left, two of the farm hands came back to feed the sheep. One of them wanted to get some more straw down from the mezzanine and I wasn't sure whether they were coming up the ladder. I didn't want to be in a position when I might have been forced to confront them, so I slipped away and waited behind the far left corner while listening out. In the end, they went for the easiest option; they got the straw they were looking from a bale already on the ground and, given it was late, decided to go home. Once I was sure the barn was empty of people, I began to make my way back, but, as I was already out and no one seemed to be around, I took the opportunity to take a look at some of the buildings nearby, especially as I knew we might have to get out quickly. I started to get a better understanding of the geography of our surroundings and where the locals go at night. I didn't realise they have a snooker hall and cinema. As far as I could tell, it looked like the snooker hall was filled with off-duty squaddies and there was a small queue outside the cinema, only three blocks from here, and then I saw Fawaz in a café with two other guys talking and drinking tea.

"From a distance, I couldn't tell what they were talking about, but the conversation looked serious and I thought he was supposed to be staying in with his family. Are you sure he can be trusted? Seems to me in reality we are pretty dependent on him for our survival here. When will we next see him?"

"Probably in a couple of hours. We'll find out what he has been up to. In the meantime, please remember there is only one boss in this field operation, and you must get used to taking instruction. I accept your first decision was to get out of the way and avoid any unnecessary contact, but using your initiative to go 'walkabout' could have put us in equal danger. We have got to hole up until I get new instructions from London. So, for now, we need to take every opportunity to either keep a low profile, or, better still, be invisible."

Dave was right. Within a couple of hours Fawaz arrived with

flasks of tea and bread. Dave realised the potential risk of Jack, the least experienced of his team, working off his personal initiative and not to instructions. He took the decision to demonstrate he had taken Jack's fears on board but in a way he felt everyone present would see as a positive action.

It started simply enough.

"What's it like being home?"

"Confusing," came the reply. Although Fawaz had spoken to Dave briefly the night before, he hadn't had enough time to share all that had happened with the team. "The place I have come back to is very different to the way it was when I left. There is no doubt that on the surface Ibrahim Sami has never looked so prosperous. My home and my family have benefitted more than most. In some ways, it's good to rebuild my relationship with my family, and, yes, because it is family, that doesn't take so much time. What is happening here is a different issue. I am starting to understand that the real reason for my father's success has been his ability to build a relationship with the military, but I don't know about how that has happened and what sustains it. What I do know is that, while he and a small group of others have new wealth, it is still the case that the majority of local people have not shared it. I need to understand better how this place works before I can understand my own place here, if there is anything for me. For now, I am using my time to build confidence with my family to reconnect with others I used to know and pick up intelligence that can inform the operation."

He then started to explain the recent catalogue of events he had learned from his father and the Chinese presence in the locality.

"There is still plenty more I need to know and will be meeting Colonel Rahman at the garrison soon. As you know, I have to be careful now I am being accepted back into the community. I have to keep some routines with the family at meal times, for instance, as well as being able to slip over here at intervals. I am starting to mix with other people in the meeting places in the town. I have prayers at the mosque and wider contacts to rebuild in the area.

Getting more engaged with what is going on is the very best way of sourcing the intelligence we need in order to realise our shared wish."

"So, who were those guys you met in the baker's café last night?" asked Jack, determined to make sure his fears were addressed.

"One is a textile merchant from Ashelqu, the next village to the north, who has a shop in the bazaar; the other is a local builder who makes his own bricks. I am trying to find out if there are other places in the area to move you to. The longer you stay here, the more chance there is of others finding out, and, as things are, I don't know whether there is anyone else in my household I could trust."

"OK, Fawaz, that's enough for now. Thanks for what you're doing. You're right.

"Jack had a close call with the two shepherds earlier. We need to get active soon and getting out of here is better than sharing the knowledge of our presence. You'd better get going before you're missed. Try to be back here before dawn tomorrow. I should have a reply from London and then we can fix our next move. While the rest of us are waiting, keep your kit bags stowed and stored out of sight. We may have to make sure we are out in the field in future at dawn and dusk to minimise any unexpected contact."

After Fawaz had left, Jack spoke up. "Guys, aren't you putting a lot of faith in him? He could dob us in tomorrow and probably get a cash prize as a result..."

Before Dave could answer, it was Jo who responded:

"Fawaz is one of us. We all have responsibilities in this, and we have to rely on each other. Right now, he is doing the most important task, getting us the knowledge we need to get this job sorted and go home. If he was going to turn us in, he would have done so by now. He is a fully signed-up member of PI, like the rest of us, and we can't get distracted now wondering whether any of us will bottle it."

The words hung heavily in the dark of the night. No one challenged her.

Overlooking the Caspian Sea and Baku Old Town district with the Shirvanshahs' Palace, the Four Seasons Hotel in the Azeri capital had that turn-of-the-century feel, reminiscent of the grand hotels on the Croisette in Cannes. Instead of a beachfront, across the busy Niazy Street thoroughfare, there was a park with mature trees, providing visitors and office workers with welcome shade in the midday heat, and, beyond, a ferry terminal and marina. Edwin Wilson had arrived a little ahead of schedule and almost immediately wished he had enough time to be a tourist. His initial impression of Baku was it was not what he would regard as a beautiful city, but from what he had seen coming in from the airport it still had a feeling of brutal grandeur and elegance. Had Baku been an old lady, she seemed to have a distinct scent of mustiness. Even away from the roadside, the smell of oil in the air from the nearby 'nodding' Russian-built Caspian oil derricks visible on the horizon to the north-east was inescapable. The concierge had already told him of the importance of the nearby national art gallery and the unique national landmark of the Flame Towers, but he had time for neither. This was business and high risk at that. In his quieter moments on the flight out from Heathrow, Wilson had reflected on the circumstances which had led to PI taking on the brief. Firstly, this was an important commission from the British authorities, part financed by France, Sweden and Canada. Secondly, evidence could prevent a new war breaking out in the region, perhaps sucking in more countries than those grouped around the Gulf.

Being in Azerbaijan was a test of a different type. The country did not recognise PI and did not have any nationals on PI's register. As a relatively new independent state, bankrolled by its government-controlled oil economy, its interest was focused on growing its customers in the international energy market. Protecting the wealth of the ruling elite and keeping its borders secure came as close seconds, which really meant focusing on the uneasy peace with its western neighbour, Armenia. Would his role at PI attract official interest? His office had secured his visa online in a little under three hours so he was assured of a smooth entry and yet he suspected the host country took a particular note of single Western businessmen arriving on tourist visas.

Bob (Mr Check Shirt) had offered to meet him, but he had preferred the anonymity of taking the trip into town by bus, instructing him to focus on delivering Dr Ehat to the hotel.

When the phone rang in his room just over an hour later, he knew they had arrived.

Wilson met them in the bar next to the lobby. Bob made the introductions and left, asking both to be ready in casual clothes at nine in the morning.

Dinner was at the Mugam Club, a restaurant set in its own mini terraced courtyard in the old town and only a short walk from the hotel. It was an atmospheric place to eat on a relatively mild autumn evening.

Ehat was an athletic build for his thirty-five years. He sported the stereotypical Mongol features which could potentially place him as a national of any of at least six central Asian states. Firm handshake, steel glasses and a piercing eye, readily analysing his surroundings. Ordering dinner was easy; most people were eating *plov*, a rice and lamb dish, itself a national delicacy.

There was the obligatory small talk, which really related to what Wilson already knew from his file. But he had gone to the trouble of meeting first for a reason: he wanted to satisfy himself Ehat understood the challenges and risks ahead.

"I will eat well tonight as I know the rations will start tomorrow," he joked before looking serious and adding, "Yes, I understand what PI does and what is expected of me in the next few days. I have been fortunate in being able to pursue an international career which has brought recognition to me as a Chinese citizen. But life is much harder now and I don't mean the day job. I have another eight months of my WHO contract in Uzbekistan to complete and then I face a hard choice: whether to return to China or not. There is no doubt China has helped me develop my career but at a price which is becoming more burdensome. My family were placed under house arrest when I first left for Uzbekistan. Calls home led me to believe all was well and my family were being cared for by the state while I was away. In fact, while in Uzbekistan I had a visit at my office in Tashkent from a Chinese official who told me my family would be looked after until my return. Unfortunately, I then got a call from a friend who works at the university in Urumqi claiming that my parents, in their late sixties, my wife's parents, my wife and my two children have been sent to re-education camps to learn the history and values of the Chinese state. Thousands of my brothers, ethnic Uighurs, have experienced the same fate; thousands more have simply disappeared. My friend advised me not to return. At the moment I cannot decide the future. I have brought credit and recognition for my work to the Chinese state and have developed a good reputation. However, this counts for nothing in the future. I am seriously contemplating staying away. If I do that, I will need to claim asylum, be pursued as an enemy of the state and would be obliged to resist. If China is engaged in Iran in a negative way, I feel it is my duty to my people to expose and stop it."

"You do know the limitations of working with us," said Wilson gently. "You will surrender your identity papers because in the event of your death your body and your nationality cannot be acknowledged. You may end up being buried where you fall, and no one will be the wiser – certainly we will not be able to acknowledge your contribution."

Ehat gave Wilson a look tinged with anger. "I don't intend to die on this mission and, if I am unlucky enough not to make it, I guess I won't care."

He pulled an envelope out of his pocket and placed it firmly in Wilson's hands.

"So here I am. This is my life. Look after my papers. I will want them back in a couple of weeks."

Twenty-four hours on and Dave found himself under the distinctive cedar tree where he had last met Gil. This night it was not raining but cloudy with a soft wind blowing off the mountains. Dave hated waiting, but knew patience was a virtue on an exercise of this complexity. He had slowly circumnavigated the tree to see if Gil was there in the expectation that, if he wasn't, his own presence would be noted, which it was... eventually. Some twenty minutes after his arrival, he heard a whispered call behind him. Yes, it was Gil, but Dave was unnerved how close he had come before he had registered his presence.

"You look pretty cool. Am I to conclude you are actually getting to like this corner of the world?"

The irony wasn't wasted on Dave.

"Funnily enough, I can think of things I'd rather be doing right now, but the chance to talk to you is sufficient compensation in itself," he replied dryly.

Gil chuckled. "Well, you have certainly got them talking back home. You'll be getting fifty extra rounds, more rations and another body in a couple of days and guess what? His name is Gul, as in the bird, or maybe that's some sort of MoD code I've missed. Are you sure you will remember the difference between me and him? Thought you'd like that. I've been told to pick him up at the embarkation point and bring him across the day after tomorrow. I suggest we meet back here then, in this very ditch. He's all yours after that."

Gil slipped away into the darkness, leaving Dave to plot his route back to the barn and formulate the next stage of the plan.

Western rock from the Shogun's radio seemed to complement his edgy driving and mood as he headed back along the coastal boulevard to his apartment. There was something about Mahta that Jamshid thought was special but he couldn't put his finger on it. What had started as a casual meeting at one of Ravi's parties seemed to have potential for the future. Despite her protestations, he was sure she had been watching his football game in Tehran. If he had been right, why did she deny it? She was evidently a successful professional woman in Iran and certainly there weren't many of them around. How had she "broken the glass ceiling" to get societal recognition and enjoy the freedoms she had? Did she have a husband? There was no sign of a ring on her finger. She must have some influential figure looking out for her. And why the interest in him? Heaven knows, a beautiful woman in her mid-thirties would not be short of potential suitors. Unusual too for the woman to make the first move, like she had done.

Despite half a day riding together and some brief snatched intimacy, he still knew very little about her. He resolved to get his laptop out again when he got home to see whether the search engine could throw any further light on her identity, but as an afterthought he realised he wouldn't make much progress. When he had asked Ravi about her, he too had seemed pretty vague. All he claimed to have was her first name and her mobile number. Could he ring her and just ask? Better not. It might put her off, making him appear too officious, like most of the rest of the male population of Bandar Abbas. No, he would just have to wait for the weekend to learn more.

The car park for his block was in the basement, a great asset on hot days when leaving a car on the street outside for ten minutes would make it unbearably sticky until the aircon started to work. His key fob lifted the barrier and he drove down the ramp to the space allocated to his flat. His mind had moved on from Mahta; the prospect of a cool shower and a can of cold non-alcoholic beer had filled the void she had vacated. Another press of the key fob locked his car as he walked to the service lift nearby. In this situation, he could afford to drop his guard. It was Sunday, after all. With hindsight he really wished he had taken the stairs. When the lift arrived and the doors opened, he found two suited men who stepped out either side of him, each slipping one of their arms under his armpits, lifting him backwards, before setting him down and standing uncomfortably close. In that split second he remembered them serving him champagne and escorting him to the door at the villa in Karaj.

"Good afternoon, Mr Turani. Mr Alrakahthan sends you his best wishes and asks if you would be available to join him for breakfast tomorrow at eight o'clock. One of us will be in the lobby to collect you at seven thirty."

Jamshid was about to point out he would be expected to be at his office desk at that time, but understood the seriousness of the invitation and the need to accept. He was minded to ask if his daughter Hanah would be there, but decided in the moment it was an unnecessary point of detail. Nodding his head would suffice. The two men then walked towards a black Mercedes, conspicuous in the half-empty car park; Jamshid to the lift. The elevator doors closed before he could see them leaving, but had a hunch they had gone. The message had been delivered and understood. They knew where he lived and wouldn't pick up the phone if they wanted a chat.

Leaving the lift on the tenth floor of the block, he reached for his door key on the landing.

As he put the key in the lock, the flat door opposite opened.

"Mr Turani, I am so happy to see you. You know that you have had some visitors this afternoon – two men smartly dressed. They looked very solemn. I thought had I not come out to see who they were, they might have battered your door. I told them you would probably be back later and they went away. You're not in any trouble, are you? They looked like the Basij to me. It's the way they stand."

The Basij Resistance Force (often referred to as the "Mobilisation of the Oppressed") claimed to be a volunteer militia allied to the notorious and feared Homeland Security Department of the Revolutionary Council, responsible for random arrests, detentions, torture and disappearances. Statistically, their work had boosted the country's prison population by 40%, and were often called out onto the streets to use force to dispel dissent.

Jamshid did not want to get locked in a conversation with his neighbour, who was obviously short of company.

"Don't worry, Mr Tawal, I met up with them downstairs. They are from the finance company wanting to look at my car. I'm thinking of getting a newer model and wanted to know about part exchange. Unless they could see it, they couldn't value it."

Although it was a spur-of-the-moment lie, it seemed to have the benefit of reassuring the old seaman.

"Oh, that's OK then. If they had been from the Basij, I would have told them to fuck off anyway," he chuckled. "When you're as old as me you don't worry about people like that. They should go out and get a proper job like everyone else. Bet they'd be as sick as dogs if I took them fishing in the Gulf." He was clearly keeping himself amused.

The humour did not spread to Jamshid.

As soon as he had closed his door, he leaned against it, wondering what calamity tomorrow would bring.

He was in the lobby of his apartment block ten minutes ahead of the appointed time. Alrakahthan's boys arrived precisely as promised. There was a nodded acknowledgement before they opened the entrance door for him and then the rear door of the black Mercedes limousine he had glimpsed the previous afternoon. A bit like a Western taxi, there was a glass screen separating the front two seats from the back. The car was already cool as a result of the aircon and local pop music played softly in the background. As he settled into his seat, he took off his sunglasses and stared out into the middle distance, letting the music play with his mind. He remembered that, like everything else in life, music had to be approved by the government. A half smile of irony etched upon his face as he listened to Arian's hit song "The Footsteps of Hope". The tune was good but be chose not to try to remember the lyrics. The journey itself was uneventful, twenty minutes or so across town to yet another apartment block. This one had a grand entrance hall with plenty of marble and mock palms. His driver and assistant, neither of whom had spoken during the short drive, climbed out, one buttoning his jacket, the other tightening his tie before opening the door and leading him in. They ascended to the twentieth floor and entered what seemed like an ornate lounge. The larger of his escorts gestured him to take a seat and returned to stand at the side of the lift door. The chair he had been invited to sit in was the sort candidates dread when they go to a job interview – when he sat down it seemed to condense under his body weight and sank lower to the floor. It was positioned in a strategic location, offering the best views of the room, itself filled with dramatic ceramics and glassware to match the monikered thick woven carpet. It was clear he was in the lair of a collector of fine arts. He was glad he didn't have the responsibility of doing the dusting. Yet among the riot of artistic icons was a huge colourful abstract painting. The mix of colours and shapes clearly had meaning for the artist, but what did it say to the viewer?

At that moment his focus was broken by a voice behind him.

It was Abdullo Alrakahthan, who shared his gaze at the painting.

SIX

"IMPRESSIVE, ISN'T IT? I love abstracts. This one is by Behjat Sadr. She was best known as an impressionist and for her use of a palette knife to demonstrate rhythm and movement, but not so many know she did a small number of abstracts, most I think are in private collections in the US and here. You know, every time I look at it, I see something different. Look at the extravagant use of paint. I think it is the texture that makes it special.

"I'm sorry to be distracted at the start of the working week but even I only get to see it once in a while. Thank you for coming to see me."

Alrakahthan held his hand out to shake in a very deliberate gesture. Almost automatically, Jamshid responded. Alrakahthan nodded to one of the men standing at the lift.

"Coffee and pastries are on their way. We are both busy people so I will get to the point. Do you recall our last meeting? Although it was short, Hanah reported that she thought it productive. She sends her regards, by the way; she's tied up with some business in Tehran. You will know we are traders – import/export. What you may not be aware of is that one of our clients is the Revolutionary Council – the government of the Islamic Republic. We provide them with a range of services – commercial and logistic – which help them to earn foreign currency to underwrite the economy. Why us? Well, we are good. Creative, you may say."

He poured coffee.

"Also, we are not a government agency. US sanctions have helped us to grow probably beyond our own expectations. My relationship with the leadership has grown over the years. My first mission for the state was to guarantee the import of embargoed foodstuffs via the stores I used to own. The next task was to maintain exports to customers for our own produce – oranges, dates, olives, pomegranates, peaches, saffron and much more. When you are a trader, learning how to interact with a market, even if it is new to you, is straightforward. As more and more categories of sanctions have come into place, we have been given the task of protecting the country's trade, keeping our economy solvent and safeguarding thousands of jobs. Today, I think we must be responsible for about 30% of GDP, one way or another. The scale of our present activities has opened more doors to us, including that of the Supreme Leader. Now I tend to be consulted about government policies to offer a view about their likely impact. It is an odd position to be in as I have no formal power, but, here, influence is everything. Providing I am responsible with my behaviour in public – and achieve results, of course – I have a level of personal freedom most citizens do not have. But one of the constant pressures I am under is to diversify and that puts pressure on my own technical resources to trade. Despite being asked to do so, I have resisted getting involved in the oil business because of the time it takes, as you well know. But the country has more challenging needs which have to be financed – nuclear power, the defence industry, disaster recovery, housing – the list goes on. We need to earn big money and we need new markets. I have spent some months researching you and a couple of others to assist in this work. People who have a flair of success against the odds. You may not know it, but your name first came to my attention through contacts in the Interior Ministry – I think your brother-in-law Abdul works there? Your father's work as an economics professor at Tehran University is highly regarded and your mother is running what I know to be the best tea house in town, which is in itself almost an institution.

"As for you, well you have done pretty well for yourself since you left the navy; you won your place at the Port Authority on merit and you have underlined that faith with our biggest single oil trade since sanctions were introduced. Naturally I have discussed involving you with my client and received the necessary authorisation, so welcome to my crazy world!"

Jamshid had noted that nowhere in this conversation had the question of his personal consent been raised; it was just taken for granted.

"So what would you expect me to do?" he asked lamely.

"Don't quit the day job. Our business operates through a loose, high-level network, and in due course you will receive details about how to access it. By being part of a network and not an organisation makes your activity on our behalf harder to intercept. You will be set objectives and critical dates for completion. Should you need to take leave from your present work duties in order to deliver, you notify me and I will arrange it. You report on your tasks remotely and payment, more than you have ever earned in your career to date, will be made to your personal account upon completion. It's simple, really, and avoids problems along the way. You will be working as one of my professional executive assistants, one of an inner circle that will attend a monthly strategy review meeting in Karaj.

"In line with our need to ensure discretion, what I have told you will not be set down in documents. In this business, trust is all. You either have it, or... you don't."

"What do you see me doing?"

"You will assist Hanah in planning and overseeing our new businesses. I said we need to diversify and the present pressure on the client is to double its receipts in a year. We need to secure high-value trades in new markets where we can operate with discretion. Think of the amount of preparation for the Yellow Sea deal. The Great Satan will get to know, in due course, by their satellites, but not until the trade is complete. In fact, you could say that is to our advantage as they are fixated with the oil market. Your present-day job will be enough of a distraction to them. We have to be nimble, open up opportunities and transact fast. That is why, for the future, managing our trades through places like Pakistan and Macau makes more sense than using Dubai, or elsewhere in the Gulf for that matter."

"What type of trades are you looking for?"

"That is for you and Hanah to assess – volumes and margins are key. If you can identify what works and make the case, we'll do it."

Jamshid's head was starting to buzz. Could he believe what he was hearing or was this part of some elaborate set up? He countered: "This research will be sensitive, even the assessment documents. How can you be happy about me working out of my present office?"

"Our technology you will use is sound – Chinese, actually – and allows you to work flexibly. If you need face-to-face meetings these can be booked here in this apartment or at Karaj. You are joining a family business *inshallah*. We share our limited resources. We have decided to set up a training scenario where you will first work with Hanah. Assuming you succeed, you will receive further autonomy. Your first assignments will be simple minerals-related – rare earth and yellowcake exports to Asia, but our growing human resources trades are likely to take more time."

"I thought you said you didn't have a big organisation."

Alrakahthan laughed. "When I talk about human resources, I don't mean recruitment and training. I mean a group of businesses related to the human condition. Some 'above the line' and others below. Do you know, as a result of our long war with Iraq, we became world leaders in the production of prosthetics? Even my cousin has a couple. Technology has moved on and a 'smart' leg means people who lost their limbs can have such high-quality replacements that you would never know they had one, unless they were wearing shorts. We also offer a kind of body spare parts service for transplants – hearts, lungs, liver, kidneys, even replacement dicks for mad men who think they don't measure up. Logistics matter as well. Profits are down in the opium markets but moving people from Asia into Europe has also grown exponentially in recent months. Personally, I have never known why they bother. I keep putting up the prices and they keep buying. It will come to a stop one day, but we must ride it while we can. One of the trickier trades which I'm having to manage personally at the moment is the arms business, which is also in our HR portfolio. This seems simple – exporting weaponry produced in this country – but most of our stuff are variants of other people's technology. Here in Bandar, missiles are a great example. Our Chinese friends helped us to set up a factory to manufacture Silkworm missiles under licence, which was OK when we were formally at war, as demand was steady. While we are at peace, we're stockpiling missiles which we can't use, so we need to sell them. Of course, our friends in Pakistan take some of them and quite a few go to Yemen, Syria and Africa, but we have to be very careful not to upset our oriental partners, who are operating in the same markets. You should start to study some of this ahead of your next family visit to Tehran. Even better for you to have a rare earth proposition lined up when you come, then bring it over to Karaj, and we'll review it. Remember appearance is all. You cannot talk with family and friends about any of this and, for those who know you, they should not see changes in your habits or routine."

"And if I fail or don't want to do this?"

Alrakahthan finished his coffee, leaving his pastry uneaten. "I don't think either scenario is likely, but if you cannot serve our cause in any other useful way there is always martyrdom. Your value to us has already increased by being party to this conversation.

Work with me and you will enjoy privileges that to most citizens would be unimaginable. I must say you should also respect my offer of working with my daughter Hanah. There are very few men I would entrust with such a responsibility."

He fixed Jamshid with a steely eye and paused. To Jamshid it seemed like the look was his personal signature on a contract, somehow more meaningful than a handshake.

"You and I must go our separate ways for now. I'll have you driven back to your apartment so you can get your car. Your communications equipment and instructions will be hand delivered to you tomorrow night."

Alrakahthan had closed the conversation and moved on – physically and metaphorically. He disappeared into the lift accompanied by one of his henchmen.

He was left to watch the lift signal reach the ground before his colleague summoned it to return.

Back in his office two hours later, Jamshid put his breakfast encounter behind him, picking up the more mundane issues in his inbox.

News of his Yellow Sea success was becoming common knowledge and he was already under pressure to ship more oil. The problem was not finding a place to sell but the means to transport it. A bit like the road haulage industry's reliance on self-employed owner truck drivers, the same applied to ships. Yes, there were the big private fleets – the Stenas and MSLs – but these had significant international contracts and weren't in the market of breaking sanctions. Finding independent owner operators in the shipping world was becoming increasingly difficult and he couldn't rely on any of them to accept loads on a regular basis. He had called many of the usual suspects, but no one was biting. He was about to leave the office at the end of what had felt like a fruitless day, when a call came through from one of his old contacts, who he had tapped up nearly two weeks before.

Yannis Yannaopolu was an independent shipping magnate based out of Piraeus. He ran a fleet of three tankers and two bulk cargo vessels. Unlike many of his competitors, he had never moved into the container business because by his own estimate he was not big enough to compete with the better-known industry brands. Yannis was a tough cookie and certainly wise enough not to do Iranian trades on a regular basis, but having his ships idle in port was not good. He would consider all cargoes to ensure his fleet was kept at sea.

They exchanged pleasantries and moans about the parlous state of the shipping industry before Yannis got to the purpose of the call.

"I have always liked you, Jamshid, but you work for a set of pirates. I never feel you really share your business requirements with me, which is disappointing when I am in a position to help. I have two of my family dropping loads near you in the next few days. If you can look after them for a short period, I think we could work something out – but you have to see to both at the same time – bulk and liquid."

The translation of his comments meant he had two ships in the vicinity of the Gulf empty of cargo. If Jamshid could start loading two ships in Bandar overnight, they could be back at sea in under seventy-two hours, ensuring there was a deal to be done.

"When are you looking to be accommodated?" Jamshid enquired, already thinking how long it would take him to get the cargoes in place.

"They could be with you in less than five days. That should give us time to fix the itineraries and price."

"OK, let's get it on. I'll have the paperwork in place at the bank in twenty-four hours."

This type of call had become rarer in recent times and this was enough to set his heart banging in his chest.

Sorting the oil for loading and destination was of course the easy bit. Jamshid arranged the contracts for this consignment with

Myanmar, but the bulk cargo would need to be rare earth ore. Finding it and getting it to Bandar in five days would be his first challenge. The next would be working out where it could be landed.

He started a search for both on his laptop.

There are seventeen rare earth elements in the periodic table, specifically the fifteen lanthanides, as well as scandium and yttrium. The fact that Iran had potentially significant reserves of over half of them had only just been confirmed by the State Mining Company at the end of last year. Concentrated in two areas, one west of Kerman, the other in the closed area near Abbasabad in the far north-west, early excavations had resulted in viable quantities of valuable ores including neodymium, used for making high-powered, infrared lasers for industrial and defence applications. Presently the quantities being produced were not able to be utilised fully by domestic customers, so already there were reserves which could be accessed.

His computer identified the managing director of the State Mining Company. He noted the name and contact details before he went home, strangely excited about the prospect of a double win: one for the day job, the other for… 'the other'.

This apparent turn of good fortune took over his mind. His doubts about Alrakahthan and the all-too-worrying risks about working for him disappeared. In front of him was a nailed-down opportunity for an early success. The next day was taken up putting in place the banking arrangements for the oil, which in this case was to be made in Chinese RMB via Dhaka, Bangladesh. He made sure he was back at his apartment early, a fact noted by Mr Tawal, who had knocked to see if he was ill.

Mr Tawal proved to be much smarter than many gave him credit for. He knew Jamshid kept a bottle of quality Bekaa Valley arak in his kitchen and seemed determined to be a nuisance until he was offered a glass. After an hour, Jamshid managed to get him out of the door, saying he had an important business call to take from Tehran. His timing was good. Almost as soon as Mr Tawal had withdrawn to his own apartment, the doorbell rang. Checking the spyhole, he saw Alrakahthan's driver.

He opened the door and gestured for him to come in. The driver shook his head and without a word gave him a supermarket plastic bag before turning for the elevator. It was an odd encounter: no words were spoken and somehow Jamshid thought even a belated 'thanks' was not justified.

All was as Alrakahthan had described. He found a mobile phone with a distinctive instruction manual that was not authored by the manufacturer.

Two hours later, he tried it for the first time. He recognised Hanah's voice at the other end.

Jamshid thought this was an opportunity for a chat. She cut him short. "You know this is for business only," she said curtly; the warmth of their last meeting seemed to have been forgotten.

He told her his news. "I will deal with the mining company. How much stock is needed?"

"Three hundred thousand metric tonnes – market price in RMB, destination Pusan."

"When?"

"Friday at 18.00 in Bandar."

"OK. We'll do this one via Jakarta. I will send you bank details."

The line went dead, but even that was not sufficient to dampen his mood.

Mahta was not in such good spirits. The freedoms and pleasure of the weekend seemed far behind her as she returned to her office as director of the 11th February Silkworm Assembly Plant, a series of low-level nondescript warehouses at the back of Trading Estate No.5 in Rajaei.

Her responsibilities were significant – 1,200 local people on the payroll, storage problems for completed manufactured product and design delays with a new locally produced warhead.

Being one of the few women in senior roles in the country, there was always talk that she had slept her way to the top, but, had that been the case, she would not have lasted a year in the job.

A professional electrical engineer and graduate from one of Iran's top universities, Qom, Mahta had joined the factory six years ago as a production supervisor, joining and subsequently leading a project team to work with the sponsors to streamline assembly methods. Her success of working with the Chinese led to a new manufacturing facility for components in Bandar and her innovative methods were taken back to Shaanxi. The Silkworm Project had been an important initiative for Iran, arriving at a time when the country did not have a defence industry of its own, but over the years Mahta and her colleagues had been instrumental in studying the technology in order to develop new home-grown products, stepping stones towards their ultimate goal of producing their own ballistic missiles. Not only did her success increase the country's defensive capability; it also resulted in huge cost savings. That said, the technology behind the Silkworm was outdated, and the Chinese were trying to extract a much higher price for the supply of upgraded replacements.

Mahta's reputation in the Defence Ministry was high – she was not only recognised for her technical knowledge, but her 'quiet' style as a Shi'a female role model had won her admirers at the highest level. Today, apart from her responsibilities in Bandar Abbas, she was also an adviser to the Revolutionary Council's Defence Procurement Committee in Tehran.

It was in that capacity that she had taken a call from Sayeed Gharbieh, head of the Revolutionary Guard Internal Security Unit, incorporating the Basij. Mahta had met Gharbieh a few times at government events in the last year but didn't claim to know him. He, like her, had something of a reputation about him, but, unlike her, it was not all positive. Gharbieh had a lot of influence working directly for the Speaker of the Iranian Parliament, effectively second only to the Supreme Leader. He built a personal aura as a hardliner, but it was never clear whether the actions he took were by personal whim or in response to decrees or instructions from the Speaker. Gharbieh liked to style himself as "guarantor" of the revolution, allowing him to take action against all threats, perceived or actual, to the authority of the government. Arrests, imprisonments, beatings and killings were the tools of his trade, but for now he was developing a new line in intelligence. It had always been a closely guarded secret that the government of the country was riven with factions, each controlled by either the Supreme Leader himself or by his deputy, the Speaker. As head of state, the Supreme Leader had ultimate responsibility of protecting the country and, in theory, had the final say on all matters, foreign policy, the economy, defence and the rest. He was known to be well informed on world events and pragmatic, understanding that keeping his people safe and well fed was the best way of ensuring loyalty. The Supreme Leader was now starting to get older and whispers about how his succession would be managed abounded. The Speaker was seeking to consolidate his role and had decided the best way to guarantee his position was to follow Gharbieh's line. The parlous state of the nation's finances was well known in government circles, and it was always easy to blame the Great Satan for its woes. Given present tensions, it was important for Iran to demonstrate it could still prosper in the face of sanctions. Gharbieh understood the commercial strategy the state was following to ensure its survival, but didn't like it. How could his country publicly fight the imperialism of the West, yet embrace it behind the scenes when times were hard? In particular, he detested Alrakahthan and all that he stood for.

In Gharbieh's mind, Alrakahthan was a corrupting influence on the pure doctrine of the state – worse still, he resented the personal camaraderie between Alrakahthan and the Supreme Leader, who he knew both shared a love of chess and Lagavulin, an obscure sixteen-year-old single malt whisky from Scotland. Maybe it was also because, like him, Alrakahthan had complete freedom from state interference in return for his services.

Gharbieh saw Alrakahthan and the success of his work as the prime obstacle preventing the rise of the Speaker to the top job.

If only the solution was as simple as arranging a hit. Alrakahthan was a difficult target – always on the move and well protected. Even if he were successful in ordering a kill, his unexpected demise would implicate himself and his boss.

No, death for Alrakahthan may be easy, but would not be productive.

He must be revealed in a plot that would lay his traitorous activities before all, justifying his public execution at the gallows.

It had been a few weeks since Gharbieh had made contact with Mahta. He told her about Jamshid and how she would be serving the national interest if she was able to get to know the oil trader and learn more about his activities. Although Mahta had been surprised to receive the call, he had apologised about talking to her about a "sensitive" matter. Although she had never met Jamshid, Gharbieh reminded her that they both knew Ravi, as both were custodians of a local war veteran's charity. Mahta knew enough not to get involved, and really did not want to have more to do with Gharbieh than was necessary. Implicit in their conversation was that non-cooperation could risk harm to her own reputation and standing in government circles.

On balance, it was better to engage than not. She told him she would get to know Jamshid and find out about his work. She didn't want to be called, but would be in touch when she had news.

Since the excitement of securing another big oil deal for the country and the Port of Bandar Abbas, Jamshid felt time had passed slowly. He had made all the necessary arrangements for the paperwork, which would show that Yannis's tanker had collected its cargo from Karachi and made the necessary arrangements for the complicated bank transfers. He had received confirmation that the money was now on deposit in Bangladesh. The ship, registered in Monrovia, would be loaded in the coming hours and it would set sail on the morning tide, calling in briefly at Karachi to change crew. Payment would be made when the ship was fully loaded and cleared for departure. Looking out on the docks from his office window, he reflected on times past when most berths in the docks were full. These days container capacity was down to 20%, with essential imports coming by tramp, mainly from Dubai or Muscat. Half the spare berths were taken up by the navy; the rest had been mothballed. Yannis's other ship, the Argentine-flagged bulk cargo carrier, had arrived in Dubai, awaiting the call to come over to Bandar. Jamshid was nervous. He felt he had made half an arrangement – brokered a deal but without the necessary ability to ensure it was transacted. He had, of course, arranged warehouse space to be reserved for the rare earth consignment, but it was turning midday and there had been no information on the whereabouts of the train carrying the load. It was not surprising really, he thought: Iranian Railways were notoriously inefficient. Under normal circumstances, he would probably have been chasing information as well, but, in the present situation, he thought Hanah should have briefed him. He clearly recalled setting the five o'clock deadline and had been told – no, *instructed* – not to contact her in the meantime. He had little choice other than to sit tight. Loading of the crude was on schedule but it looked like some slippage was going to happen on the bulk. It was now 12.30. Yannis was expecting his call to send in the bulk carrier. To make that call, he needed certainty the fulfilment would occur by the deadline. At one o'clock, he took the risk: the bulk carrier would weigh anchor within the hour. Jamshid had allocated the most distant berth, number 32. Excavators, cranes and labour were all in position. There was nothing more he could do. He lit a cigarette and stared out over Bandar. Looking out to the north-east, he saw a long goods train approaching. It was crossing the junction which would lead away from the city and into the port.

Hanah had delivered.

Friday had been a good day for this transaction. Given it was the holy day, staff were limited to essentials only. The rare earth consignment was big and he knew more questions would have been asked by colleagues seeing such a load arrive. There were few in the office at this time and those who were there were preoccupied with day-to-day tasks and certainly didn't have time to stare out of the window. He grabbed his car keys and hard hat, left the office and drove to Quay 32. Soon after, the harbourmaster reported that the ship, the *Shimmering Star*, had received the pilot and would dock within the hour, about thirty minutes behind the projected schedule. It was an advantage it would be empty on arrival so loading could commence directly from train to hold. The task was a big one: estimated loading time would be three days. He would personally supervise arrangements. His first call would be to customs to give them the special code he had been sent to ensure they did not interfere with his plans. While maintaining a destroyer on twenty-four-hour readiness, to be scrambled in the event of any US incursion into its territorial waters, the same code would be issued to the navy's command centre to stand down and not challenge the *Shimmering Star*, which had not listed Bandar as a port of call. The ship would be expected to be offline for communications between Bandar and Mumbai, where it would stop to resupply before continuing its journey to Korea. Again, Jamshid's timing had been good. Most civil maritime services had closed for the weekend, meaning there was a lack of interest in where Yannis's ship was at that time.

At ten on Sunday night, ahead of schedule, loading was completed. Once he had reported to Hanah, all he had to do was to wait for her confirmation to release the vessel. For Jamshid, it was a sleepless night. The *Shimmering Star* was the largest vessel in dock at that moment and he would have preferred that it had been able to set sail before his colleagues came into the office at the start of the working week. He certainly didn't want to be asked too many questions about it. The approval came through at 08.30 on Monday morning, just as Jamshid had decided to meet Ravi for breakfast at the usual place instead of being at his desk. Steaming coffee and pastry in front of him, he called the harbourmaster to authorise the release before turning to his friend.

"Goodness, you look knackered and it's only Monday," Ravi said. "Burning the candle at both ends? Maybe I shouldn't have introduced you to Mahta – she must be a handful! Seriously, mate, you should take it easy – go for a swim or, better still, go up to the Caspian for a bit of RnR for a few days. Better than popping pills. Trust me, I'm a doctor."

Jamshid's mood had lifted in the preceding minute. He shared the joke. "I don't know; I think I should go away, but I just can't get the time. The board are asking more and more questions about our business projections in the coming year, and I'm having to go into the office on the weekend to do the extra paperwork."

"Seems to me you're starting to think you're indispensable, just because you got that Yellow Sea deal away," his friend replied.

"Oh, but I got another biggy away on Friday, this time to Myanmar," he blurted.

"So, right now, I'm either way ahead of my targets or slightly behind, because I think the board are shifting the goal posts; that way they think they don't have to pay me commission."

"You aren't making much space for your private life then? I hear from Mahta you met up last weekend."

In that moment, he realised he had not given her a thought, such was his stress.

"Yes, we did, and it was great. I think she must be pissed off with me because I crashed my next date with her, which should have been yesterday. It's all gone a bit quiet in that direction, so I guess I owe her a call, flowers and the rest."

"What happened about those heavies you were telling me about last time? Were you being warned off for chatting up that gangster's daughter in Tehran?" Ravi said, jokingly.

"Oh, that! Well, I think it shows I'm getting paranoid. I haven't had a chance to think any more about it and no one's reminded me," he said. He changed the subject. "And what's the latest medical drama from your place?"

"Not much really – been a quiet few days – an amputation, a shooting and a couple of liver transplants. I'll tell you more when we both have more time. Let's do something useful before the weekend when we can really talk. Squash? Golf?"

Glancing at his watch, Ravi didn't wait for his friend's reply. He headed for the door and disappeared into the morning rush.

Back home in front of the TV with day-to-day work matters put aside, Jamshid knew his priority was to mend what he expected to be his broken relationship with Mahta.

It took three calls before he succeeded in making contact. He thought it was his third message which had made the difference:

"Mahta, it's me – Jamshid – again. Not only am I sorry I missed our date and didn't let you know but then I realised I couldn't even send flowers as I don't have your postal address. Let's get together, if only so you can see a grown man give a grovelling apology."

She made him wait half an hour before sending a text.

"Rescheduled our missed meeting. Same time, same place. Sunday. Last chance."

Jamshid smiled, clutched the phone to his chest and decided to take a shower.

Bob arrived at reception in the Four Seasons ten minutes ahead of schedule. To his surprise, Edwin and Ehat were ready and waiting, their bags left at the concierge desk.

"You are right to keep your kit here; it is the safest place. You

136

can collect it when you get back. Let's go. The car is right outside."
Bob strode out of the lobby, his guests in his wake.

Edwin and Ehat sat in the back of Bob's white Toyota Corolla.

The journey to the airport was about forty-five minutes depending on traffic conditions. The drive took them out of town to the north-east, heading away from the coast past the Zaha Hadid-designed Heydar Aliyev Cultural Center, famous for its towering, flowing canopy. Then on to the Heydar Aliyev Expressway to the Heydar Aliyev Airport. If Edwin hadn't noticed before, portraits of a suited, benevolent figure, left arm indicating a sense of direction, sun rising behind him, were on several billboards, especially around major highway intersections, captioned with the words "Founder of the independent Azeri state". He had died back in 2003 and been succeeded by his son, but, to the casual visitor, he seemed very much alive. His portrait gave the impression of signposting them towards the airport but also his gaze made the viewer think he was watching them as they passed. Bob noticed Edwin looking at Aliyev's image as he drove.

"It's funny but you always see the grand old man when you are leaving, not when you arrive. He's almost telling you to get out of town," he laughed. "With an image like that, his son Ilham doesn't have to try too hard to remind people who's in charge."

"What do people think about that?"

"Who knows? People don't talk about it. They're pretty well fed and have jobs. Only a few bother to read the papers and those that do probably don't believe what they read anyway. So, although this is an autocracy, citizens are smart enough to realise they've done alright out of it."

Ehat joined the conversation. "Surely people want to be free of the tyranny?"

"You don't miss what you never had. I guess Aliyev was an improvement on Stalin," Bob replied.

"You obviously know this place well," Ehat persisted.

Bob smiled as he looked in the rear-view mirror, offering a mocking look suggesting the Uighur was too curious.

"I've been here five years now and run an adventure tour travel agency with my partner, Anya. I used to be in security in Donegal at the end of the Troubles, but got bored. I came here as part of a plan to see someplace different and probably start an Irish bar. Except, when I got here, I discovered they were all Muslims and I was unlikely to convince them to start drinking Murphy's. I was about to move on when I met Anya, who was working as a tour guide. She showed me the sights and I've been here ever since, even learning a bit of the local lingo. Although not many know this country, we get a lot of punters in for the annual Grand Prix and international football games, so we get a steady flow of enquiries to go hiking. Outside the city there is some spectacular scenery and some pretty scary wildlife. In the spring, we always have to be careful of brown bears, who like coming off the mountains for the odd selfie and anything else which takes their fancy. In the winter, it's the same with wolves. I have become part of a small but growing international community and as a result understand the importance of keeping the peace. Unfortunately, there is a lot of tension beneath the surface, but not directed at the government. Nationalism is a potent force in Azerbaijan and has led to many border conflicts. I am sure you have heard of Nagorno-Karabagh? The Azeris went to war with Armenia about it. It was a stalemate, but thousands were killed in the process. If you have caused or witnessed death, you learn peace is something you must nurture and value. It isn't always a natural state of affairs and you need to work to sustain it. I joined Peace International so in some small way I could make a contribution, so this is great – a chance to help PI in the best way I know – running a trip."

Edwin brought the conversation back the immediate situation. "I thought we would be joined by Anya," he said.

"Given the tight timetable you set, she went ahead yesterday to get everything set up. She's taken Mr Ehat's stuff as well. She will meet us when we get there. When we took the others down south last time, we went in a truck. Took us six hours so that's why we've chartered a plane today. We will fly down to a place called Minjivan, which is itself about an hour's drive to the embarkation point.

"Anya has got a car and will take us first to a shooting range for Mr Ehat. After that we will go on to drop him off. Anya will return with us back to Minjivan for the flight back here in the morning, and if we're lucky we'll fit in a few hours rest before that, and maybe some hot food along the way."

"Sounds like a plan," Edwin said, glancing at Ehat. The Uighur nodded and returned his gaze to the passing landscape.

They drove past the main entrance to international departures, instead taking the next left into an unmarked and unmade road with unkept hedging on either side. Bob slowed to avoid the worst of the potholes. Presently, they arrived at a small car park next to the two-storey General Aviation building at the side of one of the runways.

Once again, Bob led the way opening the trunk.

"Just before you go in, guys, I suggest you get changed into these camouflage suits and put on combat vests. I'm doing the same. After all, I don't want us to look too conspicuous when we get there."

Having changed in the toilets, the three came out into a reception area, where an unshaven, balding man, with a waistline that looked like it had benefitted from too many pastries, sat reading a paper in his shirtsleeves and slurping coffee loudly from a plastic cup.

"*Privet, Sergei eto Bob.*"

"Morning, Bob. As you have guests, we will talk in the Queen's English."

The dishevelled character picked up his not-inconsiderable frame and gripped the nearest hand, which happened to be Edwin's.

"It is a pleasure to meet you, sir, I am Sergei, your pilot. I was here an hour ago to do the pre-flight checks. All is good including the weather so we can expect a smooth trip. Come…"

He gesticulated for the others to follow him out of the glass door to an area with seven light aircraft. He pointed ahead.

"This is ours."

Like everything else in Azerbaijan, even the plane looked unconventional, with its main propeller at the back, below a double tail fin. Either side of the nose were small stabiliser wings to complement the main span. It was painted sky blue, the standard colour of a Reliant Robin car, but with go-faster stripes on the fuselage.

"Do you know this plane? I don't think you have these in England. It is a Yak-58. I think it is the best air taxi, cheap to run, easy to fly and will land on a kopek. Perfect for Minjivan. The engine is a Vedeneyev, one of the best, which powered half the Soviet Air Force."

He stared momentarily at his shoes.

"At least it did when I was there," he added.

For such a compact plane, it was surprisingly spacious inside, and Edwin estimated it could seat six in comfort. Once strapped in, Sergei fired the engine. Despite all the stated qualities of the plane, one thing it wasn't was quiet. It was smelly too – a mixture of stale sweat and kerosene left over from the night before. It was clear the three would not be having much conversation en route.

Sergei Boroschenko wanted to look the part of a buccaneer, so he pulled a pair of mirrored sunglasses from his pocket and kissed his St Christopher necklace before adjusting his own seat belt. To those in the know, there could be no doubt on this evidence he was Russian. After a short exchange on the radio, the engine tensed and moved on to the runway. Alarmingly for the passengers, the Yak did not taxi to the far end but started its take-off halfway down. Despite the growing roar, it lifted nimbly into the air and started a steep climb, taking off over Baku and the nodding oil donkeys of the Caspian. Another surprise was the height at which the plane levelled off as it set its course to the south-west, flying just below the white cumulus clouds which pockmarked the sky.

In common with the part he was playing, Sergei held up his right hand to give a thumbs-up. He gesticulated to Bob to lean forward and shouted in his ear. Bob was nodding. Sitting back again, he recounted the message to Edwin.

"He wanted you to know that he is the best pilot in Baku and not scared of doing this trip. Yesterday, he did the same run for Anya and survived. This is because the flight passes over some small territories controlled by warlords. Now and again they like to launch missiles at aircraft just to let the government in Baku know they are still active. The best defence against this is to fly low so they can see us. Generally, they are not bothered about light aircraft, but helicopters or drones, which are run exclusively by the military, are normally targets. He says he will point out some of the riskier spots when we reach them. Oh, and, by the way, we are landing on a grass strip at Minjivan. Sergei hadn't landed there before yesterday and says to warn you it may be a bit bumpy. But, above all, you shouldn't worry because he is confident and used to fly MiG-15s for the Soviet Air Force."

Edwin wasn't sure if Bob had thought about the content of the message rather than focusing on providing a literal translation. It certainly had an impact on him. In that moment, Edwin realised he was now part of an active mission. Although he was charged with making difficult decisions about clandestine PI operations, this was the first time he had come face to face with the reality. His background in British politics had given him a theoretical understanding of international affairs and diplomacy, but this mission, the one he had personally authorised, was clearly the riskiest so far, even though his own contribution was small. Although he knew nothing about the pilot, the London office had a good file on Bob and his activities before and after joining PI. The Irishman came with high-quality references despite having some dubious links to a couple of proscribed groups in his home country and had been recommended for support operations across central Asia. He didn't know much about his partner, Anya, except she was Azeri and had probably the best knowledge of the region out of anyone on the team. He decided to stop analysing the decisions he had taken in the past and keep his eyes and thoughts firmly on what was in front. He passed on his own limited version of Bob's message to Ehat about the landing at Minjivan.

The flight plan took them south to Beylagan and Larijan before following the route of the main highway for the final twenty minutes. Sergei checked his navigation over Fuzuli but out of the corner of his eye spotted a flash on the ground. Immediately the plane banked to the right and gained altitude and speed, disappearing into cloud which buffeted the small prop. Despite the bright conditions, subsequently Edwin thought he experienced a flash, the sort you might see in an electrical storm or when a photograph was taken at night.

Sergei seemed to be muttering to himself as the plane banked again, this time to the left, dropping out of the cloud once more. Edwin felt the butterflies in his stomach. Sergei flicked a switch which appeared to be his radio transmitter and barked what seemed like an instruction and a series of numbers into the microphone. The turbulence stopped, the engine seemed to return to a more relaxed sound, the snaking path of the main highway appeared below on the left side and Sergei felt calm enough to signal to Bob he wanted a word.

"I said there are some dangerous motherfuckers down there who like to play with fireworks. Somebody must be a bit bored this morning and sent up a surface-to-air missile. Why, I don't know – being visible in the sky is usually a good deterrent. I think it can't have been a new weapon – I saw it being fired and it looked from the launch like an old type, like a mortar. They must think we're fucking stupid. It's easy to dodge. We weren't going to fly into an aerial explosion they made. Also, I noticed they only fired once, just to let us know they are there."

"Who are they?"

"Fuck knows – that's part of the problem. I've told Baku the coordinates of the attack, so it's up to them to find out. We've not far to go now, so I think all will be OK."

Edwin tapped Bob on the shoulder.

"What did he say?"

"Nothing much – this one's a bit of a moaner; air traffic control told him to move because of a military jet in the area, then told him to go back as we were."

"Did you see that burst of light back there?" Edwin asked, almost casually.

Bob decided to close down his concern.

"I'm not sure I did. That's the problem of flying through cloud – its density changes all the time, creating flashes as well as turbulence."

Ehat remained calm throughout, his thoughts clearly on something else altogether.

Looking down at the highway leading to Minjivan, Bob recalled driving the route a few days earlier. He was relieved to think he had not been stopped by the same people who had fired the missile and happier to know Anya hadn't done the trip yesterday by road after their previous experience of the drive in the truck.

Whatever the incident had been, thought of it was soon dispelled as the topography changed from mountains to hills and a few green plains came into sight.

Sergei had kept his sunglasses on throughout but now, for the first time since take-off, he smiled and gestured again to Bob.

"We're here now. Because we are landing on a field with no support on the ground, I will fly over Minjivan at low level so I can judge the wind speed and direction. I don't think we will have a problem, as the visibility is fine, but we need to check. Get the others to check their belts."

Whether the overfly was necessary or just a chance for Sergei to show off his skills, his passengers could not be sure, but they kept their eyes on the ground as they dropped to 100 metres. Now the same roar of the engine that came from their unscheduled change of direction returned, this time with vibration. It seemed to Edwin the plane was telling Sergei to land but he was resisting – holding tight control of the altimeter.

The village of Minjivan was to the right of the field, yet it was to the left Bob saw what he was looking for – a green Land Rover with his wife and two others waiting.

Sergei continued to provide a commentary for Bob as they banked left away from the town and lined up to come in from the north-east.

Bob called to his fellow passengers: "Better brace for this: remember the pilot said it would be bumpy."

Sergei's praise of the Yak at the start of the trip was justified; the span of its undercarriage made the fuselage sit firmly on the ground. The engine was cut and came to a halt well within the boundaries of the landing site. For a moment, the mood in the cabin changed as his passengers offered their congratulations which was clearly tinged with a sense of relief. It was now the middle of the day. Sergei opened up the doors to let the fresh air of Minjivan dilute the stale oil and sweat smell they had brought from the capital.

Bob had passed close to the town less than a week ago in the dead of night when it was impossible to appreciate the beauty of the location. Now he was able to take in the scene. To the right, behind the town, a hillside with a lining of deciduous trees leading to a band of a mauve-tinged heather, and then scrub. The vista reminded him a bit of the Mourne mountains, especially the view from Newry. To the left was a flat plain but it was impossible to gauge how big it was as his view was limited by shrubs and a heat haze. What was evident was this was a dramatically different landscape from the arid environment of Baku. The Land Rover came alongside to meet them. Anya jumped out of the front passenger seat to hug her husband. Interestingly, the coming together wasn't that sort of lingering passion that younger couples naturally show but was more restrained, probably because she had two men in fatigues and Kalashnikovs at the ready.

She immediately explained the situation to all. The village elder, Grishkin, sent his welcome. In return for a payment, he had put six of his guards at her disposal for the next twenty-four hours and had set up the training range for Ehat. The two who had accompanied her were to remain to secure the aircraft until they were ready to leave.

They signalled for all to get in the Land Rover, but Sergei refused.

"You hire me as well as the plane. I stay here throughout. I have brought my own picnic and can sleep in the back," he said, holding high a bottle of vodka which was in the pocket of the plane door. He also pulled out a package from under his seat and spoke directly to the guards.

"Help me get the netting over the plane. I want to keep it hidden until we go back. I'll see you back here ready to go at first light."

Bob nodded their agreement. Anya took to the wheel, Bob upfront, the other two behind. After the confines of the Yak, the Land Rover felt surprisingly comfortable as they drove across the dry grassland towards the main road.

There was none of the small talk usually associated with travelling. No 'did you have a good flight?' – all that mattered was they arrived.

"If you get hungry there are sandwiches and water in the back. We'll sort out everything else when we get to the range – it's about fifteen minutes from here." Anya called. She struck Edwin as capable. As befits a woman of her age, she had a figure not easily disguised by her sand-camouflaged uniform. With her dark hair tied back, olive skin and full lips, she was clearly attractive but not what he considered to be alluring. He imagined Bob's relationship with her must be intense; he already felt the aura of her assertiveness.

SEVEN

AS PROMISED, THE LAND Rover arrived at the end of a wooded track with a hut and another one parked outside. As they approached, two local men with the obligatory AK-47s slung and ready for use stood waiting. They nodded to Anya and the others. She breezed in. The interior was spartan but highly organised – maps, weapons, ammunition, backpack. She started the briefing straightaway. She knew nothing about Ehat, other than he was expected to be referred to as 'Gul'. She had wished she had been given another name for him as she kept getting him confused with *Gil*, the man she expected to meet at the embarkation point.

She began: "We are here to get you ready to go to Iran. My job is to supervise your weapons training. I am afraid this will be intense as you haven't long before you go to the meeting point, where the courier, Gil, will take you across the border. We will concentrate in getting you used to your weapon. Because you are on a Peace International mission you will be issued with a Makarov pistol with silencer and twenty rounds of 9mm. This weapon is ineffective in mass kill situations and its range is no more than about fifteen metres at best. It is not a weapon of threat like one of the automatics you saw outside. This is designed to make an individual killing at close range. In the field, your decision to kill must be instantaneous, so your reaction time will be critical. You will carry your ammunition in a belt and the silencer is already attached. Please put on the belt and pick up the gun. Don't worry; it's not loaded."

Gul adjusted the belt and picked up the gun. Like most unfamiliar with the Makarov, he was surprised how heavy it was.

"Do you have anything better?" he asked.

"In the event of your imminent death, you will be pleased to have this weapon. This is standard issue to FSB and, in the absence of formal identification, possession of this gun will ensure you will be considered to be from the Russian Federation. The colleagues you will be joining also have the same kit. We will now go outside when I will show you how to load it and adjust the grip for your safety."

Anya took Gul outside; Bob and Edwin watched from the window. "She seems to know her trade," said Wilson.

"She ought to," said Bob shaking his head. "She's ex-Azeri army before she went into tourism. Spent some time in Syria chasing Islamic State rebels with the Kurds a few years back. When I was in combat, we did our training in a bar over a Murphy's until closing time and then just went out and shot some poor fucker staggering home from the pub. This lady is seriously organised."

Anya deftly showed Gul how to load the weapon. "Unload, load again, unload, load again. Aim, assess distance, check for obstructions left and right, fire. Return weapon to holster. Draw, load, unload, load again, aim, fire. Keep repeating this action. You must be capable of doing this instinctively. It could save your life," she warned.

She spent some time watching Gul. As a relatively big man with a strong grip, he handled the weapon well.

Soon after, Anya's instruction changed. She showed Gul a map with a trail on it.

"This is approximately one kilometre in a circle in a mix of terrain, woodland, open field and scrub. You are to follow this trail as quickly as you can. As you go, at certain points snipers will target you with blanks. You must return fire instantly, aiming at white targets which will appear in the direction of the shot. We will monitor you throughout for speed and accuracy."

"How many targets?"

"That is for you to discover. The route should take you a couple of hours." She pointed the way forward. "Your time has already started."

She nodded to one of Grishkin's men to follow.

Gul stooped to get through a thicket and was gone.

The late afternoon sun cast shafts of dancing light and shadow through the trees. All had seemed quiet, save the occasional squawk of startled birds who were sensitive to the disturbance on the ground below. Despite the criticisms of its handlers, whatever else the Makarov was, it was, at least, quieter than many pistols. Bob likened it to the rasping cough of an old drunk. A bit old-fashioned and of limited use, in the right hands it was still an effective weapon.

Anya had followed Gul's progress, watching him move almost silently around the course, stopping occasionally to check the map reference. Grishkin's man had set targets and shooting positions in advance, firing at given points, close to Gul's position. Although this was an exercise, there was still a danger of getting hurt. Although the sniper was aiming wide, anticipating Gul's movement, there was a possibility he could inadvertently move into the direct line of fire.

The direction of the shot would change, requiring Gul to be ready to fire backwards or to the sides.

Over the route, Gul had taken twenty shots, obliging him to reload more than once. The circular track brought him back to the cabin some twenty minutes behind the target time. He saw Edwin and Bob, the latter pulling on a cigarette. He stiffened and strode towards them.

"How did you get on?" said the Irishman.

"Good, I think. It certainly has a kick." He stretched his shoulder with a grimace.

Anya and the sniper arrived shortly after.

"You scored fourteen out of twenty, which with the amount of training you have had is OK. In the time we have you are unlikely to improve but at least I think you have a chance if you get caught in a skirmish."

It was dusk. Climbing aboard the Land Rover, they retraced their route back to Minjivan but didn't need to return to the field where the Yak had landed.

Instead, they drove towards the centre of the village and stopped in a narrow street where their headlights picked out a growing crowd of local people, seemingly bringing food and drink from their houses and walking towards the central square.

With the windows down, the air was filled with the pungent smell of burning meat and the growing sound of an accordion, belting out what Edwin took to be local folk music.

Gul and Edwin looked anxious at this unexpected turn of events. Anya put them at their ease.

"Grishkin is the local head man and has ordered a party. That means everybody will be there. You are the stars of the show. Tonight, they are roasting wild boar in your honour. Although I have paid Grishkin for helping us today, coming here was also a condition of their help. Don't worry, after we have shown our faces, we'll be able to slip away."

The three men got out and followed Anya into the square. It was almost Italianate in style, bordered by a mix of rough stucco-clad, condensed two- and three-level houses with clay-tiled roofs. There were two prominent buildings on opposite sides: the one to the east was the mosque, the other a slightly elevated building with a grand staircase leading up to double doors. The casual visitor might have regarded this as a town hall, but in Minjivan's case this was the residence of the head man, a sort of unelected position normally given to its oldest living male resident, who by implication must be the wisest. In reality, the head man had no power other than the resolution of personal disputes and the ability to consult with locals on issues that concerned their lives. Again, in the case of Minjivan, the big issue was the increasing tax demands of the state. So, provided the community paid their way, the state had no real interest in what happened there.

The surrounding buildings of the square were illuminated by a huge fire pit which Bob thought would be capable of roasting at least a couple of oxen, not just wild boar.

A ramshackle mix of chairs had been assembled on three sides, with half a dozen of the most comfortable set out, below the exterior staircase of the head man's house. Next to the fire was an area where six people were dancing; next to them kids were running around, playing their own games. Between the fire and the dancers was what looked to Bob like a field kitchen where a number of babushkas were cutting up vegetables for the meal.

Through this scene, Anya walked with purpose. She had spotted Grishkin. He came forward and hugged her, almost like they were old friends. Again, the familiarity surprised Edwin and Gul – Bob just laughed. This man was no love rival. Rotund, white hair, craggy features etched out of layers of fat, food-stained tunic and old breeches, this was a man who clearly looked as though he was from a different age. Which he was.

Anya introduced Grishkin to his guests. He smiled and gripped her right hand firmly. Looking to the periphery of the gathering, Edwin noticed armed men ensuring the party would not be interrupted. His host gestured all to sit, called for tea and the next ten minutes were taken up watching folk dancing. The boar was duly cut and plates brought to all to share. And then the conversation started. The male guests were puzzled by the fact Grishkin seemed to be very emotional, almost upset.

Edwin sought an explanation.

Anya responded: "This is my home village. I lived here for the first fifteen years of my life. I used to get back from time to time when I was in the army, but then, after my parents died, not so. Mr Grishkin thought I, too, was dead and thinks us being here tonight is a sign, an omen, a miracle."

Bob had been listening to Grishkin and thought his wife was only providing a general explanation.

He thought he heard Grishkin say "Thank God you escaped..." but didn't understand the context.

Gul and Edwin seemed to be absorbed in the entertainment and the succession of locals coming to shake hands and share their leader's welcome.

Bob took the opportunity to take his wife to one side.

"Escaped from what? I heard the head man say you had escaped."

"It's nothing really. Back in the day, just after the break-up of the Soviet authorities, there was a lot of confusion here with warlords fighting over everything – drugs, women, antiquities – anything that had a value. I was in the army on duty one night when Minjivan was raided by militia forces from Iran. They were not government forces but *jihadis*, rebels or some such. They were highly organised and came and went within an hour or so. Our military was not informed until after they had gone. They shot quite a lot of the men and filled a truck with young women and anything else they could move. As soon as we were warned, we mobilised from our small satellite base at Barthaz. We had tried to anticipate where they would cross the border and we were looking to close down their exit. Literally, as we had assembled our force and were leaving the gate, we came under attack. It was mainly small arms fire and mortars but was coming from three directions. We never knew how many of them there were, but I think there must have been a hundred at least. It was happening quickly and there wasn't time to get back through the gates of the base or call for reinforcements. We were sitting ducks in our vehicles, so we stopped and moved out to engage under cover. Our base was relatively small, really only used to monitor the border.

We didn't have the numbers to take them on and our positions were soon overrun. We suffered a similar fate as Minjivan, only they didn't kill so many of us. They rounded us up and locked us in the base's main service warehouse. I was one of six females who became prisoners that night. They took us over the border as well – to Ibrahim Sami. Anyway, me and two others escaped. It was the first time in my army career that I was scared. After debriefing, I was allowed to step down and the past is past."

"What? Why didn't you tell me before?"

"This was some time before I met you and, as I said, the rest is history."

Bob had often wondered why his beautiful wife had been so capable in helping to make arrangements for this Peace International clandestine mission. She had proved she was perfect for the job, but, somehow, her explanation didn't feel right.

His own confidence had taken a knock. How could he have been with her for so long and not known?

He needed to discuss this some more but now was not the time, except he had another question that could not wait.

"What happened to the other girls?"

Anya shrugged. "I don't know – other than the fact they never got home."

Then, almost as an afterthought, she said, "They also stole some of our kit. We also had a whole Buk mobile surface-to-air missile battery taken. Radar, command centre, missile launcher and logistics component, complete with *Sprout* missiles. I'm not sure what happened to them either. I think they would have found them difficult to use. The instructions and computers were in Russian."

Bob and Gul seemed to have relaxed as the evening celebrations progressed, so much so they didn't notice a disturbance between one of Grishkin's guards and a group of about half a dozen other figures in the semi-darkness on the edge of the square. What they did notice was a middle-aged woman, one of the dancers, approaching Grishkin, whispering in his ear.

The host's face fell momentarily. He made his excuses to Anya and slowly walked up the flight of steps to his house. From where they were sitting, his guests could not see what was taking place but, presently, he returned and whispered to Anya.

She turned to the rest. "There has been a development; we have been asked to come inside the house to discuss. I think we should go." She gestured upwards with her eyes.

They climbed the exterior balustrade to the front door of the head man's house. Bob went inside with Edwin; Anya and Gul waited outside, straining to hear what was going on above the noise in the square.

The hallway, complete with double-doored front and back buttressed entrances, acted as a grand, if austere, reception room, with a bit of peeling paint, adorned with the flag of the Azeri state and Minjivan prefecture. The walls were covered with photographs of important events that Grishkin had presided over but were dominated by two portraits Edwin now recognised, one of former president Heydar Aliyev and his son and heir, Ilham. The expansive room had space for a desk, a large coffee table and six chairs. No sooner had they entered than there was the sound of heavy footfall, before the back door was flung open and two soldiers with semi-automatics followed by two other military figures, distinguished by shoulder epaulettes and peaked hats, walked in. He noted that both men, clearly of rank, were slightly smaller than the guards that preceded them, but walked in that distinctive, straight-backed, parade-ground style more often seen in the televised military May Day drills of the Eastern Bloc states.

The smaller of the two officers was the more decorated and took the lead, extending his hand to Edwin.

"Good evening, Mr Wilson and... Mr Mullen, my name is Major Valentin Ryumin, commander of the Azeri domestic defence forces, Southern Division. This is my assistant, Captain Alexander Zeitsev. It is a pleasure to meet you at last and please accept my apologies for not meeting you sooner, but in our line of work, schedules can be... unpredictable."

Edwin looked at Bob. The surprise on the Irishman's face told him what he wanted to know.

Ryumin made himself at home.

"Please take a seat. I hope you will permit me to continue in English."

Edwin and Bob sat on the same side of the table, allowing Ryumin and Zeitsev to sit opposite. Grishkin sat in his normal seat at the head of the table.

"Our job is about promoting peace and ensuring stability, across the south of this country. As I expect by now you have realised, this area has many 'fiefdoms' – all have their disagreements with each other and we encourage them to get along in the national interest, especially as, you will understand, our prime military assets are deployed on our western flank. You gentlemen are certainly discerning tourists. In choosing to come here, you have attracted our interest, especially when we saw your flight plan. Personally, I tend to think this is the best time of year to visit Minjivan. What this town may lack in hotels and restaurants is more than compensated by the warm welcome of locals and magnificent hikes we have here. Of course, this area is only just opening up for visitors and, as I know Mr Mullen understands very well, care is needed when travelling off the beaten track, as your pilot, Boroschenko, found this morning."

It was Zeitsev's turn to read the expression of their guests, adding, "Your plane was targeted by a surface-to-air missile earlier. Your pilot radioed the coordinates to the ATC and we sent a jet over to bomb the location. We have just had the reconnaissance back to show we hit a base used by Umah Ruslanov, one of our more unruly warlords, so thank you. You should know Boroschenko started celebrating when you left. We found him sleeping in the back of the plane out there with an empty vodka bottle."

Ryumin took control of the conversation once more.

"My colleagues up in Baku are bit confused about the purpose of your trip. Oh, of course, Mr Robert Mullen – '*Bob*', we know all about you, but not so much you, Mr Edwin Wilson."

Ryumin was clearly of Russian origin and his blue eyes stared intently at Edwin.

"I think it is your first visit to our country, and for a holiday on your own. I think that's sad. In my limited time off I choose to be with family and friends. When I saw your visa application, I immediately wondered whether you were looking for a meeting with a government representative, but, when I checked, nobody knew anything about it. You come as a tourist, stay in one our best hotels and never found time just to cross the road to see our National Art Collection. Your arrival understandably fired our curiosity, so my colleagues ran full checks on you and discovered you are certainly a person of interest to us." He read from a clipboard Zeitsev had passed to him. "Politician, diplomat, charity field worker, you are a leader of a non-government organisation, Peace International, with an international board of directors headquartered in New York City. Your organisation exists to prevent war through diplomacy and active field engagement, and you work closely on humanitarian relief strategies with the United Nations and the World Health Organization. You are based in London but have responsibility for Peace International's European activities." He paused. "Now, I know my country participates in European football as a member of UEFA, but there are many who regard us as Asian. So, I am assuming you think like UEFA. I think this is right as me and Zeitsev here are ethnic Russians, even if we are Azeri citizens and we are the second largest ethnic group. But I am getting off the point. I think I know why you are here and what you are doing. I also know that you have not committed any crimes on Azeri soil so far, and that according to your flight schedule you are due to leave us in forty-eight hours. So I ask myself: why didn't you engage with my government before you arrived? After all, we may have been able to make the logistic operations simpler and could have shared our intelligence with you. And now we feel a bit embarrassed. You are like a guest joining us for dinner in our house without an invitation and then going into the garden to look over the fence to see what my neighbour is doing before leaving without saying goodbye, leaving your perplexed hosts to answer complaints about the invasion of their privacy. It is bad manners and uncomfortable. Surely this is not the way you work elsewhere? If you are planning to leave us so soon, I am assuming something big is about to happen that will have implications for us, so tell us about it."

Zeitsev pulled a smartphone from his pocket and placed it on the table. "I hope you don't mind, but this is for Alex's benefit when he comes to write the report."

Edwin applied his diplomatic skills to explain the broad purpose of the mission, avoiding reference to the taskforce already in Iran and that the action was sanctioned under obscure United Nations articles. Success depended on secrecy.

"If you had come to us first, we could have helped you." Ryumin repeated his point.

The front door opened again. This time, Anya and Gul walked in.

Edwin was about to continue with his general, non-specific explanation, but stopped.

Ryumin filled the vacuum. "Captain Ramadi and Dr Ehat, do join us, I was about to ask where you were." He gestured to the guard to get another chair. "There is a fundamental point of information I must address which may aid your continuing explanation, Mr Wilson. You may not know that Captain Anya Ramadi here was Zeitsev's predecessor, running local operations on my behalf – banging local warlords' heads together where necessary and maintaining the integrity of our borders. Of course, she has now stepped back from active service but, when she gets bored of her private family life and looking after tourists in Baku, still helps us out from time to time. Her reports on your preparation have certainly helped us to understand your mission better, and I expect her knowledge has been useful to you as well."

Bob's shocked look from his wife's previous casual admission remained. Ryumin picked up on his discomfort.

"Don't look so hurt, Mr Mullen. As far as she is concerned, her day job finished before she took up with you, and it is because of you she regards service to us as a hobby, a paying hobby. I have no doubt she really loves your Irish charm. Wasn't there a British spy case in Australia once where one of the protagonists was described as being 'economical with the truth'? This is the same thing. There are no lies here, just the sharing of limited information for the benefit of all."

Ryumin knew about Gul as a result of pictures identifying him at dinner with Edwin at the Mugam Club.

Wilson continued his explanation – his reference to Ibrahim Sami and to the Chinese sparked Ryumin's renewed attention.

Wilson concluded, "Dr Ehat, 'Gul' to us, will cross the border tonight heading for Ibrahim Sami. He is the most qualified observer we could find for the job."

"How will you get him back?"

"Dr Ehat is experienced in field operations and will make his own arrangements."

"A Uighur in Iran? It will be difficult to move him quietly. Once he has collected his evidence you need to get him out by the shortest route – back here. You cannot leave him on his own. If he gets caught they will guess his entry point and we will have a serious conflict on our hands."

Wilson's explanation had not made reference to Hebbert and the others.

Ryumin glanced at Zeitsev. "You give us a real problem, Mr Wilson. You come here to supervise the dispatch of an agent into hostile territory and go home to avoid the consequences? And you, Mr Mullen, as an Azeri citizen, must understand you are facing arrest and imprisonment – that will not be good for your business or… your family. And Dr Ehat? Well, I think the consequences back home are worse for you. I am surprised a man of your reputation would run such a risk. I think we should accompany you all back to Baku in the morning and brief our foreign ministry accordingly."

Zeitsev fidgeted and stared at his boots.

"On the other hand," Ryumin continued, "I am not sure reporting you, Mr Wilson, at high level for completing the wrong visa application would be good for me either and I agree the information you may obtain could be materially relevant to the security of the state. This case has already produced a result, albeit inadvertently, with the reported elimination of Ruslanov, and it is clear Dr Ehat is taking part in this endeavour on his own initiative.

"And then there is you, Anya. I too, remember the raid on this town some years ago and am clearly aware of your own sacrifice. The night of the attack I was away in Baku and only got back the day after to supervise the clear up. You remember that as well, Mr Grishkin?"

The old man nodded.

"I promised the President not to allow such an incident to occur again and we should learn lessons for the future. Now we have a much more mobile and responsive military presence in this area with the ability to deploy forces on the ground anywhere in the country at two hours' notice. We run daily reconnaissance drone missions over our borders and send supervisory patrols to all communities with a population greater than 2,000 people every week. Despite this there are still incidents from time to time, like your trouble yesterday. It could be argued that the intelligence you obtain may help to destroy those renegades outside our borders, thus making us all that much safer. Given what I know now, Mr Wilson, I would be asking Anya to accompany Dr Ehat. Although it's a few years back, she will be familiar with the terrain but also is an expert in fieldcraft. Now she is a civilian, she cannot represent the state. For my part, if 'Mrs Mullen' here agrees to take part, my people will stand clear of your operation, on one further condition. You, Mr Wilson, and you, Mr Mullen, must remain in Baku until you can inform us of the outcome of your mission. From now on, you must regard us as a 'sleeping' partner, and share intelligence with us. We will also monitor your progress to satisfy ourselves of your compliance. Now I think it is time for you to leave if you are expecting to get to your rendezvous in Barthaz. My unit is camping at Minjivan tonight and our helicopters are parked near your plane. I have taken the liberty of relieving Boroschenko of further vodka supplies so he is ready in the morning."

It was a neat closure of the conversation, providing the opportunity for Wilson's team to leave Minjivan and for Grishkin to parade another two honoured guests to the night's festivities, where a favourite spectator sport, a wrestling contest, was about to take place.

Back at the Land Rover, Anya took the wheel with Bob next to her.

Wilson opened the conversation with Anya.

"So will you go with Gul? You don't have to. If the handover tonight was really in doubt, they could have arrested us on the spot. They may feel their noses are out of joint but they admitted this is our show."

"Yes," she answered, looking at him in the rear-view mirror. "I'd prepared a spare backpack at the embarkation point, some hours ago, as a contingency."

Bob didn't speak. He was getting the clear impression his wife had sorted all this out in advance.

Being in a Land Rover made the approach to the quarry and down to the warehouse much easier than it had been last week. Although Bob was familiar with the site, he hadn't noticed it had been fenced at some time in the past. They narrowly avoided a post as they ground their way over the rough ground towards the warehouse. He remembered their previous visit and the fact he wasn't sure if it was a farm building, machinery depot, animal shelter or grain store. Looking at it a fresh, he guessed it must have been a storage depot for military supplies.

Putting on the lights, he also noted the presentation had what he regarded as a woman's touch – everything was neatly laid out – drysuits, boots, nightsights, food. Surprisingly, arrival at the warehouse had sent Wilson's heart racing, feeling the same adrenaline rush as when he was in the air earlier in the day. This was the sharp end of his job – far from the tea and biscuits of the St Ermin's Hotel.

Bob left Wilson to fix some more tea while he helped Anya and Gul into their combat suits.

Around half an hour before departure, a sharp banging on the corrugated iron door hailed the arrival of Gil. As he stooped to enter the porch Anya was ready with her Kalashnikov aimed to deter any unwelcome visitors.

"That's no way to greet a friend. Sorry but it was too dark to for me to bring a bunch of flowers," he said.

Anya relaxed, placed the gun on the nearby table, smiled and replied:

"You're late and now I expect you are going to ask for '*a brew*'?"

Some English expressions were still new to Anya and she looked to Wilson for approval.

His laughter broke the tension of the moment.

Bob came forward to give Gil a sort of man hug which looked more appropriate for a rugby field rather than a more remote relationship started a week ago as a result of a six-hour drive. Gil was surprised to meet Wilson and was impressed by his assertion as an administrator he wanted to see what was happening on the ground. Wilson then took the opportunity to introduce Gul. For Gil, this was the chance for him to see at first hand the outcome of the message he had sent from the field on Dave's behalf. This was as expected. The difference was the gun-toting, sullen woman he had met briefly last week who looked ready to loose off at him again seven days later, and now was to accompany them over the border. He hadn't realised he would be taking two people back and should have been told. He certainly knew Dave would not be expecting the additional woman either.

Gil didn't like it. "Look, guys, getting you into Iran is my only involvement, before I have to get back to other duties. I don't know if you understand it's busy over there – every person who comes over increases the risk to us all. You know I cannot be held responsible for getting you out as well. That fucking river is a torrent at the mo and will take more time to cross than the last."

Wilson responded. "We're not making further demands on you other than to deliver our people into the country. You always knew you were coming here to collect one body anyway. In fact, Anya might make this trip easier. She is a trained soldier and familiar with the territory. Do you know how Dave is getting on?"

"When I saw him the other day, he seemed well enough but was still on reconnaissance. He seems to have found his way around and is embedding the team. He gave me the impression that although he was confident of success it was going to take longer than he thought. Maybe with these two he can move a bit quicker."

Gil opened his throat and gulped the remaining mug of tea, which was still steaming.

"OK, folks – time to get a shift on. We should hit the road. When we go out of here, you follow me in single file. Move only when I do. Avoid speaking unless I speak to you. When we get across there are anti-personnel mines and a few other treats in store, so you must at all times follow my lead."

Bob and Edwin helped Anya and Gul strap up their backpacks, helmets and nightsights.

Gil led them forward into the night.

Edwin had wanted to go with them as far as the riverbank, but Gil and Anya advised against. In the same way they could see across the river into hostile territory with nightsights, it was possible an Iranian patrol could do the same. There was no special emotional act between Bob and his wife. Bob suggested Edwin would be better employed clearing up with him making sure there was no trace left of their presence prior to departure. Tidying up just left three hours before daybreak for them to snatch some sleep on a bale before the drive back to Minjivan.

So much was happening, Edwin was having trouble keeping a check on the time. They had used most of what they had to move the project forward. Now all the pieces were in place the hardest task ahead was to wait.

They arrived in Minjivan and drove to the airstrip next to the town. The scene had changed dramatically from when they had arrived. Two giant Mi-26 military transport helicopters were parked next to their little Yak light aircraft, with their holds open. Each had brought a number of armoured vehicles and their occupants had spawned a small tented village nearby. Edwin was particularly pleased to see Sergei in the middle of an animated discussion with one of Grishkin's men who had greeted their arrival with Anya the day before. When he saw Edwin and Bob, he jogged across to the Land Rover, in a slightly ungainly way.

"Hello, boys – I think you are expected to see the major before we go. He's at Mr Grishkin's house now. While you're away doing that I will do the pre-flight checks and get a departure time from ATC."

He looked up at the growing clouds and grimaced. "I think we will be good to go two hours from now."

To Edwin's eye, Sergei still looked slightly dishevelled and was pleased he would have a bit more time to recover before he had to pilot the plane.

They drove back to the main square and were impressed to see much effort going into tidying the place, after the festivities of the night before. All the chairs had gone, a couple of men were dousing off the embers of the fire and at least four women were brushing the cobbles. Climbing the steps to the head man's house, they saw the scene had changed little, other than the fact that both sets of double doors at the front and the back were open. Grishkin and Ryumin were in the same seats, although at least the head man had taken a change of clothing.

The welcome was cordial and coffee and pastries were already on the table.

"I am glad you made it before my unit needs to redeploy. Zeitsev left an hour ago in our new Mi-24 gunship. I wish you'd seen it. It's our answer to the Apache. If any of Ruslanov's thugs are still alive, that will scare the shit out of them. I have to go back to our Stepanakert base."

Ryumin wanted an update.

"So they have gone?" The question sought confirmation.

Edwin nodded. "Yes, as planned."

"Good – so we have a deal. Let us hope your plan is a good one. You are lucky to have Ramadi on your team. She is a brave woman and a fierce fighter. But you knew that, Mr Mullen? Forgive my rudeness, but you seemed a little surprised to hear she had worked for me. You shouldn't, because she is one of the best, and modest with it. Mr Grishkin knew her when she was a girl and she proved her bravery here when the *jihadis* raided. Isn't that so, Grishkin?"

The old man took a noisy slurp of tea and then suddenly became animated. His recollection was not the same as Anya's had been.

"I remember the night very well. It was crazy. These *jihadis* drove into the town in a couple of lorries and started shooting at anybody or anything. Fortunately, it was towards the end of the day so there weren't too many people around. I lived two houses away from here back then, and she had come into our kitchen just to say hello. We had been friends of her parents. Her three fellow soldiers were parked over there by the well, waiting for her. The *jihadis* moved fast. They threw a grenade at their four-by-four and filled it with fire. They didn't have a chance. My wife shut and locked the door to the street as the *jihadis* started going house to house, ransacking anyplace they could get into, killing men and kidnapping two or three women, as I remember. Anya went out of my house into the side street on her own, firing back. There must have been at least a dozen of them. Anyway, somehow she hit one of their trucks, causing it to explode. It must have been full of ammunition. We were frightened to go out, so two vehicles were burning out of control. We called the military at Barthaz, who said they would deal with it, but the raiders were still chasing Anya. They then started to chase her out of the square towards the big field where you landed. When they thought she had escaped, they climbed back on their lorry and left as suddenly as they had arrived. One of my friends is a farmer and was returning from feeding his sheep. He saw the *jihadis'* truck just out of town with half a dozen gunmen jumping off and shooting into the wood. He went down to watch. There was a firefight, which lasted about twenty minutes, and then it all went quiet before there was shouting and screaming. Four of the *jihadi* fighters had the woman soldier cornered. They threw her automatic away and tied her up before deliberately ripping her shirt open. One of the men got back in the cab, the other three pushed her into the back and they drove off. When they had gone, my friend came down to the place that their truck had stopped and saw four bodies of dead *jihadis* left in the road."

"Then what happened?" Dave enquired. Bob was transfixed.

Ryumin took up the story. "Barthaz got the call and were taken completely by surprise, thinking it was a hoax. Captain Ramadi was the senior duty officer at that time, and in her and my absence a junior lieutenant had to deal with it. Barthaz was a small unit at best and only had a couple of troop carriers on site and a Buk mobile anti-aircraft battery. The lad sent the troop carriers up the road to head them off but didn't find them. He then sent one of the vehicles on here to Minjivan and the other was to return to base. When the returning unit arrived, they found the base had been ransacked and the four Buk units had been taken. By chance I was in Baku and was able to mobilise air support, but it happened too late. Subsequently we found tracks of the raiders' vehicle leading to the border – they had gone. Unfortunately, owing to its complicated geography and history, this area has suffered more than its fair share of criminal activity and we appealed to our neighbours in Iran to help trace the bandits and bring the people concerned to justice. Without success. But we did have some luck. Anya Ramadi had been captured and taken over the border to Iran but managed to escape. She was able to tell us she had been taken to Ibrahim Sami and sold together with three other women to the local head man. Subsequently, this head man had held her as a personal prisoner and she was abused on several occasions, apparently, by him and others. Details of exactly how she escaped have always been sketchy but, apparently, she managed to hide under the axle of a civilian transport vehicle working on border fortifications near the river. She swam back and was picked up by one of our own border patrols. Apart from being pleased to get her back, she was able to alert us to the building of a new military base outside Ibrahim Sami and we have been trying to find out more ever since.

"I have a lot of respect for her as a person and as a soldier. I had to debrief her. I remember asking her how she'd coped. She told me she had become two people in one body. One was the true happy Anya; the other was soldier Ramadi. All the bad stuff happened to soldier Ramadi. She knew she couldn't carry on. The true happy Anya came in to being when she started to work as a tour guide and met you, Mr Mullen. I can only guess she has been too upset to tell you this herself, or perhaps worried you would leave if you knew. This situation changed when Peace International first contacted you about this mission. Anya came to see me to tell me about what was going on and that she was helping you to prepare. Apart from doing her duty to her country by telling us of your plan, she saw an opportunity for her. She wanted to join your mission to Ibrahim Sami, to find this head man and to kill him. For her, his death would lay the ghost of soldier Ramadi to rest, enabling her to enjoy what was left of her life, as Anya Mullen. Knowing her as I do, I could not deny her this chance."

"So she's working for us because she wants to avenge the deaths of friends and her own suffering?" Edwin was shocked.

"I think it is true," Ryumin added. "What better motivation could a person have?"

"What do you know about Ibrahim Sami?" Bob asked.

"Clearly not enough. It used to be just a small farming community, a dot on the map, but then started to become used as a staging post mainly for drugs and people heading from Pakistan and on to Georgia. They knew the problems we have policing our southern province so they used to cross our borders at will as they passed through. But then there was a period when the Iranians got tired of these guys ripping them off and our government complaining about insurgencies. They tightened border controls and introduced physical security measures. It gave the Iranians the chance to say the illegal crossings were not state-sponsored and therefore beyond their control. For about a year afterwards it worked – the bandits kept blowing themselves up crossing minefields, but, eventually, the Iranian forces stopped replacing them. The result was a couple of corridors were created where they could cross into Azerbaijan in relative safety. The local head man started to control these corridors and charged the pirates 'market rates' to use them. He then started to invest the money, growing the town and buying a relationship with Tehran. Now, as far as we can tell, there are three people who run Ibrahim Sami today – one is the provincial governor, Moussavi (recommended by the head man), the military commander, Colonel Rahman (approved by the head man), and the head man himself – Hafiz al-Fouadi, a local farmer – reaping the benefits of diversifying his business.

"Where or if China fits into this, I have no idea, but think it can't be something which al-Fouadi has fixed. Al-Fouadi is, in reality, a petty criminal and a lucky one at that. He just happens to have been the right guy, in the right place, at the right time.

"Anya is a very resourceful person. She is the one who is most likely to be capable of changing al-Fouadi's fortunes."

He looked out of the back door. The tented village had all but disappeared; soldiers were boarding the helicopters.

"Time for me to go. Thank you for your hospitality as always, Mr Grishkin. Mr Wilson, Mr Mullen, I wish you a safer flight back to Baku with Boroschenko. As agreed, your passports are temporarily suspended. I will contact you at the Four Seasons in a couple of days."

He waived a casual salute, skipped down the exterior steps and walked briskly towards the waiting helicopter.

EIGHT

IN THE SPACE OF a few days, Jamshid was just starting to realise how his life was changing. Whether by luck or judgement he had succeeded in delivering his second two-billion-dollar deal for his employers (which carried a good bonus) and completed his first trade of equal significance for Alrakahthan (which produced an even greater return). His success was giving him another problem – where to keep his money. Although by Iranian standards he had never been poor, he now had the kind of money in the bank that would get him noticed and he needed to do something about it – but what?

Jamshid was already realising this sort of wealth brought its own problems. He needed advice, but who could he trust to help him without asking too many questions? His parents, sister, employers all failed the test. He had to find someone who was even wealthier and had no interest in his affairs. While he mulled over potential solutions, he was aware he should continue to live his life in the normal routine to avoid attracting attention, but even that was getting harder. Only that morning he had received a letter from the energy minister congratulating him on his success, stating his achievement would be brought to the attention of the Supreme Leader himself.

As if standing out in a world where most craved conformity was not enough, he realised he needed to create a cover story immediately to protect his position. His first move was something he should have done at the start. He immediately transferred the Alrakahthan money to a separate number two account. If anyone started asking questions he would say (like all good Muslims) that this money was going into a charitable activity and he was merely holding the funds to ensure Mr Alrakahthan kept his word. It was not the answer but would buy him some time. The real answer, he knew, was to talk to Hanah, but in doing so would show him to be weak and indecisive. Maybe laundering this pile of cash was a test set by Alrakahthan to really see how astute he was. He also considered talking to Ravi about it. Ravi was his trusted friend, he could talk to him about anything. But, whereas confessing to having syphilis, for example, would be OK, if a little embarrassing, explaining how he had suddenly become wealthy would not. In his heart he imagined their conversation, which would probably conclude with him saying "if you're so worried about it, give it back". That is certainly what his imam would say. He already knew that wasn't an option. Having started to make the basic administrative arrangement with the Bank of Bandar, where he had already noted the CEO was now personally available to handle his business, he would start to clear his mind and seek guidance by praying to the Prophet. Jamshid was a lapsed believer but was starting to wonder whether he should up his game and make better use of the prayer room at work. There was no doubt right now prayer was helping him to think through his options, but it was not going to take the place of face-to-face contact. Reflecting on the situation, he decided he would need to consult with someone unrelated to the present, and maybe, just maybe, he would have such an opportunity on Sunday.

His missed appointment from the week before weighed heavily on his mind. He remembered her message: "last chance". He would get to the stables ahead of schedule and arrived an hour before the appointed time. If he had expected to be waiting on Mahta, he was wrong. With the help of one of the grooms, she was packing paniers for their two horses, which were enjoying a couple of buckets of water before their journey.

He parked his battered Shogun next to a red sparkling clean Mercedes coupe, which he assumed to be hers, across the yard from the horse boxes.

"Glad you got here early – I wouldn't have waited," she smiled, tightening the girth on her chosen stallion. I'm looking forward to today. This is my favourite – Alazaha, an Arabian, the one I told you about when we met at the Apadana. He was away at the farriers when you were here last. This boy has the energy to gallop halfway to Minab! But don't worry, I'm not taking you that far. The horses have more to carry this trip because lunch is on board. Anyway, I'm glad to see you're better dressed this time," she said, a look of mockery in her eyes.

Jamshid was pleased. He had been determined to make a good impression and had spent a couple of hours downtown in Bandar looking for a proper pair of breeches. He didn't want a repeat of the sore thighs.

Having checked his saddle and stirrup, he climbed in position with skill. Just in case, he had kept his sunglasses in his shirt pocket and made a point of putting them on casually, like he would have done if setting off in the Shogun. Mahta realised he was out to impress and looked on admiringly.

"Let's get moving; we're going further today – you'll have to earn your lunch."

A nudge from her spurs and she set off at a canter along the track they had followed a couple of weeks previously. He came up alongside her for the part of the journey where the ground was firm and it was wide enough. Once again, the weather was good, perhaps even a little better than before, with a cooling westerly breeze. This was not the moment for a heavy conversation, more an opportunity to take in the majestic, if stark, vista.

"We are going up there today over that ridge." She pointed off to her left.

"I went up there last week on my own to find a picnic spot. The place I have found is just magnificent. It's one of the highest points around here which doesn't have a transmitter on the top."

They made small talk the rest of the way which petered out the higher they climbed, and the narrower the track.

"Are you sure this route is OK for horses?" Jamshid shouted. "Seems more suited to goats."

"Yes," she replied, "I think you're right. Maybe you would be more at ease on a goat next time? That is, if there is a next time."

"Why wouldn't there be?" Jamshid fell into her trap.

"That depends on whether you pass my test," came the reply.

"Which is…?"

She turned Alazaha and dismounted, starting to loosen the pannier on the side of her saddle.

"Firstly, you have to set out our picnic rug and sunguard before I will lay out the food and drink."

Jamshid hadn't seen it coming, but, as she had promised, they had reached a plateau on a ridge with views down to Bandar and the sea on one side and a verdant valley behind. It was a truly beautiful spot, complete with a shrivelled acer bush, ideal for tethering horses.

He set to work on creating their picnic hideaway.

He couldn't remember how long it had taken him to assemble, but when he stood up to admire his handiwork he realised the promised food was still in the saddle bag.

"Come on, you've made me do all this and I haven't even got a piece of bread and hummus to show for it?"

She laughed. "You've still got work to do. Sit down, close your eyes and tell me the first thing that comes into your mind."

He did as he was told and was about to answer before she cut across him.

"Keep your eyes tight shut until I say… Now open them…"

Nothing could have prepared him for the scene ahead.

Mahta stood naked in front of him, her pale alabaster skin shimmering in the heat.

He was shocked and excited, wanted to look away but couldn't. Wanted to say something but was devoid of rational thought. She kneeled in front of him and gave him a languid kiss. Even for a relatively experienced man, this was an altogether new sensation. Yes, he had snatched a kiss at their last meeting but not like this.

She proceeded to wrap her lithe frame around him, continuing the embrace while unbuttoning his shirt. Her breasts now tantalisingly nuzzled and heavy against his chest, as he became lost in her embrace.

She stopped kissing him and put her finger to his lips. Moving back, she slowly released the tension in his breeches and stole his attention again and again, enveloping him in her fragrance until he lost control.

It was his turn to take the lead, carefully, *intensely*, exploring her as if admiring one of the great precious ceramic artworks in Alrakahthan's apartment.

Every touch, every kiss, every sound, heightened and savoured in their own private world.

For here in this place, nobody and nothing else mattered including time.

In the shade of their makeshift awning they lay wrapped around each other in a euphoric clinch, sheltering from the heat of the day and the very different stresses of their lives.

Like a flower I shall embrace your love
And then switch off the light of reason
I shall place my head between your breasts
I drink love from the scent of your body.

"You know this poetry?" Mahta whispered in Jamshid's ear.

173

"Yes, it's by Sa'di from the thirteenth century – it's ironic: as a writer and poet, his favourite topic was about morals and manners – a lot of it holds true today."

"Not only a great fuck, but a cultured one at that," she observed.

It was a mad scene. In her bid to disrobe quickly, items of Mahta's clothing were spread around the place, wherever they had fallen, or the soft breeze had taken them. Jamshid had managed to keep his breeches and boots on. Recovering his shirt was the quick bit; helping her to collect her clothing took a bit longer. While he walked carefully around the surrounding boulders, he tried to make sense of what had happened. Ever the gentleman, having brought back some of her more intimate apparel, he looked away as she dressed.

"Now you decide to be shy." She laughed at his clumsiness.

After the *hors d'oeuvres* of love making, the picnic was reset in a more traditional way – salads, salamis, flatbreads, hummus and the rest, washed down with rosewater and champagne.

Mahta looked nervous when she offered the champagne.

"You do, don't you?"

"Sure, providing there are no witnesses."

With a sigh of relief, she took the cooling band off the bottle and passed it over for him to pop the cork. He registered that the fact that she could obtain it meant she was a person of influence.

"I know what you mean. Imagine how difficult it is to have sex outside marriage, even as a single woman?"

"You have to come all the way up here to get a shag?" Jamshid said with a smile.

"Only if it is an important one. Coming up to a place like this is the only safe way of doing it these days. Even then, those fucking pervs, the religious Guidance Patrol, are either following people with binoculars or listening against walls, trying to enforce sharia law. Who are they to dictate how I should conduct my private life? I think they do tests so they can tell the difference between screams in lovemaking and those of torture. In the name of the holy, how do these people live with themselves?"

He knew they had started conversational chess.

"So you had it planned from the beginning," he replied.

"Of course, but you read the signs. You could have escaped if you wanted."

Jamshid caressed her hand. "True. But you were testing me from the moment we met in the Apadana. I remember you saying you wanted to see how far I would go."

"And now I know," she said.

"Why me?" He looked at her full on.

"You're good-looking, clever and well-mannered – that's two characteristics ahead of most men in Bandar. And, despite all its contradictions, you love your country, as I do."

"How can you possibly know that?"

"Oh, people talk – at least the ones in my circle."

"Who is in your circle?" Jamshid wanted to know why other people would be interested in him.

"Don't play games with me. I know you've been asking Ravi all sorts of questions. But now I'm in front of you, we can be direct with each other. It is better this way that you find out without speaking to others who may not be as informed as they think.

"I guess I'm a little older than you, maybe four, possibly five years. I married at sixteen and had two children, both boys, as soon as my body allowed. They lived at the family home in Bandar until they were seven and eight. My parents helped out while I studied engineering at the university. The kids are both now in private school in France. My husband, Rashid, is a colonel in the Revolutionary Guard but is based up in the far north-west, where he has been for the past four years. Maybe three years ago, I was in Tehran and met up with a mutual friend, who showed me pictures of my husband at a party in bed with two other women. I have often wondered whether that friend thought they were doing me a favour, or was sent by my husband in the hope I would seek to end the marriage. For me it was neither. As you know, my professional reputation grew here, and two years ago, was cited as one of the top industrial leaders in our country, one of only five Shi'a women. I lead a research project that is helping us to design and build a new generation of ballistic missiles, I train engineers in non-destructive testing technologies – I am a role model. That position has opened doors for me in places I could never have imagined. All would be lost if I sought to annul my marriage. My husband and I have, in every sense, separate lives. We talk on the phone occasionally about the kids and even end up in some of the same meetings in Tehran, on opposite sides of the table, but that is it. As well as my day-to-day duties at the machine assembly plant, I support the government's industrial and scientific policy committees and appear at conferences representing the state when asked to do so. When at work, I look like an average Iranian citizen, wearing an embroidered black *chador*, no make-up and flat shoes. When outside work, I wear simple loose-fitting colourful clothes, jeans or whatever, make-up (providing I'm in private), hair down, heels as well as the *hijab*. Or perhaps, for you, nothing at all!" She laughed suddenly, realising she was getting too serious.

"There are aspects of life which are difficult to manage, but we all have to find a way. I have good acquaintances at work but, at the end of the day, I am the boss, so you don't have many friends there. I help Ravi run his charity for limbless ex-servicemen, which provides one outlet to meet new people, and I have my true best friend behind us now, Alazaha, with whom I share everything."

"Boyfriends?"

"As I said, it's hard enough for me to find space and time to live as a normal woman. A boyfriend brings with it an emotional commitment. If the boyfriend understood my life, and started to tell tales, I would be ruined, and my husband would have him killed. That's why I prefer straight sex, or, if I'm really stressed, masturbation gets me through."

"If all that is true, why have you told me all this?"

"Because we are here. There are no witnesses. No evidence. Because I am careful. Even if I was under suspicion, I would just lie low for a few weeks. Because I need to talk and I see in you… someone who has as much to lose in the future as me."

Jamshid was getting used to Mahta's directness.

"What do you think I have got to lose?"

"You're smart, successful and loyal. Your parents have a nice house in Lavasan, one of the smarter Tehran districts. You're getting a reputation as a top salesman. Every time you get a ship leaving Bandar with an Iranian cargo on it, people will think it's down to you. That's not a good place to be in a society that values conformity. When you produce a result, it means money in the bank for the country and that helps to keep people in jobs and that stops rioting in the street. Not everyone thinks that's a good idea. Believe me, I know. This country sets new rules for high-profile people like us, which makes it easier to catch you if you step out of line. You have to get used to leading a double life, with one hand 'under the counter'."

The champagne had finished, the food now just a collection of empty packets, and his mood was turning to a new reality.

"What do you really know about me?"

"Not that much. I know you were a sailor before you worked for the port, I know you like a game of football and a lamb tagine. I know you are not married and need a lover and…"

"And…?"

"You are coming into new money."

"May the Prophet be merciful, how would you know?"

"You're a salesman, right? If you are able to sell a couple of billion barrels of crude, that must be carrying a pretty hefty commission. The other thing I know about you is that you are honest, too honest for your own good. Once people realise you have more money than the average monthly paycheque, all sorts of people will take an interest in you."

Before he could react, she added, "Don't forget your duty as a good Muslim to help others less fortunate than you. If you are

177

sitting on some extra money you don't want others to know about, I'd put it into a charity pretty quickly. Me and Ravi can help you with that."

Jamshid made a non-committal grunt. He had really enjoyed his day, and, like their last encounter, she had given him plenty to think about.

They started to clear up and pack the saddle panniers for the return journey.

Mahta and Alazaha led the way at a steady trot. The sun had turned from shimmering brilliance to a warm glow by the time they returned to the stables.

Dismounting, loosening the saddles, emptying the panniers and leading the horses back for feeding and grooming, Jamshid watched Mahta, happy in her own world.

He had admired her beauty and candour. She was a great advertisement for "living under the counter".

He found his car keys and went to say goodbye. He started to speak. She put her finger to his lips. "We have both said enough for now. Let's treasure the moment. I will call you in a few days."

He nodded and opened the door of the Shogun to take one last look at her, before he went.

Despite all that had passed between them, she still hadn't admitted watching him play football in Tehran.

A new day started with some finches fighting for food and territory on the apricot tree outside his bedroom window. He couldn't be sure, but had the feeling they had been pulled from their slumber by the first calls to morning prayers from the mosque nearby. Fawaz's immediate priority that morning was to find another place or places for his Peace International colleagues to shelter. In some ways, the barn was convenient but was too close for comfort. If the team were discovered now, the whole mission would collapse. He had been reviewing and dissecting conversations with his father in recent days and recalled him making reference to building new houses on the edge of the village, but like so many of these recent conversations the subject had been referenced but not discussed. Where were these houses? Who was building them? How could he afford it? Who was buying? He was well aware of the need not to appear too inquisitive. He decided to make it is own business to investigate. He knew he was still in the honeymoon period regarding his reintroduction to family life. No one was asking questions about his future plans and his father appeared not to be around the farm during the days. Hanif, the farm manager married to Khalifa the housekeeper, seemed to be the most visible person looking after his father's affairs. Although polite, he appeared to be quite a distant figure who was vigilant, but not easy to engage in conversation. Fawaz guessed he was nervous about him because he was a potential rival to the management of the estate and had an unfair advantage in that he was his son. It was the day after Dave had reported that extra help would be arriving and the pressure on accommodation would grow.

He decided to walk to the northern edge of the village, in the direction of the compound. Away to the right on the side of the hill, looking back towards the main settlement, he saw a new road had been carved out, with six flat building plots marked up. As he got closer, he saw a small cement mixing tank and piles of steel poles, as well as a stack of stones and some of brick. A small crane attached to the back of a lorry was lifting panels to the first floor on one site and another had its concrete frame completed. The nearer he got the more detail he could see. There was a small dump truck, generator, site office and toilet, as well as eight people working on the site. Two with hard hats seemed to be in control, consulting the plan and pointing ahead. The others he could see were all bare-chested south Asians wearing flipflops and no safety helmets. He continued to walk towards the site.

One of the two seniors with the hard hat broke from his discussion of the plan and came towards him.

"This is private land. Can I help you?"

"Oh, I'm new to the area," said Fawaz. "I like it and am looking around for somewhere to live. When are these places going on the market?"

"I'm sorry, this is a private development; they're all sold," the foreman said, "but if you're interested, there are some smaller new places going up over there." He pointed in the opposite direction in the valley.

"Really? When will they be ready?"

"No idea, but I drove by them yesterday and there's around three or four built already. They've not fixed the gardens yet, but there was a water tanker there when I went by."

"So how come you can sell places before they are built?"

"Good question, brother – I'm not clever enough to know that. There's a notary in the village, Mr al-Hamady; he'll tell you about that. Now, I've got work to do. Good day."

While Fawaz had been chatting to the foreman, he noticed his colleague, still holding the plan, had taken a picture of him on his mobile.

Later in the day after he had walked to the other side of the village to see the smaller new builds, Fawaz came back through Ibrahim Sami's main street. It had been the fourth time he had made the journey and he had to confess he had missed the small window of Mr al-Hamady's office. To the Western eye, it looked like a small estate agent, with pictures and sketches of properties in the locality, but no advertised prices. Seeing such a business in a city like Tabriz was not unusual but here was another inescapable sign that life was changing in Sami. The properties sold had a red star on them, but it was not the sale symbol that attracted his attention, but a small note under each picture which said "An al-Fouadi development". Fawaz was starting to understand why his father had less time to cultivate land. It was clearly more profitable to sell it.

That evening, his father was home. It was another opportunity for a family get together with his mother and Shimina. This was

180

an informal gathering with a range of *mezes*, fruit juices for mother and daughter, Shiraz for father and son. After they had eaten, Dilshad and Shimina retired to another room to continue work on a *susani*, an ornate tapestry which would form part of Shimina's dowry when she married. Hafiz and Fawaz took a shisha together.

"Are you settling in OK?" asked his father, "I bet you're surprised how different life is here now."

"It's changed so much, I feel like a visitor in my own home town. So many of my friends from the madrassah either left or got killed in the wars with Iraq."

"I don't need to remind you how tough life was. After you went, I barely had enough money to run the farm and had to do all sorts to get by, but things have gradually improved. I promised myself, every time I made a profit, however small, I would invest it in another business. I also promised myself I would only invest in businesses alongside others, so each success didn't just depend on me. Today, I have investments in agriculture, property, manufacturing and personal services. All are related to the land. My businesses grow crops, produce meat, spin wool for clothing, refurbish buildings, build new ones, make bricks and pour concrete... and all need transport, which I also provide. It's a funny thing, business. You need to be big enough to make money, but not so big you lose control. If my business interests stretched beyond Khoda Afrin Prefecture I'd pull out. It pays not to *look* too successful or *leave* too much in the bank, otherwise it gets 'political' and people get fucked about. We're lucky I think to have Governor Mayor Moussavi handling that stuff. He's done well to bring new investment here, which is keeping local people in jobs and attracting new ones. We owe a lot also to Colonel Rahman, who is our very best customer. We will have lunch with them both in a couple of days. I want them to meet my son and heir."

Hafiz drew deeply on the pipe.

"Because of this, I want you to get to know these businesses better. I would like you to spend more time with me."

Fawaz was non-committal. "There's no rush, Dad. I want to get to know Sami again first to decide whether I want to make a life here."

"I get that, but don't take too long. We have plans to make."

Typical Dad: suddenly he snapped out of his passive condition and stood up from his armchair. "Tell you what, lad. Now is a great time to take a walk out. I want to show you round the guest house and Chinese restaurant. Get your coat."

It was now evening. They walked down a small, dimly lit side street to the main thoroughfare. Although most of the market stalls had closed for the evening, a parade of small shops huddled around the central café were all open. Carpets, textiles, wool, traditional women's wear, small electrical goods, hardware, bookstore, barbers and tobacconists were all doing steady business. The main entrance of the guest house hotel was at the far end of the strip. It had a semi-open lounge area suitable for pipe smokers, reception and juice bar with a giant marquetry picture of a lion, the length of one wall. Fawaz had discovered this place the previous evening when he had passed through before meeting the owner of the textile shop next door and his friend, a local builder at the baker's café. Lit by a series of lamps and filled with soft furnishings, this was a cosy place to while away an evening and for a minute he thought his father was going to settle in and continue their conversation. Instead he walked through to the reception area, signed in Farsi-Arabic script and Chinese. The receptionist, in her twenties, olive-skinned with eye liner, in a dark blue *hijab* but not full *chador*, smiled and said "good evening". She nodded to her boss as he walked by. Up one flight of steps and they arrived at the Silk Road restaurant that was just opening for dinner. Hafiz acknowledged two Chinese staff at the door and took a menu.

"Look at this. Chinese and Persian dishes. This is quality food you wouldn't find out here in the country. I told you I am looking to hold our Chamber of Trade meetings in here, so I can educate my friends to try chicken chow mein instead of *shashlik* or *kofte*. I know it is a difficult sell, but it will be good business in future, especially after meals. These Chinese really like to party, so they drink alcohol – beer, wine, arak, *anything*. They like music, poker and mah-jong, so over there in the corner I've built a games area. I employ two full Chinese families to run it all. They live in the basement. Between them they do the cooking, table service, kitchen and the games. To play, they must put down a minimum of 1,000 RMB. We charge them 500 RMB per session so they get their other 500 deposit back when they finish or forfeit it if they have unsettled debts. You should come back later and see how popular it is. But come; there is more to show you."

Instead of returning to the stairs, Hafiz moved across the first-floor landing to the lift. It showed the building had six floors in total. Entering the lift, he pressed the second floor. On arrival, the doors opened into a small gymnasium.

The reception desk here had a local man in a white running vest and tracksuit bottoms. He, too, nodded to the boss.

"The gymnasium is free to those who stay in the hotel, but non-residents pay a charge to use it. It's not that big. We just have a weights room, sauna, whirlpool and changing facilities. We should make it bigger and will do so when Sami itself gets bigger."

Fawaz could see how animated his father was becoming as he showed off his pride and joy.

"And now, son, I want to show you my hotel, my 'guest house', and what makes it special."

They returned to the lift. "The only people who can access the next floors are hotel guests with a special room key. This is not just about security. I regard anyone who stays here as a VIP. They need to understand if they come to Ibrahim Sami they get the best hospitality we can offer."

They took the lift to the next floor. Hafiz used his master key to open one of the rooms. "Here we are."

To Fawaz the room looked distinctly ordinary. Double bed, TV, beige colour scheme, couch, private bathroom.

"The thing that makes this special is the service we provide. We only have nine rooms, but each one has a manager dedicated to ensuring the guest's complete satisfaction."

Hafiz clapped his hands.

A beautiful dark-haired woman Fawaz took to be in her early twenties appeared, smartly dressed in a white braless chemise, pencil skirt, stockings, heels and make-up.

"This room manager is called Eleheh, aptly named 'like a goddess'. For a fee, she will wear whatever clothing you like… or none at all; she will serve you drinks or sit on your face; she will drink alcohol with you, smoke a joint or read you a bedtime story. In short, she does whatever is asked of her. I have taken room service to a new level. My managers are multilingual Russian, Mandarin, English. And they are discreet – when you are finished, they disappear. Rooms here cost 2,000 RMB per night, but to reserve one requires a pre-checked credit card to cover other, flexible fees. For example, for those who adhere to sharia law and expect *halal*, we can even get Mullah Yusuf round from next door to authorise a *mutah*, a temporary overnight marriage licence, especially if they bring a young companion."

Fawaz was amazed at his father's detachment. He showed his son around like he was just another investor. Iran was certainly a male-dominated society, especially outside the metropolitan areas, and he didn't have to ask whether his mother or sister knew anything about it. Hafiz was proud of what he had created, a secret world, only known to a select few, where men could enjoy their most intimate fantasies, free of the guilt and embarrassment of recognition. And all this next to the mosque.

"Where do the… er… managers live?" Fawaz couldn't think of anything to say.

"They have a dormitory on the sixth floor, with full cleaning and changing facilities. They get a day off once a week when Hanif will take them shopping out of the vicinity to different places. It all works quite smoothly, and they get a wage and all their costs – clothes, make-up, cocaine – paid up front. They serve a three-month contract, after which they can leave at their own wish. Most want to stay but, unfortunately, we tend to move them on. Anyway, I have some reading to do at home. You can stay here if you wish, as my guest. I had heard you were looking at some of my housing plots earlier. I understand you may not wish to live at home anymore, but I will give you a house if you see something you like – don't worry, we will have plenty of time to talk. But, for now, I hope you can see the kind of business opportunity that could be open to you if you stay."

Fawaz thought quickly. "You are very thoughtful, Dad. Yes, if it's OK, I will stay. I would be happy for Eleheh to look after me."

"It is settled. If I had such an opportunity at your age, I too would have taken it." He smiled. "Come home in your own good time. I will expect to have some feedback about the quality of your stay."

After the door closed, Fawaz waited for the grinding noise of the elevator and the closure of the doors as his father departed.

The girl waited, standing in an almost military "at ease" posture.

"What can I do for you, sir?" she asked.

Fawaz looked at her again. He had to admit under normal circumstances this girl... this woman, dressed in a way which showed off her figure, yet seemed almost demure in her presentation, was very desirable. But was it because she was available at his command that he felt strangely unaroused? Nonetheless, he had a purpose in accepting his father's offer.

"I'd like you to get me a beer and something also for you. Come and sit next to me. I'd like to talk."

She produced a can of Dutch lager and glass and an orange juice and came to sit next to him on the couch. She settled next to him and draped herself provocatively, her body facing him, crossing her stockinged leg and balancing one of her stilettoes on the ball of her foot.

"So what do you want to know?"

"Who you are, where you come from and how did you get here, for a start."

Eleheh, previously in a relaxed and confident disposition, became visibly more tense, uncrossing her legs and sitting forward.

"I am not authorised to discuss my personal information," she said.

"But you'd rather fuck." He had spoken brutally in order to snap her out of the pre-learned script.

"Sure." His sharp words didn't produce the response he was expecting. She put down her drink and started to unbutton her blouse.

Fawaz leaned forward and gently, but firmly, gripped her arm.

"If we are going to become friends, and I'm going to get in the mood, I need to know something about you, and the more truth you tell, the more pleasure I will get. Let's start with your name – is it really Eleheh?"

"Here in Iran it is, but it was not the name I was born with. I used to be called Nuray. I am from a small town in Azerbaijan, near the Iranian border. I was kidnapped by an Iranian clan a few years ago after I had been captured in a raid. I was just fifteen. Azerbaijan used to be a Soviet state where girls and women were respected. But not here. This is a male-dominated society. The raiders first abused me then tried to rape me, but were stopped by their leader, who said I would be worth more money if I was sold as a virgin. I was held as a prisoner for a few weeks, locked in a basement on my own. I was fed porridge once a day and had a bucket of cold water to wash in and another which I used as a toilet. I didn't understand what was happening as I didn't speak Farsi at the time. My captors spoke to me in Russian. Now and again, groups of men, three or four at a time, would be brought to see me and tried to touch me but I would scream and they'd withdraw. Then one day Mr al-Fouadi came. He seemed nice and smiled at me. I was then given to him and he brought me here to Sami. He took me to a proper house with a proper bathroom. I was able to look after myself and had a kitchen stocked with food. I was able to eat regularly. I felt better and must have looked better as he came to me one day and said he wanted me to work as a housekeeper at his farm. He brought me a uniform and gave me a bed in his servants' quarters. During this time, he never asked for sex, but one day, when he was alone in his house, he summoned me to his private room because he wanted a hot bath to ease his back, which he said he had hurt as a result of a fall.

"I had just finished filling his bath when he came in the room naked and erect and ordered me to take my clothes off and to sniff a drug, which I later knew as cocaine. I was frightened as I thought this was out of character. I had worked for him for over a year and he had shown me nothing but kindness to this point. We had sex and he was gentle with me. I didn't imagine I could lose my virginity to an older man, but I did. Afterwards, I couldn't get it out of my head, and, I have to admit, I wanted it from him again and wanted to sniff the drug which made me high. At first, he didn't want to, but I started to plan days where I knew he would be alone in the house and I would go to him sometimes with no underwear. I learned how to arouse him and we soon became lovers. The result was I became infatuated with him. He set up this hotel and told me I had a new job as a manager. Not of the hotel, but this room. I am responsible for its complete maintenance, including cleaning and housekeeping as well as room service. He told me that, if I truly wanted to make him happy, I should be prepared to fuck anyone who stayed in it. Because I was always well treated, had good health care and money for clothes, I have gone along with it. Until I realised I was not alone; over the past couple of years, other girls have come to be managers as well. We share a dormitory at the top of the hotel. Most share my story of coming from Azerbaijan, but now there are one or two from elsewhere, such as Pakistan, one from France, another from Kazakhstan. Most of the time we can manage OK. We don't have to handle money. Some of our customers are regulars – there's a soldier called Rashid who's straight – no problem; a politician called Hossein who gets pissed and just wants to wank in front of us; and then there is Yusuf, the imam next door. He likes to tear off his manager's clothes, slap her and call for her to repent of her sins before he administers her punishment with his dick. But even he has to be careful; if one of us thinks he's getting too rough we can call Hanif. When guests of interest arrive, they are normally given one of the fifth-floor rooms. These have cameras, where recordings can be made.

"But it's difficult for me to stop. If I do, I will be thrown out on the street, have no passport and no money. The real problem is the cocaine. Mr al-Fouadi knows how much we need it and knows that it is the way he can ensure control."

"The place is pretty busy, then?"

"We are nearly full most nights these days, especially since the Chinese came. There are two in particular called Mr Ho and Mr Wen." She started to laugh. "Yes, really, they come as a team. They are bi. I think they think they get better value that way. We all have to have a soapy bath together."

Fawaz had listened in amazement.

"What happens if a guest wants to take you out?"

"Where?" Eleheh looked surprised. "There is nowhere to go around here. We only meet guests in the evenings and get our day off to go shopping in Tabriz on Sundays as well as a visit to the gym on Friday afternoons when it is shut for maintenance. If a guest asks for anything unusual we can't supply, we are instructed to call Khalifa. She is our day-to-day boss. She brings fresh laundry, sanitary products and cocaine in the mornings and takes away linen and towels for washing. The rest of the time we spend in our dormitories, cleaning, sleeping or reading."

"Mr al-Fouadi tells me the girls only stay for three months at a time. Is that true?"

"Yes, on the whole. He writes contracts in his own way. Sometimes he gets rid of girls who cause trouble or make a baby and others who are 'overused'. In all cases, he makes it his job to screw them before anyone else does."

"Have you thought of going to the police?"

Eleheh sighed. "What do you know about Ibrahim Sami? He *is* the police."

"What about the girls who have left; do you know what has happened to them?"

"No – occasionally we hear Hanif talking to Khalifa about them on our shopping trips, but I have never seen them again. Hanif takes care of all that."

"You've been here longer than most; why have you been able to stay when others have arrived and left?"

"I am not sure. Mr al-Fouadi believes in clear line management. I guess I must be the head girl. When important guests like you arrive, he normally introduces them to me as I act like an advertisement for him. He is also happy the other girls come to me for help and advice about anything that helps them to do their job better. Maybe because he had a relationship with me, he is slightly scared. When he made me pregnant, our personal relationship finished. I had an abortion and afterwards he decided Khalifa should be in charge of me and the other girls. Now I never see him alone, although, when he visits with others, I still see the look in his eye that tells me he wants me. If I have any matters to discuss I have to speak to Khalifa. I am very worried about the future. When I cease to look as attractive as the others, I will be replaced and will have to try and find a way out."

"Thanks for telling me all this; you have been very brave."

Eleheh shrugged. "You asked. I needed to talk. Most men don't give a shit. Besides, you told me you got off on hearing the truth."

She learned forward and took his right hand, pressing it on her left breast.

Fawaz felt the warmth of her heart.

"And you are part of Mr al-Fouadi's family – entitled to my special service."

Fawaz leaned much from his short stay in the hotel and a little before dawn he woke finding himself lying fully clothed on the couch with Eleheh, still dressed, curled up next to him. There were three empty beer cans and a half-empty carafe of apricot juice on the coffee table. He carefully extracted himself from her arms and looked around for his shoes. Despite his best efforts, he disturbed Eleheh. She sat up sharply and reached out for him.

"Don't go – it is still night and we haven't had sex. If you leave now, I will be in trouble."

Fawaz kneeled, putting his face close to hers, squeezing her hand.

"Don't worry; I will tell my father we have had a wonderful night of lovemaking. So much so that I will insist on staying with you again and soon. I am not looking for sex, but I will be your friend and will help get you out of here," he whispered.

Staring deep into her brown eyes, he hoped she had understood how serious he was.

NINE

IT'S NOT OFTEN GIL would sit in a ditch on a cold night and feel in good spirits. His second incursion into Iran had gone quite smoothly. He could never have known the capability of his charges and was prepared to help them every step of the way, but it had proved unnecessary. Crossing the Aras river, the *de facto* border, was always a bit daunting. Gil had been surprised on their previous crossing how strong the current was and its relative depth. Without guidance, an average person could fall victim to one of the eddies, which were powerful enough to suck a man down beneath the surface for good.

Gil had taken a more direct route than Fawaz and had set up a guideline for the three of them to follow. It was slow work because the riverbed depth fluctuated, causing the three to paddle in places. The stony shore gave them a brief opportunity to rest before following the same route as colleagues had used the previous week, through the minefield trips and barbed-wire rolls. Progress was sure but measured. Defences had to be negotiated but were to be left exactly as they had been found. Even now Gil was familiar with the landscape and the deterrents he needed to concentrate fully on each move they took. Once they got as far as the treeline, the start of the fertile landscape, Gil felt more comfortable as they picked up the shadow of vegetation and had real cover. They had traversed the track minutes earlier, where Fawaz had picked up an Iranian border patrol, but all stayed quiet, save for the occasional screech of a brown owl on the hunt for its next meal. As Fawaz had showed him, Gil was moving forward and sideways, maximising the cover of each field's boundary and hedge, avoiding tell-tale boot prints on open ground. They had almost completed their first hour when Gil stopped and gestured them to lie flat. They were on the edge of a wheat field, with no apparent obstacle ahead. All three strained to pick up the noises of their surroundings. At this level the predominant sound was the wind blowing through the crop, like the noise of a whip without the crack. But, shortly after, they heard low voices. Again, Gil gestured for his followers to move to his right, go down and lie still. The voices were coming louder now and were speaking Russian. Two silhouettes now appeared close by. In fatigues, they carried automatics but had slung them on their shoulders, a clear sign they were not expecting trouble. Unbelievably, the two stopped close by, one lighting two cigarettes and passing one to the other.

"Can you tell me why we've come all the way down here, chasing some poacher? Even they aren't stupid enough to come this way. They'd get blown up in a couple of minutes."

The other replied, "Well, I haven't heard a bang; we'd better check it out and report. They're getting a bit nervous about foreign fighters passing through."

The two trudged on, their voices becoming quieter. Gil didn't move until he was sure they'd gone. He beckoned his charges forward.

Up ahead were the shadows of the first outbuildings of Ibrahim Sami, but Gil steered his team to the left. Keeping the buildings in sight, they started to move away until the great cedar came into view. They stopped again.

"Stay here – follow me on the night sight. I am expecting to meet one of your colleagues by that big tree trunk. As there's a few others knocking around tonight, I will go and make the meeting solo. Look out for the overhead arm movement. That will be when I want you to come." Gil moved on, running fast and low along the edge of the ditch. He stopped at the tree to listen.

Silence. Then, "Psst, up here!" Dave jumped down from a branch above. "Missed the welcoming committee?" he asked.

Gil snorted: "Not by much. It's certainly getting busy round here."

"*Spetznaz?*"

"Probably – Russian speakers certainly. I'm sure my unit is going to run in to them sooner or later. Anyway, London has sent you two people, both look good and up for it. A Chinese-looking guy, called Gul, and the woman, Anya, who you'll remember helped us get to Barthaz last week. They've got the standard Makarovs, extra ammo and one or two other pieces to make your life easier. All clear your end?"

"I think so; we're picking up a lot more info about what's going on. We'll be going in once we have put the picture together. In the meantime, you'll just have to wait and watch."

Gil signalled for the others to join them.

"Alrighty, Dave, meet Gul, and this is Anya who you met last week. Dave is the PI field commander on this one. You will need to update with him soonest. Now you are connected, it's time for me to go. Don't stress about our Russian friends in the wood; it's my job to pick up on them. If they are any good as trackers, they're about to go for a long walk out of the theatre."

Gil deliberately avoided saying goodbye and left their conversation unfinished. There was a possibility they would meet again if the MoD got cold feet.

Gil had been late. It was just after 02.00. Dave would get his new colleagues back to the barn and manage the introductions.

Some forty minutes later, Dave and party arrived at the back of the farm barn. A stone thrown at the window got the attention of Jack, who lowered the ladder. One by one they entered the mezzanine via the hatch. The barn was now congested with six in it and another expected. Backpacks were stowed ready at one end of the space. All shook hands and fist-pumped in silence. They waited on the arrival of the last member of the team. Despite the quiet, the air carried the static of excitement. Dave now had the team to do the job.

Fawaz arrived shortly after with flasks of tea and what he called soup. Jack had been the most enthusiastic about the refreshment and was the first to taste the piping hot liquid, spitting and spluttering.

"What the fuck's *that*?" he whispered, much to the amusement of his colleagues.

"It's a type of *naryn* – a clear broth of horsemeat. If you were having it at table, there would be chunks of meat and pieces of thin pasta in it. My grandmother used to make it and said those men who ate it would have many children. You are lucky to be having it in Iran. If you were further east it is served like a national delicacy. Seriously, it is very effective in keeping the cold out of your bones."

It was certainly known to Anya, who took the cup and had a good swig before passing on to Jo.

Dave called the gathering to order and asked Jo and Rodg to provide the latest observations of the Chinese compound.

He then gave his own update.

After contacting Gil, he had made his way across country towards Posyan, taking the bus to the east, stopping off first at the barn to change and collect Jack. He had the advantage of an old shirt and trousers, courtesy of Fawaz, and, having spent much of the night in a ditch, had the dirt and the smell of the land on him, so had the appearance of a casual farm hand – a not uncommon site in these parts. As for Jack, a few days without shaving had transformed him into a credible impersonator of a homeless war veteran. It was clearly a masterstroke as the antique bus seemed to be packed with all shades of humanity – mothers, kids, grannies, limbless war veterans, plus dogs and chickens – offering the best cover to hide in plain sight he could ask for in daylight hours. The overcrowding meant they had not been able to get seats, instead holding on to a couple of the straps protruding from the roof and leaning their bodyweight against the steel frames of seats towards the back. Such was the chaos, the driver seemed less concerned whether his passengers had paid than making sure no one was hanging off on the outside. The bus climbed the long slope away from the verdant valley of Ibrahim Sami into the barren lands of the mountains. Considering the old Mercedes was overloaded, it kept a steady jogging pace on the straight incline until it reached the dog-leg corner at the summit. At this point the bus's speed dropped obligingly to a crawl, offering Dave a glimpse of a panoramic view of the climb they had just negotiated, between the back of an old woman's head and two young girls staring at an iPad game. Jack carried a mobile with a locally purchased pay-as-you-go SIM, which would allow him to get some pictures from the reconnoitre. The bus was not due to stop before Posyan and so they were reconciled to standing the whole way. With everyone's personal space invaded, Jack found himself closer than he had wanted to an old woman. He tried to avoid her gaze but started to feel uncomfortable as she looked straight at him. For a moment their eyes locked contact and the woman gave a broad smile, revealing a gum line with half a dozen teeth protruding at odd angles like tomb stones. He thought she must have felt her smile was her best asset as to the left side of her mouth she revealed a gold molar, which sparkled in the morning sunlight. She then spoke to him in what he judged to be an indistinct tone. He wasn't sure what she was saying but decided to act like he was deaf, pointing to his ear, shrugging his shoulders and offering a vague apologetic smile.

Rather than discouraging her, she continued to talk, smiling and nodding her head. What Jack hadn't realised was, in pointing to his ear, he had drawn attention to a stud. It became clear it was the stud that interested the woman. He studiously avoided her effort at conversation as the bus crossed the brow of the mountain ridge and picked up speed on its straight descent into Posyan. His preoccupation with the woman was not shared by Dave, who, through his restricted vista, noted an armoured car and two fully loaded troop carriers passing in the opposite direction. Jack took the opportunity to reposition himself so he was now sideways on to the woman and he was able to engage Dave in a mock conversation. Realising he too was being watched, he smiled and also pointed to his ear. For some reason the old woman seemed to understand Dave better than Jack. It was true the increased tempo of the bus engine certainly drowned out any attempt at rational conversation.

As the descent started, the village of Posyan came into view, nestling in another lush valley. And, looking to the east, the outline of a runway could be made out with the naked eye.

Also visible ahead and glimpsed from their position was a rare sight in rural Iran – a traffic jam. Fortunately, the queue kept moving slowly, but Dave was pleased he was not relying on the bus to work to its predetermined timetable. Catching snippets of chatter from fellow passengers, the reason for the delay was the annual Pomegranate Parade in Posyan, which probably went some way to providing the explanation for the crush on the bus, although, to his relief, he could only see one woman with a pomegranate in her shopping bag.

The celebrated fruits, the product of shrubs cultivated in fields throughout the region to grow up to five metres, were a staple crop of the locality, their contents revealing sparkling, jewel like inner seeds, known as arils which were eaten raw or juiced. Light pink in colour, the size of a large orange, rich in antioxidants and vitamin C, pomegranates were credited with diverse health benefits from aiding the digestion to alleviating symptoms related to cancer. Not only did the parade mark a successful harvest; it also provided the opportunity for local growers to demonstrate the versatility of the fruit as a key ingredient in stews, juices and cakes, with specific varieties bred for sweet and savoury tastes. Women of all ages, dressed in their best colourful *chadors* in red, yellow and green, had formed a procession led by men in white tunics banging hand-held drums to a noisy and incoherent folk melody blasted out by trumpeters and accordionists. Behind the drummers came jugglers, behind the jugglers came a horse drawn cart filled with pomegranates and behind the cart were girls, swaying to the music, who had brought samples of dishes using the fruit, for bystanders to sample and buy.

As the bus neared the first buildings of the settlement, he noticed bunting attached to each, either side of the main road and the noise and chaos grew louder as the bus negotiated the highway, now flooded with bystanders enjoying the show.

Arrival at Posyan could not have come fast enough for Jack and he was relieved to see the majority of passengers disembark into the swell at the village's central bus stop, including his new-found admirer. It was difficult not to get caught in the moment and Jack's newly found space provided the perfect opportunity to take some snaps like any average tourist. From what he could tell, this place was smaller than Ibrahim Sami but looked prosperous nonetheless. Posyan seemed to consist of well-maintained, freshly painted low-level buildings with flat roofs, some with terraces, others with potted bacopas and verbenas cascading through balconies, the mosque dominated by a minaret, marking the centre. The bunting had been woven through orange trees which lined both sides of the main street. Dave was surprised how the departing diverse mob seemed to be absorbed by the street scene, quickly disappearing into the melee, and down surrounding alleyways. Although there were no new passengers joining the bus, the driver waited and was in no hurry to move on, adjusting his rear-view mirror, checking his phone and enjoying a cigarette. He seemed almost oblivious to the fact that some of the dancing revellers decided to continue the parade through his bus, on through the front door and off at the back, led by a musician in a white tunic with a bottle green *tagiya* hat and bugle. This impromptu conga line climaxed with two beautiful smiling girls, one carrying a large silver-coloured cup (similar to a Celtic quaich) of pomegranate juice, the other with a plate of cake slices, offering samples to the six people left on the bus. Dave didn't want to appear too friendly with Jack (especially as he seemed enthralled by the action) and deliberately sat down two rows away, but he too shared his colleague's sampling of the fruit. Once the celebrants were off the bus, Jack was surprised how quickly the street cleared and calm was restored. The parade had turned off the main street by the mosque and was filling up the adjacent small central square. The heat of the day was now setting in and whatever so-called air conditioning the bus had ceased with the engine off. There were sliding windows at the top of each frame and, despite the presence of a cool breeze, the temperature continued to rise. Dave sat impassively, looking out of the window, but Jack started to twitch, encouraged by a wasp. At that moment his attention was drawn by two soldiers in fatigues with pistols in holsters, rushing up behind the bus, shouting before scrambling on board and stuffing a couple of banknotes into the driver's hand. He took their action as his own cue to start the engine of the bus and shout his destination, "Timor Baglo", before releasing the handbrake and slowly moving off, past the revellers to the left. The two soldiers took advantage of the space on the bus perching on either side, maintaining their conversation in such a way that anyone could join in. The one closest to Jack lit a cigarette, took a drag and offered it to him. It was a dilemma. Jack wanted a smoke and would have accepted, but knew that would have brought him into their conversation. He smiled, shook his head and pointed to his ear.

"I think the guy is telling me he's deaf," one of the soldiers said to the other.

"I don't think he would be interested anyway," his colleague replied.

Because he was sitting slightly further away, the two men seemed oblivious to Dave.

"That governor mayor is a bit of an arsehole. Builds himself this little palace out of the way on the edge of the village and then tells our boss we have to guard it. Don't know why they worry about security there; any enemy would have to ask locals for directions at least three times to find it. I bet that's why no one from Tehran can be bothered to come here. Seems to think he's in charge of everything, not just the pomegranates, that tosser. The other day, he told me I had to fix a blockage on one of his toilet pipes. I nearly told him I wasn't a fuckin' plumber, and it wasn't just his toilet that was full of shit."

His friend sniggered. "But you found a proper plumber anyway."

"Yeah, and I told him to bring a fuckin' big brush."

They both laughed. His friend said, "You know we've had an easy gig here – even if we had to make our own way by bus. You could have ended up going with those miners up to the Arasbaran Protected Zone. Once you get up there, you'll be stuck for a week, watching a load of dickheads from down south breaking rocks. *Or* you could be taking another lot over on the one-way trip to the Chinese takeaway in Sami and end up on border patrol. *Or* you could be teaching those so-called *jihadis* how to set an IED without blowing themselves up..."

"Or... I could just be taking it easy at the prison. It's really funny watching those guys beg for food. There's one I always tell to do an impression of a dog. He's barking mad! At least you get to knock off on time and get to eat at the mess regularly. *Woof, woof*" He laughed. "When's your next leave due?"

"Not until the end of the month. I can't decide whether I want to go home to get the attention of my good woman or go over to Sami and buy some time with a bad one. I have a pass for the night bus to Sami on Thursday."

"Are you part of the duty tactical squad or there on your own time?"

"Thursday night is about me. I'm not going to sit in that shitty hut by the bus station waiting for a riot, drinking tea and walking around town checking everyone else is in their beds. I'm going to play some snooker, see a movie and maybe, if I get lucky, get into someone else's bed or, if not, at least into their knickers."

"Is it the weekly mixed party on Thursday?"

"Yes, doing the one mixed off-duty night per week has been the best thing Rahman has done since he took charge. Everyone else who has been on it – including you, as I remember – thought it was great. I guess I always knew it would be arranged as an alphabetical order thing. Well, it's great they've got down to me. It's only taken nine weeks..."

Staring into the middle distance out of the window, Dave was translating their conversation and memorising the passing scenery.

Jack was trying to do the same, conscious he was missing key phases. The soldiers didn't mind – they thought he was trying to lip read.

The main entrance to the garrison had a bus stop and the two soldiers got off. Dave noticed they seem to walk in unchallenged.

The bus proved to be an excellent vantage point for the base. Although it was protected with barbed-wire fencing, there were no bunds to block the view. The big feature was the runway, which was wide and about a kilometre long – big enough, he estimated, to take large passenger jets. On the far side of the runway, in one corner, was a four-storey building, itself surrounded by security fencing and watchtowers, clearly the prison within the camp. Following the panorama to the right was a large hanger with a military transport plane facing inward, next to that a fuel storage area with three mobile tankers and a fire engine and finally the control tower. Below it, what looked like a Jetstream executive jet, a bigger passenger jet with twin engines mounted on the rear of the fuselage (probably a Comac ARJ21) and what looked like a Mi-24 helicopter gunship. On the nearside of the compound close to the road was a ten-storey tower block, presumably the garrison building, and a car park with half a dozen cars and two buses. In the far corner were eight new trucks, four he would describe as off-road 'dumpers'. Surprisingly, there was no obvious signs of defensive capability, but just because it wasn't visible didn't mean it didn't exist. And, talking of visibility, no trees or cover of any kind to allow undetected observation at the base.

Dave had pretended to have fallen asleep and asked the driver if he would let him off before they arrived at Timor Baglo, the next scheduled stop, and enquired when the next bus back would be passing.

While Dave and Jack's encounter had been taking place, Fawaz had obtained vital intelligence as he recalled his own recent experience.

"It's time we were moving," Hafiz called to his son. "We'll take the Land Cruiser; I'll drive. Hanif has got other stuff to do this morning, and I don't want to arrive at this meeting with a chauffeur."

"Coming, Dad," Fawaz called, quickly putting on a black gilet over his pressed white shirt.

He ran down the stairs to meet his father in the hall.

"Is this smart enough? You did say smart but casual."

"You'll do. The colonel will be uniformed, but Moussavi will be casual and I don't know about the other guy..."

"What other guy?"

"Mr Ho – he runs the research base. I met his predecessor, Mr Chen, but he went home about three weeks ago – I've only spoken to him briefly."

"Are you sure they won't mind me attending your business meeting?"

Hafiz laughed. "Don't worry about a thing. I spoke to them individually about it. They all agreed with my point of view."

They set off on the Posyan road.

"Where are we meeting?" Fawaz asked.

"We were going to the governor mayor's residence, but, as I told him you were coming, we agreed to change it to the garrison.

It's one of the newest in the country and its development has been the colonel's pet project. I've seen him overseeing it from the time they laid the runway, and I think he always wants the opportunity to show it off.

"Anyway, what did you think of the guest house? Pretty good, isn't it? I got the idea from a place I stayed at once on the Caspian. I'd rather build something of quality that people will pay a premium for, rather than some big monstrosity that sucks up money. I thought Eleheh would be right for you. She's a smart girl and knows how to manage herself. From what I heard, she certainly took care of you!" He laughed again.

"I hope I will have the opportunity to see her again," Fawaz replied.

"I am sure you will, but don't go wasting your time and energy on her right now. There's plenty of more important matters for you to focus on, as you will understand today."

Traffic was light and they passed through Posyan village and beyond to the entrance to the base. A left turn took them to the gatehouse. Hafiz wound down the driver's window and waved. The guard recognised the regular visitor and saluted. They didn't need to speak because Hafiz knew exactly where to go, turning right onto the perimeter road which ran parallel to the public highway, only now the other side of the three-metre-high razor wire topped fence. The size of the compound meant Hafiz could drive at a steady 50kph for ten minutes before arriving at a car park in front of a ten-storey block. Parking in one of the hatched VIP spaces closest to the entrance, Hafiz, in a blue blazer and open-necked shirt, moved at a brisk pace with purpose, Fawaz stepping quickly to keep up.

"Al-Fouadi for the Colonel," he barked at the duty soldier at the reception.

"Yes, sir. Please take the elevator to the tenth floor."

Had the exit from the lift been a picture, it would have provided a perfect frame for a portrait of the colonel.

Rahman was a tall, naturally imposing figure with a waxed moustache and pitted olive skin, in the image of Clark Gable. He wore his dark green dress uniform with colours and epaulettes and with his name and the flag of the Islamic Republic.

He nodded his head in greeting, before giving a brotherly bear hug to Hafiz.

"May I introduce my son and heir, Fawaz?"

"You are very welcome, Fawaz. I am delighted to show you Posyan Garrison, the biggest and newest of its type north of Tehran."

He led father and son to a window opposite looking across the base.

"From here we run all the Islamic Republic's military operations in the north-west, including the borders with Azerbaijan, Armenia and Turkey. Our responsibilities include managing penal services for offenders against the state, training freedom fighters aligned with the state's foreign policy and providing logistical support for the state's trading and emergency relief activities. We have 500 Revolutionary Guards based here, a fluctuating number of freedom fighters under training, probably around 100 at the moment, and another 200 maximum-security offenders housed at the far end of the compound. This is not really an offensive asset, so we don't keep squadrons of fighter planes here, but have four Mi-24 helicopter gunships, two in maintenance, but two always available to scramble to remote corners of our territory if required.

"As this is primarily a logistics base, we tend to cater for heavy-duty air transport, so storage and warehousing takes up quite a bit of room. And, naturally, as a military facility we are protected by a surface-to-air missile system, which we always hope never to use."

The chime of the elevator signalled the colonel's other two guests, Governor Mayor Moussavi, dressed in blazer and tie, and another figure in military uniform, Major Ho Li Sen of the People's Liberation Army. Ho was accompanied by an interpreter and a uniformed personal guard. Greetings were exchanged, before

Rahman led his guests to an anteroom, with a round table set with places for a meeting.

The colonel had a confident, easy and informal style aimed at simultaneously making his guests feel at home but letting them know he was in charge.

"There are refreshments on the table over there. Please help yourselves, take a seat and we'll get started."

Once all were settled, he began:

"It's great to welcome faces old and new. Apart from extending the warmest of welcomes in particular, to our honoured guest, Major Ho, I should acknowledge the participation of Mr Fawaz al-Fouadi, son of our community representative, Hafiz, who will act as our project manager to ensure our future activities are coordinated. And now, Mr Moussavi, can I ask for you to provide an update on affairs with Tehran?"

The governor mayor paused to light a cigarette and took a sharp intake of breath.

"Thank you, Colonel. For the benefit of young Mr al-Fouadi here, I should say this is an informal local contact group which meets from time to time to ensure the interests of the government of the Islamic Republic and those of its principal external investor, the People's Republic of China, are fully realised in the Khoda Afrin Prefecture – this locality, which is the key beneficiary of Chinese investment in our country. The colonel commands the infrastructure and apparatus to drive the required outcomes. I manage political liaison with Tehran on inter-governmental issues, so, if we find there are matters that we cannot agree between us, I can escalate them to the Foreign Ministry. The focus of our work is to deliver the classified cooperation agreement between the People's Republic of China and the Islamic Republic of Iran that will enable a sixty-million-dollar US investment in our North West Region. My interest is of course creating jobs for local people. The colonel's focus is to safeguard the implementation of the Islamic Republic's commitments under this agreement. Mr al-Fouadi Senior is the area's leading civilian entrepreneur and has a consultative role to assist in civil compliance with the agreement's terms and conditions.

"The first phase envisaged the creation of a research facility in Ibrahim Sami, established by the Revolutionary Guard to develop fertiliser-based chemical and biological weapons and antidotes. After a number of local incidents, it was agreed the Islamic Republic would benefit from additional technical expertise and resources to develop this facility successfully. The People's Republic has now taken full control of the site and in return the Islamic Republic has agreed to cede full territorial rights. In a minute, we will review progress to ensure the full conditions of this arrangement have been implemented.

"The second phase of the cooperation agreement relates to the facility here at Posyan, which is due to be ceded to the People's Republic to be developed as an international free port as part of the Belt and Road Initiative. Apart from facilitating the global transportation of goods from the People's Republic to the Middle East region, it is expected to prime the major development in the environs of this base, leading to the construction of hotels, warehousing, component assembly plants and infrastructure links, as well as exports from Iran – in particular oil, minerals and cotton.

"In view of the sensitive nature of global geopolitics, the Islamic Republic and the People's Republic anticipate a negative reaction from both the United States and the Russian Federation, as well as their respective allies – in particular Israel, Syria, Turkey and Saudi Arabia. It is understood that the plan is vulnerable in its early stages and needs to be kept classified until its development is close to completion. Major Ho, you have been in Sami for a month now, having taken over from Commander Chen. Perhaps you could provide a review of your recent experiences."

Ho leaned forward, elbows on the table. "My experience so far is mixed. Commander Chen's mission was to consolidate the status of the site, to make it safe for our workers and those nearby. The carelessness of the previous management was a serious problem. The outbreak of anthrax in local livestock, in which I understand you, Mr al-Fouadi, were involved, as well as the potential of failing to destroy the body of a test prisoner infected with smallpox safely, was beyond our initial understanding. The very weapons you sought to create could have impacted heavily on your own countrymen, which would also have prevented the prospect of us working together if a major contamination had occurred. You, Mr al-Fouadi, are a scientific miracle to us. As we monitored you in the months since the outbreak, we are genuinely surprised you did not contract the condition. We were not so lucky with the smallpox – the soldiers who handled the body were put into isolation and had to be killed and cremated according to our rules. Since taking over the Sami site we have had to restructure its management. Commercial organ harvesting has now been restricted to a distinct unit with separate staff and management. Chemical warfare and biological warfare also have their own separate operations. We have been happy with the supply of human collateral for testing and have made our own arrangements to supervise disposal of samples where necessary. The issue is, now we have the structure to run an effective operation, we need to scale up, as proven results are required urgently. The geological confines of the site itself are limited and so we must expand by opening up new subterranean levels. Plans have been approved by Beijing and we will be flying in a specialist team to start the work at the end of next week.

"You should be aware this requires special construction and engineering skills we cannot find in Iran and, even if we were to do so, we would not be happy about the security arrangements. Talking of which, the immediate challenge for you here is to arrange the accommodation of these temporary workers. There will be sixty of them. I have taken it upon myself to visit potential sites nearby with Mr al-Fouadi, when I have been staying at his guest house." He paused, fixing Hafiz with a stare, before continuing, "I assume Mr al-Fouadi has consulted Mr Moussavi about this already. I suggest these are prefabricated units, which can be easily transported by road and stacked in position, I note each is capable of taking four persons. Please ensure these are ready in time."

Moussavi looked at Hafiz. Hafiz nodded to Fawaz to note.

"Anything else?" asked Moussavi.

"Not at the moment. Completion of our activation plans for Ibrahim Sami must take priority for now. I must say, Colonel, from what I have seen of your planning to date, you have demonstrated a good understanding of our requirements. Please ensure you keep your fuel reserves on site high in the next few weeks as I anticipate an increase in the number of flights in and out."

Rahman enjoyed the moment; a bit like being the school class "know it all", he just nodded and smiled.

"OK, if that is the end of the meeting for now, there is a selection of *mezes* and juices out on the observation deck before you go."

The major was quick to respond.

"Thank you for your hospitality, Colonel. Unfortunately, my time is limited. I must go, but I hope we can plan for a banquet when the blueprint for Ibrahim Sami is complete."

He stood, shook the hands of Moussavi and the two al-Fouadis, and saluted the colonel before heading for the elevator.

The rest waited until they heard the sound of the door shutting.

"Pompous little prick," muttered Moussavi.

"That may be true, but he's the one with the cheque book," said Rahman. "I'm more concerned we get this rare earth business under way before the Chinese takeover, otherwise they'll try and buy the rights to that before the Islamic Republic has had any commercial advantage. By the way, Hossein, what's happening with the land disposal options around the base? I thought that was the reason why the three of us had set up Golden Goose Investments – that's my pension."

"… and mine," added Hafiz.

"I have meetings at the Ministry in Tehran next week. Last I heard, they were still assessing the geologists reports from the Arasbaran Protected Zone before committing to further test extraction work. Also, the Finance Ministry needed one final piece of legislation through the Islamic Consultative Assembly in order to release the tenders for land sales. Getting agreement to excavate under a UNESCO World Heritage site is not easy; in fact we may have to redraw its boundaries before it goes ahead. Don't worry – all the documentation will come to me for implementation and I can amend it to suit our circumstances."

"That's all very well, Hossein" said Rahman, "but I think we can be clear that it is Ho who is driving the timetable. You must push things forward."

"The Chinese are creating pressure all over the place now," said Moussavi. "They know the Yankees have got us by the balls, so I think even the Supreme Leader understands we have to get on with it. These riots and highway blockages over the doubling of petrol prices have really got the establishment worried. The public don't understand why we're having to raise the price of our own home-produced product. If we don't get the land reforms and our export trade going again, we'll have to start scraping the bullion reserves and if that happens, it will be much more than ministerial necks on the line. We also need a quick win for Ho.

"Hafiz, you must get hold of these prefabs. I don't really care where they come from, I don't really care where they are built, but you must fix it. If anyone gets in your way, call me."

The Governor Mayor and the al-Fouadis shared the elevator to the main entrance to the officers' mess. The encounter with the Chinese major had left the three principals in a subdued mood, realising they had responsibilities to deliver on behalf of their country which might prove to be outside their personal control. It was clear Ho was a different character to Chen, and possibly less open to influence, but Hafiz still had the insurance of his guest house video if relationships became strained.

Once father and son returned to the Land Cruiser they followed Moussavi's white Mercedes with darkened windows along to the perimeter road towards the exit.

"What did you think of that?" Hafiz asked.

"I'm not sure I can believe it," Fawaz said. "It feels like the Supreme Leader has sold Khoda Afrin to China for sixty billion dollars and you're helping to make it happen."

"I suppose that's one way of looking at it. When I got involved, I was only trying to win some contracts to supply food to the military. I didn't have any idea what was happening before my sheep were killed. Back then I was so broke I got involved with some bandits raiding and trading in Azerbaijan, but then I started to pick up business from the military and got to know Rahman. I owe them a lot. They've helped me to change my life and, as a good Muslim, I have found ways to share my success with others in Sami. That won't change. We will still make money, perhaps even more, by trading with the Chinese. This *is* and will always be *our* country, whatever outsiders may say.

"I think you have just got your first job for me – find these prefabs and get them to Sami. I use a lawyer in Tehran who does a lot of contracts in the construction sector. He'll know what to do and who to speak to. His name is Hasan Alrakahthan. I'll give you his number when we get home."

TEN

"THANKS, FAWAZ – I think we're starting to get the picture now," said Dave.

"Have you called this Hasan – whatever his name is?"

"He was out but I've left a voicemail," Fawaz replied. "Summarising what we have learned so far:

"One: PI were right about the use of the Sami base. But we didn't know about the organ harvesting operations.

"Two: the Sami research compound was set up by the Revolutionary Guard but was taken over by the Chinese because the Iranians *fucked up*.

"Three: security within the base is managed by the Chinese.

"Four: the Revolutionary Guard have a 'low key' security post (probably about ten strong) in Sami at the bus station, which supplies personnel to man the anti-aircraft defences outside the research base and other materials into the research compound nightly, as well as making the return trip each morning.

"Five: staff at the research base are changed every six weeks.

"Six: staff at the research base have a nightly bus into Sami for off-duty and recreational activities.

"Seven: Posyan serves as a logistics support centre for the Sami operations.

"Eight: Chinese and Iranian personnel are separated in all activities (duty and off duty) and Iranian participants are reluctant.

"What we don't know:

"One: how the research base works in detail.

"Two: who are the people involved in testing?

"Three: what harmful materials are stored on site?

"Four: what steps are being taken to make these weapons operational?"

Fawaz stared at the ground through Dave's analysis and interrupted his summary: "When I got involved in this mission, I had no idea about the extent of my father's personal role. I understand enough about him to realise he was not a career criminal but was forced by poverty to participate. He isn't some big ideological strategist, just a little guy trying to get along. Although it is clear his employees do as they are told, I'm pretty sure my mother and sister are innocent victims. I think he has underestimated the situation he is in and can't get out. The only thing he thinks about is the next deal."

"This is you pulling out, right?" Jack had always been nervous about Fawaz.

"On the contrary – this thing is so much bigger, so much worse and so… *personal* to me that I want you to know my commitment is total. I just want to make sure the innocents caught up in this don't suffer as a result."

"Nice speech, friend, but life's a bitch and the floor is littered with the dead who had good intentions." Jack favoured irony above sarcasm.

Anya nodded, but again Jo intervened to defend Fawaz.

"This is your place, your country; none of us understand it like you do. It's a good sign that you are choosing to share your feelings with us. Because of your inspiration I don't mind anyone here knowing I am between nervous and scared. I hope I am on the road to becoming excited. Like your dad, I feel this is a much bigger and more dangerous exercise than I realised. The only way I will get through this is to concentrate on what I have to do."

Rodg was always better in a tight situation when he was chewing. With no gum or cheroot, he made do with a piece of straw.

"I think you are worrying too much, *bokkie*. Those who swagger with guns tend to be poor at using them. The ones I've seen here so far are lightweights. Let's get the evidence on all this and we can piss off home."

Dave was quick to lift the moment. "Couldn't have put it better, mate. We are up to date and up to strength, which means we are ready to act."

There was only one person who could call Abdullo Alrakahthan to an immediate meeting, and that person's private secretary had just been on the phone. He had been heading back to Karaj from a viewing of a new water purification plant at Qarchak, south-east of the capital. It was sometime after five, and his limousine with blue-tinted windows was stuck in a jam off Highway 44. He tapped on the glass and spoke to his bodyguard. He gazed out at a taxi driver next to him. Like most of the occupants of neighbouring cars, the cabby tried to see who was inside, but the exterior lamination only offered a mirror image in return. Alrakahthan was tired, having spent most of the afternoon studying a plan to export a kit version of a new water purification plant to Turkmenistan.

It was essentially a good product built with technology developed at Tehran University, but it was still a bit of a Heath Robinson creation, with random parts added and taken away as its relative effectiveness was assessed. The final system had not been built in mass produced 'kit' form and so it was necessary to commission the components in order to test its assembly, prior to signing the deal. Although he was confident – after all, he had spent several weeks on it – this project had been filled with annoying glitches, which if they weren't resolved in the near future could put the whole venture in doubt. With a multi-million-dollar price tag and a projected margin of 65%, he concluded that failure was not an option in this case. His next meeting was due to be at the machine tools manufacturer, but this sudden appointment was getting in the way.

He stared out at the taxi driver, who had swapped playing with the beads on his rear-view mirror for a thorough examination of his right nostril with the digit he would have been better off using to keep his missus amused. He looked at the cabby carefully; he was now looking at his finger in wonder, as through he had discovered a gold nugget. Yes, his mind was wandering, and he was trying to anticipate his next new, hastily arranged meeting. Why had he been summoned? What was expected of him? Why now? Why was he stuck in this fucking jam? This last question was directed to his bodyguard, who was fiddling with the car's satnav and gesticulating to his driver. The indicator for a left turn came on and the car edged forward seeking to leave the main highway.

"Boss, it looks like there is a vehicle on fire up ahead – it's another protest about petrol prices. We're getting off the main road and will use a suburban route through to the palace. It should be OK as most of the traffic is coming out of town."

Alrakahthan nodded and picked up his monthly performance figures. He needed to make sure he had all the numbers in his head, in advance of the upcoming Alrakahthan Enterprises (AE) board meeting. This one was especially important as it would be the first to include a non-family director, Jamshid Turani. He was nervous: he had originally expected to demonstrate the power of the family's commercial assets as a means of pressuring Turani to perform. But, already, the boy from Bandar had landed Iran's biggest single rare earth export contract, almost single-handedly, and that alone made the figures look strong. Most of his businesses were proving robust in the face of growing global recessionary pressures but taxes and payments to state enterprises had, like the domestic petrol price, become more demanding. He was trying to skip through the analysis to understand why. On the positive side, most markets were performing well where open trading was allowed. The trade war between the US and China had already been felt in Japan and the European Union and was producing niches of opportunity, especially in semi-finished goods. His Dubai sales office had proved effective in rebranding and relabelling most Iranian-produced exports as being from third-party countries, especially fruit, but motor car components had been the best performer over the past quarter. The threat of electric cars, which used about 60% fewer parts, meant that would soon decline. Despite progress in areas such as component assembly and three-dimensional plastics printing, the big money the country needed was still in commodities. The oil trade was still subject to strangulation by Washington, but not so much with gas. AE's biggest collaboration to date had been the building of the Xerxes LNG pipeline between Quchan and Ashkabat in Turkmenistan, which would shortly contribute 750 billion USD in its first full year of operation. Privately financed through Qatar, with shared revenue for both host countries, it had been built on both sides of the border by their respective energy departments citing domestic needs, thus without attracting the attention of other nations.

AE's key role was to build the last kilometre across their borders, a critical contribution, delivering a major strategic asset in five years with a rentable value. A competing project, the so-called "Peace Pipeline" planned between Iran and Pakistan, hadn't got off the drawing board despite thirty years of planning.

As Alrakahthan was realising gas was a better investment than oil in the present market, he noted how the real value of the drugs trade was slipping owing to increased competition and oversupply. He had never been that interested in the business because there were too many people involved – too many greedy fuckwits taking their cut for doing very little, especially in Afghanistan. These days, drugs were for the little guys. He didn't mind helping them out from time to time, but really he had better things to do, like his modest but growing human resources businesses. That really interested him because this was a natural phenomenon. The world was a small place and people were becoming more mobile. Without much effort already there was a natural supply line across Asia. If the Iranian authorities played hardball, the supply lines and routes would just avoid them. People were just another logistic product. They didn't need much more care than freighting a load of fresh tomatoes, just more stop-off points. His people-movement activities were showing a month on month increase of about 300%, pretty good accepting he did not have to guarantee arrival at the end destination, just pass them on to the next country. All he had to do was move them across Iran faster than any other route. And what was it about Europe anyway? Britain, France and Germany were pretty fucked up themselves. Right-wing activists had not been so close to the levers of power in a generation. Could there be future business in taking these economic migrants back to where they came from? Time would tell. Organ harvesting also showed promise, although the trend showed costs were rising. There were still problems in transferring organs to recipients quickly enough and he would probably have to invest in a specialist hospital somewhere else in the Gulf in order to dominate that market. With more thought and focus this could move from 'below the line' or 'under the counter' into positive reputation territory, in the same way he had done with prosthetics, where 'Made in IR Iran' was starting to be recognised as a quality mark, ironically against the international market leader, Israel.

Yes, AE's affairs were in pretty sound order. He would be happy about discussing it all at his next appointment due in the coming hours and repeating his comments to his board in the coming days.

His bodyguard's comments about the traffic had proved largely correct and there was little doubt that the satnav had helped them to avoid the jam on the trunk road. It was always a challenge negotiating the traffic of the city centre and the inevitable frustrations of irate and tired drivers trying to get home. Amid this noisy confusion was the oasis of calm that was the Sa'dabad Complex, a microcosm of the history of Persia, set in 300 hectares, built by the Qajar and Pavlavi monarchs in downtown Shemiran. The Supreme Leader's official residence was one of eighteen palaces contained in a parkland setting, each paying witness to an era of the state's history. The political elite had never been comfortable with the term "palace" since the 1979 revolution, and the majority were now museums open to the public. However, their grandeur was inescapable, telling the casual visitor that this was the centre of a great civilisation – past and present.

Alrakahthan's car entered via the Zaferanie Gate, the entrance reserved for senior officials and those on government business. On arrival, he was met by the Supreme Leader's personal private secretary, and subjected to the perfunctory search, but not escorted to his private quarters as he had been expecting. Instead, he was escorted to the front of the White Palace. An imposing piece of architecture, the building could best be described as elegant, or understated. Although formerly the home of the late Shah, Mohammad Reza Pavlavi, many of the outward fixtures and fittings had been removed in keeping with its present status as the Mellat Museum. As he followed the private secretary, he became aware of a number of suited men wearing the standard government-issue collarless shirt starting to appear in different places in the manicured gardens. As the density of men increased, Alrakahthan knew he was getting closer to the man who had summoned him. Passing the statue of Arash the Archer, a grand suite of thirty steps of bleached marble led up to the portico of the palace. Standing in front of the central arch was a robed figure, with glasses and greying beard, crowned by a black turban-like *dulband*. The setting sun created a warm glow, softening the white of the building into a soft cream. Had the Supreme Leader not known Alrakahthan, it was exactly the pose that he would have wanted to be seen in by a visitor. Despite his years, an upright figure in an assertive stance against a background which spoke of imperial power. Alrakahthan climbed the steps two at a time, stopping before taking the final stride. The Supreme Leader held out his hand with a ruby signet ring and the visitor bowed his head and kissed it.

"Welcome, Abdullo – were you were surprised to meet me here instead of in my personal quarters? I heard you were in the vicinity. I thought it would be good for us to take a short walk before the chill of the evening sets in. Come…"

They walked down a ramp at the side of the portico and followed what looked like a newly-laid gravel path, secluded by yew hedges.

"I have something special to show you, brother."

Alrakahthan had known the Supreme Leader since his supermarket days, when he had been asked to distribute food parcels to the poor and needy in five Iranian cities. The venture proved so successful that it had become an annual event, extending to another twenty-five locations across the country. Despite regarding the Supreme Leader as a personal friend, he understood the discipline of protocol and remained silent until such time as he was asked for a response. The pathway was straight and at the end of it, appeared to be a greenhouse. As he got closer, he could see it was more besides – the slightly steamed windows of a temperature-controlled hothouse. How many of these were in Iran? It was one of the few luxuries missing from his own household. At the doorway was the obligatory suited guard, who, despite not being in military uniform, stood to attention and saluted before opening the door.

The Supreme Leader walked forward purposely, his guest in his wake.

"In all the time we have known each other, I am conscious that I have never shown you my favourite hobby. So here we are in one of the restricted parts of the Sa'dabad very few outsiders have ever seen. This is my personal nursery, where I grow one of the most beautiful flowers in the world sculpted by nature – the rose. There are over 300 species and many thousands of cultivars. As you can see, they differ in form – some are shrubs, others are climbers and these here are bred for trailing. In this shed, I can create the conditions to mimic the seasons to ensure I always have fresh buds to look forward to, with colours to suit my mood and fragrances which remind me of happy days. Just look around you."

It was a truly remarkable sight: roses as far as he could see – an explosion of colours mimicking the spectrum, but all coordinated by shade from white, through tones of cream and peach to pink and yellow, to gold, orange, crimson and red. They continued to walk slowly, pointing out some of his favourites.

"Iran is a great place for roses and rightly a symbol of our nation – they love the sun but the real secret of growing a truly majestic flower is in the mulching. And I have experimented too. I have something here which I believe to be a world first – a crossbred blue rose which many professional growers thought was impossible to achieve. The secret is delphinidin, an anthocyandin pigment, produced here in Iran. The Americans, of course, claim to have a variety called 'Applause', which I have over there, but it only gets a slow hand clap from me; as you can see, it lacks the depth of colour of my own. Most other *so-called* blue roses are fakes, dyed from white varieties. Yes, growing roses is a labour of love and requires patience and dedication to succeed. I often talk to them and they respond producing beautiful blooms. It is a truly great way of dealing with the strains of the day and this is a marvellous spot for reflection."

Although flattered by having an insight into the Supreme Leader's private world, he was still mystified about the timing of the audience, but knew it was better to display the patience the Supreme Leader had just referred to. Fortunately, he did not have long to wait.

His host turned and fixed him with a beady eye.

"I have brought you here to share some personal thoughts with you, my brother, in my own private place where our only audience, my roses, understand the power of discretion."

He tapped his ear and paused, as if to emphasise his point, before continuing to walk slowly through the nursery.

"I think, when we have met previously, we were in my library, where, when it comes to reading, most of my time is spent reflecting on the Holy Book. For me this is more than a daily duty; it is a fixed period of deep mindfulness which can't be interrupted. During this time, I seek guidance from the Prophet to direct my actions as head of state. Never has it been more important for me to safeguard this duty. I know you share my love of books, Abdullo, and so you, too, must have read Sun Tzu on the *Art of War* – all thirteen chapters of it. It may have been written in the fifth century BC, but is no less relevant now."

Alrakahthan nodded hesitantly.

"Well, if you have ever doubted it, today the Islamic Republic is at war, and I don't mean the skirmishes of Yemen, Syria or Iraq. I mean the global war of cultures, money and ideas instigated by the United States. War today, as we know, is no longer about military might but the struggle of ideologies. The world's biggest economy does not understand us and as a result we are seen as a threat to their legitimacy by our very existence. For people to feel threatened you need to give them something tangible – a fear they can relate to. In the last forty years that tangible threat has been expressed by conflicts between armies, invasions, civil disorders or more recently terrorism – the ultimate 'catch-all' concept to create that fear. Today the tools of fear are not guns or bombs but the control of currencies, credit and assets. Trade is the glue that holds all societies together – destroy it and they fall apart. Because we dare to live in our own way that does not conform to their idea of morals and values, we attract their wrath. *Their* argument is the opposite of our intention – *we sponsor 'terrorism'*, by providing aid to poor countries trying to feed their people; *we want to have control over our own 'clean carbon-*

free' power supplies including nuclear without making bombs, so we can grow our own economy; *'we want to promote our own faith and values to suppress democracy and free speech'*, so we can promote peace, wherever we are represented in the world. My regret is that we have failed as a government to be able to engage with the United States in a meaningful way. They continually attach preconditions to talking with us which they know we could never agree to. I have even sought dialogue through mediators in Europe to create a basis for talks, with no outcome. I have concluded that the US quite likes the concept of being an enemy of the Islamic Republic because, in their thinking, they feel it makes them look more legitimate. In other words, by concentrating on us as bad guys, people fail to notice their own shortcomings. I have to tell you, this deliberate policy of 'non-communication' will result in all their perceived fears coming true. We will support freedom fighters in spheres of US influence; we will pursue the development of a nuclear bomb, even if we have no need of it; and we will support autocracies where we find them; after all, I'm not sure these days if there are any genuine democratic societies in the world anyway. And all this is a race against time, as they seek to starve us into submission by sanctions first.

"Abdullo, you, of all people, have proved that sanctions don't always work. They are a licence for individuals and companies to trade 'under the counter' at great profit. There is really only one sanction that has worked, and it hit us hard: that is, our ability to sell our oil on international markets. We have offset the damage by increasing our refining capacity, but it is still difficult for us to recover our costs. It is a fact that, despite our resistance, we are becoming poorer, but I am determined that as a proud sovereign nation we will not be brought to heel by the US. We have to find our own way to maintain our economy and keep people in jobs and food. If we fail, the Great Satan rightly expects another revolution, but it is wrong to assume that any new government would pursue different policies that would benefit the aggressor."

The Supreme Leader drew a sharp breath.

"My apologies for the sermon – I know it's not Friday. There are few I can be so candid with and I have to make the most of the opportunity. This was not the reason I brought you here. Given all that I have said, you will know the Islamic Republic needs an insurance policy against collapse. That is why I have signed a comprehensive partnership agreement with China. Only China, and not the Russian Federation, has the necessary diverse resources and expertise to safeguard the economic security of the nation. Presently 30% of our exports are with them. My plan is to raise that to 50%. The plan comes with risks, creating an unhealthy dependency on them in the future. I don't like it and there are plenty who consider I am mortgaging not just our business but our culture to a nation whose only real incentive is to use us as a lever to replace the US as the world's economic powerhouse. Frankly, I hope the fact we can survive US sanctions may lead to a change in US policy where they reconsider us as a viable trade partner, allowing us to take back part of our economy from Chinese control. But that is not where we are now. We just have to grit our teeth and get on with it.

"I can tell you that, in order to get this strategy through, I have made enemies of some of my closest associates. They could never follow my logic of integrating the role of the executive presidency with my own position and demoting the president to the office of speaker. A 'power grab', they said and failed to understand the Islamic Republic's need for consistent decision-making and a clear line of authority.

"My position as Supreme Leader must mean what it says. It's conveniently forgotten that, from time to time, I too, am subject to an elective process just like them. The Speaker remains my deputy, Ravshan Jeylani, and my chief opponent, criticising me for 'tearing the heart out of the nation'. His assistant, our head of internal security, Sayeed Gharbieh, is leading a strategy to destabilise my position, so that Jeylani can succeed me without waiting for the next leadership election, two years from now. They

221

believe we don't need help from anyone to defeat US sanctions and are prepared to start a new Gulf war with the Saudis to force them out of our affairs and divert the attention of our people from rioting in the streets. They also dislike my policies of allowing a role for greater private enterprise in tackling sanctions, which they say is weakening the power of the state. They are mad; we cannot give the Americans an excuse to destroy our country and civilisation. My way of proving that sanctions cannot break the will of our nation is the strategy that will work in the end. Anyway, I have to accept they will stand against me. For now, their opposition is behind closed doors and I have them where I can see them. However, I am sure they are working to weaken me by destroying the apparatus of my power, bit by bit. I will deal with them in time, but, as one of my closest commercial advisers, you must understand you and your family and associates are in great danger. Go carefully, my friend."

The Supreme Leader was a skilled communicator who used significant pauses as a tool of active conversation. They had walked the full length of the nursery, which had conveniently brought them back to the door which they had entered. It was dusk; the duty guard had noticed their approach and opened the door.

The predicted chill was in the air.

"What do you think of my plan to make the rose the new symbol of our country?"

This was the signal his words were now in earshot.

"With your personal seal of approval, excellency, I am sure you will succeed."

The point was acknowledged by his guest.

"By the way, Abdullo, I think there is just time for you to complete your next move in our chess game."

In his private quarters, the Supreme Leader kept a chess room with nine large onyx chess sets neatly arranged with games at different stages of play. His favourite personal visitors would be allocated a numbered chess board and invited to play for a short period as part of their audience. Being invited to play was one of the highest personal accolades the Supreme Leader could bestow and those who were understood they were likely to be granted personal audiences in the future. Some games would take months and several visits to complete. Even in his own time, the Supreme Leader was punctual in all matters. The tour of the nursery had taken an hour, and chess would take the next hour – in time for the Supreme Leader to settle down to see the evening TV news, Al-Jazeera, BBC and CNN.

Abdullo's game was one of the slower ones, the present encounter coming up to six months. In that time, he had not been clear in his own strategy. Did he want to win or just look like he made a fight of it? His opponent considered himself to be a scholar of the game and had read many books on strategies, so he could not be certain how long he had been considering his next move. Was the Supreme Leader's chess hour serious or just an excuse for him to enjoy his favourite peaty malt with convivial company? Although Abdullo had access to many of the finer things in life, he had yet to acquire the same taste for the dram as his host. Still, this was a duty he had to perform, and he did it with all the style that befitted a man of his sophistication.

In the private quarters there were no signs of a family. The Supreme Leader never discussed the subject as it was regarded as a state secret. Abdullo had heard talk that he had two wives and six children. No wonder he was happiest on his own. Where they were and how he managed his private life was 'off limits' and, despite their friendship, Abdullo didn't expect that position to change.

The Supreme Leader led Alrakahthan into the anteroom, which his host had referred to as the Chess Room, and waved him to take a seat.

The room was intimate, considering it was in a palace, and was decorated with heavy beige-coloured velvet curtains and pelmets, flock wallpaper, wall lamps, bookcases and two 'Regency' armchairs, either side of a tiled fireplace and open, blazing wood fire. The ceilings had frescoes depicting scenes from Persian mythology, including the legendary encounter between Rostam, the most powerful of the Iranian paladins, and Esfandiar, a crown prince.

The Supreme Leader noticed Alrakahthan's gaze.

"There is much to learn from Rostam and Zoroastrianism today," he said. "We are in a battle between good and evil, as he was. In this scene, however, he ends up fighting the wrong enemy. Zahhak, shown over there, with the serpents growing out of his shoulders, was the real bad guy."

Now seated and looking to a side table next to the Supreme Leader, he noted a stack of strategy books that had clearly been laid out for reference – Chernev, Seirawan, Silman, Heisman and one or two more besides.

Seeing him eyeing the books, the Supreme Leader said, "You never struck me as a man intimidated by intellect – you shouldn't worry. Despite their brilliance, even Carlsen and Kasparov made errors; they just made sure their correctional moves were brilliant."

Whisky and *mezes* arrived on cut glass and silver plates.

Alrakahthan moved his bishop to rook three.

The Supreme Leader kept his eyes on the board and instinctively reached for his glass.

"Your quarterly contribution to state funds is strong, given the external pressures – oil and gas in particular. But I also have to be mindful of internal stability. We have 8.5 million people unemployed and many of them are destitute. Desperate people are dangerous and unpredictable. I need to contain the situation until the next election. I may need you to restart the programme of food parcels you masterminded for me and I need the fiscal headroom to allow you to do it. You must expect to overachieve in the months ahead. That means you must come up with higher volumes and new, secure trades. But you cannot rely on us to do your diligence for you. That is why we allow you to make your profits. Be careful of shortcuts – for example, your new trade in rare earth minerals may prove to be a problem. Did I tell you I have signed an extension to the new economic cooperation agreement with China? They want our rare earth business and complained about your man's deal with the Koreans. I suggest you regard that business as a test transaction for the future."

Alrakahthan's response was as cautious as his chess, the whisky warming his bones better than the open fire. Alrakahthan sent his bishop to put his opponent's king into check.

The Supreme Leader used his queen to take the bishop. The businessman then brought a pawn into play to buy some time.

"Excellency, you know we face daily headwinds in the market against sanctions. Oil sales are threatened primarily by the availability of ships, but the gas project Xerxes is now performing ahead of expectations and I have dedicated a member of my team to ensure it becomes a key element in our export strategy. Rare earths could be our third commodity export, but we are still investigating the extent of reserves and the market potential. I would suggest the most helpful way of managing this, given your agreement, is to transact in RMB, not US dollars, and build client relationships, where possible, other than China, so we can influence the price of future trades. As for the food parcels, let me propose an equitable financial solution that will not impact adversely on your reserves."

The Supreme Leader countered: "You must do what is necessary, but our Chinese friends must be reassured we are making progress, particularly in these early stages. My governor in Khoda Afrin is reporting our first two deals under the agreement, the transfer of the PLA base at Ibrahim Sami and the free port at Posyan, are running behind schedule. These two projects were set up as exemplars in a remote part of the country nobody cares about. If they go wrong, we can close them down quietly. But, at sixty billion US dollars, they are potentially strong earners, in themselves important contributions to our national GDP. They could provide us with the blueprint for future cooperation. I worry that one is being run by a civil servant and the other by a soldier.

We need someone on our side with strong commercial acumen. I want you to send one of your best people to review their business potential. Politically we need evidence that this type of 'below the counter' activity is profitable and, remember, get this right and we get to the real prize – three million Chinese tourists in the next five years. *Three million*... I don't need to tell you what that will do for the tourist industry – hotels, restaurants, logistics, currency... and jobs. It will bring us bang up to date and really get the nation's cash registers ringing."

"Excellency."

The Supreme Leader moved knight to bishop, two and one.

His personal business envoy knew it was time to step back, leave his host to the TV news and head home.

The game remained unresolved.

Jamshid had mixed feelings about his return to Karaj. To begin with, he had grown hugely in personal confidence. On the back of his oil and rare earth dealings he had already proved himself as one of the top traders in the country. He had found favour with his employer and his 'private' consultancy partners, had some serious money in the bank, and had started an exciting personal relationship. On the other hand, he had stumbled into a business that he had never planned to go into, with a family he didn't know much about and he was unsure who to trust.

It reminded him of the first time he had gone sailing solo as a child off Hormuz.

He remembered the thrill and adrenaline rush of his sail on his little Mirror boat, picking up its first gust of wind and the tiny craft careering off, skimming the gentle waves for what seemed a huge distance seaward, with him barely in control. Then the worry of remembering the hard work and uncertainty of trying to tack back against the breeze to the safety of the inshore waters.

Although he had enjoyed what many considered to be a middle-class upbringing, he had still to get accustomed to his new-found wealth. It had been Abdullo who had advised him if he wanted to be taken seriously in this new world of international commerce he had to look the part, so he had resolved to hire a different top marque each time he flew in to Tehran, as opposed to the workaday Toyotas he was used to. Today, he had decided to make an impression and arrived at the Alrakahthans' villa in a red Ferrari. Even the journey from the airport had been a bit scary as he came to terms with the power of the sports car. Fast and conspicuous, this was a vehicle which defied convention and the speed traps of the police. The memory of his last meeting with the local traffic cops was still fresh in his mind. This day, not only was the sun shining; traffic was light and the journey a breeze. The only thing missing was a beautiful woman to share the moment. That woman, now *his* woman, Mahta, was supervising the production line at a missile factory some 1,300 kilometres to the south. His choice of car proved to be right for the moment. Predictably, as the one person from outside the family attending, he was the last to arrive, parking next to Hanah's Mercedes, a Porsche Cayman, Maserati GranTurismo and Range Rover Overfinch. Plucking his jacket and laptop from the back seat, he skipped up the steps of the main door, passing his keys to the door attendant. Unlike his last visit, this time there was much tighter security, similar to that he had experienced a few hours earlier when he had taken the flight from Bandar. Emerging from the full-body scanner, he was disconcerted to find Abdullo there to greet him in person, while he struggled to hold on to his jacket, laptop and shoes. It was not the smooth arrival he had anticipated. It was friendly, nonetheless.

"You must forgive the additional security measures, Jamshid. I was reminded only the other day that life can be unpredictable, as it is fragile, so we must all take extra care. Welcome, once again, to my home. Please come through and join the others; tea is about to be served."

Jamshid was also apprehensive about his initial introductions to the rest of the Alrakahthan clan. Not so much with Hanah, for that matter, but his wife and his son. He entered the same imposing but anonymous room where he had dined with Hanah weeks previously and there she was again, this time in a teal-coloured, figure-hugging single alpaca dress with navy *hijab*. She moved towards him and offered her arms to accept a light kiss of greeting on either cheek.

"Great to see you. You remember my mother, Bahar?"

"How could I forget?" Jamshid said to himself. But the truth was that the last time they met, in his mother's tea house, he had other things on his mind and not paid much attention to her.

Maybe it was because of the occasion or possibly for her husband's benefit, she looked more attractive and perhaps a little younger than he recalled. Maybe it was the auburn hair tied back but unscarved. Pale-skinned, brown-eyed and freckled, she wore a dark business suit with a "hussar-style" gold-braid jacket – clearly a power dresser, offering a sense of what her daughter may look like twenty years into the future.

"Sure. *As salam aleykum.*" He tried to avoid eye contact.

"*Mahaba*, Jamshid. I didn't think we would meet again so soon."

He had been tempted to respond "neither did I" but started to stumble over another apology.

"I am truly…"

Mrs Alrakahthan cut across him.

"I think enough has been said and done now. It gave me an opportunity to get to know your mother better and to understand more about your character."

It was a cool reception, but perhaps better than he had expected. What did unnerve him was Hanah's next introduction.

"This is my brother, Hasan. He is a lawyer and accountant and appraises all our commercial activities. He had the opportunity to attend Harvard Business School a couple of years back. We are lucky to have him home."

For some reason Jamshid had got into his head that Hasan, as the younger child, was a teenager, but what stood before him was a lightly bearded, light brown-skinned man in a sky-blue business suit and white open-necked shirt. For one so young (he must have been five years Jamshid's junior), he had developed a furrowed brow.

They exchanged greetings and Abdullo gestured for all to sit at the oval table, where he sat at the head, males to the right, females to the left. At the far end of the table was a person who had not been introduced. Jamshid took this to be a secretary who was tapping away at a laptop, seemingly disconnected from the movements and activities of others in the room.

It was interesting for Jamshid to note here was a family gathering, yet it was formally constituted, like any other business meeting. The 'chair' looked in his element, the ultimate smart but casual look in shirtsleeves and gold cufflinks. He was immaculately groomed, with a deeply black, swept-back receding hair line, created with the benefit of an expensive German hair tonic.

Tea and baklava followed.

Alrakahthan sat forward assertively, staring over half-rimmed gold-framed glasses.

"This constitutes the formal monthly board meeting of Alrakahthan Enterprises. At the outset I would like to welcome our newest and first non-family director, Jamshid Turani. More about him later. You will have seen the minutes of the last meeting and I assume we are all happy before we proceed?"

There was silence.

"Matters arising. Divisional reports, P&L, cash balances, state contributions up 32%. Excellent performances against challenging market conditions. Well done everybody. Comments? Bahar?"

"Yes, Chair. The performance of the fruit production relabelling and distribution has proved a strong anchor for us over several years now and our increased capacity has helped us to move into the valuable Western European markets. Nuts, dates and pomegranates are all category leaders. Through Dubai we have signed a new distribution agreement for Europe with Shamrock Commodities of Ireland, which should contribute another 20% on the bottom line by the end of the present fiscal. Despite religious restrictions, our Iranian sisters are spending more on make-up, for use in social situations in the home, than ever before and we are extending online availability. However, we also had some teething problems with our new cosmetics plant at Rasht, with some of our own preparations based on chemical analysis of the French proprietary brands causing allergic reactions on certain core skin types. We had to destroy fifty lines of tribute products, which caused market delays in South East Asia, but I'm pretty sure we are now over the worst. Prosthetics have just landed its biggest order for legs from Ukraine and we have opened an online business for Africa in Lagos."

"Hanah, anything to add to your paper on Xerxes?"

"Not really. This is possibly the best performing business we have ever developed. Our 750-billion-dollar target is very close to being realised. Our friends in Turkmen think they can really open up central Asia for us, starting with Uzbekistan, where the energy requirement is most pressing. I have met their Chinese partners. So far, to avoid attracting attention, I have stayed clear of their negotiations, but I had set them a target figure as a marker price."

"Are you sure the Americans are not on to it?"

"I think we should be OK, provided we only raise capacity in small steps and keep the Chinese in the background. Anything too big will draw attention."

"This is a good point to bring Jamshid into the conversation. You all know who Jamshid is and what he does, and in the three weeks since joining us he has landed our first major rare earth export with South Korea. This is above my initial expectation. The value of this trade makes it the third most important export category behind oil and gas and at the moment we have been able to make a shipment outside the sanctions regime. How did you do it, Jamshid?"

"The trick has been to export 'as mined' ore extracts, so the weight and value of its constituent parts cannot easily be identified. That said, in this raw form, it is a relatively heavy cargo to move and only certain ships can carry it. I am talking with a particular European-based bulk carrier about further transmissions and, subject to Hanah's confirmation, I think I can see my way to another 600,000 tonnes – that is, before we get to know the scale of reserves in the Arasbaran Protected Zone, presently accredited as a world environmental asset by UNESCO. If we end up going in there, we will have to get the government to redefine its boundaries and spend significant sums to mask extraction activities. That's why we really have to be accurate in our test methodologies."

"And I know you will be helping us to drain the country's oil reserves as well," Alrakahthan added.

"Hopefully yes, if I can identify the right trades to make."

"Hanah – you wish to say something?"

"Jamshid has got off to a great start but still needs to learn about our operating standards and methods. It's too early to assess his effectiveness."

This coded remark took Jamshid visibly by surprise. He looked at Alrakahthan, but the chair seemed to ignore the remark altogether and carried on.

"Thank you. Anything to add, Hasan?"

So far, he had learned that Alrakahthan's wife seemed to be running the fruits and a cosmetics business, Hanah ran the Project Xerxes gas pipeline, and he was looking to do oil and mineral deals, so what of Hasan?

"Yes, as you asked me to do, I have been looking at the strategic growth opportunities for our business and whether we should continue some of our 'under the counter' operations. You have a copy of my report. The key points are these. The state and the People's Republic of China have concluded a major trade agreement which cuts across some of our peripheral trading activities, having the effect of cutting some margins and making

231

other ventures unprofitable. The big casualty is defence – I know how much time you have given it, Dad, but it's too political in the long run. We could only play on the sidelines, moving out old stock the government doesn't want. Human transplants are difficult to do from a logistical point of view. We cannot get organs to market quick enough. We either need to link our existing business to a dedicated hospital, which is a considerable undertaking, or get out as the fees are just not competitive. People trafficking – again, quite fee-intensive and time-consuming – and drugs – the same thing. I suggest, Dad, we do the Silkworm Project and step back. I think the Chinese will want to take over organ harvesting and both the people and drugs operations will be taken over by local outfits with lower overheads than us. You are right to ask where we should direct our efforts. I am looking at two major growth areas at the moment – chemicals and tourism. I'm not sure yet what is our best route in and how we sustain ourselves in the longer term but will try to report back in the next quarter."

"It's a good report, Hasan; you raise some important issues which I want to think about. But the general direction of travel is positive. We are trusted commercial partners of the government, so it is important we stay in line with the policy objectives of the Supreme Leader. We need to steer clear of matters that would be regarded as controversial, so personally we need to limit our 'under the counter' activities to those which are low risk, high margin, such as the fruits, energy and minerals businesses. Reputationally, we need to show we are serious international players – people trafficking, drugs and small arms are *pisspot* businesses which we should leave to little guys with big egos."

He continued: "We need to position ourselves much better on the Chinese thing. I have been asked to review the governments' first two collaboration ventures in Khoda Afrin Prefecture at *er…*" He peered at his notes, "Ibrahim Sami and Posyan."

Hasan interrupted him.

"I've had a voice message from the son of a guy up there, al-Fouadi, asking for us to procure prefabricated accommodation for sixty people, a couple of days ago. My practice helped him to set up a property development business a year back and I hadn't heard from him since."

"That's useful. You'd better get on it. Source the material and sort out the payment, but don't get distracted. Hanah, you have some capacity, go up there and see what's going on. You have better experience of dealing with the Chinese. Take Jamshid with you."

It was all very well Alrakahthan laying down the law, telling Jamshid to go running up to the other end of the country 'at the drop of a hat', but his new shadow boss seemed to have a good understanding of his availability.

"Tell your bosses the government have awarded you a sabbatical to study advanced business strategies as a reward for your recent oil deals. It will be sanctioned by the Energy Department in Tehran and you will be seconded to me. I will sort out the paperwork – you concentrate on helping Hanah."

Hanah's response was equally swift: "I don't want to go up there until Hasan has procured the prefabs and that could take a couple of days. If you need to get back to Bandar, go now. I will call you back when we're ready to move."

ELEVEN

DAVE HAD BEEN REVIEWING plans to get into the Ibrahim Sami compound. He was still worried that he didn't have all the information he wanted ahead of the operation.

"The real problems are, firstly, we only have a sketchy idea about what is going on there and secondly, no information other than our own observations about the layout of the site. Much of the facility is subterranean anyway. Time is short. There really is no other choice than to get somebody in there who knows what they're looking at.

"Gul and Jo, I want you to go in and take a look around; take Rodg with you. He can look after you if things go tits up. The entertainment truck will be down from the compound around 23.30 and back to collect at approximately 02.30. That will be your ticket in and out. Rest of us need to be around to meet and greet in civvies, please – Anya, Jack, me and Fawaz. We need to be ready by 23.00."

Gul was not an emotional man. He knew such thoughts were destructive and now the need for clarity was critical. He spent the next hour deep in conversation with Dave, Jo and Rodg, anticipating each stage of the operation, before changing into their assault suits and checking their guns and ammunition. They slipped out of the back entrance of the barn with cameras attached to their helmets. Fawaz and Jack headed to the hotel foyer, close to the Chinese restaurant.

It was nearly twenty minutes to midnight before the truck and its cargo of off-duty Chinese servicemen and women arrived. Noisily disembarking, they made their way through the hotel foyer to the stairs to the Chinese restaurant. The atmosphere was starting to build with the moronic thud of house music in the background and trays of drinks ready to be consumed. Casually, from a distance in the foyer, Jack counted them in – twenty-four men and six women. Outside, the driver and one duty soldier in fatigues making sure all their passengers arrived in the right place. PLA soldiers on duty were not allowed to carry automatic weapons off site and so the two who sat upfront on the truck had pistols in holsters only. Importantly, as Jack looked at them, they looked bored, slightly envious of the fact they were not scheduled to join the fun of their compatriots. They used the short lull before their return to share a cigarette outside and were talking in lowered tones. As they finished their break, the passenger guard went to the rear to check the tailgate and walked into Gul. He wasn't going to remember anything else as the Uighur calmly knocked him out with a single blow of extreme force. The driver waited a minute and couldn't hear sounds from the back. He called to his colleague.

"Hey, Li – stop fucking about, we need to get back."

The response came back in Mandarin. "The tailgate is jammed; give me a hand, will you?"

The driver leaped down from the cab, muttering under his breath, and walked into the shadows around the back of the vehicle. He too was met with the irresistible force of the Uighur but this time, despite being stunned, staggered to his feet, just in time to receive a knockout blow on the side of his neck from the butt of a Makarov wielded by Rodg. His victim's closing grunt drowned out by the increasing noise from the restaurant. Both bodies were bound, gagged and cuffed by the South African and were deftly pulled into the back of the truck. Two of their assailants disarmed them of their pistols and climbed into the cab, putting on their stolen flak jackets. Gul did the driving, with Jo wearing the driver's camouflaged baseball cap pulled low; Rodg was in the back.

The truck engine roared into life. Gul looked at Jo and smiled as he reached for the handbrake and gear stick.

"Glad that's over; this was the bit I was most worried about."

It was only a ten-minute drive to the compound from the centre of town and only a short distance to travel without the benefit of streetlight. Turning off the Ashelqu road, the blanket of trees seemed to enhance the dark of the night before.

In the distance, the floodlighting of the base came into view.

At Rodg's advice, Gul drove steadily at around 25kph as he approached the main gate. The soldiers on duty were expecting the truck and scarcely bothered to look at the driver or his mate before opening the gate and letting them through. Rodg peered forward into the cab.

"Keep on the perimeter road anti-clockwise. You'll see another truck like this. Park up next to it."

That done, the engine was switched off.

"Leave the key in the ignition, Bud; we know where to come if we have to go quickly."

Gul and Jo removed the flak jackets, putting them on the floor of the front passenger seat.

"How are the two in the back?" Jo asked.

"They'll be quiet for a couple of hours. Thought I'd put a reverse balaclava on them to keep them warm. Now see the building to the left? Give that a miss because I'm pretty sure that's the staff areas and dormitories. I think we should go into the building over there. That's the one that seems to be where most deliveries go to."

The three ran towards the entrance to the right, running either side of the doorway. Looking through the glass door there was a lift with a sign saying "Goods In". Pressing the call button, they watched as the lights showed the impending arrival. Rodg stood ready with the Makarov. The lift was empty. Inside was a helpful inventory of services. 'Administration', 'Biolabs 1, 2, 3 & 4', 'Test Observation Area' and 'Holding Zone'. Jo chose 'Biolab 1' from the menu and the lift descended. The door opened on to a well-lit foyer, together with a big warning sign in black-and-yellow hatching, with the infectious disease symbol and graphic personal safety images, next to a wall-mounted phone. A large steel door, with a security card swipe release lock was directly ahead. With no prospect of moving forward, their first thought had been to return, but that was the point at which events took their own course.

At that moment the door opened, and a startled woman dressed in a white lab coat and face mask came through in front of them. She gasped in shock as she was grabbed firmly by Rodg, Gul talking in a staged whisper:

"Be quiet. We mean you no harm. Just answer our questions and we'll let you go." Gul knew as he was speaking that was unlikely, but it was just the way it came out. "What is this place? What happens here? What do you do?"

The nurse or laboratory technician was in shock and clearly petrified to come across intruders who didn't seem to know where they were. Her eyes were wide and Rodg kept his hand on her mouth, expecting her to scream.

"I think we'd better go back in the lift and conduct the conversation upstairs," he said.

They returned to the surface in the lit portico next to the lift. All was quiet at this hour, but Gul kept watch. Jo had the questions: "This is a secret laboratory where we make experiments with diseases and chemicals to make weapons," the distraught woman said, trying to control her rising hysteria. "We make phials of diseases to stockpile as weapons. Here we test, store and export stocks to take home."

"Why aren't you doing this at home?"

"These materials are very dangerous and if something goes wrong we would prefer it to be somewhere else. Besides, when we go home, we say we were on national service overseas. If my family and friends knew where I had been working, they would banish me for good. Also, a lot of people have died managing these materials. If people die here, it is easier for the authorities to explain we died on active service."

"You don't seem to be wearing any protective clothing."

"That is because I am not working in the production area, which is the other side of the base. This side is really administration and is the low risk zone."

"What materials are you dealing with here?" Gul asked.

"On the chemical side, mostly sarin and phosphates and the biological side mainly anthrax and smallpox. Much of our work is not discovering new agents but looking at how to produce concentrates and methods of delivery. To do this we have to use live experiments."

"What are those?" Gul guessed the response.

"The only way we can test effectiveness is to expose individuals to the agents and observe the results in terms of how long they take to become effective and what symptoms they display. This is important as we are also trying to discover antidotes and to put these into production."

"Who are you experimenting on?" He tried to hide his rising anger.

"We have a supply of people made available to us by the Iranian authorities. These are criminals. We are told that if they didn't come to us they would face the gallows. We get them delivered here from a local prison when we ask for them. Once they are infected there is no possibility of them leaving here. Either they die from their symptoms or, in exceptional cases where they survive, we kill them."

"What happens to the bodies?"

Jo took over the questioning, understanding what Gul needed to know, but could see him starting to display the emotion he had been so devoid of since his arrival.

"They are normally disposed of as part of the fuel to provide energy for the base, but this too must be done with care as we have to monitor all discharges to ensure spores from the affected do not get into the atmosphere. We had just such an alert last month when two of our soldiers contracted disease without known contact with our experiments. That is one of the reasons why all staff are rotated every six weeks. I have heard there are also some doctors here who use our operating theatres to do special operations."

"Special operations?"

"I have not seen it but one of the girls in my dorm works for one of the doctors here to do transplants, mainly livers but sometimes bigger things like hearts. There was a joke going around a couple of weeks ago, when we had a special pork banquet at the restaurant in the local town, that the heart of the pig was brought here and put into a man, but I don't know if it is true."

"What is your job?"

"I am a laboratory analyst. My job is to monitor the reproduction of diseased cells when treated by recovery agents."

"Does Iran have anything to do with the base?"

"I don't think so. They started off the work here, but we took it over because they had some trouble with controlling discharges. My bosses think the Iranians are lazy and stupid and do not respect the science they're dealing with."

"How long are you going to be here?"

"Just another two weeks. Then I can go home to my family in Xi'an."

"How did you get here?"

"We flew to an airbase nearby and came here by coach. We sleep in dormitories and eat in one canteen and we get a night out in the town once a week if we want it. It's the only chance of getting time with a guy. You know?"

"What is your name?"

"Amy Fong."

"OK, Amy. We are trying to see this base closed without fighting. To do this we need evidence of what is going on here. Will you help us?"

"Who are you? Americans? Russians?"

"We are an international charity with people all over the world. Loyal people committed to living in harmony and peace. If you help us, we will ensure the United Nations gets to know about this, which may help to close it down."

"I do worry about what will happen to us as a result of being here. Already I have seen much death. If you can stop the killing and keep me out of trouble, I will help, but you must understand, everybody here is really scared."

"We need to get a map of the facility here. Can you draw it?"

"No, no, it will take time. This place is very big and we are not allowed to go into any other block, apart from the place we work."

"So if you had a couple of days could you bring this to us? We could meet you in the town in the lobby by the Silk Road restaurant."

"My night off is next Tuesday. I will bring it then."

Gul glared at Rodg. Although he had let her speak, he was still restraining Amy firmly, hanging on her words along with the others. He relaxed his grip as though handling a porcelain vase.

Jo took both her hands and looked her in the eye.

"You have been brave talking to us. Thank you. I will see you at the hotel lobby on Tuesday night. Don't worry – I will come and find you."

He smiled and squeezed her hands reassuringly.

Rodg called the lift and preset the button for the basement. The doors closed and the three sprinted to the relative safety of the shadows behind the parked vehicles.

"How long have we got before she blabs? What do you make of that?" Rodg asked in a stage whisper.

"I saw the look in her eyes. She is too scared for herself to tell anyone. I thought her answers were pretty good," Jo replied. "We got a lot out of her and we have it on the headcam."

"It's not enough," countered Gul.

"We need data – names, times, dates, tissue samples."

"Are you mad?" Rodg said. "We can't carry that stuff – we become ticking bombs ourselves."

"Not if we carry the items in appropriate containers. What do you think they're doing? They must be moving consignments when they move people."

Gul checked the time. They had half an hour before they were due to return to pick up the off-duty soldiers back in town. Jo and Gul donned the Chinese flak jackets once more.

"Time to start to get our friends in the back ready for their return to the real world," said Rodg, pulling on his balaclava and pulling a pair of knuckledusters out of his pocket before clambering into the back. "Remember, park as close to the exact spot as the previous driver had done, back facing inwards. Keep the keys in the ignition. Get out slowly and, Gul, you wait and light a cigarette while Jo brings their pistols out of the glovebox and comes straight to the back of the truck. Then put the pistols in the pockets of the jacket and throw it and the cap into the back. Gul, count to ten once you've heard Jo, and do the same with your jacket. When you have dumped them, stay in the shadows and work yourself back to the barn, using the back entrance."

"What about you?" said Jo.

"Don't wait for me. I have a little cosmetic fieldcraft to do before I get back."

Jo looked at Gul, "What's he doing?"

"Not much – at least not until we are out of these gates," the Uighur replied grimly.

Exiting proved to be no more of a formality than the arrival had been. The truck was the same; the driver had the same soft

Mongol features. A casual smile and wave, the sidekick nodding off under the camouflage baseball cap. No need to get involved.

Rodg waited while they passed the external gate to the compound and used the tone of the gear change as his queue to get to work.

He had been impressed with Gul's actions at putting both men down. They were still out concussed, but their vital signs were OK. Using a pocket torch, he looked at their faces and hands. Neither had the requisite bruises and cuts. Both carried watches on their left wrists and, as right handers, he closed their hands to check the width of their fists before hitting their knuckles with the butt of his Makarov a couple of times to draw blood. Then he lifted their reversed balaclavas and gently removed the mouth seals, being careful to avoid any chafing of their skin. Faces upturned towards the sky, torch in mouth, he used the knuckleduster on each of them to leave severe bruising and cuts with just two blows each, swearing as the truck turned the corner, causing him to miss with his last blow and hit the floor. With one head damaged, just above the left eyebrow and the other on the right cheek, they now looked convincing as the victims of a brawl.

Gul and Jo followed instructions in Ibrahim Sami, leaving Rodg to replace their pistols and jackets, first ensuring each had some of the blood stains of the other.

The truck had now been abandoned and he could hear the sound of high spirits coming from the restaurant. It was time for the finishing touches to the bodies. Reaching into his pocket, he pulled out a small flask of arak given to him by Fawaz. Cradling each, he opened their mouths to pour the fiery liquid in and, after all he had done, this was the action that stirred them into life. Both were now coughing and spluttering as the liquid burned its way to their stomachs, but clearly had no idea of where they were and what was going on.

Rodg picked up the first body like a sack of coal and jumped down from the back, dropping his shoulder to let the body fall awkwardly forward into the undergrowth at the back. Time was now running out, so when jumping back down with the second body he carried it a couple of metres further on before dumping it, then diving himself for the cover of the undergrowth. Typically, his efforts resulted in him landing in a gorse bush, providing cuts and scratches, part of the same injury he had sought to recreate on the other bodies. He chose to lie completely still as there were now raised voices coming from above his location.

Swearing to himself, he wondered whether he had been seen, but knew if he made a run for it now he would definitely be spotted. The raised voices were indistinct, but he took them to be separate languages, Farsi and Mandarin, and not just from one or two but a group – maybe six or more, as far as he could tell. Had Rodg looked up, he would have seen one of the passengers from the bus being thrown out of a fire escape, but he certainly heard the shriek of a woman. He took his chance to roll further out of range of casual sight into the darkness and far enough away to get clear. He would have been amazed and proud of the actions of one of his colleagues, had he been present in the Chinese restaurant in the preceding hours.

Fawaz and Jack, and Dave and Anya had spent different parts of the evening at the hotel. The first pair had arrived in time to witness the arrival of the Chinese party and to check no one in the hotel had reason to go out to the bus before Gul, Jo and Rodg took control. Once they saw the evening's events getting under way, they had started to leave but were caught unawares making their exit. Fawaz's sister, Shimina, had arrived with one of her girlfriends and immediately took an interest in Jack. Despite Fawaz's best efforts, Shimina attached herself to them, resulting in the quartet going to the cinema. Fawaz's stress was convincing his sister of Jack's deafness, allowing him to interpret answers to questions she asked. Dave had an entirely different experience. His contribution had been to take a Chinese meal later on with Anya, and they were one of the few non-Chinese couples on the premises. He had been surprised how the new recruit had smartened herself for the occasion, considering she was living out of a bag like the rest of them. In black trousers, make-up and loose black hair, she wore a sheer mauve blouse and little else. From a positive perspective, it was true that the standard of the food was authentic: a relief to Dave, who had what he thought was duck in a sweet and sour sauce. Anya settled for a bowl of noodles, but what had happened after they had eaten was the bit that took him by surprise. Just after two in the morning, with the food service finished and other guests departed, the floor was cleared for dancing. Anya decided she wanted to dance and had suddenly left Dave at the table and joined the group of Chinese men, who wanted to get off with the small group of girls from the base. Anya moved into the middle of the group and targeted one of the men. At first, he looked embarrassed, but then took an interest watching her sweating, gyrating body, thinking she was a prostitute hitting on him. Having danced closely and getting him under her spell for what seemed like an eternity, she then went to a nearby table a picked up another man for the same treatment. It didn't take her first choice long to realise he was in a competition where there could only be one winner. Pushing the group of Chinese girls out of the way, he moved in, knocking his perceived rival away, and then that was it – blows were exchanged. Drinks, glasses, chopsticks, then heavier items – plates, table flower vases, bottles, ash trays and more – became projectiles. The Chinese girls started screaming, amid the din of destruction, running to the balcony at the back, followed by the melee of Chinese men. Ironically, the DJ had put on a lengthy disco rap with a fast beat, which he evidently thought would be a great accompaniment to the impromptu choreography. Two staff grabbed the till and started barricading themselves in the kitchen. By this time, Anya coolly walked over to Dave, taking his hand and walking purposefully towards the elevator. Behind her, the fighting mob first succeeded in throwing one of their number off the open balcony at the back, with others rushing down the steps to continue their battle, right next to the truck – their transport home for the night. As Dave and Anya walked purposefully in the other direction, they first heard shouts, before half a dozen Revolutionary Guards with assault rifles ran towards the scene. The couple continued their steady pace away and into the shadows with the sound of shots ringing in their ears. Dave became conscious of the closeness of his colleague and the scent of her body in the chill of the night.

There was a mood of celebration on the mezzanine in the al-Fouadi's number three barn. The first incursion into the target compound had been completed successfully without death, compromise or serious injury. It was Rodg who had been the first to congratulate Dave.

"A classic soldier's diversionary tactic you pulled off there, gaffer, and without a mark on you. I can tell you I was wondering what to do with 'Pinky' and 'Perky' on the way back. Thought I might have to drag them off somewhere in the woods, but you really did me a favour and your timing was spot on."

It was the serious-looking Anya who started, breaking out into a brief smile. "It was nothing. I knew you had to run to time, so we started fifteen minutes ahead of your schedule."

Dave took a more analytical approach.

"It was a good step forward and we were probably not likely to have achieved more. But the headcam stuff is not definitive evidence, as Gul knows. We need data and must know where to find it. It seems Jo has the best relationship with this girl, Amy Fong, and we need to concentrate on making that connection work. Despite what she says, we cannot know she will be successful in getting leave on Tuesday, so we must be ready to meet her any night from then onwards. We must also be clear we have a number of handicaps now. Firstly, Gul, it is certain they must have camera monitoring on the gate and will have facial recognition technology available. They might be able to run a trace on you. Secondly, there was security monitoring at the restaurant and, although we sat at a table below the main camera position, there will be some footage of the dancing and fighting, so me and Anya will be on there somewhere. And then there's you at the cinema, Jack..." He paused. "We'll have to wait to speak to Fawaz about that, so in the meantime I will try to get in touch with Gil so we can get the headcam stuff downloaded and out."

Breakfast in the al-Fouadi household was designed to allow the family to get together, and talk about their plans for the day, especially when Hafiz was home, but that morning circumstances dictated an unexpected change of plan. He had already been out to see his wrecked restaurant and had supervised Hanif boarding up the door. Fortunately, nothing outside had been damaged and, temporarily, it would be possible for hotel guests to eat meals in the foyer while the premises was closed.

He walked in through the front door, mobile clasped to his ear, talking with Jafar, the builder, and went straight to the table. Dilshad was already in the dining room, earlier than usual, as she had an early start in order to visit her sister in Hamadan, having just finished packing clothes and presents for the trip. Shimina was there too, especially to see her mother and to share the news about going to the cinema the previous evening. Fawaz was the last to arrive, immediately after his father, but he had his own plan to see his old schoolfriend Kolani, the carpet merchant in Ashelqu. Hafiz had expected to visit the sheep sales at Ahar that day but that was all cancelled now. A casual observer of the scene might have wondered whether it was Hafiz visiting the chaos or the chaos was following him, as he shouted and gesticulated at the phone or anyone else who happened to be in front of him or even in sight.

"Seven hundred and fifty thousand rials... *for fuck's sake!* Who are you kidding? Do you think I'm made of money? I've got a family to feed and workers to pay and you can't do it before next Wednesday? That's a week's worth of wages. Shall I tell my staff there's no wages until you've done your job? I expect they'll organise a riot round at your house, then you'll know how I feel... No, I'm not... OK, if you want, take it as a threat!"

He threw his phone onto a couch on the other side of the room.

It was instructive for Fawaz. He had never witnessed his father in such a rage.

He and Shimina were quiet.

Dilshad went to him and put her hands on his arm.

"You can make it right, my love. I heard you say earlier it's just redecorating and some new bits and pieces for the tables."

Hafiz shook the temper out of himself.

"I know, I know. It's the principle of the thing!"

There was a knocking at the door and Khalifa appeared.

"Sir, there is the Chinese officer at the door."

Major Ho did not wait for a lengthier introduction. He walked past the housekeeper into the dining room.

"Honourable Mr Hafiz, please excuse this unannounced visit, but I felt I had to come immediately to offer my sincere and personal apologies for the unruly actions of my staff last night. I have heard some accounts of the disturbance and, apart from damage to your property, I understand no other people were caught up in the trouble. My men have brought shame on our nation. All those present have been reprimanded and their leave withdrawn until further notice. The driver and his assistant who were on duty have been arrested and charged with negligence. They will face court martial and re-education on their return. I am on my way to visit Colonel Rahman to express my thanks for the Iranian Guards' help in cleaning up and alerting us to come and collect our truck and personnel. Finally, I have authorised a task force of ten people plus materials from the base to make good all damage caused within the next twenty-four hours. It will be put back to the standard it was before. One of my sergeants and team will be at the restaurant presently. Thank you and good day."

The soldier saluted and nodded to the family before departing.

"All's well that ends well," said Fawaz after the officer had left. "Perhaps we can all calm down and enjoy some breakfast. I'll come with you if you like, Dad, and meet these military workers who are going to set things right."

"Thank you, son. I would appreciate that. I've never had to deal with a situation like this before."

"How did it start?"

"Some of the guys started fighting over some woman who was with one of our other guests. Mr Choi, the manager, said she wasn't Chinese, but she was alluring. He'd not seen her before but would certainly recognise her if he saw her again."

"So, the Chinese guys were fighting over an *alluring* Iranian woman? Weird!"

Shimina glared at the brother.

"How did it finish?" Fawaz asked.

"In the end, the Revolutionary Guards from the duty guard post came down from the bus park and fired a few rounds in the air. They soon stopped fighting and sat on the ground waiting to be collected."

"What was that about their driver?"

"God knows. I heard the duty soldiers joined the fray. Apparently, they both got badly battered. Our guys found one of them slumped in a bush three metres away. They nearly missed him when they were cleaning up."

Hafiz picked up his coffee and headed for his study, prompting Shimina to change the subject.

"Anyway, Mum, I've got something much more interesting to tell you about. I'm surprised Fawaz hasn't told you about my dishy date at the cinema."

Shimina's mother reacted predictably to her daughter's baiting.

"What on earth do you mean? Fawaz, I thought you were looking after your sister."

Fawaz shook his head and buttered a bread roll.

"Well, I went down to the foyer last night with my friend Shadi for a milkshake and some of that yummy chocolate cake they do. Who is there having a beer? Your son. And who is he with? A really fit bloke I met on a bus the other day in Posyan at the Pomegranate Festival. I know he likes pomegranate cake, but he looked at me, you know, in *that* way. Can you believe it? He's young and quite light-coloured for one of us, with brown hair and this wild, sexy beard with a hint of ginger."

She started to giggle and so did Dilshad, until she realised Fawaz was watching.

"It turns out Fawaz knew this guy from the army and he went deaf by getting too close to explosive shells he was firing in Syria – or was it Yemen? I can't remember... *Anyway*, he has big blue eyes and can only talk with sign language that Fawaz taught him. Isn't that right, Faz?"

Fawaz had a mouthful of roll but made some gestures ending with one finger to his lips.

"Well, I thought I'd try and chat him up, only, according to Faz, he didn't want to talk, so I made Faz take us to see that film, *The Beginning*. Is it boring or what? I thought it was a love story, but is about a divorce. Apparently, it's won all these international awards and is one of our most famous movies. Well, if that is so, what does the world think of us Iranians? We're depicted as being bland, dutiful and dull. Well that's not me. I don't want to grow up like that. I want to wear lipstick, share my selfies on Snapchat and go dancing, not stay in reading."

"You must be careful with social media, darling," her mother admonished. "It's not just your friends who take an interest. You never know who is looking at your posts. I have heard the *Gasht-e Ershad* morality police are taking a particular interest in pictures of young women."

"That says more about them than me. What's the point in dressing up just to stay home? I want other people to see me as I want to be seen, not wearing a black blanket. *Anyway*, back to this boy. Did I tell you he has a beautiful smile? And his name is Parviz – which means lucky. Lucky he's found me! Apparently, he has just moved to Ashelqu, so guess where I'm going for my next night out? Hey, Faz, is there anywhere to hang out up there?"

Jamshid had taken the first available flight back to Bandar. Going home to check the authorisation for his sabbatical was uppermost in his mind. He remembered clearly what Alrakahthan had told him and had rehearsed the line about his recognition from the Energy Ministry. The two-hour flight south passed without incident. His car waiting at the airport, he headed straight to the office. Checking his phone en route, he had a message from his newly appointed boss at the Port Authority, Elias.

"Hi Jamshid, it's Elias. I'm not sure whether you are caught up with business in Tehran, but this is to let you know I have just received a requisition order for you from the Energy Ministry. It releases you from your day-to-day duties here at the port. I'm sorry as your boss – it seems I am the last person to get to know you – but I would like to add my congratulations to those of your colleagues. This is a great reputation success for the Port Authority and I hope we will get the chance to get to know each other better in a while. If your duties bring you back to Bandar, please give me a call. I would like to learn lessons from your achievement. By the way, your paycheques will be mailed to your home as usual. Don't be a stranger. Good luck and bye for now."

It was ironic Jamshid had taken the message ten minutes away from the office. The good news was that he could now put the day job to the back of his mind, but he would have liked to have said a couple of personal goodbyes before leaving. What would the new man be saying about his departure? His sudden absence would inevitably lead to speculation about his future in the office, but, in the scheme of things, did it matter? He was now clear, he was engaged in affairs of the state, so, in one way or another, he had moved on professionally and probably personally too.

The unexpected gap in his diary created space for the next most important person in his life in the locality, Mahta. He pressed his speed dial.

"Hi, I'm back in town. Can we catch up?"

"I'm a bit busy right now." He detected a coolness in her voice, telling him she had company. "Should be free after seven tonight."

"Fancy dinner at the Apadana?"

"Not really, I'll be a bit tired by then – tell you what, I'll come round to yours and you can fix some food. We'll see whether your cooking is as good as my picnic."

He smiled to himself. Happy memories.

Heading back up the coast road, he called the second most important person in his life in the locality, Ravi.

"Hey, what do you think this is, man? Some of us workers have hearts to fix and minds to influence."

"That's OK, then. I fit the second category. Can you nip out to the Pak Bakery in the next ten minutes?"

"If you're as good as your word. I have to be getting scrubbed up in an hour."

With his itinerary sorted, Jamshid went looking for a car parking space.

To his embarrassment, Ravi was first to arrive at the bakery and had pre-ordered coffee and pastries.

"Well, my old friend, fancy meeting you again – and so *soon*. I remember telling you that you would soon get pissed off with life up north, but even I thought you had more staying power than that. So come on, spill the beans, have you still got these mafia types on your back?" His friend gave him a mocking smile.

"Oh, that. Well, I think you were right about one thing – I was under a lot of stress doing those deals and I recognise people do funny things when they're under pressure. But now I'm stressed in a good way, and I have been asked to work on some new commercial contracts for the government on a sabbatical."

"How long for?"

"I've got no idea, but it means I may have to stay in Tehran for a while, but I will be keeping my flat in Bandar just in case I need to be in my own space from time to time."

"It's good to hear, but if suddenly you're on 'easy street', why was it so urgent for you to see me?"

"Firstly, remember me telling you I had been rewarded for some of the high-value trades I've done in recent days? Just now, I have come into money, like I have never had before and may never have again, *inshallah*. I have thought what I should do as a good Muslim and know I must share it with my brothers. I want to give a special donation to the limbless ex-servicemen's charity you run, *today*."

"That's very kind, Jamshid, but it doesn't have to be today."

"Oh, yes it does. I may not have the opportunity for many weeks to come, so I want you to give me the bank account details, and I will arrange the payment."

"Hold on a minute, how much are we talking about?"

"For now, ten million rials. Maybe more in the future."

Ravi was used to living life on the run and his multi-tasking – in this case talking, eating pastry and drinking coffee – stopped.

"Wow! That's more than a little pocket money."

"Well, it's burning a hole in my pocket and I want to do the right thing for me, my friends and my country. It's the sort of money that will help a lot of our heroes start to live a normal life and I just cannot get over how many are out there now on the streets. I know you and the other trustees will ensure the money is spent wisely giving those guys a better future."

Ravi scribbled some numbers on a paper napkin.

"Here are the account details. I won't try and give you a lecture about charity starting at home and all that bollocks. You are big enough to know what you are doing, so all I can say is: thanks. I'm sure your actions will be noted by the great and the... not so good.

Your money is likely to result in a multiple new order for prosthetics, made by our own technicians in our own country, because, when it comes to it, we, not the Americans, Europeans or the Chinese or Japanese, are the world leaders. By the way, how's things with Mahta? I've not seen her for a while and probably won't catch up at our trustees' meeting next week as I have to go over to Muscat for a medical conference. Last I heard, you guys were getting it on."

Either Ravi could read his friend's face well or maybe the horses had been talking.

"I saw her last a couple of weeks ago and, yes, I think it's going well. She's a really interesting lady."

"Hah! Not surprised you haven't won any awards for acting. Remember, you can't do anything in this world without someone seeing! She's 'bezzies' with my sister-in-law, a vet who specialises in horses. She reckons she's got 'the hots' for you. Be careful, my friend. It's one thing stoking a fire, but much harder to blow it out. Anyway, seeing as you are about to turn the tables on me, I'm going before I have to confess to my own sordid relationships. Did I say 'relationships'? The plural was just a slip of the tongue." He winked and headed for the street.

Jamshid waited for a few minutes, logging the charity's bank account details into his phone. When asked to do so, he used his thumbprint to authenticate the transaction.

It had been a while since Jamshid had been required to do any serious cooking in his kitchen, so he had been to the local supermarket to collect all the ingredients to make a classic *Ghormeh Sabsi*, the iconic Persian lamb stew in a special home-made lemon herb gravy with kidney beans and basmati rice. He remembered it was a favourite dish of his mother's and she had made him practise making it before he left home. He recalled her telling him about the importance of getting the three flavours right, the melange of local herbs, fenugreek and dried limes. The real secret, in his experience, was cooking off all the ingredients, then putting it all in a casserole dish to 'mellow' for a couple of hours. He had still kept a couple of bottles of Shiraz in his flat in case of a special occasion, and, with a dash of his arak in the pot as well, all was set for a wonderful dinner.

Next came the packing of a fresh overnight bag, tidying up of the bedroom, clean sheets, a single rose in a small vase, a shower, but then the doorbell.

Checking his watch. He saw he still had an hour and a half before Mahta's scheduled arrival. He opened the door a fraction too soon.

"I thought I heard noises from your flat. It's been so quiet this week. I always like to hear you moving about so I guessed you'd gone away. I thought those men from the Basij had got you. You hear these stories of ordinary people disappearing just like that. Without so much as a by-your-leave. You can never be too careful these days in my experience. I always look through the spyhole before I open up."

While dispensing personal advice, old Tawal had gently shuffled one of his slippered feet into the ridge of Jamshid's door, preventing him from closing it without knocking the old man over.

"Been in Tehran, have you?" he continued, "Dirty place, if you ask me — too much traffic and too many rude people. I wouldn't swap my home in Bandar for a place up there. No, you can't beat the sea air here. It smells so fresh, but breathing in all that salt makes you a bit..." He paused, licking his lips, looking beyond Jamshid. "Thirsty."

Jamshid smiled and readily understood the fastest way of sending his neighbour home.

"Would you like a drink, Mr Tawal? I could put the kettle on."

"There's no need to go to all that trouble," he said, walking towards Jamshid's kitchen.

"Would you like a small drop of something else?"

"I have been known to take a small glass of arak now and again."

Jamshid had left the bottle out while cooking and decided to get to it before his uninvited guest, who opted instead for taking a tumbler off his draining board.

Glass filled moderately, old Mr Tawal walked to the window to admire the sea view, and the growing sea haze.

His tone changed to a lower, more conspiratorial level.

"You know, I'm not the only one who misses you. There was another shifty-looking bloke in a suit and collarless grey shirt here on Wednesday afternoon. Wanted to know where you were. This one didn't look like that gangster who came up here last time. He had scuffed shoes and a fat belly. I wondered if he had come up the stairs. He looked a bit sweaty, like a tax inspector."

"What did you tell him?"

"Just, if he was looking for you, to leave a message in your box down at reception. He was another one who looked a bit rude. When he set off back, he took the stairs like he wanted the exercise going down. I heard him farting as he set off."

"Happens to the best of us. Don't worry, Mr Tawal; I have tried to tell my friends where I am and, if any strangers arrive, your advice is the best, but now you must drink up as I have to prepare for a business meeting." Jamshid shepherded the old man towards the door. "I am very fortunate to have such a trustworthy neighbour as you, Mr Tawal. It makes me feel my home is safe when I'm away."

His hand was now at his neighbour's back and with the door ajar he was able to steer him onto the landing. He made a point of shutting the door firmly to send a signal he did not want to be disturbed again. Secretly, he took the old man's advice and looked through his door spyhole. Tawal slugged off the rest of his glass and shuffled back into his own flat.

TWELVE

HIS NEXT VISITOR RECEIVED a much warmer welcome.

In a black dress with a separate red jacket, brass buttons and two-tone black and grey *hijab*, topped off with a Burberry raincoat and make-up, Mahta had come directly from work.

He took her hand and kissed it.

"Is that what I have been looking forward to for the past week?" she asked testily.

Walking in, throwing her handbag on a nearby chair, she went to him, arms around his neck, and kissed him in a way that said she really meant it.

He responded, "Is that the way you normally start a business meeting? If so, we've clearly got a lot to discuss."

Their eyes danced with each other like two butterflies playing in the spring sunshine.

"Let me take your coat."

She walked to the window and gazed towards the sea on the lights of the corniche.

"Some view. Glad I don't live here. I wouldn't get anything done."

"Well, as of today, I don't need to anymore. I've said goodbye to the office for now and have started a sabbatical, courtesy of the Energy Ministry. Now my Bandar home is purely for pleasure."

"For how long?"

"That's the question. For as long as I'm able to keep bringing in the big trades. Drink? I've got a bottle of Shiraz over there which blew its cork when you came in."

"Better decant it, then."

She didn't need to be invited to sit. Having scanned the room, she had picked a sofa where she could stretch out and kick off her heels.

He brought over a couple of wine glasses. "*Salamati* – so how's the day job?"

"About as good as when I saw you last – except with one notable success – I think I've found a way of re-boring the casings for those Silkworms I've got stacked up all over the place. If I'm right – and as you know, I get paid for being right, we can convert the lot for the new generation of home-produced Shahin ground-to-air missiles and I'm pretty sure we can use the same detonators. I'm waiting to get the clearances from the Defence Ministry. They seem to be in a ruck about whether to go my way, which will give them new missile capacity through reverse engineering, at the fraction of the price of upgrading the Silkworm system."

"Why do you think they might not do it?"

"You should know. When it comes to earning currency, their legs go to jelly. There's talk that they have lined up customers for all our old stockpiles. If it's true, it's worth millions, but they risk getting their balls mangled in the process."

"What do you mean?"

"It's now outdated Chinese technology. If we manage to sell our kit and the Chinese find out we've done so, there will be trouble. Possibly double trouble. Firstly, China will reserve the right to sell its tech (however outdated) to countries it approves of. There is no guarantee they will like Iran's customers, but, even if they do, there is another problem. Why would China accept a country operating their out of date defence tech when, *if push comes to shove*, the Chinese themselves would like to sell them the latest kit direct? No, when it comes to defence sales, it becomes a really dirty political game."

"But won't the Chinese want Iran to have the latest kit?"

"Certainly, and that's the trouble. We would be swimming in bombs, missiles, tanks – whatever – of their latest designs. They would give us credit too. We would still have to pay their asking price but, right now, we don't have the money. In reality, it's a zero-sum game – one way or another, the mullahs will end up mortgaging the country to stay in power. Question really is: are we going to spread the pain by borrowing less from a wider pool of lenders or just mortgage ourselves to the Chinese and become a vassal state in the game of global geopolitics? And, even then, there's no real choice, American sanctions have just about snuffed out every other potential supplier we have. Although the Russians don't really give a shit about the sanctions, they like to keep their relationship with the world banking fraternity cool. Sitting on the side lines without committing to Iran gives the Russians much more influence on how things finally work out in Syria and Iraq. Overall, you could say we are between a rock and a very hard place, so fill my glass, and tell me how you will solve all our problems, Mr Supersalesman."

Glass poured, he responded, "Well, that's what I'm trying to do in my own way. I'm working for the Energy Ministry, indirectly helping to build our exports and get more cash in the country's coffers. They have set me on planning rare earth aggregate exports. I've got to do some market testing and study the projection of reserves, so it is one of the few jobs more complicated that fixing unregistered oil trades. But potentially well paid if I can put together some deals."

"Who's buying?"

"I'm not sure yet, but I have heard they've appointed a representative in Tehran – a 'hot shot' US-trained young lawyer called Alrakahthan. I think the ministry are setting up a meeting after I have been to this wild place in the middle of nowhere…

this 'Arasbaran Protected Zone', which has a special environmental designation. They've got a colonel from the Revolutionary Guard looking after it at the moment but, clearly, he's a soldier and hasn't got a head for business. And it's good for you that someone in high places thinks I'm worth employing, as I saw Ravi earlier today to tell him your charity for limbless ex-servicemen has just got a new donation of ten million rials, my commissions for recent oil trades."

She had looked thoughtful as Jamshid explained the challenge of his new job, but swapped a pensive face for one of delight with his news.

"You remembered our conversation about being a good Muslim and you've acted on it! On behalf of the charity, how would you like me to express my gratitude?"

"I'm sure you'll think of something."

It was Jamshid's turn to smile.

Dinner was served in his modest kitchen diner.

"Well, I'm sorry the service is a bit slow and the surroundings may not be what your used to, but I did promise some good food, so I think you must score me at least a six out of ten for effort."

Mahta gave him a mock critical stare as she forked her first mouthful, which made Jamshid realise she must be a tough negotiator in the day job.

"The secret of a good *Ghormeh Sabsi* relies on the quality of the cut of lamb. Shank like this is the best; it just falls off the bone, and I'm pleased you didn't over-boil the rice. This is not a dish you can cook with a pre-packaged sauce, so I can only assume you have a good teacher. Your mother? This is the sort of dish mothers teach their kids to make. But, hey, you've done great! The more I see, the more I like, so cooking can be added to your CV alongside your appreciation of poetry and culture." She laughed. "By the way, I have to say, the poetry you recited on our picnic was really romantic. Did you learn it to get off with me?"

Jamshid flushed. "No – I just try to be well read. You never know in life when these skills become useful."

She smiled, sipping the Shiraz and responded:

"You inspired me to rediscover some of our country's classic poetry. I picked a verse for you, just for tonight:

At last I was recaptured by your love
Resisting had no effect
Love is like an ocean without a shore
How can one swim there oh wise one?
Love must be taken right to the end
Many unsuitable things must be accepted
Ugliness must be seen as if it were good
Poison must be taken as if it were sugar
I was disobedient and did not understand
The harder you pull, the tighter the rope.

"It's by Rabia Quzdari – do you know it? It made her famous throughout the Samanid Empire, and was inspired by the story of a young Balkhian woman, Roya, who eloped with her slave, Baktash. It was based on a true story of tragic love and was considered a masterpiece of its time, some 800 years after the birth of Jesus."

"Wow, I didn't know it, but it's beautiful. Reciting a poem is like carrying a picture gallery in your head. You can keep repeating it and, every time you do, you feel something new." He put on some music. "Have you heard this? It's Rana Farhan – the live jazz version of 'Drunk with Love', recorded in New York."

"Are you sure it's OK? I don't want to disturb your father next door."

Jamshid tensed slightly at the remark, but dismissed it. "The walls up here are thicker than you might think," he observed, putting on the smart speaker.

Dinner finished, they moved to the lounge with the remnants of the second bottle of Shiraz, a couple of fresh glasses and what was left of Jamshid's rapidly emptying bottle of Bekaa Valley arak.

Mahta picked up her handbag and took out a small pouch with a ready-rolled cigarette.

"Do you mind? This is no ordinary smoke. I like one of these occasionally after a good meal. Together with the booze, it helps my digestion." She lit up and took a deep breath, letting the smoke out slowly. "I've just seen the future. I predict I'm going on a trip. Come with me now." She passed over the burning weed. "Take a deep breath and let go."

Mahta had been right. Her "after dinner digestif" was his entry into a slow-motion world of pleasure which he seemed not to have the ability to control. Through the drug induced haze, he was barely aware of what was going on, except he reacted to the warm familiarity of her kiss and the perfection of her body, face, neck, arms, breasts, abdomen, thighs, legs and feet, all open and available to his touch and more.

Sex this time was somehow more mysterious than the last. There was something premeditated about their first assignation, a deliberate coming together, but this was different, somehow more nuanced, erotic, intense, as though they had bought into an experience provided by some unearthly power which was directing their actions. They were not in bed, the venue for respectable lovers, but on the floor in his lounge, on a sheepskin rug.

Two hours, four hours, however long it was, Jamshid opened one eye to stare around him. The scene looked like an accident, but vaguely similar to their outdoor liaison – clothes strewn around the room, empty Shiraz and arak bottles and glasses horizontally and haphazardly spread around, a used and unsealed condom, and the smell of stale smoke and musk in the air.

At some point earlier, he recalled they had looked out on the lights of the corniche, but now, as he sat up, he became aware of the city street lamps switching off, street by street, the sky moving from a deep navy to dark pink, anticipating the arrival of the sun. Struggling to his feet, he saw his lover, lying on her front, legs apart. Alerted by his erratic movement, she groaned and stirred.

Unsteadily rolling her over, he picked her up and carried her gently to his bed.

Once wrapped in the warmth of the duvet, she sighed as she nodded off once more. He went to the lounge and started tidying up, stopping in the hall to check the messages on his mobile.

"Flight fixed at 11. Car will collect at 9." Out of the corner of his eye, he saw her handbag with her mobile half out, screen lit. There was a notification message – "How did you get on with lover boy?" and an anonymous telephone number. He was going to ignore it but, seeing he had his own phone to hand, he tapped the number into it. His head was a mess: a hot shower and shave would focus his mind.

Maybe he had been noisier than he thought. As he finished brushing his teeth, Mahta put her head round the door.

"Going so soon?"

"There's a car coming to pick me up in thirty minutes. You're welcome to stay. Just drop the lock before you go." He restarted the shower.

"No, no, I've got to get a change of clothing before I go to work. Can you call me a cab?"

"Sure. There's a rank outside by the concierge desk on the ground floor. Just turn up and they'll take you."

They passed in the doorway of the bathroom. Although completely nude, she had collected her handbag. To save her modesty, Jamshid left the pile of her clothes by the door as he hunted for his favourite linen jacket in his wardrobe. Although not a natural tie wearer, the unexpected nature of his trip made him think he should take one, so he selected a sober-looking, plain gold woven silk version and stuffed it into his pocket.

Wallet, watch, keys, passport, sunglasses, cologne, handgrip – he was ready to roll, and surprisingly, in that time, so too was Mahta. As she walked with him to the door, he appreciated how, *despite* no make-up, and *in spite* of her *hijab* and dark glasses, her natural beauty had not been completely disguised. Waiting for the elevator, she gave him a gentle kiss on the cheek like a nervous schoolgirl.

"Call me when you can. Don't make it so long," she whispered.

She walked purposely out of the building, climbing into the first taxi she saw.

Edwin had kept his luggage and his booking open at the Four Seasons. He had politely declined Boroschenko's kind invitation to take him out that night to see 'the real Baku' as a way of celebrating their safe return. Bob was relieved to find his Toyota as he left it, but nonetheless did the precautionary checks to see whether it had been tampered with in their absence, following their unexpected encounters with Ryumin and his people. Although the car was 'clean', Bob knew his licence plate would have been shared by the security agencies and his movements would be closely monitored for the time being.

Having said their goodbyes at the terminal, Edwin and Bob headed for the city centre.

"I expect you had already worked it out that, as soon as the official introductions had been made down there, you and I would have been completely checked out. In my case, they will have been through my apartment, my little office, my email and social media stuff, as well as your bags at the hotel. I think Ryumin is a genuine guy who is serious about wanting to help, if only because there were no tracking or explosive devices on the car."

Edwin raised an eyebrow.

"Oh, the Azeris are very polite people. They are reluctant to tell you to your face if they don't like you. It's not beyond Ryumin's brief for you and/or me to have had an unfortunate accident… but, then again, they were pretty keen to get Sergei to fly us back." Bob smiled as he picked up signs for the Expressway. He dropped Edwin at the hotel and they agreed to meet an hour later in the lobby before walking round to a steakhouse and beer garden behind the Interior Ministry, popular with tourists. A few steins of German pilsner and some Brazilian steak skewers raised their flagging spirits.

"So, boss, what now?" Bob asked.

"Well, as a precaution, I've got to brief the MoD, inform my office, and then decide what the next moves are. The conversations will be difficult. The client was a bit 'lukewarm' about this one when I did the first briefing and won't welcome the embarrassment of a high-profile Brit being, in effect, held hostage in a place where relations are sensitive. I guess I'm in for a *bollocking* on a personal level, even though there won't be any comment publicly."

"What happens if the whole show goes 'tits up'?"

"It's always best to be positive, so I will be hoping the team comes through. If they don't, for whatever reason, then we'll just have to see what success we can pull from the wreckage."

"And for you personally?"

"Reputationally, it will be damaging. I got this job at Peace International thanks to some effective 'behind the scenes' lobbying. Those supporters will either fall away or actively distance themselves. PI will want a European director with a clean pair of hands, and there are plenty of those up in the Scandi countries, and... my contract does give them the flexibility to do what they like in terms of 'gross misconduct'... oh, and then there's the blacklist."

"The what?"

"The blacklist. Although some regard it as an urban myth, there is a blacklist, kept by the head of the civil service that any permanent secretary can access. If your name is on it, you are certainly unofficially blocked from the higher levels of public service."

"You're joking, right?"

Edwin looked at him cynically. "You can't be that surprised."

"I'm not – I just don't get the secrecy. Thought you guys had a Freedom of Information Act? I heard about it on the BBC."

Edwin laughed.

"That's all part of the secrecy architecture – it's window dressing, a distraction. There are lots of legal 'fig leaves' which excuse the authorities from answering questions they don't like, especially if they think it's not in the 'public interest', or, to be accurate, their *personal* interest. The real reason why the public service blacklist is denied was because, a few years back, some freelance construction workers sued their employers for not hiring them because they had been labelled 'agitators' for having acted as whistle-blowers about individual companies' site safety practices. They proved their case, won damages and changed employment legislation as a result. How can the government, which stands for the rule of law, admit that it operates in the same way? And that is why it is an urban myth. There is no 'smoking gun' trail of documents or evidence that supports it and so nothing can be proved, and yet it happens. No, if you get blacklisted, it's early retirement or stacking supermarket shelves for you, or perhaps, in my case, opening a bar over here."

Bob looked shocked. More beer arrived.

Edwin continued: "You know what is really funny? Some of the top people in Whitehall regularly screen their staff for what they call 'difficult to manage' employees and there's nothing underhand about it, apart from the fact they will always deny it, if asked. What they do is to allow them to access a private intranet service. This allows them to share their problems and concerns, making comments in a so-called 'secure' environment where they can be anonymous. Those unfortunates don't need to give their names, as the intranet server identifies who they are and where they work. Theoretically, if they call their line manager a 'wanker' in the street without witnesses, that's OK, but try doing it anonymously online and you're out. I remember a private competition once between the various department permanent secretaries to see who was the most complained about. They all thought it would be the pensions people, but – what do you know? – it was the FCO, so that tells you something. It's this sort of instance that makes foreigners love us – if you were a public servant in China, you would be quietly shipped off to a correctional centre to be re-educated. In Russia, you would just disappear."

"My former associates would want you to feel the pain of your mistakes. Doin' your knees was popular in my day," said Bob. "What's the plan for tomorrow?"

"British Embassy first, then I guess back here." He paused. "I mean over there," he added, waving his arm in a dismissive way, "across the street at the Interior Ministry. I've put in a call to get an appointment. I am sure Ryumin will have arranged a reception committee and will be monitoring transmissions out of Iran. Don't worry about Anya; from what I have seen, she is as capable as anyone else in that situation."

"You know, in a strange way, I'm not worried about her at all," said Bob, staring down into his rapidly emptying glass. "She has a different take on love than me. Maybe I'm a romantic, but when we got together it seemed like a good marriage. You know, love, sex, companionship and all that. And perhaps it is, but now I wonder whether it is more a marriage of convenience for her. I've learned some things in the last few days I knew nothing about. I've got to thinking she saw this situation as a means of taking revenge on this bandit right from the start. The risk is not her getting hurt but how many she'll take down before she gets back. Your man Dave will have his hands full there; she's not a great one for taking orders.

"Tell you what, why don't we meet back here when you're done with the embassy tomorrow, and we can sort out the locals together? Sure, we'll both do better when we've had some kip."

Away from the chatter and beat of the beer garden, the city centre was relatively quiet. Bob was feeling the stress of the journey and the effect of the beer. He left his car and hailed a cab. Edwin wandered slowly back to the Four Seasons, wondering whether his own career would finish on the banks of the Caspian. He wondered if he would ever get used to its acrid industrial fragrance.

"What the fuck is going on? Who's in charge around here?"

Hafiz's mood was darkening once again as he took he took another call in his study. With the help of Major Ho and the soothing comments of Dilshad, he had started to come to terms with the issues of his restaurant and its imminent repair. Now, out of the blue, another problem had come to torment him. He was starting to realise that the day would not be his best. Privately a superstitious man, he was well aware that bad luck usually came in threes and what was facing him now was problem number two – a consignment of economic refugees was being sent from the covert "logistics integration centre" in Marshad. At this time, he could expect it at around 23.30 local. Breaking down the problem further, he noted the consignment was a week early and was larger than the twenty he had agreed, and, because of the known border restrictions, they would need to be passed on, perhaps via Mardanagom into Meghri, Armenia. This was a much riskier, thirty-hour undertaking using connections he only used occasionally, and was much more expensive in time, money and the rest. Irritatingly, this crossing would need a locally based guide and was not always reliable, especially when this batch would be carrying backpacks of opium, even if it was unrefined. Upon reflection, Hafiz preferred to drive them from Sami across the southern tip of Azerbaijan to Vezhnaly, an "out of the way", sleepy hamlet on the back road to Nrnadzor, Armenia. There were more calls to be made to his link in Armenia, so they knew they would have to do the pick-up some eighty kilometres east of the usual exchange point. There was no way round it: this consignment would be 100,000 USD, cash on delivery. He had a Pakistan cell to text with his terms. No confirmation – the courier would just have to dump them in Sami and take the consequences. No pay days for anyone. If the cash arrived with the consignment, the cargo would be transferred to another trailer on the edge of town and moved on in a matter of minutes. There was no possibility of any incriminating evidence getting left on his doorstep. He put his head round the office door into the dining area. Dilshad and Shimina were still there, Fawaz had gone.

He called out, "Khalifa, are you there? Can you find Hanif and get him to call me on the mobile?"

His head was in a different place; he ignored the presence of members of his family. He went back to his desk, switched on his computer and started to watch the CCTV recordings from the previous night. He began to imagine what was the third piece of bad news coming his way.

Mahta sat in the back of the taxi headed first to her apartment before going into the office.

Gripping her phone, she had skipped through her appointments for day and started catching up on her messages. One was clearly more urgent than the rest. She noted the cynicism behind the text.

"I told you I would call when I had news. Don't send me stupid texts."

"Well, it produced an early answer so maybe I'm pleased I sent it," was the dry response.

"Tell me what you know."

Mahta recounted their conversations.

"That Energy Ministry stuff and the contact with the younger Alrakahthan tells me what I suspected. Things are clearly moving faster than I thought in Khoda Afrin. I think I will have to put the brakes on all this for a while."

"Don't do anything dumb," she said. "It's taken a while to get close to him and the conversation will finish if he suspects me of spying on him," she said.

"I certainly wouldn't underestimate him. If he truly is an apprentice of Alrakahthan's, then he will be as interested in you as you are with him. When do you see him next?"

"It's open for now. I guess next time he's in Bandar."

"Call him up in a couple of days. Now you are an item, he will think it strange if you are not in touch."

The line went dead.

A faint smile played on the craggy features of Gharbieh's face as he reclined on his swivel chair in his office. He pressed the intercom to his secretary.

"Get me the cell phone number of Rashid Rahman."

Alrakahthan always believed in using commercial flights wherever possible as a means of avoiding attention. Jamshid had been given the same advice. These days he took the Iran Air shuttle service between Bandar and the new Tehran International so regularly he was on first-name terms with some members of the crew. Whereas there were few frequent flyer benefits available, it was normally the case he would get a front seat a distance away from the mothers, kids, grandparents, religious pilgrims and others who climbed aboard with what seemed like all their worldly possessions shoehorned into the compact spaces around their places. The flight was towards the end of the early-morning rush, so there were recognisably fewer business people than usual and the seat next to him was free. Not so long ago, an opportunity like that would have allowed him space to spread out papers he was working on, but no longer. Alrakahthan liked his people to use the latest technology and now Jamshid was poring over plans of the Arasbaran Protected Zone on a tablet. The 72,460-hectare area covered mountains up to 2,200 metres, high alpine meadows, semi-arid steppes, rangelands and forests, rivers and springs. Trying to follow the key for the concentration of mineral deposits in the government's geological survey was complicated. The document chronicled that Arasbaran was home to 215 species of birds, twenty-nine species of reptiles, forty-eight species of mammals, and seventeen species of fish. But where exactly? A unique characteristic of the Arasbaran forests was the ubiquity of edible wild trees, including concentrations of hazelnut in particular. Large walnut and rare *Cornus mas* trees were recorded as growing wild alongside streams, and more exotic plant species and herbs with application in traditional medicines significantly added to its ecological importance. No wonder he would need to explore whether its boundaries could be redrawn to allow mineral extraction.

He fiddled around with the zoom feature to get a close-up on some of the deepest concentrations but was frustrated that the file close up kept reverting to the masterplan image.

Dumping the tablet on the seat next to him, he stared out of the window at the bland and largely empty vista of the airport environs, hangars at the periphery, listening to the standard safety announcements. While his eyes and ears were casually occupied, his mind was focused on something else entirely – Mahta. What should be her place in his life? Who was she really? Why was she interested in picking up with him? And what could possibly come out of an association with her?

For a start, he knew that his mother wouldn't like her in the same way she had approved of Hanah. Mahta was older, and more worldly and independent.

Unusually, this was a woman succeeding in a male-dominated society. To do that, she needed to be better in so many respects than her male peers. Better educated, better trained, intuitive. He could easily see Mahta was someone that others would seek out to consult, rather than her trying too hard to make connections. She spoke with authority about culture and world events, as well as the day-to-day, and was confident in the bedroom, not like the subservience often advocated by the Iranian societal demands of family and religion. Back to why she hit on him. She was either stupid or very clever. Most evidence pointed to the latter. Was it her intention that he should regard her as a spy and, if it was, what was she really trying to tell him? She had retained her rebuttal of his charge that she had been in Tehran watching him play football. Did she think, if she continued to deny it, he would either accept her explanation or even forget it? Then there was the issue of his apartment. He never told her where he lived, and he was pretty sure the only other person who could have told her, Ravi, hadn't done so without his permission. And what about old Tawal? How had she known he had an elderly neighbour and how on earth had she concluded he must be his father, when from the earliest times of their association he had told her his parents lived in Tehran? These errors, if that was what they were, seemed elementary mistakes of spycraft. Having said all that, there was no doubt their assignations had been fun, the sex had been great (and educational), and he had also had the benefit of peeking into her clandestine world.

He remembered she had originally described herself as a teacher. Wow! Some teacher! She was now telling the state how to build a new cut-price generation of ground-to-air missiles at a fraction of the cost of sanction-busting alternatives from China, Russia or elsewhere. That knowledge could be of interest to Alrakahthan, so maybe it was a more even trade after all, if acquiring commercial information was the order of the day. Strangely, he had concluded he had been wrong to trust Mahta, but wondered whether trust would feature anyway in their future relationship.

This jumble of thought had filled much of his flight time to Imam Khomeini International. Upon landing at Terminal One, he crossed the Persian Gulf Highway and into the lobby of the austere curved tower block of a well-known global hotel chain. The foyer, although open and airy, was tinged with the typical beige and brown colour scheme which infected its fixtures and fittings. This was a hotel that was not designed to be a destination, more a temporary utilitarian refuge to escape the punishing daytime heat of the concrete jungle outside.

Hanah and Hasan were in the lobby locked in an active conversation, but Hanah was quick to register Jamshid's presence. Dressed in a one-piece linen trouser suit with *hijab*, in a tone of brown complementary to her surroundings, sunglasses and white branded designer trainers, she looked ready for action, provided that action wouldn't involve too much exertion tramping through undergrowth or open fields.

"Hi, Jamshid – looks like we're in for a busy few days. Hasan has sourced the necessary prefabricated shelters for Sami and we've picked up some trucks to move them with. We've had to charter an Antonov An-22 out of Kiev to load it all. It's a bigger commitment than we thought. It's costing 50,000 US dollars an hour just to fuel it up! You and me will go with the trucks up to Baku to collect the prefabs and from there we will fly direct to Posyan. We've put in a request for full refuelling on delivery, to allow the immediate flight home. Once we are there, it should take us three days to get the units in position and that is just two days ahead of their requirements."

Hanah rightly looked as though she had resolved a major logistical headache.

Her brother, himself 'power dressed' in his sky-blue suit and open collar, looked in a hurry to move on.

"Just be aware, Jamshid, this consignment is being undertaken by the humanitarian protocol already in place between Azerbaijan and Iran for earthquake relief. Hanah has the paperwork and flight plans lodged. That way we can procure these items below a market price, at short notice, subject to charging them back to the government when we move them on after the Chinese have finished with them, so you need to make it clear we are only loaning these, and reserve the right to remove them when the reason for their deployment has been realised."

Considering the scale of the task they were undertaking and with half the Alrakahthan clan present, Jamshid asked where their parents were.

"This is just a handover by me to Hanah. You will support her in any way she requires in Khoda Afrin. That is what is agreed. This is a busy time for all of us and we each have different things we need to be doing in different places. Remember what we discussed in Karaj. Stick to the plan and it will work out well for us all."

Jamshid wasn't sure if Hanah's clever little brother was in fact issuing a reprimand to him, a director of equal standing in the family enterprise, but this wasn't the time to find out. He was well aware of how little he really knew about the family and the "little brother" in particular.

The conversation proved necessarily brief as two black Mercedes pulled up outside. The lead driver, distinctive in a white short-sleeved shirt and black tie, walked into the reception and was spotted by Hasan.

"We all have to go now," he said, leaning forward to kiss his sister on the cheek.

"Look after her, Jamshid – this is a tricky job that will need both your skills to resolve."

Stepping out into the dry heat, his driver ushered him into the air-conditioned comfort of the first car and prompted the driver of the second to step forward to collect Hanah and Jamshid's grip bags.

Hasan set off without waiting towards the city. Hanah's driver turned his car around and headed for the airport perimeter road, while she checked her phone. Jamshid got the feeling he should be quiet until spoken to.

"Our plane is almost loaded. We have a take-off slot of 13.15."

He sat back looking across the airfield at the looming hangers and planes not just from Iran, but from some forgotten parts of the world – Kyrgyzstan, Tajikistan, Ethiopia and Nepal, as well as China, Japan and Pakistan.

"That's ours, over there," she pointed with understandable childlike excitement – this, the woman who preferred to travel by executive jet when her father wasn't around. Their car was waived through a private security gate and onto the apron.

The hulking shadow of the giant, four-engined turbo prop carrying the flag of Ukraine with its distinctive twin tail fins, had been in sight for a while. But, at fifty-eight metres long, this cargo leviathan of the air looked like a hangar itself, especially when loading, with its twenty-four wheels lowering the fuselage almost to the ground. As they approached, its nose cone was being closed, giving it the look of a more conventional plane from the side. Although its mouth was closed, it had still to 'pull up its trousers'.

The Mercedes pulled up at the rear close to the entrance ramp. At first glance the cavernous hold appeared empty and devoid of people. Getting out of the car in the shade, Jamshid was able to see two trucks being locked down at the furthest point by four boiler-suited technicians and another four men in white shirt sleeves and epaulettes walking towards them, the first waiving his greeting.

"Madam Alrakahthan, Mr Turani! Good day. My name is Captain Viktor Shelepin of Donbass Air; I am in charge of your flight. May I introduce my team, First Officer Lyudmilla Shimok, Chief Engineer Katalinsky, Second Engineer Ignatiev, Flight Controller Ballitsky and Loadmaster Renko. We and the rest of our freight handling crew are delighted to be of service. It is a pleasure to welcome you onboard our Antonov Antei; we call it 'the Beast'. I'm not sure you are familiar with these things, but this aircraft is always admired wherever we go, as it is the largest turbo prop – that is, propeller-driven – plane in the world and ideal for your use today.

"I am pleased to say the paperwork is completed and I have had confirmation from my bosses in Ukraine that your deposit of one million US dollars has been received. It is a condition of transit that I see your passports. Thank you. There are just a couple of small details before we go. First the insurance waiver, on behalf of the Islamic Republic and, secondly, the fuel indemnity guaranteeing refuelling for our return home to Kiev from Posyan. Please come with me to the flight deck so you can witness our fuel level and sign the final authorisations."

Loadmaster Renko collected their bags from the driver and caught Hanah's eye.

"Yes, Madam, as loadmaster I am responsible for the stowing of all freight on the plane, from the largest to the smallest." She smiled, as the group followed the captain into the hold and up a flight of stairs to a passenger area with seating for thirty in rows of sixes and forward to the cockpit with space for the air crew of five. Amongst the banks of switches and dials, Shelepin leaned forward and tapped one of the main gauges to the left of the main flight console, which was indicating full. Hanah signed, took a photograph on her phone of the dial and followed the flight director to the passenger area.

"We're closing the doors and have permission to start engines. We are on time. Captain Shelepin will come to visit you during the flight to Baku, which will be two hours thirty. Please check your belts."

What differed from a normal commercial flight was there was no discussion about what to do in an emergency. Whether because it was a cargo flight or just the cavalier attitude of the crew, Jamshid could not be sure.

"Don't worry if you see the propellers turning in opposite directions – it looks a little strange but gives us the balance and uplift we need. I will see you again when we get to cruising altitude."

What the plane's VIPs weren't told was the rising sensation when the wheels were raised to take-off position, but, amid the noise of the propellers taking up power, they experienced the lightness of the airframe as they taxied to the runway.

During all the preamble for take-off, Hanah had said little to Jamshid. He detected a contradiction in her manner between wishing to demonstrate her authority on the project and a nervousness about undertaking a solo mission on the edge of her own competence. Did she want to work as a team or merely retain him for use as some sort of emergency backup? Jamshid had hoped to see her father in Tehran before they departed to share what he had learned about the Silkworms, but now it was probably too late, and was the fact Mahta had told him so openly about a matter of state secrecy some sort of test, to see if he could be trusted? Anyway, the moment had passed, and it was now time to give complete attention to what was ahead.

As the plane levelled out at 30,000 feet heading north-north-west over the Caspian, he thought it time to discuss their plan.

"We won't leave the plane at Baku as the Azeri handling agent will come to us with the cargo. All we need to do is eyeball the goods and check the manifest. We'll be airborne for Posyan soon after, flying over the sea to avoid security risks. They have a lot of rogue operators in the south of Azerbaijan." She looked down at her laptop. "I'm not sure if you are aware, but our government has signed agreements to lease the Ibrahim Sami research Base to the Chinese for twenty-five years. The Supreme Leader has also agreed a joint venture with them at Posyan to turn it into a global logistics hub for their Belt and Road Initiative. In essence, that means extending the existing Revolutionary Guard complex into a commercial cargo airport with warehousing, component assembly plants and hotels in a poor region in the far north-west. Our cargo today is basically a loan of construction workers' accommodation to extend the Sami facility underground. We will then add the cost of the supply of these units, plus our commission, to the Chinese quarterly account. Good business for us, demonstrates Tehran is a credible partner by getting things done quickly and allows the Chinese to accelerate their own plans."

"Why aren't the Chinese bringing in their own prefabs?"

"Apparently they could, but it would take them longer. This is about cash flow. Our government wants them to hurry up with work at Sami, so they can motivate them to bring forward the plan for Posyan, which will make Tehran much more money as that will be a joint venture and Alrakahthan will be a lead contractor. I will be doing that. You're here to build our own trade out of Posyan. If we are to facilitate the export of rare earths from the Arasbaran Protected Zone, Posyan will be the exit point. That's why Dad wanted you on this trip with me. First, we check the installation of the temporary units at Sami; secondly, I get a chance to view the Posyan development masterplan, which no contractor has yet seen; and, third, you get to research extraction proposals for the Arasbaran. We're being met by the guys in charge. Colonel Rahman, base commander at Posyan for the Revolutionary Guard, the

Governor Mayor of Khoda Afrin, Hossein Moussavi, essentially the Supreme Leader's man, and a Major Ho, the commandant at Sami."

"What about al-Fouadi? Where does he fit in?"

"He's a prominent local farmer and entrepreneur. He doesn't get the strategic importance of all this but is playing all ends up, to make fees. He has a grip on the local labour supply – that is, skilled workers, not those held in the prison on the Posyan base. He dabbles a bit in the 'under the counter' trades we used to do – guns, people, and drugs – as well as having legit interests in property, retail, entertainment, manufacturing and farming. He's small fry, an amateur who knows a little about a lot, someone who could be useful on the ground if needed. I've not spoken to him personally but Hasan took him as a client doing small land trades when he first came back from Harvard. He seems to think his son, Fawaz, is a better bet for us to be working with."

There was certainly enough in the briefing to keep Jamshid occupied for the rest of the journey despite the efforts of the Ukrainian crew to provide what they thought of as "customer service".

Coffee and cake with the captain was one thing, but when the vodka bottle came out it was time for the clients to make the most of their Islamic heritage by proclaiming their abstinence.

Prevailing winds helped to shorten the journey to Baku, touching down in the late afternoon, yet the taxiing to the cargo warehouse took another twenty minutes in the failing light.

Open-framed containers of prefabricated buildings were ready for loading, exactly as Hanah had predicted. The client's job had been to inspect the loading and count the units before signing the manifest to authorise the trade. When the tractors loaded the final sections onto the plane, Jamshid watched as the team of loadmasters checked the weight positions and anchors of each consignment before signalling they were happy to proceed.

Hanah had taken delivery of the prefabs. It was time to fly south again.

THIRTEEN

FAWAZ ARRIVED BACK FROM Ashelqu and went looking for his father. Despite his diverse range of business activities, Hafiz had resisted the temptation of hiring a secretary himself, nervous about any other person knowing precisely what he was up to. For those formally constituted businesses, he was always prompt at settling tax demands and saw them as the price of avoiding too much official attention on his activities. Staying close to Governor Mayor Moussavi was also part of that strategy. Any opportunity to support or engage with Moussavi was a chance to secure his position as a leading figure in local society. It was ironic that the closest person to him was his "general manager", Hanif. Hanif had worked for Hafiz since he was a boy and had always fulfilled every request of his boss in a diligent and timely way. The result was in practice, it was Hanif who managed his "under the counter" transactions on his behalf, whether that related to the team of girls at the hotel, people smuggling or drugs. These were steady activities, not requiring huge intelligence but efficient administration, especially the collection of cash, which Hafiz used to launder some of his joint ventures, such as property, manufacturing and food sales. Hanif was perhaps the only person who would know where Hafiz was at any particular point in the day. He knew he had changed his diary in the light of recent events and so keeping in regular, hourly touch had never been more important than now.

It was no surprise, then, for Fawaz to find them both in his study at the house, but more surprising to see them both staring at the CCTV images from the restaurant riot.

His father was replaying sequences of action like some TV football pundit analysing in minute detail what was taking place.

"You're not still looking at that, are you? Why not leave it to the police?"

"They are fuckwits – even worse than Rahman's guys. I have to pull together my own evidence and will tell them what to do as a result."

"What have you learned so far?"

"This was no casual incident. A fight was started by this woman."

He froze a frame on a woman with long dark hair, wrapping herself around a couple of unsuspecting off-duty Chinese squaddies.

"Look, you see she concentrates on just two of them going from one to the other. The guy who was with her just watches on."

"Who's he?"

"Dunno – the table booking is in the name of 'Akdeniz'. Apparently, they just walked in off the street."

"Turks?"

"Possibly – I didn't know there were any Turks staying locally. Maybe there were, but not with me. Hanif will make some enquiries."

Fawaz saw the worry on his father's face.

"What's the matter?"

"I'm not sure. I have tried zooming in on her face, but the picture goes grainy. You know, the more I look at her, I just get a sense I have met her before. Sounds stupid and I can't place it, but I just feel I know her."

Hafiz nodded to Hanif. His general manager started to leave. Fawaz held his hand up, gesturing him to stay. "I came by to let you know some good news. Your contact, Alrakahthan, has come through with the prefabs you promised to Rahman and friends. They are being flown into Posyan tonight before being delivered to Sami tomorrow. Although their office called me as I had put through the request, they told me they have confirmed the arrangements with the governor mayor's office. Have you agreed where they are going to be sited?"

"There is a cleared plot with access to drains on the road just outside the perimeter boundary of the Chinese compound under my ownership. Ho knows about it and is putting in place the necessary security arrangements. I was due to call him to thank his team for the speedy refurbishment of the restaurant and to invite his workers down for a free night out. I'll pass on the news, if Moussavi hasn't already done so. In the meantime, can you get in touch with Rahman and find out how he thinks he's managing the delivery here from Posyan?"

It was Fawaz who was the first to leave. When he was gone, Hafiz turned to Hanif. "And, as if we didn't have enough going on, we've got to move this consignment of people through here tomorrow as well. You are clear, Hanif, on what you need to do? We cannot afford any fuck-ups."

"Yes, sir, I am sure it will be OK. At the livestock sale at Ahar, we got our best market price for sheep so far this year and didn't require too much of your time, beyond authorising the sale on the phone, so I expect the people transfer to proceed in the same way. As you instructed, the necessary connections have been made."

"On you go, and thanks. I'm not sure we would be getting through all this without your help. I'm just going back to the restaurant to review the refurbishment work before I call Major Ho."

Fawaz walked casually out of the house and called Rahman. At the Posyan base, the name al-Fouadi was well known. He got through to Rahman directly. As he suspected, Moussavi had already told him about the delivery and he had sanctioned the necessary resources to move the prefabs to Sami. He agreed to call when the cargo arrived. Checking his surroundings to ensure he was not being followed, he slipped down a narrow passageway and into the number three shed. Being towards the middle of the day, most of Dave's team were taking rest, but he woke him to provide an update and then moved on to pray at the mosque before going to the laundrette.

With Dilshad now away on a family visit, Fawaz once again became the focus of Shimina's attention and she had started to follow him, not with a real sense of purpose but because she decided she had little else to do. Fortunately, Shimina did not pick up Fawaz's trail until he left the mosque but was puzzled seeing him going into the laundrette, especially when he had Khalifa to take care of 'that sort of thing'. Empty-handed, he must have been going to make a collection, so maybe he was making plans to press a favourite shirt – maybe he had met a woman he wanted to impress. The shoe shop opposite was always a source of attraction to Shimina, and a convenient place from which to observe the launderette and its customers. She saw him leave with a heavy package, walking towards home. She kept following him at a discreet distance. When he turned into the side street towards their house, she decided to make herself known.

"Hey, Faz – that's a lot of shopping for a guy like you. Are you getting supplies in for Eid?"

Fawaz, normally so careful, had been tripped up by his own sister. Inwardly flustered, he thought quickly and remained cool in his answer.

"It's nothing really, just a favour of cleaning some uniforms for the garrison. There were a few who got caught up in the rough and tumble at the restaurant; I said I'd get their uniforms cleaned as a thank-you. I'll have to run over to Posyan soon to help with the transfer of materials back to Sami. Said I'd drop them in when I was passing."

"How boring – I thought you were doing something interesting like meeting your sexy friend, Parviz – that's why you went to Ashelqu, wasn't it? Not helping Dad."

"Well, I did say I would help out any way I could. It's the best way of learning the family business – and I am entitled to keep my own friends without you hanging around."

"I am sure he would have appreciated it. I think he fancies me – it's a woman's intuition. Have you spoken since we went to the cinema?"

"No and no. I think he has other interests." He rolled his eyes to the ceiling.

"What a waste," she replied. "If you were to ask me who my ideal man might be, I'd probably have said Parviz."

"Well, don't worry. I don't think anyone is asking you that question. Why don't you…"

"Yes?"

"Why don't you bake a cake, like you did for the Pomegranate Festival? I know plenty of people who would line up for a slice. Dad might even pay you to bake one for the hotel lounge."

"Well, I just might, and why aren't you going with Hanif to Armenia tonight?"

She tossed her own conversational grenade into the conversation, but this time Fawaz was prepared.

"Firstly, if you were thinking about that courier job, it will take too long and would stop me doing what Dad has asked. Secondly, I have no knowledge of that part of the world and would, in all likelihood, cock it up. Thirdly, Hanif has already had instructions from Dad and he knows what to do. Now that's enough of the questions; you'd better get to the kitchen or go to market to get what you need. I'll be back later. Go on, GO!"

His surprise had not been about the talk of Armenia, a subject which by its very nature in Iran implied some form of illegal trade in people and drugs, but the timing. Why would Hafiz fix a trade anyway, today of all days? It was a recipe for disaster. Satisfied he had new information to impart, he retraced his steps to the number three barn to alert Dave and his team.

Dave did what he did best: strategising. He worked out what resources he had, where they needed to be, and what needed to be done. Thanks to Fawaz's briefing, he had nearly all the information necessary to complete the mission. Except two things. Firstly, he had to understand how and when Rahman would move the prefab consignment to Sami, and secondly, the location of the administration block within the compound. They only had to wait for Jo to be able to meet with Amy, or so he hoped, and then he would commit to the serious deployment.

It was Tuesday.

Hafiz's rollercoaster mood was on the up after he had visited the restaurant.

Although the colour scheme had now changed to a purple (not his choice but clearly based on the paint Ho had been able to procure), it didn't look wrong. Plates, glasses, table decorations were all in place. He had no doubt some of his customers would regard it as an improvement – purple looked good after dark. He was a man of his word and arranged an early-doors party for the Chinese workers, Ho had already agreed to schedule early leave and even promised to make a personal appearance, but Hafiz wasn't going to wait for that. He called the compound directly, but was disappointed to learn that Moussavi had already informed Ho about the delivery of the prefabs and it was he who told him about Rahman hosting a briefing meeting the following morning at the Posyan base. Hafiz reacted as though he had known all about it all the time, but was privately irritated to have been informed by the Chinese commandant, in his own country. He spoke to Moussavi, to ensure he received his share of the credit for arranging the consignment in the first place. He was walking out through the hotel reception when he met Fawaz.

"Keep your diary clear: we are attending a briefing meeting organised by Moussavi at the Posyan base at ten in the morning.

You can drive." He was clearly still in a mood and avoided a longer discourse with his son. Had he done so, he might have had some curiosity about why his son was there at that hour.

Fawaz had come to see Eleheh, who was nervous about getting reacquainted with Hafiz's son.

"I have to be careful about leaving here and talking to anyone," she said.

"It's OK. We don't need a lot of chat. Are you ready to leave and if so, how many of the others would do the same? Talk to the girls and let me know. All you need to do is to make a booking in my name in the restaurant for eight tonight with the number who want to go. I will check the reservations book at six, but will cancel once I have read the number. Clear?"

"There is no point. We have no documents and nowhere to go," she replied.

"You can still have a better life. Think about it."

He left in a hurry, not noticing a woman in a full black *chador* quietly enjoying a cup of tea and reading a volume of the official modern history of the Islamic Republic in the foyer lounge. It was now late afternoon and the woman was letting the cup of tea last a long time. Passing Fawaz was a mixed group of young Chinese, those who had helped redecorate the restaurant. They were excited to be at the hotel earlier than normal, with four hours' extra leave and no bills to pay. They gathered waiting to be called to the first-floor venue, and were met by the restaurant manager, Mr Choi, who greeted them in Mandarin. Clearly his speech of welcome was heartfelt and humorous and lasted a good ten minutes. He gestured the group to follow him but one asked to visit the women's washroom first. The lady with the *chador* watched carefully, recognising who the girl was, before getting up and following her in.

Checking her make-up in the mirror, Amy looked almost as startled as she had done when Rodg had grabbed her at the compound, as Jo removed the face covering and smiled at her.

"Nǐ hǎo. Nǐ hǎo ma?"

Amy looked into her small clutchbag and pulled out a small folded square of paper, leaving it next to one of the basin taps.

"Gěi nǐ." She returned the smile nervously and left to join her friends.

Jo picked up the folded square, secreting it in her robes before leaving herself to meet her colleagues at the barn.

Arrival at Posyan was, in itself an interesting test. The Antonov Antei was one of the biggest aircraft to land at the base and Captain Shelepin was bringing down "the Beast" in the face of an easterly headwind. As they made their final approach, the tension in the engines was palpable. As they touched down, the vague silhouette of hills on either side told first-time visitors, even if they were landing in the dark, they were in a valley bottom.

There was the inevitable shudder and shake as the wheels supporting the aircraft connected with the ground, taking responsibility for their continued forward motion. Metered application of air brakes, combined with two of the four engines shutting down immediately, and the other two cut to 15%, was slowing it down, helped, no doubt, by the full weight of the airframe. Although the plane didn't really give the passenger a sensation of speed, the full length of the relatively smooth runway was needed. As the plane turned, the lights of the airfield boundary were clearly visible at close quarters on the right. A third engine was cut, leaving just one to provide the necessary thrust for taxiing.

Hanah and Jamshid stared out like children on their first holiday trip looking for signs of life in the dark as they moved towards their directed parking position. The dull sodium lights of hangers were seen first, then a neat line of four military helicopters and then a brightly lit administration block, at which all engine power was cut. The loadmaster crew waited for the green cabin light before moving to the goods area. The flight deck door opened and Shelepin emerged.

"Lyudmilla is finishing things off now. We'll soon be dropping the wheels to ground level and will open up at the back."

"Thanks for getting us here," said Hanah, with a sense of relief that suggested she wasn't as experienced a traveller as she liked others to believe.

"Happy to help. The ground services team here are on standby to empty us out, fuel us up and get us fed – after that, we'll be on our way. All in all, we have a take-off time for Kiev at 04.00. Come – let's see who they've sent to meet us."

Hanah and Jamshid followed Shelepin out of the back door of the passenger area onto the gantry and then down a flight of steps to the hold. The back-door ramp was just being lowered and the cold night air rushed in to greet them. At first it was something of an anticlimax as there was nobody or nothing to be seen just the blackness of the night. It must have been a good ten minutes before they could see the lights of a procession of vehicles heading out towards them. First to arrive were a couple of Mercedes, followed by a truck of armed soldiers in fatigues, who immediately took up positions around the plane. The lights of a second cavalcade of vehicles could also be seen approaching, still a little way off. The driver of the first Mercedes leaped out to open the rear door and a tall figure in military dress uniform climbed out, putting on a pair of gloves before adjusting a peaked cap. A somewhat smaller man with a less impressive moustache and Western-style suit and overcoat came out of the other side. The uniformed figure strode towards the ramp.

Hanah and Jamshid were at the front, Shelepin, now fully uniformed with his own peak, just behind; his team of loadmasters lined up across the back in a military "at ease" position.

The formalities consisted of a lazy salute, which the loadmasters interpreted as an instruction to stand to attention, and Colonel Rahman extended his hand, directing it in the first instance to Hanah.

"Welcome to Posyan, Madam Alrakahthan, Mr Turani. My name is Colonel Rashid Rahman, commandant here. May I introduce you to Governor Mayor Moussavi of Khoda Afrin Prefecture? Please follow me. Your luggage will follow and my ground services director, Captain Abbas, will liaise with the pilot and crew to unload, refuel and the rest. This way..."

He led Hanah to the first Mercedes, leaving Jamshid to join Moussavi in the second, after the two guests had waived their goodbyes to Shelepin.

The two cars left the pool of light created by the cargo deck of the plane and into the pitch of the night. As Hanah's eyes adjusted, she realised the base seemed to have a variety of buildings around it and where they were headed, albeit one of the closest, was the most prominent.

"I am sure you and Mr Turani must be tired. We have arranged rooms in the officer quarters here for you to take some rest. I have taken the liberty of organising a briefing for ten o'clock in the morning. All relevant local stakeholders will attend in order to share knowledge about the transfer of goods to Ibrahim Sami. We can talk afterwards about arrangements to visit the Arasbaran Protected Area and indeed the future for this site. I am also pleased to advise that, during the night, your cargo will be loaded for immediate transhipment tomorrow after our meeting."

Their car pulled up at a side entrance, the rear car door was opened in perfect coordination with the opening of the main building door.

"Let me escort you both to your quarters and my adjutant will bring your luggage shortly. The governor mayor will leave us now, but will return in the morning."

Brief handshakes exchanged, Rahman led the way to the accommodation block and the officer's quarters before wishing his guests goodnight.

The arrival had happened with understated quiet efficiency – exactly the impression Rahman sought to create.

They gathered on time in the morning in the Posyan base's operations room. Rahman had prepared a full presentation for his guests and had flicked through the slides to ensure he had all the material he needed. Gathered with him were Moussavi, Ho, the two al-Fouadis and Captain Abbas. Even in this semi-private forum, there was protocol to be observed, which required the formal introduction of Hanah and Jamshid.

"Gentlemen, it is a pleasure for me to introduce our special guests – Madam Hanah Alrakahthan and Mr Jamshid Turani, who are here to represent the interests of Tehran in this endeavour."

There was a short round of applause as they entered the room and took their seats.

"There are three principal areas to discuss on our agenda. Firstly, the extension and excavation work to the Sami base, secondly, the further development of this site, and third, mineral extraction in the Arasbaran Protected Zone.

"I shall run through some slides on all three matters before opening up the discussion for your respective input."

After the presentation, Hanah was invited to comment.

"Thank you, Colonel. Firstly, it is a pleasure for us to be with you today. The Islamic Republic of Iran regards these three projects as the first stages of detailed economic cooperation between us and the People's Republic of China. I am confident, as the Islamic Republic's appointed technical advisers, that, as important milestones in our collaboration are achieved, senior ministers from both countries will come to view and celebrate our achievements, but today is about setting the foundations. With some of our work covering important aspects of defence, it is with regret we cannot publicly acknowledge the true extent of our shared endeavour. However, for now, in this room, let me record our appreciation for the first results, which have established the confidence to go forward.

"The Ibrahim Sami base was, as we know, established by the Revolutionary Guard as a research facility into fertiliser-based chemical and biological weapons. However, the pace of global development in the sector outstripped our country's ability to manage its research effort. Our cherished dream of production was unfulfilled as a result of not applying the stringent levels of control required in its early stages. Our brothers and sisters in the People's Republic recognised the obstacles we have had to overcome and have assisted us to manage our resources effectively, avoiding any further potentially unintended scenarios. We have responded by inviting the People's Liberation Army to play a lead role in this effort, improving environmental security and sharing expertise in return for offering sovereign rights over the site on a twenty-five-year renewable lease.

"But, to create the momentum, the Chinese side proposed a major extension of the facility, stating its value could only be realised through rapid, world-class development. On our side, we had to rush through the necessary planning authorisations and demonstrate we could procure the requisite construction-related materials and equipment in under a month. Here today, on trucks ready to leave this base for Ibrahim Sami, is evidence of that. Having delivered on our word, we opened up a further condition of the agreement between our two nations, allowing for the lease of this military facility for conversion into a global free port as part of the Chinese President's Belt and Road Initiative. This opens the way to the building of logistics warehouses, aircraft servicing facilities, component assembly sites and hotels, offering unparalleled growth and employment opportunities in this remote part of our homeland. We are truly inspired. And finally, as this vision takes shape, we envisage underwriting this shared endeavour by opening up our extensive untapped natural assets in this wider locality, including unexploited reserves of cobalt for batteries and rare earth ores in the expectation that our Chinese brothers and sisters can be sure of a consistent supply in uncertain times. It's time to get this work under way today."

Another round of applause.

"And I will be personally involved in all stages to ensure the plan is realised," interjected Moussavi.

The group looked to Major Ho Li Sen to respond.

"On behalf of the People's Republic of China, may I thank you, Madam, for your kind words. We are pleased to share your vision, but must add a note of caution. For all these ambitions to be realised we must collectively identify and neutralise all potential threats to our plans. The commercial value of the endeavour we have estimated to be costing around sixty billion US dollars. That valuation is only relevant if we strictly adhere to agreed project dates. Failure to achieve these may result in us reviewing, downscaling or cancelling our plans. And, further, a key aspect of delivery depends on a stable political environment in the locality. We cannot afford to be distracted by threats of civil disorder or terrorism. We expect you, as our hosts, to address this matter, and, depending on the circumstances, you will understand we may make our own moves independently to protect our investments. Already, we believe we have identified a terrorist threat from a Muslim minority sect in our own country to our activities here and must as a consequence review our security arrangements. I will deal with this matter separately after this meeting."

Ho's explosive comment landed without warning. For a split second there was silence and nervous looks exchanged between those present.

Moussavi was the first to react.

"Major, if you will share your evidence with me, I will instruct Colonel Rahman to root this out right now. We pride ourselves on providing a safe environment in Khoda Afrin. We have fortified our international borders and use our detainees at our prison here on the base to assist our initiatives, offering a free labour supply on extraction and infrastructure projects, such as the runway here, as well as human test subjects for weapons trials at the Sami base. Because we supply murderers, rapists and other high-risk prisoners to your projects, we have avoided the need for public hangings and floggings, which in turn has resulted in an increasingly calm and positive civil society. Mr al-Fouadi is typical of the local entrepreneurs thriving in this new environment. Wouldn't you agree, Hafiz?"

Hafiz, too, had been wrong-footed by Ho's remarks and started to bluster.

"Er, yes. There is no doubt, as a result of increasing government interventions in the prefecture in recent years, I have benefitted. I am a farmer by trade, growing crops and livestock, and have recently gone into pigs, as well as diversifying into small-scale manufacturing, property development, retail, hospitality and logistics, to name a few. With each of these businesses have come opportunities to employ my fellow countrymen, giving them regular wages and opportunities for training. Future Chinese workers will also benefit from a unique welcoming atmosphere and, as you know, my opening of the Silk Road restaurant, a destination for authentic spicy Szechuan cuisine, and our cinema shows a movie in Mandarin at midnight three nights a week."

Rahman returned to the central issue. "Before we proceed, Major, you should be assured that all discourse in this room is confidential. What evidence do you have to support your claims?"

Ho looked at him directly. "You will be aware we employ a range of security measures at the Sami compound. One element of this is remote facial recognition technology. Our scans showed one of our workers displaying the characteristics of a significant engineer scientist from the Uighur Muslim minority, our prime terrorist threat. This individual and his family and relatives have all participated in various stages of our specialist state education programmes for such people. He had valuable and unique knowledge which qualified him to receive special dispensation to travel abroad to participate in a World Health Organization project in a remote part of Uzbekistan. We are now trying to contact him urgently and have taken measures to detain all his family members back home. It is not the policy of my government to sanction any Uighur to work on this project, so you could say, until we have established the whereabouts of the man, citizen Dr Gulman Ehat, he must be regarded as a clear and present danger."

Despite being annoyed by this unexpected departure from the script, Rahman moved on to take control of the situation. "Alright, Major, we will look into this matter with you. Can you provide us with a picture? We can then arrange to circulate it to our guards and public places. We have limited low-loader capacity and I don't wish to delay sending equipment up to the site."

"You may proceed, Colonel. My people have allocated storage space for essential construction equipment within the compound. The land presently occupied by your anti-aircraft battery will become the new construction site and the prefabricated components will be stored closer to the highway junction at the amelioration site. You are responsible for the security of all items stored close to the compound but outside the boundary fence. Further, during the scheduled period of power outage for the connection of essential services, I expect you to double the allocation of guards, both patrols and checkpoints. I regret not being able to grant you access to our compound, Madam, and Mr Turani, but, given the circumstances, I am sure you will understand. I am hosting a table at the Silk Road tonight and would welcome you both as my guests."

"Just before we finish." Moussavi intervened to put his seal of approval on arrangements. "Where, Colonel will the anti-aircraft battery go?"

"As a temporary measure there is a flat plateau above Ibrahim Sami town centre that Mr al-Fouadi is preparing for a luxury housebuilding project. It is the next closest flat accessible site to the compound but lacks the cover of its present position. When the facility is built at the compound, the four vehicles will be relocated to the amelioration site. It's rather a symbolic asset really – Russian technology. We've had some problems adapting it for our use and maybe your technicians can take a look at its computer control system, which has caused our people some headaches. It doesn't work like our own Thunder surface-to-air missiles we have here."

"Why have it then?" Ho asked.

"It was an asset we acquired as a result of a border dispute some years ago. We have kept it as a deterrent while trying to see whether we can reverse engineer it to our benefit, so I will be happy for your people to take a look."

"We will see. There may not be time this trip. The first priority is to prepare the accommodation blocks for our construction and subterranean engineering teams who are flying in from Xi'an next week. The personnel inventory does not include missile experts but maybe we will have a couple of spare places and can bring others with us. I will check. Madam, gentlemen…"

Ho had decided it was time to close. He had other business with Beijing.

After the meeting had broken up, Rahman turned his attention back to his special guests.

"Madam, Mr Turani, I understand you are with us for a couple of days and Mr Moussavi and I have planned a series of meetings and tours to coincide with your schedule. Today we will go to Ibrahim Sami to review the transfer of your cargo to the site. Despite being unable to access the compound, I thought it useful to give you a tour of the environs, which will provide some context for your future planning. Tomorrow, we will separate, with you, Madam Alrakahthan, spending time reviewing investment plans with the governor mayor, and you, Mr Turani, accompanying me on a tour of the Arasbaran Protected Zone. I understand, from your earlier request, you will be collected by helicopter for your return to Tehran. Mr Moussavi and I have cars ready to go to Ibrahim Sami in one hour, allowing you some time for refreshment before we leave. Should you require anything further during your stay, please let me know."

Rahman's cool, efficient approach to planning was already winning the admiration of Hanah.

"There is one further request I would have, Major. I need to take a view on the further commercial development of Ibrahim Sami and understand there is a hotel there which you own, Mr al-Fouadi. If possible, I would like to spend tonight there, especially as we are dining at the Silk Road."

Back in the Land Cruiser, Fawaz started the drive home. His father, subdued, stared at his mobile and muttered, "Moussavi is always asking for favours then fucking me over. I have spent months creating the site for that housing development at my time and expense, just to be told it will now become a private car park for a load of fucking missiles. Yet more cost and delay. Well, that's it, I haven't got time for all this. I need cash flow. Fawaz – I've asked Hanif to deal with the people consignment tonight. Rahman said the road in from Posyan will be open again at six, which suits me well. Because our usual crossing points are closed, I'm going to drive down to the border ahead of the consignment in order to check there are no fuck-ups. Ho wants to be dinner host, and, with me, your mother and Hanif away, you'll have to manage these prefab deliveries to the compound and the moving of the missile battery. Better fix the best two suites for the posh bird and her bloke. Might be a good show if you put them in a camera room. Seen her sort from Tehran before. She only wants to stay over because fucking at a military base is difficult. Rahman is providing all the people you need to manage the logistics – all you have to do is show them where everything is to go. You'd better go and find Jafar and tell him. Rahman won't want any casual builders on that site until further notice."

"How long do I get him to call them off for?" Fawaz asked.

"Well, based on what we have heard, it must be at least a week or those workers have got to be transferred to the prefabs. I won't have to pay for idle hands."

It was a bright, cloud-free morning in Ibrahim Sami and, considering the hour, the small centre was unusually busy. Notices about the pending road closure on the eastern approach from Posyan had made those visiting the market loaded up with provisions arrive earlier. The modest guard post in the town by the main bus stop had quadrupled in numbers and soldiers were starting to take up positions at strategic points along the roadside. So too bystanders, in the main women, children, old people, ex-servicemen, and beggars, all wanting to witness the spectacle to come. Something of this magnitude didn't happen in this locality very often so the streets were starting to get taken over by the curious, including Dave's team.

There was a real sense that their plan was about to enter its final stages. With the benefit of the sketch plan of the compound, interpreted by Gul, Jo and Rodg, Dave was confident they were ready. Yet again they had discussed the risk of violence and use of weapons and the potential implications. Those with soldiering experience, including Anya, didn't worry about it and just focused on deconstructing the plan at each stage and searing the details into their memory. But Dave had the impression that Jack, the least experienced of the group, might become a problem. He recalled, in their quieter moments, it was Jack who tended to be a dissenting voice, and more likely to take an initiative with risky and unpredictable results. When the action started, all needed to be clear on their individual roles. Fawaz had been kept out of this aspect of the work for his own protection. Dave had explained that, although most of their interest was at the far side of town, where the road turned northwards to Ashelqu, the better positions for close observation would be as the traffic moved through the town. Since his arrival, the overarching impression Jack had formed of the locality was the number of war veterans, some disabled, either sheltering from the sun in doorways or begging close to the market area. Issues with Iraq had been mothballed, not entirely resolved, yet it was clear Iran had paid a heavy price without securing a result. It seemed such a waste but he could not be distracted. Dave understood the best form of surveillance was hiding in plain sight and so was happy for Jack, in his ragged clothes acquired from the laundry, to sit out on the roadside and pick up fresh dust and deposits of diesel engines.

He regretted Fawaz going for realism by gathering some old clothes before they had been washed. He was unnerved being on the street in the heat of the day smelling of someone else's sweat. He needed a clear mind in his position – it was too risky for him to carry a headcam and so he carried a scrunched-up piece of paper and pencil just in case he saw something he might have forgotten to report.

All was set fair. He had positioned himself close to a slight bend in the road, offering him what he thought was the best view of the approaching convoy. What he failed to understand was, in this part of the world, begging was a commercial activity like anything else, and each person had their place and only got an improved position if a person died, moved on or won a fight for it. This was to be his experience.

Edwin had announced his intention to call at the embassy the previous evening and, having dropped a few higher-level names in the FCO, had secured a meeting with an attaché called Mark Clinton-Brown. Who Mr Clinton-Brown was and precisely how we would be able to help wasn't clear, but Edwin's experience told him it was important to be demonstrative about the nature of assistance required. The building, an anonymous eight-storey block with reflected windows in Khagani Street behind the House of Government, was only distinguished by a modest union flag and a surly security guard in a booth behind a turnstile, itself in turn, behind some tall, utilitarian iron railings. Security was a mix of the expected and unannounced, involving the copying of his passport, electronic body searches and palm-scanning. Twenty minutes later he was admitted into the main reception area, his eyes greeted with a number of exhibition flat panels extolling the virtues of British commercial exports, a solitary, bored-looking receptionist and an instant coffee machine, plus a long bench with no backrest, perhaps the sort of thing you might see at a lower-league football ground back home. Wilson could see the process for gaining admission had been super-formal. He didn't expect different treatment once inside and wasn't disappointed by the reaction. Thank goodness he had communicated his requirements prior to arrival. Clinton-Brown greeted and escorted him into an inner office, which appeared to consist of a warren of workstations and, at the far end, a Perspex bubble with a telephone in it. The unusual juxtaposition of a futuristic bubble with what appeared to be a domestic telephone from the mid-1970s made him smile. Was this the principal instrument for managing British influence in Azerbaijan?

"Our presence here has increased over the past three years," Clinton-Brown explained. "We see huge mutual trade benefits for us here, especially post-Brexit, and, of course, given the ambiguities of dealing with the Russians, it is always helpful to have an oil-exporting friend we can turn to when necessary, so I hope Peace International doesn't bring further complications."

He had said enough to suggest he was already briefed on the circumstances of Wilson's visit but said nothing further.

"We have a line to London as requested. Please use the red phone." He gestured towards it.

The bubble had a ready-moulded seat for one, which Edwin suspected was deliberately not designed for comfort, yet hearing the calm intones of his friend Roddy on the line from the MoD made him feel more at home.

"Well you have been a busy boy," his friend began. "I have been following your progress from time to time, especially since we had a request in from Baku regarding your identity status. You should be pleased. They were certainly pissed off when they first contacted the FCO, but I get the impression they've warmed up a bit since. They have some military commandant who's come across you and by all accounts he was quite impressed. We've heard they're inviting you to stay on for a little while until the Peace International mission is settled and I get the feeling they see some advantage to them in your efforts, so that must be positive. You must be careful about this Ehat chap, though. I hear he is becoming hot property with our Asian friends – he could end up causing you a bigger problem than you expected. Anyway, you are on the side of the angels on this and my eyes and ears on the ground will do what they can to ease your progress – at least keep the other players off your back. Do remember, Eddie, it's all to play for. Officially we will remain in denial about what you are doing and if it goes tits up you'll probably have to see if you can get the Canadians to bail you out through your New York links. But, if I were you, I'd enjoy the sunshine and hold your nerve."

It had not felt like a conversation, more of a statement. He was being left out to dry and it was up to him to check the weather forecast. His next meeting, however, gave him cause for optimism.

Bob was waiting outside the House of Government when Wilson arrived. "How did you get on?"

"Being held at arm's length as they think I could be a bit whiffy – I get the impression they'd like me to take an early bath."

Bob laughed. "Well, as they say on the best football shows, it's a game of two halves and there is still a bit to go."

"You sound just like them," Wilson smiled, as they walked into the Interior Ministry.

They had a fifteen-minute wait before being escorted to a meeting room, which seemed to be at the far end of the building. Having taken a lift to the fifth floor, Edwin and Bob walked along a very long corridor. They were shown into a large room, plain but tastefully decorated in green Lincrusta with wooden venetian blinds, dominated by a large candelabra, and those all-seeing eyes of the president gazing down on them from his standard portrait on the wall at the end of an oval table. Through the only other door opposite came a tall, dark-haired olive-skinned man in a light-grey business suit with black, pointed, highly-polished shoes, carrying a lever-arch file.

He looked distracted and in a hurry.

FOURTEEN

"GOOD MORNING, GENTLEMEN. PLEASE be seated. My name is Maxim Nubulatov. I am a minister with responsibility for what you would call 'homeland security' and in charge of your case."

Edwin glanced at Bob; he hadn't realised his activities had been elevated to the status of a government "case" – the omen, he felt, would not be as positive as he had hoped.

"I should begin by thanking you for taking the initiative to come here. I did have it in mind to send someone over to the Four Seasons to find you, so you have saved us a little time. Let me come to the point: I am up to date with what is going on – I have a very comprehensive report from Major Ryumin, so I am happy with that. Before we discuss, there are a couple of points which are not clear from the documentation. Let me start with what I understand to be the central point of your endeavour. How did you become aware of the chemical and biological weapons research facility at Ibrahim Sami in the first place? And, secondly, I know you have sent a number of people over the border into Iran but I need to know how many, as I am assuming those people may well have violated the terms of their visas."

Edwin responded. "Peace International is a humanitarian organisation with members and supporters around the world. It is not unusual for us to be notified of serious human rights abuses by all sorts of individuals who have access to the World Wide Web. In many cases, we do not have the resources to investigate all the allegations which are brought to our attention, but sometimes, in the most serious circumstances, we will receive donations from governments and individuals that allow us to follow up these enquiries. I should make clear we are not some sort of international militia. Ours is not to pursue violence but to document evidence to share with those who can decide how best to respond. Ibrahim Sami was the result of a tip-off received from a private source within the Islamic Republic of Iran."

"Who is paying you?"

"Money for this mission is drawn from central funds held in our headquarters in New York City and includes donations from a diverse range of member states and individuals. It is not uncommon for states to sponsor projects they deem to be of interest to their own affairs. In this case, funds have been drawn from donations from several countries including the UK, France, Sweden and Canada."

"How many of your activists have passed through Azerbaijan to take part?"

"Six. Three British, one South African, one Chinese, one Iranian. All on tourist visas. I have retained their passports while they are out on the assignment."

"Please arrange these to be brought to my office as soon as possible. Again, it will save me having to enforce my request, which I would prefer not to do."

Was this a subtle way of being told to surrender the passports or else prison awaits? Edwin guessed it was and nodded his acquiescence, clear his friend Roddy in London was not prepared to engage in a "dust up" on his behalf.

"And how do you communicate with your people in the field?"

"We don't. They are the ones who understand what is happening on the ground. We cannot influence that, so we must wait for them to contact us. In this case, they have a burner cell phone, which Mr Mullen has. When they have either achieved their objective or returned to Azeri territory or even elsewhere outside Iran, Mr Mullen will hear. My expectation is that because of the passport situation they will return the same way they departed."

Nubulatov continued, "This situation is difficult for us and I think Major Ryumin told you that. We uphold the rule of law and as you have already been told, we understand you and your colleagues have only incurred minor infringements to your visa status on our soil. While recognising these are technically crimes against the state and must result in punishment, the government is also aware you have brought an issue of potential importance to our national security to our attention, and, independent to us, you are taking actions which we would be minded to support.

"We both know that Azerbaijan has not always been a backer of Peace International and has previously declined the opportunity of membership, especially as we understand you have also received false reports of unlawful imprisonments here in the past, which I am pleased to note you have not taken steps to pursue.

"I have to say again we are disappointed you chose to embark on this particular 'initiative' without seeking our advice in advance, but we cannot worry about that now. However, your work to date has helped us to neutralise one of our more troublesome local terrorists and to refocus on addressing significant crime issues in our rather complicated southern border region, when for so long now we have had to be looking to the west and Armenia.

"We have subsequently increased our efforts to intercept radio and cell phone communications in Khoda Afrin Prefecture, which are helping to build up a picture of what is going on over there. As a result, our intelligence operatives have discovered information that will allow us to make a significant move soon.

"We are meeting today because I wish to propose a way of sorting out this mess to the benefit of all.

"Firstly, we will become members of Peace International without paying fees but will offer you logistical support to complete this exercise. When it is over, you must publicly acknowledge our role and, by implication, guarantee that enquiries made to you by reactionaries in this country are not followed up.

"Secondly, you and Mr Mullen will travel back to Barthaz and liaise with Captain Alexander Zeitsev, who has been delegated to set up a temporary forward base to manage the return of your people. He is under an instruction to contact you at the Four Seasons in order to make arrangements.

"Thirdly, as your team return to collect their passports, each will be sentenced to a period in detention, which will be suspended, based on the time that has elapsed since they first entered the country. Alternatively, they can opt for immediate deportation, which will carry the sanction of life bans from entering the state in future. Your own passport will remain suspended until we are satisfied all outstanding issues have been addressed.

"Finally, you are at liberty to refuse these terms, but my people have been speaking to your embassy. It is agreed we are on the verge of a new era of economic cooperation and it is not in the interests of either the UK or Azerbaijan to face any potential embarrassment from this situation. I think you will conclude there is really only one way to go on this matter."

Leaving the ministry, they crossed Malokan Park, a picturesque leafy green oasis on the way back towards the Old Town and the Four Seasons. Ironically, at this hour, it seemed to have been turned into a sort of downtown smokers' shelter, with a concentration of coffee shacks and a collection of stressed taxi drivers taking time out from the clogged surrounding streets.

Edwin wanted to keep moving, but Bob looked in need of a nicotine fix.

Coffee and Sobranie in hand, he asked, "Do you want to drive down there? I can get the car loaded but it will be around six hours."

"We'd better wait until I hear from Zeitsev. It's clear our hosts want control of all this and it looks like we've pissed them off enough at this point. We can't risk getting carjacked en route. Besides, if the military is getting involved, I think they will want us there more quickly then we could manage ourselves. If there's no message when we get back to the hotel, I'm going to do what Ryumin suggested and take a look at the National Art Collection across the road. As a tour guide, I'm sure you will be able to tell me what I'm looking at, so when I next see him I'll have something positive to say."

The noise of the wind and the rain shower was helpful cover to Gil as he edged his way forward. From his position he was now just a matter of metres away from two crouched figures, one staring through binoculars, the other fiddling with a magazine on his AK-47 assault rifle. They had been talking in lowered tones and were clearly oblivious to the fact they had company. Gil made a side wave of a gesture towards one of his colleagues to cover his approach. Gil sprang forward, landing on one of his quarries' back and knocking the other sideways. Surprise had given him the advantage of claiming one of their weapons, while the other was persuaded to relax by having an M16 carbine in his ribs.

"*Zdravstvuj*, boys. I thought it was time we got to know each other. You FSB people all speak English, I know, and I wouldn't want you to misunderstand my intentions by me speaking Russian to you. It seems you and we are interested in the same things, yes? I've not known a small piece of forest to have so many secret soldiers in it, all trying to stay out of each other's way, have you? I must admit, I'm surprised we didn't meet sooner. Anyway, I didn't drop by to find out how your mother was – just a bit curious about why you would be grovelling in the bushes in western Iran with us?"

"Who the fuck are you, *Americanski*?"

"I like to think we're a bit better mannered than them – we're British and a little shy of meeting the locals. But always happy to talk to other foreigners like you."

"We are here on private business – it doesn't concern you."

"This is a pretty small place. I can't help thinking your private business might be something we might have an interest in. You never know: we might even be able to help. It's never a bad thing to have an offer of help, especially as you won't be doing anything until we let you go."

"We are Russian Federation Special Forces Tactical Engagement Team. You get the word 'team'? There are more of us about, who will come looking if we don't come back to our camp."

"Where's that?"

"On the ridge over there," he indicated with a nod.

"You guys aren't Soviets anymore, so why are you here on the border?" He pressed the muzzle of his weapon into his captive's ear.

"We are here to claim back stolen property."

"What?"

"We have a big and very expensive four-piece anti-aircraft missile protection system here, loaned to Azerbaijan that was stolen by some Iranian gangsters, some time ago. They are trying to disassemble and reverse engineer it for their own purposes. Fucking pirates. They have left it here unguarded. We are going to take it home."

"If it's theirs, why are you doing it?"

"The Azeris are scared of the Iranians. They think if they do it, it would start a war. If we do it, they can't complain. They already owe us for half their air force."

"How will they know it is you?"

"Hah! We are proud Russians – we don't hide what we want to do. We will leave our calling card. And, if you try to take it off us, you can be sure we will come after you too. What are you here for, English? The sunny weather?"

"Do you know, your Chinese friends are building a chemical and biological weapons base with the Iranians? Right here. Bet you don't fancy having the locals getting their hands on that. It will give you worse problems than you've got in Ukraine and Georgia. We're here to fuck it up – *just a little*, but enough to make them go off the whole idea. We know all about your Buk missiles and their air pressure detonators. As far as we're concerned, we don't want the responsibility of trying to get one of your old rust buckets halfway across Europe – so what's there not to like? We can both do our thing and who knows, perhaps help each other along the way."

"What help do you want from us?"

"Firstly, keeping out of our way would be good. We don't want to shoot you by accident. And, second, don't go and grab the Buk trucks too quickly. If you wait until we have left our own calling card, you'll get a free run to the frontier – assuming you are going to use the Ashelqu channel and not Barthaz."

"When are you going to act?"

"In the next couple of days. Keep looking through your binoculars and you'll see the story unfold. If you just want the Buk system, we'll leave you alone to take it. If I were you, I'd talk to your mates up on the hill about it. We could just be the best thing that's happened for you today. But be warned – if you get in our way in the next forty-eight hours you could get damaged. Oh, I see you have a flask of vodka in your pocket. Could you share a drop? Our army is a bit stingy on basic rations, and we could toast our new friendship. Cheers! And now we will leave you. My mate somewhere in the dark round here has got you covered, so no sudden movements. Give us five minutes and you can hope you won't see us ever again. I will send your regards to our Queen."

Abdullo Alrakahthan was in his car stuck in another Tehran traffic jam, this time heading north by the Pasargad Bank on Sattari. It was an entirely normal scene. Thick fumes, frustrated drivers and blaring horns. He seemed to spend most of his working days in cars reading briefing papers on his way to his next meeting. His cell phone started to buzz. The caller was coming up unrecognised.

"Yes?"

"Good morning, Abdullo."

Alrakahthan knew he was taking a personal call from the highest person in government.

"I am on my way to the Consultative Assembly to give the National Day address. I have been lobbied to include something about the revolutionary struggle against the Great Satan and the fact we will not be blackmailed into submission, but the members are not going to like my message about the need for fuel price hikes and food shortages, as it will play to the narrative of our enemies. I have decided that the best message of defiance we can issue is to show how caring we are, looking after those who are being hurt the most by our present challenges. So, I want to go ahead with another round of emergency food parcels, as we discussed at our last meeting. We need to follow the same specification and distribution arrangements as before. My people have forecast that, to do this successfully across the country, we will need 8.5 million units. Can you get this sorted and let me know when we will be ready to release? I won't need to explain too much today, but it will constitute a promise that we will need to deliver upon, so come back to me soonest please. We also need to be careful about how we account for this; I don't want the details published."

"Excellency, my company is always at your disposal. I will make the arrangements and provide a full budget statement, but I would think it will not be more than a 20% increase in the unit charge, especially if I am able to manage fulfilment via Dubai. Rather than drawing down funds from the state exchequer, it may be better for you to look at a package of 'sale and lease back' of state assets. That way you can fund your initiative without further negative pressure on reserves. Did you realise, for example, that if you were to consider the sale and leaseback of, say, the old Silkworm assembly plant in Bandar Abbas, that in itself could provide all the resources necessary? In addition, it would leave a discretionary margin clear to cover necessary unanticipated disbursements. All it would need is a decree from your office."

"Yes, but if you take over an armaments factory you will inherit production obligations to the state. Are you sure you can cover this?"

"My people have already profiled the project as part of my company's five-year plan. I cannot see there is a problem. If I take over the Bandar site, for example, I can retain the management and continue to meet state commitments as well as investing further in the business. It's a *win–win*."

"Alright. Make an appointment to come and see me with a fully costed plan. I will talk with Jeylani."

The phone went dead. Abdullo called Hasan. He smiled as his son reported receiving a new order from a national charity for prosthetic limbs – the biggest yet.

Ryumin was right. The National Art Museum of Azerbaijan was indeed a sight to behold.

"I thought you were going to show me around, not buy an audio guide," Wilson said mockingly.

"Art is a subjective thing. It would be wrong for me to force my views on you." Bob smiled.

"Do I get the feeling you haven't been in here much yourself?"

"Well, it must have been a year, but you're right: I shouldn't leave all the artistic stuff to Anya. As an immigrant, I should appreciate it more. You've got two buildings to choose from here. One is European art, the other is Eastern. The real difference is that the European one feels more like a collection – like someone thought about it. I'm told the Dutch/Flemish gallery is the best. There's stuff in there from Franz Hals to Pieter Claesz. Not a lot of people know that. The Eastern one I suspect is what will interest you more though. That's got Persian, Turkish, Chinese and Japanese artefacts, plus quite a lot of nondescript Russian pictures."

"Why nondescript?"

"Anything good that was here the Russians took to St Petersburg when the Soviet Union collapsed, with the possible exception of the Shishkin. Still, there's one or two others in there that might look OK in a front room in Surrey."

Bob was getting to know his boss, who instinctively walked towards the second building and the Azerbaijani Rooms with their antique and medieval ceramics and carpets.

The visit proved to have been a welcome diversion for the pair, masking their own separate thoughts about the task ahead. For Edwin, he'd found himself far more engaged in detailed operational planning than he had been before and as a consequence had developed a keener sense of risk and personal responsibility for his work. He was now committed in a way that his own future was now directly locked in with the outcome of Hebbert's team in Iran. For Bob, it was personal in a different way. He had committed to building a new life in Azerbaijan and much of that rested on the relationship with his wife, whose own future was uncertain at best. Their visit to the National Art Museum had filled up a couple of hours, a good break from the day's realities. Returning to the Four Seasons, Edwin found the message he had expected had been delivered. It was time to refocus and press forward to a conclusion.

A car arrived to collect them from the hotel the following morning and followed the now-familiar route back to the airport – the former president still seemingly keeping an eye on them during their journey. They dressed casually, looking more like tourists than businessmen. Their uniformed driver had a stern look about him. He clearly didn't have much English or, if he did, was not the sort to engage in idle banter. Edwin wondered if he was in for another encounter with Boroschenko when they arrived, but this time their car was ushered directly onto the main apron and driven to the steps of a military helicopter away from the civil aircraft and terminal buildings.

This machine looked different to the transporters they had witnessed in Minjivan. It was smaller, probably more agile, and bristled with guns and missiles on its two truncated stabiliser wings. It had an observation gunner's bubble window at the front, below the flight deck.

"Welcome, Mr Wilson, Mr Mullen. My name is Pavilinsky, skipper of this Mi-35 gunship. You will be joining our mission on the southern border. This is a military operation and so you must understand there is an element of danger. My job is to offer you the best protection I can and so I would ask you to respect and act immediately on any instruction I give. Please put on the overalls, helmets and protection vests and climb aboard. One of my guys will get you strapped in. We should be on our way in ten minutes; the weather is calm and it will take us about an hour to get there. Captain Zeitsev will meet us for the briefing."

"I think we have been warned we are travelling on a flying bomb, so not to expect much in the way of creature comforts," Bob quipped as they were shoehorned, then fixed into two narrow seats in the back. "And, if you think this is tough, we're probably sleeping on those hay bales in that shed in Barthaz tonight," he added.

Pavilinsky had not wasted time. Having collected his cargo, he donned his own helmet and went up front to start his pre-flight checks, as the side door was closed behind him. Although Edwin was grateful for the ride, Bob had picked up on his apprehension about flying by helicopter so close to a potentially hostile border. At the very least he assumed they would be monitored by Iranian radar, which could make them a target for hostile fire. There was little point about worrying. He was in someone else's hands now and he guessed his fellow travellers also wanted to live to tell the tale. It is always difficult to estimate altitude especially from a helicopter, but he guessed they were flying at about 500 metres, especially watching the crew manning their weapons as if expecting attack. It was noisy and cold. There was no point in a conversation. Best to close his eyes and zone out until arrival.

Bob remembered his two most recent visits to Barthaz, both after dark. He tried to remember the terrain, which he recalled was gravelly, sandy and marsh-like. Probably not the best place to land a helicopter. He realised how fast-moving their situation had become as Pavilinsky identified the quarry site that they had originally used as their jumping off point as the best place to land. In the light of day, he noted it was only hollowed out on two sides, creating a plateau before the open ground fell away. Previously deserted, at the far side, Edwin saw an army personnel carrier, and further in the distance the warehouse and a large green truck with a telescopic aerial on it, but no sign of anyone else on the ground. Once the helicopter was down, the rotors lost their methodical beat, creating a local dust storm until all power had been switched off.

Pavilinsky climbed down as the side door was opened and gesticulated to Edwin and Bob to release their safety belts, leave their helmets and follow him across the arid quarry floor.

They reached the top of the track leading down to the warehouse, the Aras beyond and, on the horizon, the far bank of the river which was the Islamic Republic of Iran. Climbing up the hill to meet them was the familiar face of Captain Zeitsev.

"Good to see you once more. Come into the shed. I expect it's changed a little since you were last here."

It certainly was different. To begin with, it was the first time Bob had seen the place in daylight. Moving away from the apparent protection of the quarry escarpment, the track leading down to the warehouse was more exposed than he thought. No trees or other natural features in sight but a mix of heathers, boulders, marsh and sedge. The track itself seemed fairly indistinct; in the good places concrete slabs dictated its course but was already under attack from local vegetation. In other spots, the route was reduced to concentrations of crushed rock, but, because it was limestone, it was deteriorating in its boggy surroundings. Mostly, this sort of terrain was only suitable for the most capable four-by-four vehicles or caterpillars. The warehouse seemed a newer and much more substantial building than Bob had thought, with quite a large area of still-good-quality hardstanding at the front. The walk from the helicopter had been more tolerable, as, although cloudy, the weather was dry. Entering through the small door of the closed corrugated-steel vehicle entrance, the scale of change in recent days was apparent. Banks of radio equipment had been placed to the left-side wall, with six operators with headsets. Towards the middle, a giant table with large-scale maps. To the right were what looked like a tented community with sleeping space, a TV and a canteen. At the back, an armoured troop carrier. Half a dozen soldiers in full combat readiness, AK-47s slung from forward positions, roamed the interior but, surprisingly, neither Edwin nor Bob saw much evidence of soldiers outside. This had the impression of being a low-level deployment. Leading the way, Zeitsev walked purposefully towards the canteen.

"Coffee?" Zeitsev nodded to an orderly, and the four of them sat at a table on camp chairs.

"Firstly, may I pass on my apologies from Major Ryumin. He is on manoeuvres elsewhere but has said he will be joining us as soon as possible. In the meantime, I am authorised to brief you on our activities since we last met in Minjivan and discuss with you the next steps we have decided on. Flight Lieutenant Pavilinsky is involved in this and will share our conversation. I should begin with a word of thanks to you, Mr Wilson, for drawing this matter to our attention. I think it fair to say we underestimated the significance of the situation across the border and we were not sufficiently prepared. The ministry in Baku has instructed us to take all necessary steps to secure our southern frontiers but, as you will be able to see shortly from the maps on the table, it is a huge and wild area, with most of the actual borders being not much more than marks on a map. It is true that the significance of what is happening in Khoda Afrin should have been documented earlier, as we had been aware over the last couple of years that the Iranians were taking steps to fortify their front lines with minefields and razor wire. We assumed at the time that this was not much more than a social employment initiative by their government, using penal workers and others as part of community sentences. One of our most immediate tasks has been to undertake a thorough review of their border security arrangements using drones launched from here. Their preparations have proved more extensive than we first thought, which has raised concerns among our defence strategists in Baku. After all, the Cold War era has passed. For our defence against Iran we have tended to rely on our network of military airbases around Bilasuvar and Beylagan, which have shadowed the two official crossing points at Parsabad and Ardabil. Observers are now reporting new defensive works on the Iranian side as far north as Jafar Abad. This area has not required the benefit of a formal frontier crossing before, but what is interesting to us has been the creation of a limited number of undefended corridors north of here, which are being used on a rotary basis for smuggling. Although we cannot be sure, because this activity fits a pattern, we think it must be instigated or controlled by the state. The most southern corridor we have discovered is at Ashelqu, not far from here. Some time ago we had a mobile surface-to-air missile system stolen by bandits from over near Minjivan, which we were able to trace to the crossing at Ashelqu and subsequently positioned at Ibrahim Sami. We asked the Iranians for permission to send a team over to collect it on several occasions, but responsibility and access have been denied. A complicating factor has been that the missile system was leased to us, but the hardware is owned by the Russians, who are displeased by the present impasse. We believe they have sent a clandestine task force in to assess the chances of recovery, but our intelligence suggests they were infiltrated into the theatre via Turkey, not through us, so we can't be sure what they are doing. If they do risk a snatch, it will be via Azeri territory, so we have to remain vigilant. However, smuggling and theft aside, the present activities of Iran's guests, the People's Liberation Army from China, represent a threat we cannot ignore. We agree on the strategy of Peace International to collect evidence of their clandestine activity, as we think securing and publishing evidence of what they are doing will cause a serious foreign policy headache for them. We understand you had some local help to cross the river here into Ibrahim Sami and have assumed that help is no longer available to you, but those who crossed now have the knowledge and confidence to return here shortly. We will maintain a presence to assist in their recovery. In the meantime, we are using this facility to listen in to all communications traffic in the Ibrahim Sami area, including landlines, military frequency radios and cell phones. The information we are collecting is helping us to build up a picture about what is happening on the ground.

"We have learned that significant machine tools and materials to assist the expansion of the research & production compound have already been airlifted into Posyan and that technical construction teams will arrive direct from China next week, so they are fast-tracking it. One of your group's members has already been identified as a local terrorist threat. Apparently, Ehat, the Uighur, came up somewhere on their facial recognition technology and they are crapping themselves trying to find him. We are assuming your people on the ground know this so it is logical they will attempt to complete their mission in the next forty-eight hours. We have also learned that the local head man, al-Fouadi, is facilitating a people and drugs crossing further south, headed for Vezhnaly, in the next twenty-four hours. We have moved the necessary resources to monitor and then intercept. The instruction from Baku is that we must be resolute in intervening against any unauthorised incursion into and through our territory, and so we have put in place the necessary equipment and troops to ensure success. We intend to use these opportunities to gain maximum

313

publicity to warn off those who abuse our friendship and drive out these warlords who are damaging our communities and peaceful way of life."

"These aren't the only groups out there," added Wilson. "Somewhere there is a small group of British special forces tasked with observing my team on the ground. Think of them as sort of unofficial protection for the Peace International crew. They can kill if necessary, whereas we have no authority to take life unless our people are in personal danger."

"Will they know we are working together?" asked Zeitsev.

Edwin knew he couldn't worry about something he could not control.

"I don't know. Probably. London is clearly aware of the situation, but how they talk to their field operatives is a mystery to me," he replied.

"Let us hope, then, we don't end up meeting them by accident. Azeri forces will not shoot over frontiers, but we will fully engage all unrecognised entities using or crossing our territory."

Zeitsev's statement was drawn verbatim from an email from the Interior Ministry and didn't feel like an idle threat.

Hafiz had spent more time than usual running through the forthcoming people and drugs transfer with Hanif. He was irritated this job was going to be much more expensive and complicated than his preferred route from Ashelqu, a well-trodden path where all the risk factors were under his control. He had picked up from Rahman that the growing sensitivity of the border area owing to the increased Chinese presence meant that his "unofficial" trading corridor would be suspended for the foreseeable future. Unfortunately, his paymasters in Marshad were not interested in his local security problems and were just expecting him to solve the puzzle. All he had to do was to get forty travellers to Vezhnaly in Azerbaijan in the next twenty-four hours. Then it became someone else's problem. Although the final thirty kilometres the other side would be by road, getting his precious cargo across the border by a new route would not be easy. He had taken the same attitude as his paymasters and decided he would have to throw money at the problem, even if it meant making a dent in his profit margins. Some careful research had led him to an engineering business south of Ibrahim Sami in the village of Karranlo. Here, he had found an ex-Revolutionary Guard officer, Seyyed Jevadi, injured out of the army, who had set up a workshop, servicing army vehicles, specialising in locally produced, doubled-axled Khodro diesel trucks. These 'monsters' had all the attributes of heavy all-terrain vehicles but their ten-speed gearboxes made them equally effective on roads. Frantic calls over the past forty-eight hours had established that Jevadi had three in his workshop which were due to be returned to Posyan the following week. When Hafiz had enquired whether he could '"hire" them for forty-eight hours, Jevadi had laughed and said it was more than his job was worth, but Hafiz was a persuasive negotiator and, as the cash fee rose, along with the realisation it was going to be paid in US dollars, the mechanic had become more accommodating. He had guessed why Hafiz was so keen, but worried about entrusting the vehicles to his care. He had pointed out that these trucks were 'moody beasts' at the best of times and required drivers who really understood their personalities – more to the point, people who had enough nous to get them going if they broke down. Hafiz had agreed to hire two of the three trucks and drivers, and thought that would be the end of the matter. But the engineer was not done, seeing the opportunity to get a bit of work for some of his friends in the locality.

"Do you know the road to Vezhnaly? It's tricky. There are all sorts of bandits and wild men up in the hills there, the type who will shoot and ask questions later. You're going to need some armed guys who can scare them off."

"How many?" asked Hafiz, resigned to the realities of the situation.

"Well, I think you should allow four per truck."

"Hold on a minute. If I want to hire a fucking army, I can go elsewhere. I'll take two per truck and that's it."

Terms agreed, Hafiz would travel to Karranlo ahead of the main consignment to make the necessary payment to Jevadi. He would then wait for Hanif to arrive with the merchandise in a truckload of pomegranates. His precious cargo would then be transferred under cover in Jevadi's workshop, before setting out to cross the Aras river south of the village at its shallowest point. Hafiz himself would join the lead vehicle as he would have no prospect of recovering his money unless the transfer to the next courier was made in Vezhnaly. The plan had plenty of risk, but it was the only solution available in the timescale he had. If all went well, he would be back home with a new pile of cash in just twenty-four hours.

He had managed a brief chat with Fawaz before he set off, asking him to attend the meal with the Alrakahthan woman at the Silk Road and to ensure Jafar got the prison labour promised by Rahman to get on with building the prefabs and connecting the electricity and water supplies outside the research compound. Any problems would have to wait until he got back, as he could not be contacted in his absence.

"Everything will be fine," he told his son. "Just take it in stages. Avoid taking unnecessary decisions if you can, but, if you have to make choices to keep things moving, do what you need to do."

Fawaz had been home long enough to know when not to ask questions. He readily recognised this was one such situation, especially as he understood why his father was going away.

FIFTEEN

IT WAS A RELATIVELY short drive down to Karranlo, but Hafiz knew to prepare. There was a special concealed safe in the cab of the Land Cruiser below the driver's seat, big enough to accommodate two briefcases with unspecified amounts of cash. Transferring the money from the house was a task that took time in itself, which required the careful counting and labelling of amounts to be paid and stacking them in the right order of payment. Another briefcase, the payment to Jevadi was kept in the footwell of the passenger seat, together with a sleeping bag and drinking water. In the back, a couple of jerry-cans of diesel, filled the day previously. He hesitated before loading the final piece of essential equipment, a Glock 9mm semi-automatic pistol, into the glovebox, with a burner cell phone for emergencies only.

It was late afternoon when Hafiz arrived at Jevadi's garage, itself a large steel structure capable of accommodating twice the number of vehicles presently occupying it. Jevadi had already got two teams of mechanics working on the vehicles that would be going out that night effectively stripping them down and putting them back together.

As Hafiz approached, Jevadi nodded towards a small office in one corner.

On the mechanic's desk was a map of the surroundings of the Aras river with marks and arrows.

"The trucks will be ready for midnight – serviced, loaded, crewed and fuelled as agreed. What about the cargo?"

"My man will be here with a trailer at 23.30 as arranged, so we should be able to leave on time."

"We will be crossing the Aras at this point." The mechanic tapped his finger at a nondescript feature on the map south of the town. "We will go this way. Although the river here is a little deeper than I would like, we will use the foundation mountings of the old bridge to run grappling hooks from the front of the vehicle, which we can recoil into the front axles of the trucks. It will be slow and noisy. It's probably going to take a couple of hours, even if it goes without a hitch, but it will be the most secure way of getting the trucks over there. We can hitch up to the footings on this side of the river for the return."

"How deep is the river?"

"Based on a measurement we took yesterday, about three-quarters of a metre. I guessed you would be wanting to take your Land Cruiser across? If so, we will adjust your suspension and fit new wheels and tyres. We have everything you need, but you know it will slow you down once you get onto a proper road."

"What happens on the other side?"

"There is an 18% incline over the first 300 metres or so – a mix of mud and shale so there is enough material to get some traction. Your Land Cruiser's four-litre engine and certainly the Khodros have the power to get up there. We will carry extra chains to ensure there is no problem."

"And what of the crews?"

"I am supplying drivers, co-drivers, mechanics and two fully armed guards for each vehicle. As well as automatic weapons, we will also carry grenades and tear gas bombs. Those teams will be here at 22.00 and will be under your control for the duration. All have to be paid prior to departure. I trust you have the money?"

318

The coming hours dragged for Hafiz, who wanted to get on with it but knew that success depended on meticulous planning. He was clear they would not be leaving the shed until he had personally checked all the preparations. He knew he needed to be patient. He sat in Jevadi's office killing time, watching the TV news. Nothing much of interest there, just the Supreme Leader blethering away to the Assembly about the need for Iranian citizens to continue their struggle to ensure the success of the revolution and that, despite the activities of the Great Satan and their friends in Israel and elsewhere, the Islamic Republic would not be crushed by the evil revisionist forces of the West. What made the Islamic Republic a global beacon of hope was its sense of compassion for its people and respect for its war heroes, he was saying. Hope meant making sure every Iranian citizen had a basic right to food, injured war veterans had access to mobility, and rationing of fuel would improve the environment for all. Yes, he thought, 'hope' was also about holding on to power no matter what, just like Moussavi. Free food parcels would be handed out for only the second time in their history, to 8.5 million people who qualified to receive them, all those who had lost arms or legs in wars would get free prosthetics, and those who moaned about increased fuel prices would soon see the benefits in terms of their health. A fitter, stronger nation was ready to play an important role on the world stage, collaborating with its friends and neighbours, especially Russia and China. The speech was dragging on and on, killing off any enthusiasm his audience may have had for his core message. It certainly motivated Hafiz to switch it off and go and watch Jevadi's mechanics finishing their checks on the Khodros. Twenty-two-hundred hours came and went. They appeared to have done a good job. Hafiz's Land Cruiser was adapted and the crews arrived. He shook hands with each, handing them a black plastic package – their wages for the trip. Morale was high; these guys were clearly ex-military, understood the territory and knew how to behave. For the first time, his nervousness was dissipating. With one hour to go, it was time to open both entrances and exits to the garage and fire the engines of the Khodros. One started first time, the second coughed and died. Once, twice, some shouting and cursing, and a final inspection under the cowling produced the ignition all were seeking from the second vehicle. Coming in the dead of night, the noise would ensure the nearest neighbours were disturbed, but, given the density of the blue-hazed exhaust fumes being kicked out, no one was likely to venture out to watch. The drivers and mechanics started loading the cabs, the guards standing around with their AK-47s, chatting and smoking.

Jevadi walked over to Hafiz, who was standing by the shed front door away from the dirt and smell.

"We've lined up the Land Cruiser as the lead vehicle across the river. I want you to take one of my guys with you, who will guide you over and attach the chains from Khodros One to the far bridge footing. That will give you a head start on getting up the incline to the road. Don't worry, you don't have to take him beyond the far bank. His job is to supervise the truck crossings. He's quite capable of getting himself back here on his own."

At that moment there was even more noise from the back of the shed as a new, higher tone of truck engine added to the cacophony and a fresh set of headlights on full beam temporarily blinded Hafiz as he looked towards the source of the commotion. A Scania S series tractor pulling a trailer with "Fruits of the World" emblazoned on it came into view. Lining up next to the two Khodros, the driver added the airbrakes and killed the lights; the new vehicle shuddered as the engine was closed down.

Hanif jumped down from the cab.

"I left the driver at the bus station in Sami. I told him we'd return his truck in an hour."

Jevadi walked over to meet him.

"Leave it with me – I'll get one of my guys to do it on their way home. Where's the merchandise? You can get them on board straightaway."

Hanif crawled underneath the trailer unit and fiddled around before releasing a small trap door and shouting, "Out, out!"

One by one, the figures of people emerged into the yellow sodium light. Crawling out from under the trailer, they stared around, bewildered and disoriented. The first were grabbed by the guards and walked quickly to the first of the Khodros. A steel arm with a rope attached protruded from the rear, the guards indicating they should use it to pull themselves up into the back. After the first two or three were on board they helped the others to climb up. The guards took their cue from Hanif, shouting and gesticulating for them to hurry. These people, mostly male economic refugees from Pakistan and other neighbouring easterly states, already understood the disciplines of their plight, clutching heavy backpacks stuffed not with their possessions but narcotics destined for Europe. The transfer of the 'merchandise' took around fifteen minutes to complete. Jevadi pointed to one of his team to move the Scania out and back to Sami. Leaving the fully loaded Khodros ready to go, Hanif and the guide joined Hafiz in the Land Cruiser, which with its new elevated wheelbase stood almost as high as the cab of the Iranian trucks. Jevadi slapped the side of the Land Cruiser and beckoned to the first Khodro to follow. They were away and on time. In the Land Cruiser there was silence as Hafiz listened to the instruction of Jevadi's guide. Hanif kept looking out behind, to check both trucks were following. They had become used to the light of the warehouse and were now pitched into the dark of the night. It was cloudy and without moonlight; it took a while for their eyes to adjust.

Looking out into the churning waters of the river, Hafiz was concerned their guide would find the crossing point but was soon reassured by the sight of a concrete buttress picked out of the darkness by the Land Cruiser's headlights. The car then turned right off the road and down a shallow embankment to face the torrent. The first Khodro lined up directly behind. Hafiz's guide then leaped out to take the coiled chain and hooked it to the back of the Land Cruiser. Climbing back in, he told Hafiz to drive straight into the river.

"Don't worry. Keep in low gear and steer into the current. It will feel like you don't have full control, especially as there are a few rocks on the riverbed that may make it a bit bumpy, but keep going forward slowly. The chain to the truck behind is attached. If we got into trouble, they could wind the chain back and pull us out, but that shouldn't be necessary. Also, don't be frightened by the noise of the water – you will think you'll be flooded out before you even get to the middle. I think the rushing sound of the water is the most frightening. You must ignore it and keep moving forward steadily."

Despite the new height of the Land Cruiser, its headlights could only pick out the white foam of the seething waters but the steel chain they were towing almost acted like a drag anchor, stabilising their vehicle. Hafiz kept the revs high and pressed forward into the chaotic blackness. Jevadi had said it would take two hours to cross the Aras and, in the case of the Land Cruiser, the trip had taken forty minutes. The most anxious part of the journey was, as predicted, the midway point where the roaring waters, sounding like a jet engine, threatened to breach the door seals of the car, but they had held firm. Gradually, the waters started to recede, but there was precious little in their line of vision to tell them where to go once they had landed on the bank, until their guide excitedly pointed away to their left – another concrete buttress with the iron eye, the destination for their hooked chain. "Welcome to Azerbaijan." He smiled, opening the door and jumping down to release the hook and dragging it to the buttress. He then started signalling with a torch behind him towards the waves and then ran back to see Hafiz pointing further left to the bottom of the incline, which would lead them up to the road to Vezhnaly.

The hook and chain proved an inspired tool for crossing the river with each Khodro. The trucks had the double strength of pulling in the extended chain to the front axle while pressing forward in low gear through the torrent, knowing they were aligned with the far bank.

Hanif joined Hafiz up front in the Land Cruiser to negotiate the climb away from the river. Jevadi's new tyres came into their own as the Land Cruiser got a grip on the new terrain and negotiated the brush and light vegetation blocking their way, with only modest wheel spins en route. Finally pushing out of the undergrowth, they arrived at a layby next to the narrow road which lead towards to mountains of Azerbaijan's southern interior. They had four hours before their timed rendezvous. Now was the time to wait for their merchandise to arrive before moving on.

Hafiz lit a couple of cigarettes and passed one to Hanif. He wasn't sure whether he felt relief or excitement for negotiating the first hazard in their dangerous journey, but he did know he wouldn't do it again. The two listened for the sound of straining diesel engines from the river below.

The man sat cross-legged on the pavement, waiting to see the convoy pass. Looking down the road, a cloud of dust was visible on the horizon, so he wouldn't need to wait long, but it proved to be too long. For him, his reason for being was to observe the convoy and note anything out of the ordinary which could affect their plans. But some of those around him had a different agenda. It was not uncommon for military convoys to throw coins to those on the street when they passed, so getting a good position to view the procession of trucks was important to the local beggars, who competed to look the most in need. Two came to sit either side of him and kept staring. He couldn't understand why as they insisted on getting uncomfortably close and seeming to block his view. He had been forced to shuffle forward from the pavement into the gutter – too far forward for the liking of one of the Revolutionary Guards policing the street to ensure none of the on lookers got into the road.

"Get back, you dog!" shouted the squaddie, jerking his rifle butt backwards into his face.

As he recoiled, the two beggars on either side saw the opportunity to get rid of this new interloper, landing blows on him as he was off balance. His head hit the kerb, but he could vaguely remember the blows kept coming and kicking feet were added to the mix. His beating could be nothing more than a sideshow to the main event approaching but it was serious enough to spark the attention of a *chador*-clad woman nearby, who started to scream. He could vaguely remember someone dragging him back from the roadside, then another figure in black bending over him to help lift him up. His face was blooded and he was now semi-conscious. What happened next was only told to him afterwards. Some way further down the road on the opposite side, two other women in *burkhas* were talking in lowered tones.

"Look – it's Jack. He's been beaten up and two women are taking him away. I'll try and follow them. Can you find Dave and let him know?"

One of them then bustled across the road as if needing to pay a visit to the bakers.

Making her way to where he had been, she saw two black cloaked figures supporting Jack and dragging him away. She watched as she saw them take him into the big house set back from the road. There was no chance of following. The property was protected by iron fencing, yet one of the two women had a key that had let them inside. There was nothing more to do other than to note the house and keep watch. A difficult task in itself as the first trucks from the convoy rolled into town.

Jack's unexpected rescuers were Shimina and Khalifa. Shimina had immediately recognised him from their recent visit to the cinema and had called Khalifa to help her get him off the street. Now inside the family home, they propped him up in the kitchen and started to wash his wounds. Still concussed, Jack did not have full control of his faculties and was unable to remember being taken to a room, stripped and put into a bed. The comfort of a soft mattress, the first he had experienced in nearly two weeks, lulled him into a deep sleep.

Fawaz had instructed special arrangements were to be made at the hotel for the welcome dinner for Madam Alrakahthan. Mr Choi had been asked to prepare a traditional Chinese banquet table in a secluded corner of the restaurant for the cabal of local decision makers. It had been agreed that Major Ho would host, accompanied by a female translator, Sergeant Amy Fong. His guests would be Hossein Moussavi, governor mayor, and his wife; Colonel Rahman, Fawaz, and Jamshid Turani, as well as the guest of honour. Seven of the eight places were filled by the appointed hour.

Major Ho liked to keep things precise.

"Mr Turani, we are looking forward to welcoming your colleague, Madam Alrakahthan. Will she be joining us?"

Jamshid looked momentarily flustered and had no warning of his colleague's absence.

"Er, yes – I'm sure she will be along shortly," he offered and smiled nervously.

Further blushes were spared by his boss making what proved to be a premediated and dramatic entrance.

Sweeping into the room, Hanah was a commanding presence. Hair loose, earrings, make-up, perfume, black sequinned dress, velvet jacket, dark stockings and shiny heels: her appearance would have attracted attention in Paris or Rome, let alone Ibrahim Sami.

"Major, please accept my sincere apologies for keeping you waiting. I just had to take a call from my office in Tehran."

"Not bad news, I hope, Madam."

"Not at all, but communications are never straightforward on the road. Our internet connections seem to suffer from power outages and always at the most inconvenient time. My business is talking to the government about trying to introduce improvements and better monitoring, but we continue to encounter bureaucracy and inefficient decision-making. I think our government thinks the best way to control the internet is to switch it off. No wonder people get pissed off, especially if you are trying to watch a movie. I keep telling the officials in Tehran they should follow your example – China seems to be the only place in the world where bureaucracy seems to work for all. You have a great internet and no Facebook."

Moussavi looked uncomfortable and changed the subject.

"Madam Alrakahthan, may I introduce you to my wife, Ziba? She is active in supporting women's rights in the workplace and has done a lot in recent years to boost employment opportunities in Khoda Afrin. I think she is the secret of our economic success."

Hanah shook hands.

"I am proud to meet any activist for women's rights. Especially one who is prepared to stand up to male domination."

She noted the cold stare of Madam Moussavi. This was a natural woman-to-woman hostility that few men understand, based on envy. Both were influencers in their way, one a younger challenger of convention, with the bonus of devastating looks, the other an older supporter of conformity, who had seen better days. How could an Iranian female citizen such as Hanah act with the apparent freedom to dress like a Western woman in a way that advertised her attractiveness to men in such a blatant and *public* way? Ziba noted how all the men at the table and many beyond had sucked in the vision of Hanah Alrakahthan like it was a treat. For Hanah, although clearly aware of the power of her *persona*, the effort was directed in one quarter. Alrakahthan Enterprises wanted to be the preferred developer of the Posyan free port and she would focus on winning Ho's support, whatever that would take.

Dinner was a complicated choreography of ritual, banality and intuition.

It was Ho who provided the ritual with the words of welcome.

"I wish to express my appreciation to Madam Alrakahthan and Mr Turani for their commendable contribution to the acceleration of our project here in Ibrahim Sami. Whilst I understand there is some work still to do to get the accommodation blocks built and connected, your astonishing effort to get the necessary materials here at short notice is truly impressive.

"It is a matter of personal regret that, owing to the sensitive nature of our work in the compound, I cannot permit a tour of our facility, but I will look forward to continuing our dialogue, Madam Alrakahthan, tomorrow regarding plans for the free port back in Posyan. I am sorry also Mr Hafiz could not be here, but it is still an honour to welcome his son, Mr Fawaz, who has taken responsibility for organising the construction teams, which will start on site in just a few hours from now. News of these two initiatives has been welcomed by Beijing and allows us to be confident about bringing our own specialist engineers in next week to start the detailed construction work within the compound. Of course, I recognise that you, Mr Governor Mayor, have ensured the necessary legal permits have been put in place, and also you, Colonel Rahman, have managed the security aspects of the deployment in the area as a whole. In essence, our collective effort is a great example of what we can achieve together and we can all take benefit from. I ask you to share a toast to our great shared enterprise."

Moussavi added the customary banality and took it upon himself to reply for the assembled company.

"Major Ho, our shared enterprise here is a great practical example of the cooperation between our two states which, only a couple of hours ago, the Supreme Leader referenced in his 326th speech to the National Assembly. Our combined resources and expertise will be a force for change, not just here in Khoda Afrin or the Islamic Republic but across the Gulf region and beyond. The Islamic Republic is a practical and responsible partner that delivers on its commitments. In our two ambitious projects, not just here in Ibrahim Sami but also at Posyan, we can be confident meeting our investment obligations, secured against the vast rare earth export extraction potential of the Arasbaran Protected Zone."

The intuition came from Hanah. "Absolutely, Mr Governor Mayor, I am delighted to have brought my colleague, Mr Turani, along to review the potential reserves and draw up extraction proposals from the six test sites. Alrakahthan Enterprises has a proud record of working as a principal development partner of the Islamic Republic and would humbly offer its services to the People's Republic of China to assist the development of the Posyan free port. We offer expertise in design and construction as well as logistics and manufacturing. You spoke of the Supreme Leader's speech earlier today, which made reference to two major initiatives. Firstly, the distribution of 8.5 million food parcels to deserving citizens, managed through AE's national logistics network through Star supermarkets, and, secondly, fulfilment of our national pledge to provide the latest world-class prosthetic limbs to our many thousands of war heroes who need them – manufactured by my company. Nobody understands the Islamic Republic of Iran better than Alrakahthan Enterprises. You can be sure of my personal attention, if you invite us to become your preferred development partner."

Colonel Rahman tapped the table in appreciation. Others followed; more specialist dishes arrived at the table, together with more Yellow River wine – red and white, acquired tastes but still potent in their effect. The night wore on, conversations became more personal.

"Major, how did you come to be assigned to Ibrahim Sami?" Hanah's quiet interrogation had begun.

"It wasn't a surprise. I am a doctor by profession, a soldier second. Our work here relates to medical activities where I have a degree of expertise," Ho replied.

"How long are your deployments?"

"I am here until further notice, certainly until such time as the redevelopment of the compound is complete, but within that, I do get two weeks leave every six months, so I have a chance to see my family then."

"Would they ever be allowed to travel here?"

"No, but I wish it was different. Iran is a very beautiful country with a rich heritage. It is a pity more people from around the world don't get to see it."

"Do you?"

"I am starting to make visits to the Arasbaran, but we are very busy, so I am limited to day trips."

"Does it get lonely?"

"Well, if I want to talk Mandarin, I can always come here or go around the corner to see a film, but part of the pleasure of being here is to meet informed citizens such as yourself, who can give me a taste of the true Iran."

Hanah smiled, edging her perfumed neck fractionally closer to Ho.

Moussavi and wife had made a point of engaging Jamshid, understanding the importance of his work to their future income.

"...And you're looking at the test sights tomorrow, Mr Turani?" Ziba asked.

"Yes, Colonel Rahman is taking me on a helicopter tour."

"But you are confident the reserves are there?" Moussavi was more direct.

"Subject to verifying the surveyor's reports, yes. The real issue will be how to go about arranging mining operations without compromising the UNESCO designation. I might need your help with that. I think we may need to redraw some of its boundaries to give us the access, but that is a matter we will look at tomorrow."

"What sort of equipment do you envisage needing?" Moussavi was keen.

"Clearly much more than you have at the present test sites, but it is too early to say. We can at least be confident we can get the necessary kit here via Posyan, once we have got clearance on what we're doing."

"You have my card, Mr Turani. I am the government representative for the locality and specialise in preparing all necessary documentation. Call as soon as you are ready and I will prioritise a meeting with you."

Rahman was bored. He had confirmed two trucks of prisoners and guards would be delivered to the accommodation block site at 06.00. He would collect Madam Alrakahthan and Turani from the hotel before returning to Posyan. Moussavi and Ho would join her to hold a meeting about the free port, but he would fly Turani to the test sites in the Arasbaran. Fawaz had told him Jafar would be in charge with a team of construction supervisors and made his excuses to leave to check everything was ready. As Hanah appeared distracted, Fawaz made a point of reminding Turani it was the al-Fouadi business which was uniquely positioned to supply local tradesmen to work across the three projects. The completed connections for the delivered prefabs the following day would demonstrate their capability.

And that left Rahman with Amy Fong.

Hanah was clearly focusing on Ho and he was certainly warming to her attention.

Rahman smiled at Amy. "Permit me, Sergeant: cigarette? Probably better we step outside. I don't think your boss will mind if we are gone for a few minutes. We can discuss the morning's deployment."

She glanced at Ho and noted he was preoccupied.

"Thank you, Colonel." She stood up, adjusted her skirt, which had ridden up as a result of being at table, and walked towards the restrooms. Rahman followed her down the stairs and outside. It was not a moment for conversation. Both knew why they were there and were short of time. They got caught up in the frenzy of the moment against the wall at the side of the building, before returning ten minutes later.

Ho was relieved to see his driver/interpreter. "There you are, Sergeant, I wondered where you had gone."

"Sorry, sir, I think it was something I ate." She looked worried.

Rahman, standing behind her, smiled. "I hope you will excuse me, Major, Madam, Mr Governor Mayor, Madam Moussavi, Mr Turani, but, like Mr al-Fouadi, I too must leave to prepare for tomorrow."

This proved the general signal for all to leave, and time for Hanah to play her final card, whispering in Ho's ear, "Do you have to go, Major? It seems an unnecessary journey for you to have to make at this time of night. We seem to have much more to discuss."

She sensed him wavering before he stood and saluted her.

"Unfortunately, all good things must come to an end. I look forward to our next encounter in the morning."

Turning on his heel, he walked away, Sergeant Fong in his wake.

Hanah and Jamshid were the last to go, taking the elevator.

"Damn, I wanted to get him to mention us in his reports to Beijing," she muttered as the lift door closed.

"What makes you think he hasn't already done so?" Jamshid countered, "I don't think he would be spending time with us otherwise."

They walked down the corridor to their rooms.

"Well, that means there's one more job for you before you turn in," Hanah said testily, moving behind him and pushing him through his door. "Fuck me."

It was said with as much passion as a military drill.

The secretary knocked and entered the office.

"Madam Professor Engineer Rahman, there is a group of men from Tehran here to see you. One of them has provided this card."

Mahta pulled her attention away from her computer screen and looked at it.

"Hasan Alrakahthan, Director, Alrakahthan Enterprises, Karaj, IR Iran."

"Why can't he make an appointment like anyone else?"

"Maybe it's because he has come from the north," the secretary ventured.

"Especially because he's come from the north," Mahta countered. "OK, I'll give him ten minutes."

Hasan, although polite, was not used to waiting and started through her door before the secretary could leave.

"Madam Rahman, thank you for seeing me. I have heard so much about you. I have come from Tehran with some important documents for you. Specifically, this." He placed a stapled paper with a dozen or so sheets attached. "This is Executive Order 560433 from the Office of the Supreme Leader, authorising the sale and leaseback of the 11th February Silkworm Assembly Plant of Bandar Abbas to Alrakahthan Enterprises for ten years, commencing today. I am here to take control of the business and will, in effect, become chairman. You will retain your position of chief executive, reporting to me. I have brought in a team of auditors to check your accounts in the first instance. I would be grateful if you will arrange temporary office accommodation at your earliest convenience today as I don't want these guys sitting around longer than necessary in your reception. I will return tomorrow so we can discuss our plans in more detail. In particular your ground-to-air missile refurbishment programme. In the meantime, I would like to review your business diary so we can prioritise your time and please make sure my people have full and immediate access to all your business records. Your cooperation is appreciated and I look forward to seeing you at ten in the morning."

He didn't wait to test the reaction, which was just as well, as Mahta stared, looking with disbelief at the document left on her desk. Firstly, why had she not been warned this was happening? Secondly, there were fifteen missile production facilities in Iran. This wasn't some giant national munitions takeover. Her factory had been specially selected for transfer. Again, why? Thirdly, this action was unusual, legitimised by executive order from the Office of the Supreme Leader, carrying his personal signature and official seal. Normally such an action would have required legislation from the National Assembly. Finally, what was Alrakahthan's intentions? Wasn't he the supermarket king that her absent lover, Jamshid Turani, worked for?

There was work to be done and calls to make. Her secretary was called in and told to find a room, furniture and equipment in one of the recesses of the main storage warehouse for Alrakahthan's pen pushers. She picked up the phone to Sayeed Gharbieh.

"I've just had a visit from one of the Alrakahthans telling me the Silkworm factory is now leased out to them for ten years, and I'm to work for them. Don't tell me you didn't know."

"I'm not happy about it. The Supreme Leader forced Jeylani to agree so he could announce the food package scheme yesterday. I advised against, but Jeylani is getting fixed on being the Supreme Leader's natural successor at the next election and decided it wasn't important enough to rock the boat, so we're stuck with it."

"What is it between the Supreme Leader and Alrakahthan?"

"Not sure, other than he thinks Alrakahthan gets things done quicker than the normal government channels would, and the supermarket king gets richer as a result. I think he trusts him too much… and he's getting too big for his boots. That will make him vulnerable. Still, I think I have started something which will slow him up a bit. Keep me in touch with what they ask you to do. I'll see if I can cause them a few headaches along the way."

Gharbieh was well known for never finishing a phone conversation. The line went dead.

Mahta then tried Jamshid, knowing she would have to leave a voicemail.

"How are you getting on up north? Miss you. Just to let you know, as of today, we have the same boss, Abdullo Alrakahthan – apparently the Supreme Leader has sold us out on a ten-year lease to him. Did you know about it? If not, can you find out why and let me know? Looking forward to seeing you soon. Dinner at mine next time."

Edwin and Bob sat at a table in the makeshift cafeteria area of the Barthaz warehouse, watching a grainy cowboy film from the 1970s on a communal TV rigged up on top of a bale. Reception wasn't great and the dialogue, although in English, had Azeri captions. The picture kept on breaking up, frustrating a comprehensive understanding of what was taking place. Pity poor Azeris watching the same broadcast in the area. The text in their language flashed upon the screen so quickly it was hard to follow. Both men tried to ignore these impediments and concentrate on the action as it was the only diversion from the waiting game they had been obliged to join. It must have been almost a couple of hours since they had last spoken to Zeitsev. Although they had seen him regularly at a distance, talking to members of his operations team, after a while they noticed a change in his body language. He certainly appeared more animated and was talking quickly into a microphone attached to a headset. An active conversation had ensued for about ten minutes before he ripped off the headset and came over.

"Gentlemen, it appears our collective timing is good. Things are starting to happen. We have had confirmation that the bandit, al-Fouadi, has crossed into military sector 7 in Azerbaijan, from a position south of Karranlo within the last hour, en route for Vezhnaly with his cargo of people and drugs. We think we have identified a collection team heading to meet them from Armenia. We will monitor them both, document the transfers and allow both parties to return towards their respective territories before intercepting them. Major Ryumin is running this initiative and expects to come here as soon as it is resolved. There is also increased chatter coming from Ibrahim Sami. Apparently prefabricated housing for construction workers has been delivered to the research compound and local workers are assembling it over the weekend. They're building it on the site outside the base where they kept our stolen Buk missile system, so we are trying to find out where it has been moved to. Engineers from China are being flown into Posyan in seventy-two hours together with 'tunnelling components' – we are not sure what they mean by that – but we will continue to listen in. They are still looking for Dr Ehat, but this building project is clearly a big thing. An extra 200 Revolutionary Guards are being sent into the border area ahead of construction commencing next week, suggesting to us they may be carrying a bigger threat of defectors or absconders than normal, especially when it is known over there we don't operate to the same security methodology. It means they are probably using prison labour. Finally, it is interesting that al-Fouadi has advocated a crossing point some twenty kilometres to the south of here in a 'high-risk' area, rather than looking to come across further north at Ashelqu. It suggests that corridor is being closely monitored on their side and they don't know about the Ibrahim Sami–Barthaz route your colleagues have used. I would expect your people to be aware of all this, Mr Wilson, especially when planning their return journey. Given all the factors we are aware of, it seems the next forty-eight hours will be the optimum time for your people to enter the base, collect their evidence and depart. In the meantime, we are continuing drone surveillance over the border area and have our own rapid reaction force ready to respond to any unexpected challenge."

"Thank you, Captain." For the first time, Edwin had the sense he was being fully informed. "How do we assist your efforts?"

"By staying here. For those coming out of Iran, there are few available options. We are sure they will be driven towards us, so being ready here to receive any returnees is the very best thing you can do. We will need to process them in line with our ministerial orders and there is a possibility some may also need medical attention."

SIXTEEN

THE SKY HAD TURNED a light shade of pink when Jafar arrived at the compound construction site with his team of supervisors. The task ahead was straightforward; the concrete platforms for the accommodation blocks had been laid months earlier, making the task of fitting together the already furnished and moulded units a matter of process and suitable for the unskilled workers, drawn from the Posyan prison camp, to undertake. Each of his supervisors would act as a foreman, demonstrating how to put the units together and snag checking. The harder part of the day's work would be connecting up the water, sewerage and electricity, which could only be linked to the mains services in Ibrahim Sami, not those used by the present compound. Plans thas should have been retained for this purpose by Khoda Afrin Prefecture didn't exist, so Jafar's team would have to estimate their position. The service pipes were buried under the road to Ashelqu, so it would be necessary for some excavation work to happen from the main road junction points to the accommodation blocks, raising the prospect of collateral damage to the town's existing infrastructure. New heavy-duty power connections would need to be laid into the compound itself to allow the Chinese technicians to utilise their own equipment for excavations and tunnelling operations.

At 06.00 Rahman arrived on site with two truckloads of workers and a third of Revolutionary Guards to watch over them. Split into four teams, they were briefed by Jafar's people and set to work. It had been agreed that, when the service team laid the power lines to the compound, the gates should be opened to allow a small group of workers in to make the necessary connections to the base's independent power plant. Although access would be granted, Jafar needed to advise the gatehouse how many individuals needed access, together with their identity papers. During this short period, supervision of workers within the compound would be provided exclusively by Chinese soldiers. Jafar couldn't say for sure when he would need access to the compound but at the earliest it would not be before 15.00. The Chinese side had seemed happy with that and now was the time to get on with the job.

Rahman had moved on to the hotel for breakfast. He had plenty on his mind and had decided to eat alone before announcing his arrival for the benefit of Hanah and Jamshid.

He chewed on his pastry and methodically applied himself to draining a pot of coffee. Strangely, all things considered, he felt on good form but whether that was because of the quality of the dinner the night before or the subsequent attention of young Sergeant Fong he wasn't sure. Today was an important one for him – professionally and personally. Better for him also that it proved unnecessary to rouse his guests. They had arrived in the foyer on time as agreed.

The journey back to Posyan was uneventful. On arrival at the main base reception, his adjutant took charge of Madam Alrakahthan, offering her a tour of the base prior to the arrival of Moussavi and Ho.

Rahman and Jamshid Turani proceeded to the tarmac to a waiting Mi-17 reconnaissance helicopter. Both needed to put military jumpsuits over their clothing, together with protective vests, boots and helmets. Sitting in the back, they had good vision from the portholes and their headsets were plugged into the internal radio system. Jamshid had brought his tablet computer with him and took a few moments to talk to Rahman and the pilot about particular sites he wished to look at.

"That's fine," said Rahman, "but I also think you need to get this area into some sort of context. There are other sites of relevance you should see while you are here. I will talk you through it during the flight."

Jo and Anya reported the news of Jack's beating to Dave in a side street two blocks away from the barn. Neither had been able to identify the women rescuers but it was clear they had been taken to al-Fouadi's house.

"Well, we know that will buy us a little time, as Fawaz said his dad was away on business and his mum is staying with her sister. Assuming the farm manager is away with al-Fouadi, Fawaz must have been left in charge. I'll try and find out what's going on, but, in the meantime, we stick to our plan. We really haven't got any more time to delay." The two women set off back to the barn to prepare ahead of Dave, Rodg and Gul.

It was late afternoon when the group gathered at the barn mezzanine for their final instructions. Fawaz had always said he was not going to return with the PI team and Dave decided it would be in their shared interest for him not to attend the session as his contribution of local intelligence had been fulfilled. Everything from now on had to be delivered with precision, especially that they had now lost the services of Jack. Almost because of Jack's unscheduled withdrawal, his colleagues had plenty of questions. What condition was he in? Would he be turned into the authorities? How would he react if tortured? Could they rescue him? Would they be discovered as a result? Dave had no answers other than to say detection, even death, was a certain risk of this type of operation which would not draw any distinction between those with military experience and civilians. Although the youngest and least experienced member of the team, Jack had signed a contract which provided cover in the event of death or serious injury. In this situation, if he could remain undiscovered for the coming twenty-four hours, his detention would not compromise the outcome of their mission. He would get a message to Fawaz to establish what was going on and then decide how to respond. He scribbled a note on a piece of paper, folded it and put it in his pocket.

Dave had reported collecting footage of the convoy from a tiny headcam illustrating the scale of the construction convoy, which he transferred to a memory stick and zipped into his flak jacket. All were now dressed in Revolutionary Guard military fatigues with caps and standard-issue boots, with holsters for their Makarovs. Gul and Anya had acquired AK-47s, which Dave didn't like but had not challenged as he recognised it was part of their uniform and would not raise suspicion.

"Alright, everyone, you each have your tasks, working together and independently in the hours ahead. Try to keep your hats on to cover your faces wherever possible as you will be passing CCTV points at intervals. You know what to do if all goes well and also what *not* to do if it goes badly. We will attempt to leave in an orderly way from here after dusk tomorrow and Gil will be on standby to help us back over the river to Barthaz. Good luck and thank you."

Anya and Rodg were the first to leave, headed for Posyan on the back of a moped "borrowed" hours earlier from the main bus stop. Having first checked the front alley was clear, Dave, Jo and Gul checked their headcams before leaving through the back hatch, circumventing Sami's main street and heading cross country on foot north towards the compound.

Rahman tapped the pilot on the shoulder, indicating they were ready to go. The radio microphones and headsets sprung into life with chatter from the pilot to the control tower. The first target location, at 39°08'N and 47°02'E, was entered into the flight computer and they took off, climbing to an altitude of 300 metres.

"I must admit, I have been looking forward to doing this trip," Rahman said. "When you are up here, you really understand what a wild and beautiful part of the country this is. As a Revolutionary Guard officer, I feel a strong duty of care to protect the Arasbaran, not just for the Islamic Republic but for the world."

"Yeah, I know all about the UNESCO thing. They seem to have drawn some pretty arbitrary lines on the map. But I'm not sure you have to worry too much, Colonel. According to the charts, much of this area is difficult to access anyway, so any commercial mining would have to take place on the periphery. I can't see us moving heavy equipment into the centre."

"I hope you're right. Our Chinese friends are pretty inventive. If they get development rights, I'm sure they wouldn't think twice about dropping the necessary kit."

"That's the point, Colonel: we're not looking to sell development rights on this one. Although it would be easier, it would get the Supreme Leader into all sorts of shit with the UN. If there's any mining to be done, it will be a job for us, and the cost would have to be charged out in export fees. Right now, the Chinese are trying to control the world market in neodymium iron boron, used to make magnets for jet fighters and missiles, and we might be sitting on 20% of that market. Even if we don't mine it, its value in export credit guarantees would make it easier for us to get loans either from Beijing or Moscow."

Their itinerary had been carefully planned. Eight stops in a clockwise direction to photograph each test site and to mark potential access points, interspersed with spectacular lush and varied terrain.

They flew on over high alpine meadows, semi-arid steppes, rangelands and forests, rivers and springs, landing close to the test sites and walking the rest of the way.

Mostly their conversation related to technical issues from geology to radon gas emissions, interspersed with the odd question any tourist would raise.

Taking off from their fifth stop, Jamshid asked, "By the way, I couldn't see too many settlements on the maps – are there many people living down there?"

"Probably about 20,000 nomads living off the land in around sixty villages. They tend to resist contact with the outside world. I get to meet their leaders every now and then, normally when they want something. They come down to Khalibar, the main town at the northern extremity, when they have something to say.

"I think we will be hearing from them soon. They keep sending letters to the Supreme Leader wanting funds for ecotourism, which would be worth a lot to them. I think he is going to have to answer sooner rather than later. This area has been a hotbed of revolutionary politics, so he has to be careful not to piss them off. Arasbaran, or Qaradağ to use its old Turkic name, was one of the epicentres of the Persian Constitutional Revolution. Its tribes were heavily involved in armed conflicts; the revolutionary and anti-revolutionary camps were headed, respectively, by two local warlords, Sattar Khan and Rahimkhan Chalabianloo. In 1925, when Reza Shah deposed Ahmed Shah Qajar and founded the Pahlavi dynasty, Arasbaran's relative importance waned. Shah insisted on a policy of cultural and ethnic nationalism and implemented a policy of cultural assimilation, or assassination, as some called it. He renamed Qaradağ 'Arasbaran' to deny the Turkic identity of the inhabitants. Consequently, Arasbaran was no longer in the focus of national politics."

"That was then; does anybody care now the Supreme Leader is in office?"

"It is a generational sore just below the surface. These people think they have a bad deal. They need money and investment to heal their sense of injustice."

At that moment the tone of the helicopter's engines deepened and it descended towards a green meadow. Rahman pointed at the map. "This is your point six; the escarpment over there is the best place to start the boron extraction, if that is your highest priority. We are just three kilometres from Jafar Abad, easy access for a service road and right on the edge of the UNESCO designation. It would also link in with the two other sites you prioritised, Toali Sofla and Tatar Sofla."

"What about the environment and the wildlife?"

"What about it? Open meadow, brown bears and Caspian red deer. We have enough to keep the naturalists happy. Come, let us move on. I have a surprise to show you before we go back."

They flew east towards Khalibar, through rich green and wooded valleys, this time landing on a narrow ridge.

"Time to do some walking," said Rahman, releasing his guest's seatbelt and taking off his own helmet.

The scenery was more mountainous. Up high above them was an ancient fortification built into the rock.

"This is Babak Castle, also known as the Immortal Castle or Republic Castle. Remember it from school? It is probably the most beautiful and most historical location in the whole of the Arasbaran. Carved out of a mountain top, it has been identified as the stronghold of Papak Khorramdin, the leader of the Khurramites in Azerbaijan, who fought the Islamic caliphate of Abbasids. Rugged, defiant, and impregnable, many regard it as a national symbol of our country.

"It's accessed via a series of broken steps that lead to the top of that hill, over there. Then, the easiest route is a long, dirt track. No signs lead to the castle. At the end, the route turns left. The first sign of the ruins appears on the left, leaving two peaks to cross. The first peak has views of the castle. After ascending the second peak, with additional ruins, the trail passes sheer cliffs on the right with no railings. From the castle, the surrounding Arasbaran oak forest, jagged cliffs, mountains in the distance, and Iranian history combine to inform the visitor's perspective. The last stretch is a narrow passageway and a 200-metre corridor-shaped temple. We can't go all the way now but even a small part of the journey is rewarding just for the view and air quality."

It was mid-afternoon, the sun was high and now the helicopter's rotors had come to a halt it was almost perfectly silent, with the exception of the gentle breeze in their faces.

They were at the top of a deep wooded valley walking towards a stone strewn path leading higher up towards the castle.

"I knew I was right to look forward to the day," Rahman began. "As I was saying, I don't get too many opportunities to get up here myself, and, when I do, I always see something new."

"Thank you, Colonel, for taking me. I have a much clearer idea about how we can develop our plans and am sure I will need to return before too long."

"This is both a beautiful and dangerous place. The beauty is easy to see; the danger is not. Now and again, I have to send a search and rescue helicopter up here to find missing climbers. Normally by the time the request comes in, when we find them they are dead. There are many paths here with loose stones and sheer drops. It is too easy to meet your end in a place like this."

"Well, at least you can take the road to heaven having had the sight of this view as your last memory," Jamshid joked.

Rahman turned and looked him in the eye. "Mr Turani, my bosses at the Ministry of Internal Security in Tehran – the Basij – asked me to bring you here for exactly this purpose. They have told me all about you. Frankly, they are pissed off and so am I. Since you started doing oil trades at the Port of Bandar Abbas, they decided to groom you to become an overseas agent of the state. They spent time and money monitoring you, not only at work but at home via your neighbour, Tawal, and your friend, the registrar at the Omm-e-Leila hospital. It was going pretty well. Even my wife, who I think you met, first at the Apadana restaurant, Professor Engineer Rahman at the Silkworm site, gave you high ratings in your assessments – she even came to Tehran to watch you play football to see if you knew anyone dodgy, but then something went wrong. You met your now colleague, Hanah Alrakahthan. We saw you kiss her at your mother's tea shop in Tehran, and meet her subsequently at the Milad Tower and visited her home in Karaj. You then met with Abdullo Alrakahthan in Bandar and agreed to work for him. He bought you, Mr Turani, and you fell for it. He gives you impossible amounts of money which you can't spend legally and sets you to work to support his international business interests most of which would not be legal if conducted here. He is clever, *your* boss. He has built a solid relationship with the Supreme Leader, exploiting the fact he doesn't trust his closest confidants, which is why he and his family are not under arrest. Now *my* boss at the Basij, Sayeed Gharbieh, tells me you have started an affair with my wife, when all she was instructed to do was to get to know you a little better. He is expecting me to kill you as a result. In your favour is the fact that I have always thought Gharbieh to be a self-serving worm. He would not tell me this sort of information without a reason and that must be to stop the Chinese investment, make the Supreme Leader look an idiot and get his own man, Jeylani, into the top job. Also, he wouldn't know the fact that my wife and I lead separate lives now and she is of an age where I know I have had the best of her. Just imagine that!

"I fuck who I want, when I want – I can't be surprised she does the same. So I have to say, if you want my leftovers, why should I worry? Then there is my own future – again, Gharbieh doesn't know, I have put money into buying land the Chinese will need around the Posyan base if they are going to build the free port. I will not be able to sell it unless you and Madam Alrakahthan succeed in opening up the Arasbaran. So, given I don't like you, I must admit I may need you, *for now*. What to do? Should I just leave you here, come up with a cock-and-bull story about you walking in the wrong place at the wrong time, then send a rescue helicopter to find you the day after tomorrow still alive? Probably a waste of all our time. Better I tell Gharbieh you recommend mining in the middle of the Arasbaran and get him up here to take a look. I can then arrange for him to go on his own hike to the heavens, *inshallah*."

At that moment, there was shouting from behind. Turning, they saw their pilot running towards them, waving his arms.

"Sir, we are requested to return to Posyan immediately. There seems to have been a breakout from the base detention centre."

They turned and ran the way they had come and scrambled aboard.

Helmets and seat belts on, Rahman barked, "Get me Abbas!"

The convoy of the two Khodros and the Land Cruiser had assembled at the side of the road to Vezhnaly above the incline from the river. Hanif had gone to check with the drivers they were ready to proceed and that their security teams were ready, if needed. All was well in the back of both vehicles now the passengers had been given the opportunity to have a pee.

The drivers had now become accustomed to the dark and knew they would need to travel without lights, but at least the road was straight and down a slight gradient. Hanif had warned there were two tricky pieces of driving to come where the road would be subject to dog-leg turns, probably without any warning signage. Given the weight of the loads and, in the case of the Land Cruiser, the change of suspension and tyres, the journey was slow, at around 40kph. They reached the first of the dog-legs, a left turn, just over an hour since moving off. The two Khodros responded to the brief hazard signal from the Land Cruiser, their drivers stepping down to inspect the corner. The second, to the right, came ten minutes later. The result was that the convoy had now entered a new valley that would take them directly to their destination. Despite the dark, the outline of the surrounding hills was just discernible, but the surrounding scene was black. A light drizzle had started making the road surface greasy and increased the noise from their tyres. No wonder Hafiz had saved money on the security. It was clear to him that no one would be roaming the hills this night. Some five kilometres from their destination, Hafiz picked up the first sign for Vezhnaly, but a slightly bigger arrow above it saying Armenia. This was the point he reached for the burner phone to make a call.

"Usman, this is Hafiz. I will arrive in twenty minutes. Be ready."

"Check." The call finished.

Vezhnaly itself seemed little more than a random collection of homesteads, with a couple of warehouses in the middle. An HGV with Armenian plates stood waiting at the side of the road to continue the journey. Four men dressed in black, two with Kalashnikovs, stood chatting next to the truck. They came up to the side of the Land Cruiser.

"Glad you could make it," their leader said with a bit of irony.

"I thought you would come closer to us."

"We have problems our side at the moment; there's a lot of military activity, which forced us to change our plans," said Hafiz. "But, still, we are here. Here's the money, plus the extra commission as agreed."

As a case was passed over, on cue, Hafiz's security men made themselves known.

"Tell your boys to relax; we just wanted to check the money. Now we can get the merchandise loaded and get on our way."

Their truck didn't seem to have any features to hide the load. People and backpacks were loaded into the trailer, the door shut and locked behind them.

"OK, so now we go. See you next time, Hafiz. Pleasure doing business with you."

The whole handover process had taken ten minutes.

The Armenian truck started up briefly with its lights on before switching them off and being swallowed by the dark of the night.

Hafiz broke the tension of the moment, "Allah be merciful! Praise to the Prophet for getting us here. Let's go home as quickly and safely as possible."

It took another ten minutes to turn the three vehicles around to retrace their journey. There was clearly a sense of relief shared by his crews. Once passed the dog-legs, the road was straight back up the hill. Without the weight with which they had arrived, they were able to make a similar speed on the home run, except lying right in their way was an armoured car with a blue flashing light.

"What do we do, boss?" asked Hanif.

"Keep going. If we stop now it will take us an age to get started again. Send the hazard signal to the guys behind and get low. I guess they will start shooting as soon as they realise we aren't stopping."

"If we go to the left, we can miss the armoured car but there's no chance for the guys behind," Hanif said, dropping a gear, putting his lights on full beam and accelerating towards the gap.

It was the last thing Hanif said to Hafiz before the AK-47s opened up, bullets tearing into the Land Cruiser, but Hanif still had control as two of their assailants leaped out of the way just before the first of the following heavy transporters collided with the armoured car, shunting it to the side of the road as the second crashed into the back of the first. Soldiers repossessed the centre of the road, firing at the departing Land Cruiser.

"You OK?" shouted Hafiz to his driver.

"I've been hit but I can keep going. I'm not sure how many shots we've taken but we still have a working engine."

The top of the hill was in sight and the incline to their crossing point was near. Hafiz was feeling a strange sense of exhilaration as his adrenaline kicked in. Suddenly, he saw a bright spotlight in the air to his right, heard a high-powered whoosh, a flash of light and an unreal feeling of weightlessness before the black returned.

Events in Vezhnaly were being followed closely at Barthaz. Edwin and Bob had been given headsets to listen to the calm commentary first from Ryumin's spotters, then his task force members and finally the familiar voice of Pavilinsky. They had heard that the Armenian truck had been intercepted within ten minutes of leaving Hafiz, and had surrendered in the face of overwhelming force. The drugs with an estimated street value of thirty million US dollars had been confiscated and forty-eight illegal economic migrants delivered to a temporary Red Cross camp to the north of the village under armed guard. Arrangements were in place to repatriate them via Baku in the course of the coming days. The damage had occurred on the other side, preventing al-Fouadi's run to the river crossing. Two soldiers had been killed and five wounded as a result of the overturning of the armoured car. Apparently, gunmen in the back of the two Khodros had continued firing and were only silenced as a result of grenades lobbed into the back of their vehicles. No prisoners had been taken. Finally, it had been reported the Land Cruiser had broken through Ryumin's cordon and had got within a kilometre of the border before being taken out by a missile fired from Pavilinsky's helicopter gunship.

The pilot reported no signs of life.

As Bob took off his headset, Zeitsev waved him to put it back on. There was more chatter coming out of Ibrahim Sami.

As anyone in the building trade knows, construction of even the simplest buildings has its problems and Jafar was coming to terms with progress at the end of the first full day's work at the Ibrahim Sami compound. The prefabs themselves were fine, stacked in blocks of four storeys as intended, but the work to put in the services was more complicated than he had expected. He had a team looking for the line of the storm drain at the junction with the Ashelqu road. It was the best clue to establishing where exactly the service cables were buried. Despite his best estimations, there was no doubt there would be no alternative than to dig a channel across the whole road, effectively cutting it for as long as necessary. This required permission and he had called Moussavi's office to get clearance. Although he got it, permission came with a catch. It could only be closed overnight, which would require one of the four construction teams to keep working under floodlights. He knew the importance of the work and the need to meet the challenging timetable set originally by Hafiz. Fawaz had just told him to do what he thought was right. So pneumatic drills were brought into use as night fell together with big 'Road Closed' signs. They had to dig down to a depth of one metre to see anything, so the job would take a long time and even when completed it was likely the temporary road surface would provide an assault on any vehicle's suspension system. As expected, the road, previously relatively free of traffic, seemed to get busier when they started digging. Jafar recognised it would be the end of the working day so he would try to keep one lane open as long as possible. His team were probably a quarter out into the road when another motorised military convoy came towards them with headlights blazing and horns blowing. The driver of the first military truck slowed, pointing to a sign in Farsi script which said 'Priority: On Operational Deployment'. The vehicle was wide and there would be little room for it to pass without using the verge on the far side of the road. Looking at it, it was clear that if these four articulated trucks could not pass, there would be a horrendous traffic snarl up and Jafar would get a bollocking and possibly have to pay a penalty fee for holding up the military. It wasn't worth the bother. Nodding to the driver, he signalled him to move his vehicle over to the verge as far as possible to clear their excavations. Moving very slowly with revving engines and copious amounts of exhaust emissions, the vehicles made it through. Quite who these guys were or where they were going was of no interest to Jafar. For him, it was one problem less.

The movement of the Buk mobile missile system was creating a lot of excitement in Barthaz as they followed its progress to Ashelqu, newly fortified with extra Revolutionary Guards in preparation for the arrival of the Chinese construction workers. As the Buk units approached the town, none of the military deployed there gave it a second look even when it turned off the highway towards a copse of trees near the river. A couple of guards watched, expecting it to park up under cover and the crew to come over for a cup of tea, but it didn't stop and kept driving forward towards the Aras and the closed frontier with Azerbaijan.

Suddenly panic spread amongst the Revolutionary Guard unit patrolling the crossing and shots were fired, firstly in the air but then at the vehicle itself. Machine-gun fire, even when aimed directly, had no chance of piercing the body armour of this machine and so the drivers kept going, leaving the shouting and shooting in their wake as they crashed into the foaming waters.

The scene was being observed by a drone, with Ryumin patched into the coverage. Ryumin knew that the Buk could not be prepared for use while it was on the move. He was not going to stop it coming into to Azerbaijan, but he did want to know where it was going. An order came to Pavilinsky to scramble to the scene, at least to let the drivers of the Buk units know they were being monitored. His fear was it would stop in the heavily wooded area without coming out on the other side where there was the main road to Minjivan.

He need not have worried. Although there was no communication with the Buk units, it was clear the drivers had a destination in mind. Crashing through the forest, they emerged at the main road and turned towards Minjivan – Pavilinsky's helicopter tagging them all the way.

Bob and Edwin remembered being there themselves and recalled the big open field next to the town with its grassy airstrip. Following the coverage from the drone, the Buk units arrived at the field, drove in and lined up at the far side under the cover of a dense thicket of trees. The combined cameras now turned to infrared in the growing gloom, which provided a surreal sight for the viewers. Four figures left the Buk units and started sprinting towards the middle of the field, just as Pavilinsky reported a light aircraft nearby coming into land. Ryumin ordered Pavilinsky to stand back to let the plane land, then instructed him to bring his gunship down as close to the Buks as possible.

"Do not intercept target. Acknowledge."

"Copy, control."

The distinctive shape of the Yak-58, with its reverse thrusting propeller, needed no introduction to Edwin and Bob. It was Boroschenko, only this time it was clear he didn't intend to stop. With the propeller still revving, he turned the plane around, the four figures from the Buk units climbed in and he was off gathering speed for take-off.

"Let him run, Pav." Ryumin was calm.

The little Yak banked to the left after take-off and headed into low cloud.

"So who were those guys?" Bob asked.

"*Spetznaz* – Russian special forces," said Zeitsev.

"They've been knocking around this area for a few weeks now. Moscow have been worried that the Iranians were going to reverse engineer the Buk and steal their tech. They were moaning to us about not doing anything to get it back when the bandits led by al-Fouadi first stole it. But, if we'd done what they wanted, we might have sparked another war and we have our hands full watching the Armenians. I bet their ambassador will be knocking on our president's door in the morning."

"Good work, everybody. We're just mopping up over here now. Let's get everyone together at Barthaz by 07.00 in the morning. Out." Zeitsev's team exchanged high fives and cheers as his commanding officer signed off – it had been a hard but successful day.

Fawaz had returned home, having checked on the progress of Jafar at the compound, and the letter box outside his father's house as he had remembered to do whenever he was away. The box appeared empty but for a screwed-up piece of paper in the bottom. He had been tempted just to throw it away, but intuition told him to unwrap it. He was glad he did. Reading it, his heart thumped in his chest. He unlocked the iron gate, hastily relocking it after entering and hurried into the house.

"Shimina, Shimina, where are you?"

His sister appeared at the top of the stairs. He briefly saw Khalifa on the landing moving into one of the bedrooms.

"Come down here now; we need to talk."

She pointedly glared at him and as she slouched down the stairs, Fawaz put his finger to his lips and gestured for her to go through the front room and into his father's study.

"Are you completely mad? What on earth were you doing bringing that... beggar into our house? Dad will do his nut when he gets back."

"I'm not the one who is mad. The man we rescued is no beggar. He is your friend from the other night, apparently living in Ashelqu. His name is not Parviz. He is not even Iranian; he is a British spy."

"If that were true, bringing him in here is even madder. If he is found, we'll all be in trouble. Anyway, why do you think he is British?"

"He was concussed. I picked him off the street with the help of Khalifa and together we got him in here, cleaned up and into a bed. While we were doing it, he started mumbling in English. There's not many people here who even understand English, certainly not Khalifa, but I remembered a bit from school."

"Khalifa doesn't suspect?"

"She thinks it strange, but she doesn't know he's a spy."

"He isn't a spy. He is a friend... a friend I met at university, a medical researcher. I asked him to come here to help me with a project."

"What project?"

"Remember, when I was away, Dad's problems with the dead sheep? It was caused by some sort of leak from the compound up the road, now occupied by the Chinese. The government called them in to make it safe but cannot get rid of them. Now they are extending the site to make chemical weapons here. I am trying to stop them and to get the Chinese to go and take their poisons with them."

"How do you know?"

"I haven't got time to tell you everything, but you must trust me and you can't tell Dad. He is making money out of this. We need to hide Parviz somewhere secret while he recovers."

"There's something else you should know," Shimina said quietly, "I have now seen him all over, close up. He's really fit and I want to look after him."

"Forget this nonsense. Is he awake? I need to talk to him. Keep Khalifa out of the way whilst I do."

Fawaz left the study without waiting for his sister and climbed the stairs in threes. Jack was in her room.

"Hello, mate, how's it going out there?"

Although his head was heavily bandaged and his face swollen, he was perfectly lucid. "Your sister's been looking after me. She is beautiful. I thought so when I first met her on the bus at the Pomegranate Festival, and again the other night, and haven't changed my mind. She is the sort of person who makes me want to reconnect with my Iranian great-grandparents and improve my Farsi. If I wasn't in this situation, we would have been dating by now."

"Things are difficult and you're not helping. The others have left to finish the job. If you're found here now we're all in the shit."

"I thought your father was the head man? Surely this house isn't going to get searched by anyone anytime soon?"

"He's away and I'm not sure what is going on. There's talk of some trouble back at Posyan and there's a few jumpy guards around out there. Can you walk?"

"Not that far."

"OK. I'll find a wheelchair and get you moved. For the sake of us all, don't leave the house until I get back."

Fawaz left immediately and headed for the street. He had to work out what to do.

This was never part of the script.

It was now dusk at the Posyan base but the place was a hive of activity. Arc lighting was being put in place at the far corner of the airfield; armed guards were swarming at the perimeter; soldiers with dogs dispersed into the hinterland. The timing could not have been worse, as two truckloads of prisoners were being returned from construction labouring duties in Sami. The returnees were directed to an aircraft hangar and told to sit in lines with their hands on their heads. The contingent of trainee Hezbollah fighters were drafted in to supervise them. Captain Abbas knew Colonel Rahman would demand a status report on his return. He would need to know who had escaped and how they had managed it. The initial results were not encouraging. At the first roll call, it was estimated sixty-two had absconded, squeezing through a double breach in the security fencing bordering a nearby wood. The tale of some prisoners already interrogated sounded like some sort of insanity. One in particular, claimed that during their evening meal a T-shirted woman with dark hair came up to an outside window and pressed her chest against the glass and pointed to a fire exit nearby. Normally all fire exits were alarmed, but, according to the witness, no one cared about that, but when the door was opened no alarm sounded. There was a jam in the doorway with people trying to get out and the two guards on duty in the refectory were easily overpowered in the spontaneous stampede. Once outside, a white T-shirt had been left by a breach of the fence in the inner perimeter and a red one left marking a gap in the outer. A lot of the prisoners just climbed through and started running in all directions, as reinforcements arrived to secure the situation. The inmate telling the tale had not gone because he wasn't able to get out quick enough. He had reasoned that he would quickly have been recaptured and tortured as punishment or, worse still, sent to the Ibrahim Sami research base.

Rahman had frowned when he heard the reports. The furrow on his brow deepened when he heard that the guard at the Moussavi residence had been overpowered and a group of prisoners were holding him and his wife hostage.

The first task was to secure the prison and maintenance teams were dispatched immediately to repair the boundary and investigate the malfunctioning security alarm. Secondly, escaped prisoners had to be traced and recaptured without delay. Abbas had been prompt in sending out dog teams but so far no one had been picked up. Thirdly, the situation at the Moussavi residence had to be quantified and the siege broken and, fourthly, the present additional security obligations of his men at the Ibrahim Sami compound and the Ashelqu border crossing had to be maintained. On top of all of this, there was also the mystery of the redeployment of the Buk mobile ground-to-air missile system. Who had authorised its movement, and was it true it had been driven into Azerbaijan? Taken together, Rahman knew he had just a few hours to address all these issues as failure would result in Gharbieh sending elite troops in from Tabriz and him being relieved of his duties.

On his return from the Arasbaran, Jamshid had met up with Hanah at the Posyan base. Both were aware of a deterioration in the local security situation but not any of the detail, other than a bland comment from Rahman that military manoeuvres in the area overnight meant they could be delayed making their return to Tehran in the morning had they returned to Ibrahim Sami. He would arrange to have their bags collected from the hotel and they would spend the night in the 'secure environment' of the officers' quarters. Up to that point, Hanah had been satisfied with the outcome of the meeting she had with Moussavi and Ho on the future of the free port. Jamshid had responded by highlighting those sights close to the Arasbaran which looked like the best for mining activities. He also told her some of his private exchange with Rahman.

"Gharbieh will only succeed if the Supreme Leader fails in his policies. Our job is to ensure he doesn't," was her response. "Our next task will be to ensure Madam Rahman's plans for missile refurbishment are fast-tracked, which will be good for the state and our balance sheet. What will Gharbieh say then? We're a threat to state security?"

SEVENTEEN

THE CONSTRUCTION WORK AT the Ibrahim Sami compound had continued through the night, with the result that eventually Jafar had located all the connecting service cables and pipes necessary to complete the development under the road. The work had taken much longer than expected because of increased military movements on the route between the border and the Posyan base. Jafar was sick of the constant moans of the drivers about his essential works and had independently decided that one lane would be kept open throughout the excavations. As this work progressed, guard duties had changed outside the Chinese facility and its gates had been kept shut, but, in line with Ho's orders, it was now opened at Jafar's request to permit access to connect external power and water. Six Revolutionary Guards, four prison workers and Jafar's technical services foreman were given access and escorted to the compound's independent power generator. Distance and the route of cabling was duly marked out and drilling work began immediately. The Guards kept watch as two bored Chinese soldiers watched them in turn. From time to time, the Iranian soldiers walked out of the compound singularly or in twos to take a break. After they had done this, three or four times, their Chinese shadows lost interest, preferring to engage in their own conversations to relieve the monotony. Had they remained alert, they would have noticed three of the "Guards" did most of the wandering and one or two of them chose to take their absence from the drilling to disappear elsewhere across the base. Dave, Jo and Ehat were taking the opportunity to walk in and out of the compound at will, familiarising themselves with the layout provided for them by Amy Fong. It had been planned that the time to connect the power was at dusk and amid lots of shouting and gesticulating by Jafar's people the final cable was plugged. Almost as predictably, the power surge blew out the substation, pitching the area into darkness, except for emergency lighting at the base's entrance. As the fuss and confusion mounted, the three moved into the main building and headed for the data centre. The power cut had released all the security doors, which made their movement easier, and in the half-light of the base corridors the sight of three soldiers in fatigues walking through, appearing to be checking air vents, did not raise any suspicions. The data room was filled with monitors showing six locations they had not seen or had access to. Three of them appeared to be hospital wards, two looked like operating theatres and one looked like a simple jail with four inmates – men – sitting down, staring into the middle distance. Dave and Jo set to work loading memory sticks to download camera coverage from the previous twenty-four-hour memory logs. Some of the computer instructions were in Chinese and Ehat helped with the translation. The speeding copy of the footage providing a fleeting glimpse of what was happening here. Patients being forcibly injected, others strapped down experiencing what appeared to be fevers, bodies with terrible lacerations and what looked like burns. There was no time to absorb the horrors of these images. Their attention was applied only to copying them. They had been there twenty minutes when voices could be heard in the corridor outside – a man and a woman. Ehat moved to the door. Although the voices were indistinct, it seemed the man had said his goodbyes to the woman and after a split second the door into the data centre opened. The figure entering was grabbed by Ehat.

It was Sergeant Fong.

She was as surprised as they were.

"Wow! How did you get in here? You are very brave. They will kill you if they find you. I came here to copy some material myself. I want to defect. Please take me with you. I can be useful. If you want to tell the world about what goes on here you need witnesses not just film. That's why I can help you. I understand all the systems we operate on this site."

"Who was the man you were with outside just now?"

"He is our chief engineer investigating the power problem. The base is on emergency supply which can be retained for up to six hours. He has that time to get the lights back on, but he is good. I don't think it will take him long."

"Where is Major Ho?"

"He is in a teleconference with Beijing for the next fifteen minutes. We are under strict instructions not to disturb him during these times."

"Are we collecting the right material?"

"Yes, I think so. I have come to copy some of the medical reports which relate to the experiments you have recorded. Please let me use this main computer."

Dave got up and moved to the door with Ehat.

"Make it quick, I don't think Jafar will be able to keep us all in the dark for much longer."

It was another ten minutes to collect what they needed. Dave and Amy Fong led the way out, Jo and Ehat following. They took the emergency stairs back to the surface entrance, which was only some sixty metres from the gatehouse.

A mixed group of Chinese and Iranian soldiers and workers were involved in a major disagreement about the power cable. Others were erecting arc lights over the area between the base generator and the guardhouse. Voices were raised and then a first blow before a melee ensued. It was the ideal environment for Dave and his team to slip into the shadows and away across the road, over the safety barrier and down into the anonymity of an almond orchard.

As the hours passed, Colonel Rahman was becoming more confident about not having to call Gharbieh. The prison at the base had been secured; thirty of the abscondees had been recovered. Moussavi had been rescued from a mob by promises of prison transfers and visits but only after his guards had shot five of them dead. He still had eight on the run, the mystery of the missing Buk unit and reports of fisticuffs at the Chinese compound to resolve. He called Ho.

"How are things, Major? I hear you've had a disturbed night. Is everything OK? Do you need any more help?"

Ho was under pressure but remained diplomatic. "I have always appreciated local people's willingness to make us feel welcome and to help us when they can, but tonight has been a test for us all. Al-Fouadi's men did a good job assembling the accommodation units for our construction teams next week but really made a mess of the service connections, calculating the cable loads incorrectly and blowing out the substation. We have been on emergency power for two hours now, which is unacceptable. When my chief engineer complained, one of the Iranian workers assaulted him. We have taken pictures, Colonel, and will expect you to make arrests."

"But it has quietened down?"

"Yes, al-Fouadi's son came by to check the work. He seems to have sorted the problem out – for now. Apparently, the man who threw the blow was one of your conscripted prisoners. I am told we should be on full power within the hour and the trench will be filled thereafter. If this is another example of the good faith of our Iranian partners I will be satisfied. If not, I will call you again in the coming hours."

Yellow alert status would be retained until the morning. Rahman needed a couple of hours' sleep.

Fawaz was short on sleep too. In the course of the next few hours the mission would come to a close. The Peace International team would leave and he and his family would plan a new life in Ibrahim Sami, hopefully without a Chinese biological warfare factory on their doorstep. He was surprising himself by his ability to manage business at home without his father. If Fawaz was honest enough, he was becoming worried about his continued absence, as he found himself with daily decisions to make, everything from arranging for produce to be collected for market and buying feed for the sheep, to authorising weekly paycheques for his staff and trying to work out how to reclaim money from the government for organising local labour crews to supervise construction at the compound. He had called the family bank in Tabriz to explain that his father had been unexpectedly delayed on business and that there were urgent transactions he needed to undertake on his behalf. It wouldn't be a problem as they had received certified copies of his identity and signature from his father only the previous week. It was one less thing to worry about. He recalled Dad refusing to take his mobile with him and knew he would be facing his own anxious moments, wherever he was. He understood too that the Alrakahthan visit was now over, as Rahman had sent a car to collect their bags, and knew Jafar had more or less completed the work at the compound as his father had instructed. He was also pleased that he had been able to smooth over the misunderstandings between Jafar's workers and the Chinese military without the situation escalating. Now, all he had to do was to figure out what to do about Jack and his sister, Shimina. Firstly, he needed to get Jack out of the house before his father got back. He hit upon the idea of moving him into the mosque. Of course, Mullah Yusuf would be likely to object, but a friendly reminder about his special hotel stays should take care of that. As for Shimina, he would have to take some time to explain truthfully what was happening, but at least that could wait until the Peace International team had left.

He was about to leave home to visit the mosque when the phone rang.

"Fawaz, is that you? It's Seyyed Jevadi, I run the truck workshop at Karranlo. I do some work with your dad over the border, now and again. I helped him get across the Aras yesterday to get to a meeting. I have heard there's been a serious road accident over there and some of my own people who were travelling with him have been killed. I'm informed your farm manager, Hanif, is definitely one of the fatalities and your dad is missing. I'm really sorry, lad, I don't know much about the circumstances, but the information is sound. When I get more I'll call."

The news had the same impact on him as he imagined it must have had on his father. He focused on Jevadi saying his father was *missing*, not dead. He must hold on to that for now and keep focused on the tasks at hand in the hours to come.

His conversation with Mullah Yusuf went as he had expected. He had started by saying his father's working trip had been extended and that he was responsible for the al-Fouadi businesses in his absence. Although, by his own admission, he was not a regular attendee, he had taken the opportunity to tour the mosque and noted its improved interior decoration as well as joking that the new sound system to announce the call to prayer was now so loud he thought no one in Ibrahim Sami had a legitimate excuse not to attend. Both items had been funded by his father, perhaps, thought his son, as a method for compensating for his considerable personal misdemeanours. Yusuf replied that his father knew what it was to be a good Muslim. He, Fawaz, had enjoyed taking responsibility for his father's diverse commercial interests and that the hotel had proved to be the most interesting, especially noting the calibre and frequency of its main customers. However, it was a busy place, and a friend of his had been beaten up in the street recently and needed somewhere quiet to rest where he would not be disturbed. His friend had a strong sense of shame and wanted to recover in an environment where 'discretion' could be assured. Could the Mullah offer suitable accommodation for a few days? It would be appreciated by the whole family. Yusuf could expect the man to be delivered to the mosque after midday prayers.

The main street was much quieter than it had been twenty-four hours earlier. There was no convoy of trucks, no audience waiting to watch it all go by. All that had been delivered and installed at the compound was ready for the next big influx from China due in the coming hours. Walking back to the house, he had bumped into Hashmi Kolani, 'the Carpet King', and decided to take coffee in the hotel foyer. It was a convenient moment for a brain dump – after all, Kolani was an old friend who had his own experience of hard times.

It had only been a couple of weeks since they last met but Fawaz was surprised how much more he had to share – he had talked about working for his father, his fears about his disappearance and his connections with Moussavi, Rahman and Ho.

"I just have a feeling he got involved in all this by accident and was out of his depth. I remember a few years ago he got involved with a raiding party that went into Azerbaijan and came back with all sorts of stuff: money, icons, girls, even some Russian missiles. It had been organised by Moussavi before he was appointed governor mayor. I know he rowed with my mother about it and he said he had to do it because he was broke. Since I went away, he's clearly made a lot of money in a short space of time and having looked through his records, most of it now looks legit. The stuff that wasn't seems to relate to his cross-border cash trades, which he only really discussed with Hanif, who is now dead, according to Jevadi. I don't know how he can know that but if my father is still alive he must be trapped somewhere in Azerbaijan and I have no means of finding him."

Kolani observed, "Your father has a big reputation round here and is nobody's fool. He would understand the risks of going west, better than anyone. Certainly, if he is stuck over there he will be figuring out a way to get back. He would expect you to keep things running in his absence, so just do it, tell the family and let events take care of themselves."

Fawaz estimated there was just four hours to go before the Peace International team would meet at his number three barn and prepare to leave the country. He had checked the mezzanine to see if their drysuits were ready for the trip back across the water. Apart from his own, he expected there to be one spare for Jack. He would need to tell Dave that Jack would have to stay on for a few days at least until he was able to make the trip. He also wanted the group out of the country before he told Shimina the full story of his return to Ibrahim Sami and the realities of his father's disappearance. The previous twenty-four hours had felt tense in the town following Rahman's decision to bolster border protections following the theft of the Buk missile system and the Posyan detention centre breakout. Word of mouth was much more efficient than the local newspaper and Fawaz's neighbours were worried, despite house-to-house assurances provided by the military, that there were still eight 'murderers' on the loose in the locality. No one knew the route down to the Aras from Sami better than Fawaz but he was clearly aware more care would be required that evening given the increase of foot patrols. There was no way of knowing in the time available where and when the guards would be out so it would be a slow 'caterpillar' movement through the razor wire and minefield when the time came. Members of the team had been lying low since completing their operational duties the night before. For safety, they had sheltered outdoors at different locations in the vicinity and were set to gather at 21.00.

All arrived at the appointed rendezvous within a few minutes of each other and quietly got to work putting on their kit for their final trip. Fawaz told Dave about Jack, but Dave had asked for his drysuit anyway as Amy Fong was now one of their number. Given the increased patrols, Dave had also instructed that they wait for Gil to arrive to lead them to the river crossing. It was now time for goodbyes, hugs and promises to keep in touch, because, after all, that's what people say at such times, regardless of whether they mean it. Together with Jo, Rodg, Anya and Gul, they strapped on their backpacks. They waited in anticipation in the semi-darkness of the ground level tubular light for Gil, watching the dancing shadows cast by the sheep jostling for their evening feed. Fawaz locked the main barn and returned under torchlight to the house, alone with his thoughts to face his own new and pressing personal challenge – his future relationship with his sister.

Entering the house, he found her, curled up on a settee watching a nature programme on TV.

"Shem – we need to talk. It's important."

"If you want to give me another lecture, don't bother, I know the script," she replied.

"No, there's something really important to tell you. Hanif is dead and its likely Dad is too."

She continued to stare at the TV.

"Did they go to Armenia?"

"I don't know other than the fact they didn't get there. Apparently, they were involved in a major road crash in Azerbaijan."

"Why did you say Hanif is dead and Dad is likely to be?"

He told her about the call from Karranlo.

"And how does he know?"

"I think he got a tip-off from someone over there."

"So Dad may be out there trying to get home and hasn't bothered to take a mobile. And there's no point in us going to search for him because he could be anywhere if he is alive."

"Yes."

"Great. What do you expect me to do?"

"Firstly, we must look after Mum. She will have no idea. I'm pretty sure Dad never talked to her about any of his trips across the frontier. It will be a complete shock. I think she is better staying at her sisters, so we need to plan to go and see her together if we hear nothing more in the course of the next few days. We must also speak to Khalifa."

"And what else?"

"Until he gets back, I have to be head of the household and manage the business."

"How boring is that?"

"Grow up, Shemmy – we both need to keep it together for Mum's as well as Dad's sake. I need your assistance, especially, making sure all the bookkeeping is done. Will you help me?"

"OK, but how about *you* helping *me*?"

"What do you need?"

"If you are going to be head of the family, you need to understand I am now a woman, not a girl, some piece of meat to be traded like the sheep in the barn. I am eighteen years old. So many of my friends have already been given to gnarled old men to be brides – raped and banished to a kitchen either to cook meals or have their horrible offspring. I am tired of going through the market on my own and being groped or leered at. I don't want to be defined by my sexuality in our male-dominated society.

"Mum doesn't really get it but it's different for my generation. I want to study and get a good job. If I have to lose my virginity, so be it, but at least I should choose who and when. The way things are, I know my life won't get better until I have slept with a man, when I can wear his ring and take control of my life. I am telling you I have met that man: he is your 'spy', Parviz, the one you took to the mosque earlier. This could be my best chance of happiness. If you can't approve, please don't stand in my way."

Fawaz sighed. "His name is Jack. He comes from Manchester in England and has an Iranian granny. He's a journalist and came here to write a story about the Chinese base. I travelled back here with him a couple of weeks ago. I don't think he would be serious or has any intention of staying once he has the story, precisely because he could be arrested and put on trial for espionage."

"If he has an Iranian granny, he could get an Iranian passport. If he had a good Iranian wife and kids, that would be everything. If you are in charge here, you will need a replacement for Hanif. Why not Parviz? What's not to like about that?"

"You're going much too fast."

"Sometimes, you have to seize the moment."

"Well, that is for another day. I will think about it. We need to talk to Khalifa before talking about a replacement for Hanif. You'd better call her in."

The journey to the riverbank, although relatively short, proved to be as tortuous as Dave had anticipated. Running low and sheltering at intervals in ditches the group had only moved about 200 metres before encountering the first foot patrol. More alarming to Gil was the fact that these two were conscripts, nervous of being in the dark in an unfamiliar place and tempted to loose off at anything they thought was out of the ordinary, which meant only total silence could be a calming influence. Frustratingly, they were static and must have been expected to be part of a rigid cordon of security. Having waited patiently for ten minutes, Gul silently crept up and nodded to Gil, who seemed to instinctively understand what he had in mind. Taking both boys down silently, they offered little resistance to the two blows they sustained. Doubtless they would have a headache when they came round, but certainly would have no recollection of how they ended up in a ditch in a soggy uniform with their weapons intact.

Gil had been more methodical than when Fawaz had first led them into Iran, crouched and feeling his way across the disturbed topsoil. The SAS man was confident in negotiating the minefield, having previously used a cotton thread along the zigzag route they had to follow to the water. Also, when he had brought Anya and Gul across, he had fixed a thin steel guidance line, allowing users to attach their belt hooks themselves in order to take the shortest route through the torrent without being swept away. Having checked his charges were together and ready to cross, he flashed his torch to the far bank and waited for it to be reciprocated before signalling Dave to attach himself to the guideline. One by one, they waded as best they could through the maelstrom, supporting each other on their journey. As the waters receded, smiling Azeri soldiers took each by the hand, disconnected them from the line, removed their backpacks, wrapped each in heat-retaining aluminium blankets and escorted them to a waiting van. Gil's eyes had acclimatised to the conditions. Rodg had been the last to make the journey and, once he saw he had reached the far side, Gil waved and disappeared, back into to the shadows of the Iranian bank.

The feeling of euphoria was unavoidable and infectious. For the past couple of weeks, the small Peace International task force had been under unrelating and constant pressure in hostile territory. They had achieved their prime objective and managed to do it without firing a shot, meeting the highest aspirations of their sponsors.

The bus transferred them from the water's edge, up the bank and up onto an undulating track to the warehouse where the whole operation had started. This time it all looked very different, with a number of military vehicles parked outside and a tall portable antenna dwarfing the building.

One by one, they climbed through the hatch into the warm sodium-lit "cavern" greeted by general applause from the Azeri soldiers and handshakes for each from Edwin and Bob, and the newly arrived Major Ryumin. Dave Hebbert stood for a moment, surrounded by his team, holding his right fist in the air with three memory sticks in it. He could imagine Gil saying, "It was the feeling Jordan Henderson must have felt when he lifted the UEFA Champions League Winners trophy for Liverpool." A special moment which would not be recreated – for Edwin and Bob too, but for other reasons. For Edwin, the successful return without fatalities had been in the end a vindication of his strategy, one which in subsequent weeks his sponsoring governments would be able to support, even if it had been at the expense of a 'wild card' – the support of the Azerbaijan authorities. For Bob, it was about the safe return of the woman he loved. He could not be sure whether their unannounced personal presence in Barthaz had taken his partner by surprise or whether there was more to come out that he didn't know. The tension in her body when they hugged, told him she was still in military mode.

Showers, changes of clothing, food and drink followed ahead of the formal welcome and debriefing from Major Ryumin.

It was 06.50. The Azeri commander provided an overview of the actions of the past forty-eight hours; although some were familiar with parts of it, no one had the whole story. He had been quick to thank Edwin for offering his full cooperation on behalf of Peace International and explained that Azerbaijan had been pleased to be of assistance. The next step would be in-depth interviews with each member of the team that Zeitsev would conduct and Edwin would sit in on. Reports would be produced, copies of the memory sticks would be taken and studied, and their passports would be retained for a short period as agreed with Peace International for 'administrative reasons'. Later in the day, they would be transferred by helicopter from Minjivan to Baku and accommodated until further notice at the Four Seasons. The situation in Ibrahim Sami was described by Ryumin as volatile, necessitating ongoing monitoring. The temporary installation of the Barthaz listening post would be retained, with the border monitored by drone inspections and his 'rapid reaction force' would remain on standby pending further instructions from Baku. The status of Sergeant Amy Fong would be the subject of separate review, although her importance to the success of the mission, providing eye-witness testimony and documentary evidence, and Edwin's insistence she would become a member of Peace International staff, were noted.

Having completed his review to the assembled company, Ryumin stepped forward to Dave, shook his hand once again and spent a few minutes in informal conversation with his team, before moving on to Edwin. He put his arm on his shoulder and walked him away purposefully into one of the recesses of the warehouse.

"After a poor start, I am really pleased our cooperation has worked out so well," he began. "I recognised you as a man of honour and you have rewarded my trust. I had a call with Minister Nubulatov a couple of hours ago and he is briefing the president about now. Of course, you must wait a few days while we assess the information you have brought back, but I do not foresee any problems in following through on what was previously agreed in principle. As a thank you, we will also propose a positive solution to Ms Fong's status. We will expect to be informed about your plans for public communication in advance for obvious reasons."

Edwin nodded. "You know, Major, I must report to my own board in New York City first and then share the information with our sponsor governments. When I hear back from them, I shall revert to Mr Nubulatov's office. Does this mark the end of our association?"

"Yes, I think so. We are moving into the arena of politics. As a military man, I regard this as being outside my personal comfort zone, so I am pleased Nubulatov is taking this matter forward with you. Although I don't expect to be involved, I will take a scholarly interest in the next steps. Although I am based in Stepanakert, I may be called to Baku before you leave. Alternatively, it is a personal ambition to visit your country soon as a tourist, so maybe our next meeting will be over a pint of your beer, looking at your Buckingham Palace."

He put on his peaked hat, offered a casual salute which looked more like a wave, and nodded to his driver he was ready to leave.

During their exchange no one had noticed one member of the Peace International team slipping outside and even if they had they would have assumed it was for a smoke. In this case the person departing hadn't got the pleasure of a cigarette in mind, but had spotted a Russian-built UAZ jeep outside with keys in the ignition. The engine roared to life and the vehicle sped back to the main road, turning left and heading south.

Anya had reflected on Ryumin's concluding remarks and, in particular, his comments about intercepting al-Fouadi. She had been incensed by his casual comment about him being missing, *presumed* dead. That was not the same as *being* dead and neutralising al-Fouadi had been the reason why she had joined the Peace International mission in Iran in the first place. She was a soldier and hadn't signed up to the 'no kill' ethos of the organisation. Yet she had played a key part in its success – creating the diversion at the Chinese restaurant in Ibrahim Sami and inspiring the breakout from the detention centre at Posyan. She had waited for the opportunity to confront al-Fouadi but it hadn't materialised. She had only just put the idea out of her mind when they started their journey back from Ibrahim Sami, but here now might be an opportunity to finish the job, once and for all.

There aren't too many roads in southern Azerbaijan and so she could be confident, eventually, she would find the location of the helicopter attack on the Land Cruiser. That part of her task was easy. After a thirty-minute drive, the mangled, burned-out frame of the car came into view, towards the top of an incline on the road from Vezhnaly. It had been moved to the side of the road and a short distance beyond were the tell-tale scorch marks of the missile induced inferno. But what else? There was nothing more to be seen. She parked the UAZ next to the wreckage and climbed out. The morning sun had just risen, illuminating a mountainous valley of sedges and heather. Visibility was excellent, but there appeared to be no sign of movement in any direction, except for an eagle circling on thermal currents high up away to her left, where the ground fell away towards the Aras river. The view was magnificent. It was a perfect opportunity for a hike, except she had none of the necessary equipment, other than a pair of stout boots. She walked a little further down the road to the point of impact and stared at the tarmac looking for clues about the fate of the Land Cruiser's occupants. Upon reflection, she reasoned that in an explosion bodies could have been thrown a considerable distance, perhaps fifty metres away. As the road itself hugged one side of the valley wall, it would have been obvious if a body had landed in that direction, but, if it had been the other side, where the ground fell away, it would be harder to find. Stumbling down from the roadside into the shale and scree of the surrounding terrain, Anya found herself walking down towards the river. She stopped every few minutes to listen for any sign of life. She was only greeted with silence. She walked on, now some eighty metres from the roadside. Still nothing, so maybe Ryumin was right when he blurred the distinction between missing and death. Turning to retrace her steps, she noticed a self-seeded sapling, which looked determined to grow in the barren environment, and on it was a torn strip of cloth which looked like it had come from a shirt. Closer examination showed it had dried blood on it. Someone had passed by recently. Drawing her Makarov, she continued to stumble down the slope, imagining what she might have done in similar circumstances, and then she saw it, about another 100 metres on was a small shepherd's hut. It had to be the place. She approached as quietly as possible, but her presence was given away by stones falling under foot. For the first time she heard the sound of movement coming from the hut. Now scrambling towards it, she used the handle of the weapon to smash open the door, standing back, expecting to be met by a volley of shots. Instead, what she heard was a soft moaning. The light of the day pierced the gloom of the interior and sitting up against the back wall was a bloodied and dishevelled figure in a ripped shirt and trousers – Hafiz al-Fouadi.

It was difficult to know who was the most surprised, Anya at finally discovering her target or Hafiz, anticipating rescue in the middle of nowhere. It was clear he was in a bad way, but he seemed capable of understanding his situation.

"Well, Mr al-Fouadi, isn't life strange? I never thought we would meet again and even if we did not under these circumstances." She looked down at the stricken figure. "I came to Ibrahim Sami to see you. Just last week I had a really great meal in your Chinese restaurant. I love spicy food."

She saw a look of understanding emerge on Hafiz's face. He had now remembered the CCTV. "I bet you're still trying to place me. Here's a clue." She unbuttoned her shirt, releasing her breasts. "Now do you remember? How could you forget? You and your thuggish mates kidnapped me when you came to Minjivan a few years back when you took the anti-aircraft battery.

"I recall you telling me what an amazing pair of tits I had, before you raped me the first time, and then how you said you couldn't get them out of your mind when you did it again upstairs at the mosque in Ibrahim Sami. I know in a strange way I should thank you because, although you planned to ruin my life, I wasn't prepared to accept it. Your depravity was a weakness. You wanted to lock me up for your private use. If you had shared me around, I would have been dead years ago, but because you were complacent, and kept me locked in a room most days, I worked out how to escape and made it back home. I was trained as a soldier and that gave me the determination to overcome the ordeal and rebuild my life. I am now married to a caring man who has no idea of the torture you subjected me to. Plotting my revenge has added focus to my life and now I can look forward once more, knowing I have ensured the end of my torment. I can tell you that those who blew you up the other day believe you are dead already, so there's little more I can do to add to your punishment, except this final humiliation.

"Look at me, al-Fouadi – think how much you want me, even now. You've got to admit, I'm in good shape. And reflect on how powerless you are to do anything about it."

Hafiz's eyes became animated and he started to grunt and whimper.

"What was that? Will I help you recover and find peace? Not my job," she said buttoning her shirt once more. "No, it's time for you to talk with Allah and make your peace. You must hope he will be more merciful than me. Good luck!"

She drew the Makarov and fired a single shot at his head. The gun pulled to the right, hitting him in the chest. He was gone. She dragged his body by his boots out of the hut, leaving him on the ground, and opened up his shirt to the elements, a passing advertisement for hungry carrion-loving raptors, or local wolves. She would have no more use for the pistol, emptying the barrel of bullets and throwing it further down the slope. She walked slowly back up the hill to the roadside and the UAZ.

This valley would forever be haunted by the ghost of Soldier Anya, not that of the criminal al-Fouadi, who no one would remember.

She had a better, more positive future to contemplate as Anya Mullen, tourist guide in Baku.

It was afternoon in Ibrahim Sami. Fawaz visited Jack in the mosque.

"Are you feeling better? I am ready to get you down to the river crossing for Barthaz when you're ready. I told them you might not make it for a week but these last two days at the mosque have been good for you. I think you will be ready sooner rather than later."

"Thanks for all you've done, mate. It can't have been easy. I heard the guards doing house-to-house calls last night. Was I right in hearing there are still some prisoners on the loose and two of the soldiers got beaten up on patrol a couple of nights ago?"

"Yes, that's right. Had those guards not been attacked at the edge of the farm, I don't think they would have come knocking but, as they did, I gave them a complete tour to keep them satisfied, although they didn't want to spend any time in number three barn. Said it smelled of shit!"

They both shared the joke.

Fawaz turned serious.

"You know it's now pretty certain my Dad's dead along with his farm manager and I am legally his successor? The business is much bigger than I thought. I cannot see how he found time to run it all. It's likely that I will have to pick up whatever he agreed with Moussavi as well if all this Chinese investment actually happens. My mum is so upset she doesn't want to come home and is staying at her sisters, so I need all the help I can get to keep the estate operating. I've already assured Mr Choi and his family they can continue running the restaurant and asked Dad's senior receptionist, Eleheh, to focus on managing the hotel business to take the pressure off our housekeeper, Khalifa, who is grieving for Hanif. I need Shimina to step up and take more responsibility but she seems preoccupied, *infatuated* with you. I never did understand her that well, but I have seen she has grown up a lot while I've been away, and I think this might be a bit more than a fad, or 'crush' as you might say in English? She seems to have some romantic idea about you staying in Iran and marrying her. She even suggested I should make you the farm manager and you qualify for an Iranian passport. I cannot know if everything she hopes for would ever come to pass, but I do know she thinks a lot about you and she has asked for my help. If her feelings are misplaced or you think life is going to be better for you in England, go now. Life is hard enough here, and, as you look a little different to the locals, you will always have to be looking over your shoulder if you stay. However, I will help you to leave if you want, and we can say no more about it. She'll move on given time."

"Yeah, I understand what you mean. Starting a relationship here, of all places, was not part of my plans, but she is certainly special. Although there is nothing waiting for me back in England, I know staying would be tough and there is much to learn. I'd be a fool if I said I was confident. I need to think it through. Can we talk again in the morning?"

Fawaz nodded and left to join afternoon prayers.

Abdullo had sent the company helicopter to Posyan to collect Hanah and Jamshid.

Jamshid assumed that their visit had been a success, not least because Governor Mayor Moussavi and Colonel Rahman had attended in person to see them off, and neither gave any impression of the strains they had been under in the past twenty-four hours. Considering the directness of Rahman's personal comments the previous day, Jamshid felt a certain warmth in Rahman's farewell, not just a handshake and a salute but an awkward hug to the shoulder.

Moussavi appeared to be positively enjoying the occasion, having rumoured to have been effectively trapped in his own residence, albeit with Madam Moussavi, for a few hours the night before. In the same way as his gardener had hosed off the spilt blood on his driveway overnight, he seemed to have shrugged off any potential embarrassment from the prison breakout and had lost none of his enthusiasm for working with the Alrakahthans in order to bolster his own position and influence.

It was a good sign that Moussavi never missed an opportunity to make a speech.

"Major Ho sends his apologies for not being here to say goodbye. He called to say he was unavoidably detained on an administrative issue at the compound, but that he intended to make a full and positive report to Beijing on the content of our discussions. From our point of view, that was the primary objective behind your visit and has created the right conditions to move our shared plans forward, so, on behalf of Khoda Afrin Prefecture, we must express our thanks to Alrakahthan Enterprises."

It was left to Hanah to reply.

"Thank you too, Mr Governor Mayor, for your welcome and assistance. I hope this is only the first of many visits. We will write to you and Major Ho confirming our willingness to submit tenders for work on the Posyan free port. With regard to the rare earth mining and export prospects, we have left you with copies of all the geological reports and our assessments of the most accessible points for the commencement of operations. This now must rest with you as all depends on your ability to redesignate the boundaries of the Arasbaran Protected Zone. Should we be able to offer further advice, please call."

It was a rare recognition of their achievement that Abdullo had sent the company helicopter to collect them. Boarding the gold-coloured Airbus H175, Hanah and Jamshid had a sense of relief as the door closed behind them and they took their seats in the luxurious interior cabin. They had retained the credibility of the Supreme Leader's commitment to developing trade with potentially their country's most important commercial partner, put themselves in a position to influence forthcoming tender contracts for the Posyan free port, demonstrated their expertise in a new and highly profitable rare earth business, and made a potentially important connection in the local labour market. In addition, Jamshid had learned that almost everyone he had worked with prior to joining the Alrakahthans had abused his trust but, more importantly, he had passed his personal initiation test, set by his new boss. What it would mean for his future prospects, only time would tell.

As they took off, Jamshid asked, "When do you think we'll be back?"

Hanah looked pensive. "When we have got hold of a copy of Ho's report. I can see I will need to spend some more time working on him to get what we need."

The rest of the journey was in silence. Abdullo had taken the opportunity to provide sealed copies of AE board papers for them to digest before landing.

On touch down at Mehrabad they were taken straight to Karaj arriving thirty minutes ahead of the appointed time. The chairman was impatient to begin and so, with his wife, Bahar, and son, Hasan, in place, the board meeting commenced.

Each gave their report; the conclusion of the session was that, as the nation's economy continued to falter and struggle in the face of international sanctions, the businesses of Alrakahthan Enterprises continued to grow strongly, year on year profits up 32%. They had consolidated their position as the pre-eminent private-sector procurement partner of the Islamic Republic. From illicit oil exports to prosthetic limbs and laboratory equipment, repackaged fresh fruit and vegetables to semi-finished goods, such as washing machines and gear boxes, niche market opportunities were being relentlessly harvested by the Alrakahthan commercial machine.

Even the increased tension with the Great Satan was spawning a new industry with the temporary acquisition of the 11th February Silkworm Assembly Plant, which was about to pioneer the refurbishment of obsolete ground-to-air missiles.

Their secret – *the primary objective* – mortgaging urgent domestic needs to drive export potential and secure profits in safe havens, around the world, out of the reach of government regulators.

It was a foreign policy any state would have been happy to own.

EIGHTEEN

THE TIME HAD COME to break the news about the deaths of Hafiz and Hanif to the governor mayor. Fawaz had not been sure how to do this, especially from attending meetings with his father and Moussavi; he had formed the distinct impression that the two had a much deeper bond and understanding that spanned many years, which he didn't know about.

His message would be simple. His dad had gone and, as a result, he was in charge. If Moussavi thought there were matters that required a response from the al-Fouadi businesses, he would be pleased to be informed in order to ensure an appropriate response was made. He would pick his words carefully because he could not anticipate the likely reaction. With his father's Land Cruiser gone, the only other roadworthy car to hand was a Mitsubishi L200 pick-up, used from time to time by Hanif to pull a trailer with livestock. He had personally hosed it off outside the front of their house so it would at least look respectable before he drove to the governor mayor's residence. Fawaz told Shimina he was going to Posyan as she left the house to go to the market and enquired about Khalifa.

"I think she is still in shock. I have told her not to worry about her duties for now. We'll just have to work it out a day at a time."

Fawaz nodded and started the ignition. If he was travelling with a purpose, so was his sister. The al-Fouadis were more fortunate than most. Living on a farm, they were not short of meat, fruit or vegetables, but bread was a staple. Next to the baker were the random stalls of the market traders and one of those was run by a local woman who made her own jewellery. Shimina had often admired her wares and had her eye on a simple but elegant ring with a deep red gemstone that looked like a ruby. Given its price, Shimina was sure this was only a costume piece, but she loved it all the same. Unlike her recent visits, which had resulted in browsing but not concluding in a purchase, this time it was a short, business appointment. A brief haggle over the price, a thick pile of rolled rial notes passed over and the ring was hers, disappearing for now into the inner recesses of her *chador*. Carrying the bread, the next stop was at the mosque, but she had deliberately avoided prayer time, which would have meant she could only have entered via the back door. Entering at the front, she left her shopping and shoes and went in search of the imam Yusuf. An animated conversation in lowered tones took place and Shimina then produced another roll of banknotes from her *chador* and placed them into his hand, her other hand closing on the top of his. He then took a book, pen and paper and led the way up a flight of stairs along a short corridor into the room where Jack had been recovering. The door closed behind them. Fifteen minutes later, Mullah Yusuf emerged, crossing the corridor to his office. After a short delay he returned with a signed and sealed document, shook their hands and departed.

Shimina smiled.

"From now on, I will only call you Parviz. Parviz is the future. Jack is the past. It's time to go home – to your home now."

They returned to the empty al-Fouadi residence, and Shimina helped him up the stairs to the room he recognised when he had first been taken in. It was light, airy and fresh, with an en suite. He took a shower, and, while he was washing, she stripped off and joined him, and they embraced. It seemed that the shower was powered by the Aras itself, judging by the time they took, but, when they were done, their relationship had changed.

She looked radiant, like this was the dawn of a new life.

"I thought you would like to give me a ring, so I chose one that I like for now, until you have earned enough wages to get me one yourself."

She put the ring in his hand. He put it on her left hand.

"And now you have work to do."

She laughed, got up and brushed her long brown hair.

Shimina had moved to the kitchen to prepare dinner for Jack and Fawaz. Her brother arrived just before dusk, looking drained. The meeting with Moussavi had been much longer than he had planned. He was not as surprised to see Jack as Shimina had expected and guessed her news ahead of her confirmation.

"Hi, Faz – I want to introduce you to the newest member of our family. This is Parviz. I found him at the mosque today and bought a one-year *mutah* – an official marriage licence – from Mullah Yusuf before bringing him home. Yusuf performed the ceremony straightaway on the promise of payment in US dollars and I always knew where Dad kept a stash.

"Parviz and I have done a deal. We have decided on a trial marriage. He will study the Holy Book with me and the imam. He will work here, as I will, and together we will make the House of al-Fouadi strong again. If he feels he cannot settle, I have agreed we can divorce and he can return to his old life in Britain. If he stays, we will plan another big wedding celebration, even bigger than the Pomegranate Festival. And, before you ask, I have my ring and, yes, we have consummated our union, this very afternoon. I can't wait until Mum is recovered so I can tell her. She knew of my feelings and I know how happy she will be once the pain of Dad's death eases."

Jack looked intently at Fawaz.

"What's not to love about your sister? She is a beautiful, fun-loving person who has already shown me a different side of life here. I hope I will be good enough for her. In the meantime, I'll work hard to support the family firm."

Her brother nodded his acknowledgement. It was time to find another bottle of his father's Zagros Shiraz to toast their future happiness.

Fawaz could only imagine what Hafiz would have said, but he knew how important this was to Shimina and had accepted he couldn't understand the difficulties of being an attractive single young woman in the local community. Personally, despite her annoying habits, he was impressed that she had found her own solution to her problem. After all, if anyone else had told her what to do, it would have been a disaster. Importantly, he would benefit too, having secured his sister's commitment to the al-Fouadi business and finding a new farm manager he could trust.

What's more, having collected Moussavi's shopping list of requirements, he was even more certain there was a busy year ahead that would require their collective effort to deliver.

With the monthly Alrakahthan Enterprises' board meeting concluded, Jamshid planned to return home for a few days. Hasan took advantage by asking him to call at the 11th February Silkworm Assembly Plant to check progress.

"We can follow most of what they're up to online, but the big question rests with Madam Professor Engineer Rahman. We have yet to see her detailed proposals for taking forward the missile refurbishment plans, especially so we can better understand her cost projections. We need numbers." Hasan spoke the language of accountancy, capable of sucking the interest out of any innovative commercial proposition.

"I'll make it my business to drop by. I'll call you from the AE apartment, once I've got my head around what's proposed," he replied.

After such an intense couple of days in the north-west, he had become accustomed to travelling with Hanah and discussing their work as they went. She was now bound for Ashkabat to discuss increasing oil exports on Project Xerxes as well as trialling their new water purification technology. Their next encounter would have to wait a week and looked likely to coincide with his next visit to see his parents. He would miss her, especially as he thought he was only just starting to earn her trust. It was time to refocus on his connections down south. Despite being responsible for reviewing a major growth area of AE's business, the luxury of the company helicopter was not offered a second time, although Hasan did give him a lift back to Mehrabad airport.

Arriving back in Bandar, he took a taxi back to his apartment in the rising heat of the late morning. The sunny weather provided the excuse to get reacquainted with his Ray-Bans upon leaving the terminal building, giving him a bit of personal privacy to reflect on his new situation. Much had happened in his life since he was last here and the experience would inevitably impact on many of his long-term friendships.

Arriving at the main reception of his residential block, he was initially surprised to have been greeted by the concierge with a bundle of mail which had built up over the past week. The surprise was the volume of letters he received, even if they were mainly bills and junk. Often, Mr Tawal would collect his mail while getting his own and slip it under his door when he got up to the tenth floor, a trick he had long perfected with his walking stick.

He commented about it to the security man on the front desk, who replied, "Yes, it's a shame he's not here to do it anymore."

Jamshid was unaware Tawal had plans to move and said as much in reply.

"He didn't move out, just went to a better place," he was told.

Strangely, Jamshid had not been close to him, but he had known him as a neighbour (albeit an annoying one) for the past five years. For him, Tawal was almost part of the furniture of his block.

"What happened?"

"He had a nurse who comes in to check on him weekly, just to make sure he's eating and drinking OK. We loan her a pass key. Last week, when she let herself in, she found he had passed away in an armchair in front of the TV. Apparently, it was peaceful."

"Did he have any family?"

"Yes. A son who is a teacher in Kerman who came here a couple of days back to sort out his affairs. His flat is on the market; we had a couple come and look at it yesterday."

"What about the funeral?"

The guy on the front desk shrugged his shoulders. Jamshid sighed, took his post and went to the elevator. He wondered about Tawal's state of mind at the end: was he as happy as he had been, draining the last of Jamshid's Bekaa Valley arak, or was he troubled, being pressurised to supply reports of his comings and goings to the Basij? He would never know. In a strange way, the death of Tawal felt like the closing of a chapter, a turning of the page, a point of no return. He opened his apartment door carefully, forensically observing the interior before touching anything to see whether all was as he left it when he was last there.

He had sent texts to both Mahta and Ravi, determined to see them both and to confront them face to face with the fact that he knew they had informed on him. He could only imagine how they would react.

Mahta had been as good as her word and responded that dinner would be at hers at 20.00 the following evening. Interestingly, she had been careful to add the address to her note without him prompting her for it. Ravi would be at the Pak Bakery in downtown Bandar later that afternoon.

Afternoon was a good time to come to the Pak and it was a first for Jamshid to be there at that hour. The normal crush of commuters grabbing coffee and pastries had been replaced in the main by women who had been shopping or collecting their children from school. Although Jamshid thought it was a pleasure not to be jostled for a seat, the premises remained a noisy, slightly chaotic place with staff and customers balancing teas, cakes and ice creams between the main counter and the tightly packed tables.

Ravi had already found a seat and ordered tea and baklava by the time Jamshid arrived.

"Sorry to have kept you waiting," he panted.

"No worries, I got through my last surgery for the day, so it's home to sort out my paperwork after we finish here. Anyway, it's good to see you. It must have been all of three weeks, so more than a social call?"

"Yes, I feel my feet haven't touched the ground since."

"I thought you were seconded to the Energy Ministry and working with the Alrakahthans on some commercial projects?"

"Keep up. I know that you have been reporting on me to Tehran. I met someone senior in the Revolutionary Guard who told me as much last week. I was hoping, one friend to another, you would tell me why?"

"Well, I'm not sure I would regard it as a breach of trust as you do. Is there any privacy left in the Islamic Republic these days? If you are a medic, I can find out about your employment record at a touch of a button in the office and I am sure it must be the same in most walks of life. I wouldn't regard my activity of 'reporting on you', as you put it, as negative. After all, when you start a new job, employers normally require a character reference and I didn't see anything strange in that. In fact, since you made that fabulous donation to the Prosthetics Fund, I had more enquiries about you from people who are getting limbs and who just wanted to express their thanks. This job you're doing may be exciting, but I wonder if this is part of your paranoia we talked about last time. Did anyone follow you here? You know our society has always existed on a steady diet of suspicion and intrigue. Seems to me you're a bit sensitive to it at the moment. Remember, it's only money and the worst may never happen. So get over it, and spare me the detail about what you've been up to. But is it true you've been working with that Hanah Alrakahthan? I saw her picture in the paper the week after you left and was thinking she must be one of the most eligible women in Iran, if not the Gulf region. She could check out my operating theatre any time."

"I have been there once, it's true, but I can't keep it going when I'm dating Mahta."

"Too tiring?"

"No, just can't get my head straight. One wants it as a hobby; the other wants a relationship."

"Ha. Choose the one you don't work with every day. That way, when it goes tits up, you're not out of a job – and don't move to Tehran, by the way. Then they will have you by the balls, and make your life a misery, not to mention your mum and dad dropping by when they feel like it."

It seemed like good advice.

Mahta's place was in an upmarket block on the third floor on the corner of Shrinkadeh Street. It was easy to find but finding a nearby parking space less so. He had spent at least twenty minutes trying to find a place that was both legal and safe. Out of habit, he had not arrived empty-handed, having picked up some very expensive flowers from a street stall on the next block. Maybe his trip north had given him a feeling of paranoia, but he had a sense he had been followed. Normally, government employees tasked with such jobs were not skilled at the covert arts, so he thought it odd he had not been able to spot any dodgy types in his wake. Besides, based on what her husband had told him up in the Arasbaran, the government were no longer interested in him, so maybe he shouldn't worry.

Arriving on Mahta's doorstep, he got the clear impression she lived more comfortably than the day job suggested. Forget she had been running a government munitions factory; this sort of accommodation would cost more besides, perhaps representing an additional hefty contribution from her absent Revolutionary Guard partner.

Mahta hadn't planned to disappoint. The regulation *chador* and no make-up had been substituted for a more casual, softer Western look. A figure-hugging mauve jersey, jeans and white trainers combined with hair tied back in a ponytail, gold shell earrings and matching necklace complemented her mascara and lipstick.

"Well, the wanderer returns," she said with a grin and gave him a kiss as a reminder of their last meeting. "I guess, under the circumstances, I need to treat you with a new respect. Are you getting the taste for life in the north again?"

He held her briefly by the waist. "I don't really know. I think I like having a foot in both camps. That way life stays interesting."

Dinner consisted of *Khoresht-e gheimeh*, diced lamb combined with yellow split peas, dried limes and saffron with fried potatoes washed down with a bottle of Persian Tradition Isfahan Chardonnay, an unofficial souvenir from an international engineering conference in New Delhi earlier in the year.

"I don't get the chance to do much cooking unless the kids are back from France, so I hope you like it," she said. "Cooking and horse riding are just the greatest ways of taking my mind away from the day-to-day hassles of the workplace. That and, of course… you."

The comment was the invitation he had been seeking to start the dialogue he came for. "It's nice to know you think of me as a distraction. I thought I was more of a mission for you."

"How do you mean?"

"Well, let's say in the last few days I have met your husband and heard all about Gharbieh. I didn't realise I was of so much interest to the government."

Mahta seemed almost stung by Jamshid's remark. "I expect you have learned much about life for the privileged in the Islamic

Republic. There aren't many people in positions of influence who haven't been compromised in some way by the state. That is our system. Some us have no choice in getting caught up in the game. Despite my qualifications and expertise, had I played my cards differently, I could have remained an ordinary wife of a Revolutionary Guard officer, beaten and raped at will, and kept in some back room as a virtual prisoner, like so many are. My background gave me a choice to take a different path, but that too had conditions. I never sought you out to spy on you, but the authorities wanted to know more about you and saw I had an opportunity to win your trust. They told me that I had to test you out as a potential agent of the state, as they wanted to send you to a number of international energy conferences. They wanted to know whether you could be tempted by money or sex, as these were the risks of being an agent as the state saw it. In their eyes, you failed because I was able to seduce you and also because your potential was leaked by a government official to Alrakahthan who decided to get you for his own organisation. Maybe, Jamshid, you understand we all have to find our own routes to surviving in a society ruled by an ideology, not reality. Maybe also it's time for you to understand yourself. You are fortunate, you have skill and opportunity, but are you using it well? Does it make you happy?"

Jamshid should have expected her assertive response and realised how well Mahta understood his state of mind.

"I don't know what makes me happy, yet. My life is ambiguous. I have a skill in doing deals and making money; I understand that international sanctions may appear to be bad news for the country but they're good for Alrakahthan Enterprises. We find ways of getting things done and make good profits as a result. Gharbieh and his cronies are wrong to say corporate business is disloyal to the state, and people like me have somehow failed or given in to temptation. It is the reverse. Alrakahthan is keeping the country afloat, allowing the Supreme Leader to assert we will not succumb to the threats of the Americans.

"We want to harness solid commercial propositions where we find them, to develop new trades that will keep people fed and in jobs – not rioting on the streets – and I think that's what you want too. It's no accident your factory has been leased to AE. That was the price for organising the second wave of 8.5 million food parcels that the Supreme Leader announced a few days ago. Alrakahthan in effect bought *you*, bought your *skill*, bought your *idea*, which will strengthen the state and create new export possibilities. It matters so much right now that he has asked his son, Hasan, to look at fast-tracking your plan. And, yes, I am here for two reasons. One is to work with you to put some figures together for him to get you the finance you need to make this happen…"

"And the second?'

"Because I needed to remind myself about why you matter to me."

They went to bed.

Six hours later, breakfast was no more than a cup of coffee.

Jamshid sat in her kitchen while she was in the shower and picked up copies of two old newspapers, *Resalat* and *Javan*. In both cases pages had been folded out to reveal stories about Hanah Alrakahthan. Both articles referred to a speech she had given at Tehran University some months ago calling on the importance of women contributing to the economy by taking up new training opportunities. Each carried a separate picture. In *Resalat* she was pictured laughing, in a brown *hijab*, shaking hands with students. In the more conservative *Javan*, at a lectern in black *chador*, wagging her finger. Looking at the pictures, he was struck how her natural, high-cheekboned beauty seemed not to be dimmed by her formal dress.

Mahta came into the room and saw what he was reading. "You can't be surprised I've taken an interest in your boss," she said, towelling her hair. "I wanted to see what I was up against."

"How do you mean?"

"Well, I presume you have also slept with her and you are wondering whether you are better with me as a result, or whether you like the idea of having us both."

Maybe it was because it was first thing in the morning but Jamshid didn't offer the denial Mahta expected.

"She is different to you. I think if you knew her you would respect her intellect but dislike her because she is amoral. Is that bad? I guess it depends on your point of view. For her, sex is not an expression of love; it is power. Sex to her is a weapon and someone like me is kept around for target practice to keep her sharp, especially if she has a business target in her sights. I cannot imagine what a long-term relationship with her would be like. I know my mother would love the bragging rights in the tea house, but from a business point of view I think I would be compromised as the only director from outside the family, and that would create extra pressure I don't need from Abdullo Alrakahthan himself."

He had always known it was an issue in the back of his mind but he hadn't understood it before, let alone articulated his feelings. He had been impressed with his own clarity of thought.

"I like the distance between Karaj and Bandar. I like the life here. There is much more for us to achieve. Missiles are just the beginning. Let's sort these numbers at the factory this afternoon, tell Hasan and let him worry about it. Together, we can build a shared future the way we want it to be."

He kissed her, grabbed his coat from a hook by the door and walked out into the day, reassured his personal relationships were intact and his commitments to the Alrakahthan business were under control, at least for now.

NINETEEN

SOME WEEKS HAD ELAPSED since Edwin had returned to London from Baku. The Azeri authorities had been true to their word, prosecuting the Peace International team members who had infringed their electronic tourist visas with a combination of fines and suspended sentences. All paperwork was resolved within ten days, permitting the return of their passports and travel documents. Captain David Hebbert was offered a desk job as a procurement consultant at the Department for International Development on the recommendation of the permanent secretary. Dr Gulman Ehat avoided personal sanction from the Chinese authorities as he had arrived in Baku without a visa from Uzbekistan and the Azeris saw no reason to delay his departure, allowing him to return to work at the WHO Aral Sea site as he had originally planned. Jack Vass had been reported as missing, presumed dead. Bob and Anya Mullen's Baku-based travel agency continued running English-language city tours and adventure treks. Amy Fong had been given a temporary Canadian visa to allow her to travel to Toronto, where she had relatives who offered to look after her when she discovered she was pregnant. Dr Joanna White-Smith, departmental head of biochemical remediation, returned to Oxford's Thornberry Institute of Environmental Toxicology with the evidence recovered from Ibrahim Sami to start to analyse the data, in advance of presenting preliminary findings to the Peace International board. Rodger Mbenza had expected to travel back to London with Edwin, Dave and Jo, but got a text in the transit lounge at Istanbul Airport, where he said his hurried goodbyes, changing flights to go to Beirut, with the promise of a lucrative personal protection contract with a well-known international business figure. Nobody knew what happened to Gil and his SAS colleagues, last seen on the Iranian side of the Aras river.

Edwin Wilson had enjoyed considerable reputation benefit amongst the sponsor governments of the mission since his return from Azerbaijan. Looking back on it, he noted the whole mission had been different from other international investigations he had commissioned previously. It had been the first time that, as the organiser, he had chosen to engage personally 'on the ground', where, to an extent, he had been exposed to the same personal risk encountered by each member of the team. It had given him a new insight into his organisation's responsibilities and the consequences of his own decision-making. Since his return, he had been congratulated for his achievement, not least for avoiding the embarrassment of failure either from not finding the evidence PI had sought, or from fatalities or capture.

But, despite this, the primary objective had been to publish evidence of Iran's clandestine collaboration with China and to hope, by so doing, to oblige both parties to halt their work on biological and chemical weapons at the Ibrahim Sami site. To that extent, the job was not complete.

Preparation of the initial report had taken Dr White-Smith longer to prepare than had been originally envisaged, not least because of the volume and quality of data obtained. In addition to the material initially collected by Dave and colleagues, an unexpected bonus had been supporting reports from both Beijing and Ibrahim Sami collected by Amy Fong. The level of detail in these documents was such that Jo's team at the Thornberry had needed to spend extra time cross-referencing sources.

It had taken almost three months to get to a formal interim report, and Jo had made a personal appointment to present it to Edwin. It told the full story of the Ibrahim Sami compound, whose original reason for being had been inspired by Saddam Hussein's testing of chemical and biological weapons during the Iran–Iraq war. The record showed the tension there had been between Iran's regular army, many of whom had been Saddam's victims and the Revolutionary Guard, who were supporters because of the technologies' relative simplicity, low cost and effectiveness. Ibrahim Sami was selected as the base for research owing to its remoteness and a recognition on the part of authorities that, if anything went wrong, it was away from all main centres of population. A molecular scientist called Dr Quassim Varshad of Tehran University had been put in charge of the covert operation, specifying the facilities required to set up the research. He had personally selected the team of biochemists to join the project, including Dr Muhammad Ghani, who had been part of Saddam's advisory group. The initial plan had been to identify the top three chemical agents and biological germs that could kill the greatest number of people but were capable of being delivered in a controllable way. Once prioritised, the next stage of the plan was to look at production, storage and deployment.

Identifying the substances to work with appeared to have been the straightforward part. In each case, they were administered to victims in controlled conditions to observe how death occurred and how quickly. There were also some references to the testing of antidotes, but these seemed to be inconclusive and inconsistent. The records showed that initially tests had been conducted on animals, rats, dogs, pigs, sheep, horses and latterly people, with most subject to autopsies prior to the corpses being incinerated. Jo's report detailed a broad range of substances used ranging from phosphorus, concentrations of phenols and sarin, as well as samples of manufactured chemical agents, such as novichok.

Smallpox, bubonic plague, rabies, ebola and anthrax featured in another extensive list of biological weapons assessed. When it came to people, there were very complete records regarding the identity of individuals selected to be part of the tests. In the main these were criminals accused of more serious crimes, including rape and murder, and one or two others who had been charged with espionage. Records described how individuals were identified by a duty judge on the Revolutionary Council in Tehran and transferred firstly to solitary confinement in the capital's high-security Evin jail before being called to Ibrahim Sami. In each case, they had been moved to the detention centre at Posyan air base as a pre-admission holding procedure. Notes showed the authorities were required to ensure at least ten prisoners were to be held for appointments at Ibrahim Sami at any one time. Interestingly, Jo's report made reference that, during the period where records were available, the government's preferred method of capital punishment, hangings from cranes in public squares, had been largely suspended, unless a sentencing judge had specifically requested it. The records described a range of procedures for infecting the subjects, hourly reports on their symptoms and demise, as well as a discussion paper looking at whether death may prevent the harvesting of human tissues for potential transplants.

Outside the controlled conditions of the Ibrahim Sami experiments, there appeared to have been poor guidance regarding the disposal of test materials. Documents had shown that a number of military technicians had died having contracted symptoms and been quarantined having been in contact with carcasses scheduled for destruction. Warnings about how such procedures should be managed had either not been given or not clearly understood. This had resulted in two major incidents which had caused major alarm. The first had been when the body of a victim of smallpox had been left outside the compound next to a main road for collection by the local prefecture's refuse collection service. Although the mistake was notified, the body collected and incinerated within the base, the incident had created a local military alert. The other had been an error in the test sample for anthrax, which resulted in an infected sheep being released into the flock of a local farmer, causing multiple animal deaths and subsequent environmental remediation.

It seemed this second incident in particular had not been well received in Tehran, where questions were raised about the ability of the Revolutionary Guards to police the compound and ensure its safety. The Revolutionary Council had subsequently decided Varshad was not sufficiently capable of managing the safety aspects of the brief and the country needed external support to manage the site. He lost his job as a result. It appeared that the Islamic Republic approached Russia and China to provide assistance, but, in the end, China had offered to provide the necessary help at no charge, the Russians having offered a menu of services, each with a price tag. Further investigation of the Chinese offer led the mullahs of Tehran to accede to a request from the Chinese to assist their security by granting a twenty-five-year lease to Beijing, making the Ibrahim Sami site sovereign Chinese territory. This allowed the occupants complete freedom to run the compound as they saw fit while continuing to take advantage of their hosts' seemingly inexhaustible supply of people for experiments. In recent years, the unusual opportunity that Ibrahim Sami presented allowed the Chinese to export some of their own investigations into the delivery and control of naturally mutating diseases, previously conducted in the western Xinjiang Autonomous Region, home of the Uighur people, to Iran. With their growing commitment to Ibrahim Sami came recognition of the strategic value of north-west Iran to the Chinese, in particular the new but relatively underused airbase at nearby Posyan. Whereas the Chinese investment in Ibrahim Sami was clandestine, the potential of Posyan could be very public as part of their global Belt and Road Initiative. This would deepen relations between Iran and China and legitimise Beijing's involvement in the locality.

The realisation of outcomes at Ibrahim Sami had been held back owing to the size of the facility and the evident problems the Chinese were experiencing in managing the safe and controlled release of these airborne weapons. That meant that the original vision of the compound manufacturing weapons seemed some way from being realised, and the existing research facilities needed radical extension, with new secure underground testing facilities needed. It had taken the Chinese longer than had been expected to come up with a specification about what was required, and it was clear the majority of the new facilities would need to be built underground, requiring specialist teams and construction equipment. Details of the most recent blueprint was enclosed in the report's appendices. There was evidence Iran was assisting the Chinese, firstly by providing temporary accommodation for Chinese workers from earthquake relief supplies donated by Azerbaijan but also by providing additional construction labour to improve access arrangements to the compound. In particular, there were a number of papers specifying the commitment of the local Khoda Afrin prefecture to offer a wide variety of logistical assistance to the Chinese mission, as well as a memo from the base commander to his bosses in Beijing, praising the willingness of the host authority to help but expressing criticism of their understanding of the nature of the support needed.

In conclusion, Wilson read, the Thornberry draft had certain proof of 487 documented deaths at the site and circumstantial evidence of another 245 cases where the cause of death was suspicious. More worrying to Edwin was the intention behind the plan. Why was China researching weapons, potentially of mass destruction, in contravention of at least half a dozen international treaties, and what was the intention of the Iranian authorities in promoting their deployment? He doubted there would ever be answers to these critical questions.

More importantly, the Thornberry Report provided vindication for Peace International's activities, predicting that its publication would ignite a robust international debate about the development and use of these weapons.

As far as Wilson was concerned, the report had been worth waiting for. It was hard-hitting and evidence-based, offering Tehran and Beijing very little wriggle room over its contents and intent.

The task of bringing it into the public domain would be another challenge.

Firstly, he had to arrange to forward copies of the draft to the sponsoring governments for assessment and to provide them the opportunity to raise questions relevant to their interest. He knew this might involve some 'horse trading' over some of the words used that might offend some national sensitivities, but this was a critical part of the job.

Secondly, he would need to propose arrangements for its publication, likely to be at the United Nations next quarterly plenary, if one of the sponsoring governments were willing and able to back it. That too might also include the appearance of eye-witnesses, potentially Jo White-Smith, Amy Fong and possibly Gulam Ehat, at an open hearing.

However, these were questions for another day.

For now, he had to write a letter summarising his own comments on the draft and the way forward to accompany this first iteration and get it to the appropriate quarters in the governments of the United Kingdom, Canada, France, Sweden and, of course, Azerbaijan.

He would have to sit tight for a few weeks longer for their considered response and, hopefully, approval.

The first returns were back with him after just three weeks, with four of the five sponsoring nations offering their unequivocal support. Minor irritation had been expressed by the late inclusion of Azerbaijan as a report sponsor by some of the original commissioners and surprise expressed at their inclusion as a new member of Peace International. Predictably, the Azeris were the ones who took issue with some of the report's contents – specifically comments regarding the reasons behind the location of the facility so close to their border. Their response had contained an unusual offer.

Would Edwin Wilson make an appointment to attend the embassy in London for a teleconference with Minister Nubulatov at a mutually convenient time?

An appointment was made the following week, and Wilson was treated as a VIP guest upon arrival at the embassy in Kensington Court.

Participation in the discussion was limited to just the two of them, with the ambassador acting as an unofficial chair of the debate.

The Minister was suitably direct. "Mr Wilson, I must commend you and your people for an excellent job and drawing our attention to this potentially serious situation. You will appreciate, unlike the other sponsoring governments, we feel very strongly about this matter, as if this lands badly (and we think it might), as a front line state we may have to deal with the consequences. Having visited our southern region, I don't think I need to remind you about local sensitivities and security issues involved. We take both seriously, especially as we have to focus so much on the challenges from Armenia, and the occasional mischievous interventions of our Russian cousins. Having considered this matter carefully, my president has decided to use your report for a series of bilateral contacts with his opposite numbers in the Islamic Republic of Iran and People's Republic of China. We do not consider it to be in our interest to embarrass either government, but to press them privately to change tack and remove this threat to us and others in the region. Our belief is, if they are approached in the right way, we can be optimistic in expecting them to change their strategy. We will also have to tell them that, if we do not receive a positive response, then we will need to join with the British and the rest to publicise the report as you have proposed, as well as making efforts to ensure we have mitigated any threat to our territory that we see arising from the further development of the base at Ibrahim Sami. We also believe in the spirit of peaceful co-existence, a central tenet of Peace International. The Iranian and Chinese authorities should amend the remit of this base to become a complete medical research facility into infectious diseases, allowing our own medics to work alongside them at the compound in the interests of all humanity in the region and beyond. We cannot know what the Iranian and Chinese attitude to this may be, but in this situation we think it important to take the initiative. We are fortunate at the moment to enjoy positive, enduring relations with both countries. Therefore, we insist you delay publication until such time as our diplomatic approaches have been made and answered. We will also take the opportunity of advising colleagues in the UK, Canada, France and Sweden of our views and trust these will be respected. I will be in touch with you directly in the course of the coming weeks, but you should be clear on our final position in the meantime. Once again, thank you and your colleagues for your work. I hope to welcome you to Baku once more in the near future."

Edwin walked back to Notting Hill Gate tube station, through Hyde Park, past Kensington Palace. Although disappointed, he could hardly be surprised.

He saw a picture of his old friend Roddy in his mind, reclining in an armchair at the St Ermin's, wagging his finger and saying, "I told you so."

Now the initiative had passed elsewhere.

But, as Nubulatov had suggested, if the *primary objective* had been achieved, did it matter?

Two weeks on and two other developments occurred relevant to his interest. The first was a news release from the President's Office of the Republic of Azerbaijan announcing a state visit to Baku by the Supreme Leader of the Islamic Republic of Iran, including a schedule of matters he would discuss with his guest. Top of the list was new frontier security cooperation, and the establishment of a new global centre of research in north-west Khoda Afrin Prefecture into infectious diseases financed by the governments of Iran, Azerbaijan and the People's Republic of China, together with a private concern called the Alrakahthan Foundation, 'in the interests of global peace and humanitarian advancement'.

The second was in the form of a strange email received from a Yahoo! account, submitted via the comments section of the Peace International website.

"Hi Eddy, how are you? With my mate Sammy, enjoying the sunshine. Bun in the oven. Wishing you well. Jacko."

Edwin had a week to submit his bi-monthly board report to New York on European operations. At least his fellow directors would get to read the Thornberry Report, even if no one else did.

ALSO BY THIS AUTHOR:

"THE END OF THE ROAD"
Everyone has secrets, but some want to leave them behind...

COMING SOON!

About the Author

West Yorkshire-based Martin Venning is a project
communications and strategic investment adviser working
in the property and construction sector with 20 years'
experience engaging with businesses in the UK, continental
Europe and Asia. He trained as a journalist as part of his
undergraduate studies and writes for pleasure.

mvenning.net

For exclusive discounts on Matador titles,
sign up to our occasional newsletter at
troubador.co.uk/bookshop